The Girl from Simon's Bay

By Barbara Mutch

The Girl from Simon's Bay

The Girl from Simon's Bay

BARBARA MUTCH

Allison & Busby Limited
12 Fitzroy Mews
London W1T 6DW
allisonandbusby.com

First published in Great Britain by Allison & Busby in 2017.
This paperback edition published by Allison & Busby in 2017.

A CIP catalogue record for this book is available from the British Library.

10 9 8 7 6 5 4 3 2 1

ISBN 978-0-7490-2130-6

Typeset in 10.5/15.5 pt Sabon by
Allison & Busby Ltd.

The paper used for this Allison & Busby publication has been produced from trees that have been legally sourced from well-managed and credibly certified forests.

Printed and bound by
CPI Group (UK) Ltd, Croydon, CR0 4YY

For L

Prologue

England, 1967

The letter had passed through careless hands.

Once pristine, it was now grey and randomly creased, as if it had been crushed into a ball, aimed at a waste-paper basket, missed, and been trodden upon.

How long did it lie there, she wondered, waiting to be swept up and discarded?

Or idly rescued and thrown back into circulation for one more try?

The scrawled words, in different fists, with different coloured pens, were perhaps an indication.

'Gone'. The first annotation, in neat black capitals.

Then, 'Address unknown'. Overwritten – gouged – in red.

And finally, 'Return to sender!' Impatient, underlined green, with an arrow towards the address on the back flap. ('Don't waste my time' surely the unwritten postscript.)

Ella's gaze wandered over the desk with its carefully arranged possessions, as if they might provide the answer to a question – suddenly brought to the fore by the letter – that she'd never been brave enough to ask.

An embossed leather notebook on top of a Manila folder.

A picture of her as a baby beside a brass shell case holding pencils.

A silver inkwell that was always kept full despite the arrival of ballpoint pens.

A lustrous seashell, its jagged spine rubbed smooth from handling.

'Dad? Did she give you the shell?'

Chapter One

Simon's Town, Union of South Africa, 1920s

'Lou!'

Infant waves curled towards me over the crystal sand. Footsteps thundered from behind. I reached out both hands to seize the oncoming water with its lace of bubbles and fell forward. Cold, green liquid gurgled into my mouth, lapped at my forehead and just as it started to trickle into my ears, a pair of familiar hands grabbed me around the middle and pulled me clear.

'Lou!' my pa, Solly, hoisted me over his shoulder and gave me a brisk pat on the back. 'You can't swim before you can walk!'

From the vantage point of his arms, I could tell that the sea stretched in white-edged ridges until it collided with the mountains, or raced impatiently around them to merge with the sky overhead. I'd already met the sky. I saw its blue dome every day when Ma put me down to rest beneath the palm tree outside our front door.

This sea was far more exciting than the sky!

I twisted in my father's arms and yearned downwards.

Solly looked back triumphantly at my mother, Sheila, sitting cross-legged on a blanket well up the beach, and waved the arm that was not holding me from plunging back. 'She wants more!'

Unlike me, Seaforth Beach was shy. It hid between massive grey boulders rounded like eggs thrust up from the ocean by some giant, divine fist. Boys, including my best friend Piet Philander, used to scramble up their smooth sides and do risky bellyflops into the shallows, praying that the water was deep enough to cushion their fall. But before the shock of cold seawater, the best thing about Seaforth was its sand. You could make perfect, five-finger impressions of your hand or your rounded tummy in its sparkling skin. It even tasted pleasantly gritty.

'No, Louise!' Ma scrambled to unload my fist.

At the high-tide mark, the sand gave way to a crust of shells. When no one was watching, I'd hide one in my pocket and press it to my ear in the night to bring back the rush of the waves.

It took twenty minutes to walk to the beach on my father's shoulders from the family cottage on Ricketts Terrace. 'Careful, that child!' Ma shouted, as I craned dangerously around to watch her panting in Pa's wake. Motor cars were only for rich white folk who drove from Cape Town to gawk at our views. Everyone else walked – whether it was to the beach, or the dockyard where Pa worked, or up through the proteas and *kek-kekking* guinea fowl to admire False Bay, christened by indignant seamen who mistook it for Table Bay at the northern end of our peninsula. It was a happy fact that if you visited the Cape you were never far from the mountains or the sea – even if you couldn't quite identify your whereabouts. And it didn't matter if you were rich or poor, they swelled your heart with a bursting pride. The mountains even put up with the white-painted towns that spread up their slopes or pressed against the shore with tarmac fingers. We lived in one such town close to the spiny tip of the peninsula. Keep going south, Pa would bellow cheerily, and say hello to Antarctica.

'Who is our town named after?' my first-grade teacher used to ask.

'Simon van der Stel!' we chanted, rolling our eyes at the obvious answer. Who in the world wouldn't know that? 'The first governor of the Cape.'

When I woke up in the mornings, instead of running into Ma and Pa's bedroom and worming into bed with them for a cuddle, I'd climb onto the table by the window in our cramped sitting room to make sure the sea was where it had been the day before and hadn't been stolen from me in the night. After all, the water rose and fell, and sometimes drowned the sand completely, or pounded against the rocks and frightened the boys out of their bellyflops. Wind – that livelier version of the breath that passed between my lips – seemed to be responsible for a lot of this erratic behaviour. It whipped the swells into towering crests and drove salt spray into your eyes to make them sting. When the sea and the wind joined forces like this, it was time to bolt the door of the cottage and wait it out.

'My pa is in it,' Piet Philander whispered with a mixture of pride and fear, as we stood with our noses pressed against the windowpane and watched the palm trees bending in half and willed his father's fishing boat back to shore. Even though Simon's Bay – our scoop of False Bay – was protected by mountains and should have been calmer, everyone knew fishermen who'd died on the water. Piet's grandfather was one, taken by waves that pounced out of nowhere like the silent leopards that hunted on the Simonsberg peak above our terrace and kept me awake at night with the imagining.

'You can stay with us if—'

I took Piet's hand, feeling the hard skin of his palm. Piet helped his father with the nets. If you've never fished, you won't know that when wet rope runs through your hand it tears the flesh like a serrated knife through a peach. Eventually, the skin learns its lesson and mends itself into a tough, scarred shell. Fishing was in the Philander family, but sometimes I felt that Piet hated fish as much as I loved the sea.

The boats that steamed in and out of the Royal Navy dockyard were much sturdier than the Philander fishing boat, and better able to cope with the Cape storms. When I was older and more sensible, Pa explained that the navy boats were warships and their job was to defend the choppy sea route around Africa from something he ominously called 'foreign powers'. This necessary exertion ensured that Simon's Town was a thriving port, with the navy at the pinnacle and the rest of us serving in layers below. Pa's steady job meant that we sat about halfway down this pyramid, below the professional navy but above the poor black labourers who lived in shacks across the mountain and couldn't read or write like we could. And we were especially lucky, Pa used to say, wagging a finger at me and Ma as we sat at the kitchen table. Brown mechanics such as him earned far more working for the even-handed British than for mean employers in the world beyond Simon's Town. Out there – Pa flapped his arm dismissively at the rest of South Africa – they take off a discount for colour.

I admired the navy for a deeper reason than money or fairness, a reason connected to the surging tides and to Piet's grandpa's fate. Whatever the weather, the navy's warships managed to stay upright. They didn't flounder or sink, or casually fling men off their decks. Instead, they cut through the waves with dash, immune as arrows. And, as an afterthought, left behind a wake of filmy bubbles far more ordered than those tossed from the waves at Seaforth Beach.

Chapter Two

When I turned seven, we had a birthday party at the cottage on Ricketts Terrace. Piet came, and my classmates Vera and Susan and Lola, and friends of Ma and Pa. Ma once explained to me that children had to be grown carefully and gratefully year by year, so a birthday was as much a celebration for the adults – in having kept the birthday child alive and well so far – as for the children. The lady grown-ups at my party drank tea, the men drank pale liquids that induced livelier behaviour, while we ate jelly and peaches and a birthday cake made by Ma with a doll encased in a round iced sponge to mimic a ballet dancer's full skirt. Ma didn't often go to so much trouble at home, she tended to be too tired at the end of each day for smart cooking. And I couldn't learn ballet because lessons cost too much, but I'd once admired a picture of a dancer.

'Thank you, Ma,' I kissed her afterwards, as we cuddled up in my tiny room at the back of the cottage. 'It was so pretty, I'm sorry we had to eat it.'

'Now you're seven,' Ma said, stroking my hair, her forehead relaxing out of its normal creases, 'you'll have to help more round the house. Put on the vegetables when I'll be home late from work. Take the washing off the line. But no ironing till you're ten.'

There was a tap on the door.

'I've got another birthday treat for you!' Pa sat down on the edge of my bed. It had taken him a while to shoo away some of the noisier grown-ups, especially Vera's mother who'd moved on from tea.

'Tell me, Pa, tell me!' I squirmed onto his lap.

'Tomorrow,' he promised. 'It's only for girls who are seven-years-and-one-day old.'

When Ma dressed me the next day in my best Sunday frock made by Mrs Hewson next door, with yellow puffed sleeves and a matching ribbon in my hair, Pa said, 'My! Don't you look a picture?' and folded his newspaper and stuffed it down the side of his chair. 'I remember when I first laid eyes on your ma . . .' He winked at her and Ma's lips curled up at the edges as she scrubbed washing in the sink. Pa loved Ma in an open way, with hugs and winks and smacking kisses. Ma was less generous.

'You can't give too much,' she cautioned when I asked why, 'otherwise they take you for granted.'

Pa took my hand – I was too big for his shoulders now – and we set off down the dirt track that led to St George's Street, past the mosque where the muezzin floated his call to prayer every dawn. 'Some of our neighbours pray to Allah,' explained Ma, 'and we pray to Jesus. So the Terrace is always well looked after.'

Pa lifted me over the stream at the Hewsons' to save my black T-bar shoes from getting muddy.

From the station came the enticing whistle of the morning train to Cape Town, followed by gauzy curls of smoke that bloomed and dissolved, bloomed and dissolved, against the green mountain. So far in my life I had only ever been on a train once. And then only as far as Fish Hoek, which was nothing like as grand as Cape Town, people said.

'Where are you off to, Solly Ahrendts?' Mrs Hewson yelled from her front door. Mrs Hewson was hard of hearing. Perhaps Mr Hewson got tired of shouting at her and that's why he left.

'Bye, Ma! Bye Mrs H!' I turned and waved. 'Where are we going, Pa? On the train?'

'You'll have to wait. Maybe we're just going for a walk?' He gazed about innocently.

'Then why am I in my best dress and shoes if it's only a walk? I'm hot—'

'Patience, child.'

Pa led me across St George's Street, crowded with more pedestrians than motor cars, and then beside the wall guarding the Royal Navy base. As we walked, passing men called out to Pa, 'Day off, Solly?' or 'She spoken for yet, Solly?' and tipped their caps to me. One patted my head as we went by. I wasn't bothered by their attention, although Ma would hurry me away if it happened while she was with us. I thought the men's interest was out of politeness to Pa. He was well known. After all, the stone for the navy wall had been quarried out of the mountain above Ricketts Terrace by Grandpa Ahrendts. Not alone, of course, although Pa liked to say it was his father's contribution that was the most significant.

'I started at the bottom, Lou, like he did,' Pa used to say when I sat on his lap and asked him how it was when he was growing up. 'I wrote an exam and they liked my answers so much they made me an apprentice and then a mechanic. Fancy that! Remember,' he wagged a finger at me, 'if you work hard, you can go far.'

It was a message he often repeated: if you work hard, you can go far.

But he didn't say how far I would reach. Ma was a cook for a navy family. Vera's mother was a cleaner. Mrs Hewson sewed. It seemed to me that none of those jobs allowed you to go further than the point from which you started. Perhaps it was a rule that girls didn't progress like boys did.

It was thc discount for girl-ness.

We turned towards the iron gates that gave entry to the dockyard. Queen Victoria's initials wound across them in curly lettering, spelling out 'VR'.

'Who was the greatest queen in the world?' Again, a regular first-grade question.

'Victoria!' we shouted. 'Queen of the Empire and of South Africa! God save the Queen!'

We waited by the gate. Heat from the tarmac rose through the soles of my T-bars.

The gate swung open.

'Pa?'

He looked down at me and winked. While others in my class had been on the train more than me, no one had ever been inside the dockyard – not Vera, not Susan, not Lola, or

Piet! Perhaps, I thought wickedly, not even Queen Victoria Herself when she was alive – after all, Simon's Town was two weeks' steaming from Buckingham Palace and you couldn't leave an empire to run itself while you visited one tiny part of it.

'Come now,' said Pa, 'stop daydreaming and mind where you walk. We can't have you messing your dress, or your ma will make me wash it myself.'

We pressed on towards a crowd of noisy sailors. And then I saw her, above their bobbing heads: a vast grey ship rearing out of the water, her deck bristling with guns, her two stout funnels flanked by wire towers. Colourful bunting reached from her bow, over her funnels and dipped down to her stern – I already knew the anatomy of ships – making her look as if she was dressed for her own birthday party. Shamefully, in the private excitement of turning seven, I'd forgotten about the arrival of the most famous ship in the world.

'HMS *Hood*!' Pa yelled reverently over the hubbub. He reached out a hand as if to stroke her soaring flanks. 'The flagship of the Royal Navy. Thirty knots in most weathers. Aren't you a clever girl to have a birthday just when she came to call?'

'HMS *Hood*!' I rolled the name around on my tongue for the thrill of saying it. Some of my first words had been ships' names, culled from my father's conversation: *Nep-tee-une, Vy-per*. Piet said I knew more than all the officers in Admiralty House.

A hooter blasted imperiously from behind us and Pa pulled me back.

A black motor car swept by and drew up to let out smart ladies in hats and uniformed officers in gold braid who paced up the gangplank and saluted the quarterdeck as they stepped on board.

My heart lurched in my chest.

Maybe they would tell us to go, even though Pa worked here? There were unwritten rules about who belonged where. Sometimes it was to do with what colour you were or how much money you had. Other times, it was about who you knew so that your colour or your money didn't matter. A ripple of applause drifted from above. The smartly dressed officers disappeared inside the ship. This seemed to be a signal for the sailors, who fell into chattering groups and headed for the Queen Victoria gate without paying us any attention. No one leant over *Hood*'s railings and ordered us to leave.

I stood up straighter and let go of Pa's hand.

'They've got an aeroplane on board!' Pa chuckled, not at all bothered by the disturbance, 'it's called a Fairey Flycatcher, and it takes off to check for enemy ships over the horizon. You know we spoke about the horizon – the furthest you can see?'

'A Fairey Flycatcher!' I shivered. Mostly I wasn't scared of smart, impatient folk – why should they bother with me? – but I was secretly afraid of the sinister black-and-white flycatchers that swooped through the proteas around Ricketts Terrace. We called them butcher birds because they speared their insect prey on barbed wire before eating them. Curing them, Ma liked to tease; waiting till they were just a little crispy, like raisins . . .

'Lou?' Pa gave me a nudge. 'Say goodbye to *Hood*, now, and let's get on.'

I blew a hasty kiss at the vast ship with its hidden fairy aeroplane and wormed through the crush after Pa. I'd never seen a real plane, like I'd never seen a real ballet dancer. Only a picture of one, fragile as a dragonfly. Pa said its wings were clothed in magical gossamer that could lift it above Simon's Town, above the heat—

'Mind!' Pa caught me as I stumbled on a set of rails that led to a crane with the neck of a giraffe. Why, I gasped, were so many machines in this place built to resemble animals or birds? Maybe it was to encourage them to go faster or reach higher, like wild creatures. To poach their energy. A giant hook lay among a tumble of chains on the ground. I quickly crouched down to feel if it pulsed with some special, savage power . . .

'Don't touch!' Pa glanced about, then pulled out his handkerchief to wipe the rust off my hand before I might wipe it on my dress. 'That crane rolls along to where the ship's moored – see? It bends its head to lift up the cargo' – I giggled as Pa mimed a heavy load, staggering under its pretended weight – 'then swings it on board.'

He held me aside as a fresh squad of sailors marched past, their blue bell-bottom trousers flapping about their legs. Without breaking stride, they nodded to Pa and grinned at me. I waved at them.

'Now what have we here? Hold my hand!'

I started back. It was as if the same almighty force that had thrust up the rocks on Seaforth Beach had now chosen to punch a hole in the sea, drain it of water and set it as a trap for trespassers to fall into.

'This,' Pa swung his free hand over the gaping hole, 'is a dry dock. It's where we bring ships that need to be out of the water to get mended. We dug it out of the sea and lined its sides – with granite stone all the way from England, mind – before they could collapse.'

'Why are there people down there?' I craned forward to see tiny figures scurrying about. Pa tightened his grip on my hand.

'They're fixing a wooden cradle at the bottom, exactly the shape of the broken ship. Then,' Pa's voice rose with pride, 'we open the gates and let the water flood in – whoosh! The ship sails in, we pump out the water and it settles on the cradle.'

I stared at the massive gates and pictured the water tumbling in, licking the edges of the dry dock, hungrier than the tides at Seaforth, pouring into your mouth, filling your ears, drowning you before anyone could grab you and pull you clear . . .

'Pa?'

The men were gathering together, and then they were lifting someone onto a stretcher and slowly climbing out of the hole, every step a draining effort to keep the stretcher steady. Pa pulled me away and shielded my eyes as they staggered to the surface and lurched past us. I peeped through his fingers and saw a man with a crooked leg. White bone jutted from his flesh. Blood trickled onto the canvas of the stretcher. He was moaning.

Pa waited until they'd gone before he released me.

'Will he die?' I sometimes saw death in Pa's face when he came home. I didn't ask him about it, but I knew someone had died. And I'd send a prayer to Jesus, and to Allah just in case, to thank them that it wasn't Pa.

'Of course not!' Pa squeezed me and put on a cheery tone. 'It's easy to fall down there. They'll take him to hospital and patch him up. Now, Lou,' he pointed at the dry dock walls, 'see those crests? See HMS *Durban*?' Around the inner perimeter stretched a row of badges painted in bold colours and decorated with swags like Ma made on her hand-cranked sewing machine.

'Once a ship is mended, it's allowed to paint its crest on the wall. It's a tradition, like your ma making smoked *snoek* just as her ma before her. Or old Mr Phillips along the Terrace, whittling pipes.'

I stared at this latest wonder of my seven-years-and-one-day treat: a slippery dock carved out of the bright, restless sea that I loved, and decorated with the painted crests of ships returned to health. And I knew it was a sign.

I grabbed Pa's hand with both of mine.

'When I grow up, Pa, I'm going to mend things, too!'

Chapter Three

Piet Philander sat on the grass above Seaforth Beach, and rested his forehead on his bare, drawn-up knees. He often came here at night. The sea flowed in and out with regularity, the moon travelled steadily and luminously across the sky, and the sound of breaking surf concealed the shouts and breakages that arose from the Philander cottage up the lane.

It wasn't that Piet was abused.

His father didn't actually beat him. Or, he didn't set out to beat him. But sometimes he fell over and if Piet was in the way then Piet fell over, too. This happened when Piet was trying to help, trying to get his father to sit down, or trying to get him out of his sea boots and into bed. So Seaforth, with its predictable tides watched over by a benign moon, became the antidote to the chaos that gripped the cottage at the end of the day. In the summer, when it was warm, he often took a thin sheet down to the stretch of grass above the sand, and rolled himself in it and slept there beneath the palm trees, with the sea in his ears. Piet never told anyone about this, except Louise. And then only to say that he did it because it was too hot to sleep indoors.

Amos Philander, Piet's father, was a fisherman, as his father had been before him. As would Piet, Amos liked to boast. The family owned a creaky boat that went out most days to lay nets and then he and Piet and whoever happened to be around would pull them in from the shore. If the weather was fair and Amos was sober and the catch was good, he swiftly spent his earnings in the nearest liquor store. That translated into a lot of stumbling about, some shouting, and no chance for Piet to get to sleep that night. In fact, he didn't sleep much at all, worrying about his father and whether there would be enough money left over for food and, from time to time, a school uniform. Piet couldn't help growing but growth cost money, even if you bought from the second-hand store. And you couldn't arrive at the Arsenal Road School in clothes with holes, the teachers turned you away at the gate.

Piet helped most afternoons with the hauling in of the nets. It was hard, aching work especially if the sea was running high and currents pulled at the ropes, dragging them away. But it was worth it when the net scraped onto the sand laden with silvery fish, jumping and thrashing. Fishing was a living. Well, just about.

He used to hover nearby when the catch was sold, hoping to persuade his father to part with some of the money that changed hands.

'We need milk and bread, Pa, and I need money for a

shirt,' Piet urged, 'otherwise I must borrow from Uncle Den or the Ahrendts.'

'Try your Uncle Den,' Amos chortled, 'he's rolling. Now help me with these nets.'

But Uncle Den wasn't rolling.

No one was rolling.

Life was a struggle unless you were lucky enough to work for the Royal Navy. When word got out that there was work in the dockyard, the queues for jobs used to stretch from the Queen Vic gate all the way to the station. The last time that happened was when the *Hood* had been in, and extra hands were needed to help load stores: eggs and fresh vegetables from the farms at Murdoch Valley, and cases of Cape wine. The Royal Navy not only paid well, it ate well, too.

The morning after the night before, Amos Philander was always apologetic.

'Won't happen again, Pietie, I promise. But since your ma died . . .'

'Ma would be angry,' Piet answered back, under his breath.

'Now you mind your tongue!' Amos growled. 'You know nothing about anything.'

'I know something—'

'Leave it,' Uncle Den pulled Piet away. 'We'll manage.'

Uncle Den waited until Amos had moved off. 'I check his trousers before I wash them, Piet.' He winked. 'Sometimes Amos forgets money in his pockets!'

Uncle Den was Piet's father's older brother. He'd come to live with them when his wife died. At first, Den helped with the boat but then he hurt his back. So now he swept the cottage once a week, did the washing when it piled up, and cooked whenever there was enough money to buy fresh vegetables to go with the fish: *galjoen, snoek, kingklip* if they were lucky. He also kept the peace between Amos and Piet. What else could he do? Piet needed a mother. Instead, he had a father who drank himself silly trying to forget her. But life was never meant to be fair. Piet would have to learn. After all, if he wanted to inherit the boat from Amos, he'd need to keep his father sweet.

'Piet,' Den coaxed, 'give your Uncle Den a hand with this washing. Hang it out – you know how my back hates bending and stretching.'

Piet came over and grabbed the pile without a word.

Den sighed. Piet was a good boy at heart. And he had a friend in Louise Ahrendts, the pretty, barefoot daughter of Solly Ahrendts up on Ricketts Terrace. They spent their weekends beachcombing, usually with either Solly or Sheila in attendance. If he, Den, had a daughter, he'd also never let her out of his sight. Everyone thought boys were the most valuable commodity, but girls, in Den's opinion, were priceless. And if Piet played his cards right? Solly had a steady job, his wife worked, there was income. And Louise looked like being an only child.

Piet pegged a shirt on the line Uncle Den had strung up with creaking difficulty between the cottage and the peeling trunk of a gum tree. Before Den arrived, he and his father used to spread their wet clothes inside the house to dry. But Den was getting old, and Piet dreaded what would happen when he and his father were once more alone in the cottage above Seaforth. He could run away, but then he'd give up his right to the place, and to the boat and to the patch of Simon's Bay they called their own. It would be different if he stayed at school, but already Amos was talking about how Piet would leave in five years' time when he turned sixteen to man the boat full-time. Piet often listened hungrily to Solly Ahrendts describing how he'd won an apprenticeship at eighteen with the Royal Navy and gone on to become a mechanic, with regular pay at the end of each week that didn't vary with the Cape weather or if the fish were choosing to rise or not.

And then there was Louise.

His Lou, with perfect golden skin, almond eyes and long dark hair that swirled down her back like the running waterfall above Admiralty House. Piet wasn't very good with words but you didn't need words to notice how people couldn't take their eyes off her. He saw it all the time. Fishermen stared at her when they saw her down by the boat, his classmates' fathers stared when they saw her on the street. Men looked at Louise with a kind of greed.

There was one other possibility.

Already he'd been sounded out by some of the flashy types who hung around the boats from time to time, men who carried knives in their pockets that weren't for gutting fish.

'Looking for pocket money?' they would say, flashing a roll of notes. 'Anytime, *jong*, anytime . . .'

Chapter Four

While Ma and Pa guarded me from one birthday to the next, the wind regularly tried to uproot our Ricketts Terrace cottage. Ma fretted – with a pleading glance upwards to whichever of Allah or Jesus happened to be watching over us that day – that our place groaned and listed like a weary soul not long for this world.

'Enough,' Pa muttered, with a glance at me, 'you'll frighten the child.'

If, like me, you were born in Simon's Town you understood the power of wind without being warned. Wind was in my bones, especially the murderous kind that barrelled over the shoulder of the Simonsberg in the hot glare of summer. Like the unwritten rules about colour or girl-ness, there were unwritten rules about our wind. If the sea inside the harbour wall was choppy, we were probably safe. But if waves were actually cresting and breaking, it meant a black southeaster, a blow so powerful it could sweep you off your feet, drive fishing boats onto the rocks, even uproot a line of cottages. And it could last for days.

'Inside, Lou!' Ma yelled as I tried to help her rescue washing off the heaving line. 'You'll get blown away! Inside!'

When it ended, a stinging, apologetic rain would arrive and wrap the battered Terrace in mist and reduce the Simonsberg Mountain to a ghost. As a child I dreaded the attack of the black wind, but at least it came at you directly. You could feel it, and set your back against it. The silent creep of the mist was a more subtle assault. To me it was like a snake, a cobra uncoiling through the grass, a threat that might engulf you when you least expected it, when you thought the worst was over.

Today, though, the wind was biding its time behind the Simonsberg and the snake-mist lurked only in my imagination. Piet was taking advantage of the calm by skipping pebbles into the sea at Seaforth Beach. It was low tide, too shallow for bellyflops, and the water rippled satin-soft around our feet. A formation of sleek terns wheeled in the sky and came in to land on a distant rock. Children looked up from their sandcastles to watch Piet's thin wrist draw back and flick the stone low and hard to make it hop on the surface, dancing two, three, four times before sinking; then taking the next one out of his pocket, aiming, drawing back, flicking, in a rhythm that seemed formed of one smooth movement rather than several separate ones.

Draw back, flick, skip! A low fizzing arc, a trace of silvery droplets . . .

Piet and I became friends soon after I fell in love with the sea. He taught me to find the spell to make stones skip, and how to surf the curling breakers safely when the wind was up. I couldn't teach Piet anything as powerful as that, so instead I taught him about the sea's quieter side, its ethereal whisper when you held a shell to your ear.

Yet lately – in fact since the last heavy southeaster – his throwing seemed less joyful, less skilful, more about flinging than aiming. And he lost interest in my seashell sounds. No one else noticed because Piet could always attract admirers even when he wasn't trying. But I could tell. I could read Piet's moods like I could tell the turn of the tide.

We'd swum earlier on, him churning through long swells beyond the protruding rocks, me treading water a little way back among the brown kelp fronds that swayed in the current, their roots anchored to the seabed.

'Piet?'

Next to me, on the sand, lay three perfectly round sea urchin shells that he'd dived for and brought up from the depths. Each was a pale, delicate shade of stippled green, lighter than a Granny Smith apple but not as yellow as a Golden Delicious. Most urchins were already chipped when you found them, but Piet prided himself on knowing where the intact ones hid, protected under a rocky ledge or between plush anemones. Piet knew the seabed like a farmer knows his land.

'Piet!'

I loved Piet, just like I loved the sea.

This time he heard me, loped up the beach and flopped down at my side, leaning back on his elbows and turning his face up to the sun. His black hair was plastered to his head in a neat circumference where Uncle Den had cut it with the help of a kitchen bowl.

'What do you want to be when you grow up?'

He picked up a handful of sand and let it dribble though his fist, making a tiny, golden cone.

'I suppose I'll be a fisherman.'

'But that's not what I asked,' I tickled him in the side. 'I asked what you wanted to be, not what you had to be!'

He shrugged, reached for another handful of sand and made a second cone. 'Don't know.'

I hugged my knees to my chest. A gull swooped down to peck at a rope of seaweed. I'd learnt to wait, with Piet. Sometimes for words, mostly for him to do something. Perhaps he already had? Maybe the wild flinging-stones-into-the-sea was what you did when you happened to be a boy and you hated the life that seemed picked out for you. I could understand that. But you didn't have to accept it without a fight. Surely he knew that? I tried to help him along.

'Remember when I went to the dockyard? When the *Hood* was in?'

He nodded.

'Well,' I leant against his bony, sun-warmed shoulder, 'I saw the dry dock where they fix ships and I said to Pa that I wanted to fix things, too.'

I'd never talked about my dream to anyone before. It brooded in my heart, day after day, too uncertain to be shared, like a Fairey Flycatcher in search of a distant, clouded horizon. And too bold. A Terrace girl studying beyond school . . .

'But you can't work there!' Piet scoffed. 'They don't take girls in the docks!'

'I know that, silly! I don't want to fix ships!'

Piet shifted around to look at me. His tanned face was intense but also strangely hesitant.

'I want to fix people, Piet,' I bit my lip and plunged on, 'I want to be a nurse. A sister in a hospital, maybe even a matron!'

'What!'

'Everyone thinks I'll be a maid or a nanny but I want to try for more—'

He looked away.

I waited for him to say something – even to tell me why I was wrong to be so forward – but he just stared at the lively waves breaking towards shore. I opened my mouth to ask why he wasn't keen for me, but he turned his narrow shoulder and stared up into the rocky face of the Simonsberg. A breeze eddied down from the mountain and whipped up dry sand, sending it stinging across the beach. I found myself shivering. Maybe ambition was like the black southeaster, or the slithering mist that followed it. An attack. A trap. I'd never thought of my dream like that.

I picked up a handful of sand and dribbled it through my fingers.

'Is something the matter with Piet?' Ma raised her voice to me as she brushed my hair before bed a week or two later. The wind had returned, blowing for three straight days, making every conversation a shouting match. Even Pa and old Jack Gamiel, taking an evening *dop* in the sitting room, were yelling at one another as if they were deaf.

'No, Ma.'

Ma and Pa knew Piet was often hungry and they knew Amos neglected him. But hunger and neglect were not things we spoke about. After all, there was hunger and neglect in varying doses all around us and you couldn't fill everyone's need. If Piet had shown black eyes or weeping wounds apart from his scarred hands, then Pa would have gone round to the Seaforth cottage and shouted at Amos. Instead, Ma regularly invited Piet for supper. In return he promised to look after me when we walked to and from school past the *skollies* that lurked in Quarry Road and the smooth men in motor cars who might snatch a pretty girl right off the street, although Pa said this was Ma's imagination overheating. But Ma declared that while boys could mostly look after themselves, you could never be too careful with a daughter. Even a barefoot one who could probably out-sprint any unexpected kidnapper.

'Piet's fine,' I reached out to finger the collection of shells that paved the top of my bookcase. Green sea urchins, spiral *alikreukel*, toothed cowries. Grown-ups had probably forgotten what it was like to have best friends: you protected them, you were loyal to them and kept their secrets, unlike most grown-ups who loved to gossip about theirs. 'He just gets tired working the nets.'

'*Ja*,' said Ma, and kissed me goodnight. 'Fishing's no picnic.'

But it wasn't about tiredness.

He'd eventually wished me luck, but with an edge in his voice. And, as the wind built in the coming days, he began to turn away, hoarding his own secret. Not in hope, like me, but furtively. Sly as a leopard hiding its kill in the branches of a tree. Then last week, with clear skies overhead and only the slightest hint of the coming blow, I tried to bring him back.

'Let's go to Seaforth!' I whispered, with a backward glance to where Ma was engrossed with sewing new kitchen curtains. 'We can swim and we'll be in time to see the boats come in—'

'No,' he cut in swiftly. 'I don't feel like it today. And

Pa has enough people to help him.' He looked towards the glittering sweep of False Bay and thrust his hands into his pockets. 'I'll see you tomorrow.' He edged towards the front door. 'Bye, Mrs Ahrendts.'

But Piet loved to swim! The sea was our shared playground, the heart of our friendship. I felt a stealing fear. Maybe getting older was less about compiling years and more about what you were forced to leave behind. The bite of salt on your lips, the glide of water between your toes . . . The friends you'd grown up with?

I ran out of the door and caught up with him. 'Piet!'

He turned, his black eyes defensive. There was a hole in his shirt, on the elbow, where the cloth had rubbed too thin to survive. I caught his arm. The sinews strained like wire beneath my hand. 'What's wrong, Piet? Is it your pa?'

'No,' he shrugged me off. 'You go if you want to.'

I watched him stride away, across the stream at the Hewsons', past the mosque, then down Alfred Lane without his usual look-back-and-wave, and became conscious of a deep and uncomfortable clutch at my heart. It wasn't a feeling I'd had before, even for the butcher birds that watched me, or the mist that liked to wrap its damp fingers about me.

You go if you want to.

He wasn't worried I might swim alone, something we'd always vowed not to do because you never knew what could happen, a freak wave rising out of a flat sea, a shark gliding close to shore . . .

You go if you want to.

He didn't seem to care.

Chapter Five

Even though Ma gave me an opening, I never told her that Piet had stopped caring for me like he used to. One word from me would have stirred Ma into indignant action – she was always aching for the chance to tackle Piet's pa who was surely the cause of all the trouble in the Philander household. And through her fuss, Piet might have been prised from his secret plans.

Instead, I let Ma believe we were as close as ever.

And I told myself he'd come back to me, that there was nothing to worry about. I just needed to wait. After all, everyone knew boys grew up differently from girls. It was the way they were put together, the way Jesus intended them to be: stronger, sometimes moody, sometimes trying things they never should have in order to know how far they could push before they fell.

Yet I knew, somewhere inside my own growing heart, that I was neglecting Piet.

Not in the careless way of his pa, but out of my own selfish distraction.

I was only fourteen, but all around Simon's Town, parents of girls my age were staying up late and letting candles burn down while they considered their daughters' future.

My future.

Possible jobs were discussed and, most importantly, marriage prospects.

Did he have a good heart? Did he have money – or parents with it?

Was there madness or drunkenness or flightiness in the family?

There was no time to waste. I must come out with my ambition before it was too late.

Perhaps I could cry, to add weight? Ma and Pa might pay more attention if there were tears. I already knew they didn't imagine a future for me that went beyond marriage and domestic service. That was how far I could expect to go, even if I worked hard. I should be mindful of – and grateful for – my place on the pyramid.

How could I tell Ma and Pa it wasn't enough?

That I wasn't grateful. Or mindful.

Yet I couldn't say I was neglected, like Piet. Why, when there was money to spare in Ma's tin savings box in the kitchen at the end of the year, Ma and Pa took me on a train trip to Cape Town, third class, to see the New Year's Coon Carnival.

'Much taller than the Simonsberg!' I craned out of the window at Table Mountain, soaring above feathery cloud.

'Such a crush,' yelled Ma as we pushed our way down Adderley Street. 'The whole Cape's here!'

'*Daar kom die Ali-ba-ma!*' sang the painted Coons in their satin costumes.

The outside world left me in raptures.

In a rash moment, Pa promised to let me complete my schooling through to eighteen. Most girls left earlier, as soon as they'd been promised in marriage, especially if it was to an older man who might have patted them on the head years before and asked if they were spoken for. Girls, you see, became a burden unless spoken for. But even if I stayed at school, marriage was the target once I finished, with a domestic job hopefully fitted in on the side.

'You'll be well treated working for a navy family, Lou,' Pa said, when my future employment was discussed at the kitchen table, 'and better paid than out there—' he waved his spoon northwards.

'It's more than that, Solly,' Ma interrupted, ladling out tomato soup. 'They'll keep you on once you have children, they won't throw you out. Lou will need to contribute.'

A prospective husband's fishing, she was implying, wouldn't bring in enough to feed and clothe a family. Piet, it seemed, had already been cleared as a potential husband.

'I told your pa you'll be happier with a boy you know,' Ma confided later in the privacy of my room, 'rather than some older stranger with more money.'

'Ricketts girls don't get fancy jobs,' Vera scoffed on the subject of work, teasing her hair into a frizz above her head. 'We're here to make babies, Lou, so you better get used to it.'

My friends were already eyeing up the local boys they knew and the occasional smooth types in cars, setting their caps at the ones seen to be the most promising, and hinting of their interest to their parents. 'You're lucky to have Piet in the bag,' Vera giggled, giving me a little pinch. 'You don't have to try so hard.' She'd perfected a turned-out foot pose in front of the mirror to attract boys into the back row of the Criterion bioscope or around the side of Sartorial House, where the models in the window wore uniforms and gold-braided caps set at rakish angles that imitated her intent.

But I needed to test my dream before coming out with it.

'Mr Venter?' I approached my schoolteacher one day after class was dismissed.

I couldn't ask Mrs Hewson next door, or Mr Phillips along the Terrace who had grown-up daughters and ought to know about ambition and marriage and if they could be reconciled, or my Sunday school teacher who might know Jesus's opinion. They'd all be so astonished by my question that they'd have to tell Pa or Ma.

'Yes, Louise?'

I took a breath.

'Sir, what must I do if I want a career? If I want to become a nurse?'

'Well now,' he puffed out his cheeks, holding a book halfway between his desk and his briefcase, 'first you must study hard to get a good matric, then you must apply to a nursing college. What do your parents say?'

I hesitated. Girls, of course, didn't ask about careers without the support of their parents, especially poor girls who lived in wind-blown cottages and ran barefoot to the beach. But if I admitted I hadn't spoken to Pa or Ma, he might not answer my next – and most important – question.

'How much does it cost to become a nurse, sir?'

He looked me over, from my collar to my shoes.

I blushed. Ma darned my uniform, but the darns were so neat surely he couldn't see them?

'I don't know, Louise,' his tone softened. 'Perhaps you could work while you're training, to cover your tuition.'

My heart gave a tentative surge. If I could find after-school work as a waitress downtown, or as a part-time cleaner for a navy family, perhaps I could save enough in advance. Fourteen years old was surely sufficient to earn a proper wage.

'I want to apply to the Victoria Hospital,' I blurted.

We'd passed the Victoria on the train when we took our New Year's trip to Cape Town. It was named in honour of the same queen whose letters adorned the gates I'd walked through on my seven-years-and-one-day treat. Wouldn't it be right – I tried to quell my excitement – wouldn't it be fitting to go there?

'No, Louise,' he resumed packing and closed his case with a snap, 'rather try somewhere else. You'll struggle to get in to the Victoria.'

'But, sir? If I get top marks in my matric, why won't they take me?'

He looked down at his hands resting on the top of his briefcase, spread his fingers as if inspecting his nails, then glanced back at me with a kind of pity. I hated that. I didn't want anybody's pity.

'You'll be competing with white girls from the best schools in the country,' he said, with a passing glance around our classroom. 'Even if you study hard, you may never reach the required standard.'

I looked at the cracked but serviceable blackboard in dismay, at the pile of textbooks we shared, one between two students. I'd never felt deprived before; poor, certainly, a little too brown, sometimes. But never deprived. Not while I lived between the sea and the mountains, with the diamond-bright sand beneath my feet.

'I'm sorry,' he said as he buttoned his jacket and took up the case, 'but it's best you don't make the mistake of going after something that isn't possible.'

I bit back tears.

'Yes, Mr Venter.'

He stopped at the classroom door. 'You're an excellent student, Louise. It's not your fault.'

I nodded and lifted my chin.

'Thank you, sir. Good afternoon, sir.'

The sun was fierce on my head as I trudged along St George's Street past the dockyard where I'd first nurtured the seductive hope, foolishly allowed it to grow . . .

The palms drooped like collapsed umbrellas. The sea smouldered beneath a white-baked sky. It was the sort of day when fire could spring up on the mountain like an avenging genie and threaten to burn down our cottage and then there would be more to cry over than just a dream going up in smoke.

I wiped the sweat from my neck and stopped outside the post office.

If you work hard . . . Pa's words goaded me from the glaring sea, the baked sky.

I queued in a line of white ladies to look in the post office's telephone directory. One of them smiled at me, the others paid me no attention. Their daughters would never hear what Mr Venter had just told me. I wrote down the address at the back of my homework notebook where Ma, who signed off my work every night, wouldn't see.

'Louise?' called Lola from across the road. 'Coming to the bioscope?'

'Sorry!' I shouted back. 'I have to help my ma.'

'Goody two-shoes!' she yelled.

'Lazybones!'

Back home, I threw off my uniform and pulled on shorts and a shirt.

I'd show them!

I'd show them all.

I hauled the dry washing from the line and folded it and piled it on Ma's bed. Then I moved my shell collection off the bookcase, dusted the surface, wiped my sweaty palms and put down a piece of lined paper. I usually did my homework at the kitchen table but what I was about to create required secrecy, even though Ma and Pa weren't due home for another few hours.

The muezzin's afternoon call drifted from the mosque.

Ricketts Terrace
Simon's Town

Dear Matron, I began in my neatest handwriting,

My name is Louise Ahrendts. I am fourteen years old. I live in Simon's Town with my parents and I go to high school. Since I was seven, I have dreamt of becoming a nurse. I want to dedicate my life to the sick and to those who can't take care of themselves. It would be an honour to be allowed to apply to the Victoria Hospital for training.

I am already the top student in my class, but I know I must work much harder to compete against many clever girls from all over the Union. Can you please tell me what matric results I must get to be accepted, and how much money it will cost to become a nurse? I can't ask my parents to pay for my career, so I will work after school for the next four years to save enough to pay for myself.

With sincere gratitude for your earnest attention,
I remain,
Yours faithfully,
Louise Ahrendts (Miss)

Sometimes, in my effort to be neat, my pen slipped and made a blot and I had to start again with a fresh sheet of paper. Also, my fingers were so hot the ink smudged if I didn't let each line dry before going on to the next.

On the seventh try, it was perfect.

'What are you doing, running about in this heat?' Mrs Hewson grumbled from her spot on her front step as I dashed by. I hadn't bothered with shoes and the stony track bit into my feet.

'Posting a letter,' I shouted, newly emboldened.

Surely no hospital could look down on a girl applying four years in advance – wherever she came from or whatever mix of Malay, Hottentot and European blood painted her more brown than white?

The last collection of the day was about to be made. Even now the postman would be approaching with his sack. My letter could be sorted and put on the train today – why, if Matron wasn't too busy she might write back to me within a week!

I ran across St George's Street, hovered for a moment, looked about to see if anyone was watching – especially any nosy friends loitering near the bioscope – then quickly kissed the letter and slipped it into the red box. It made a light thud as it hit the pile of post inside.

The tears that had threatened earlier tipped into my eyes.

Do certain moments carry magic within them?

To be caught and treasured before they blow away on the southeaster?

I wanted to tell someone. I had to tell someone – maybe if I found Piet and shared this moment with him, if I took his hand with its hardened skin and asked him to come back to me—

Workers began to stream out of the Queen Victoria gate, bumping into me as they rushed for the train. These days Piet often hung around the back entrance to Runciman's General Dealers, hands in pockets, feet scuffing the dirt, waiting for a chance to stack shelves or unpack boxes. I wiped my face with the back of my hand and joined the flow hurrying along Grandpa Ahrendts's stone wall towards the station. The fiery aroma of curry from the navy canteen drifted over my head.

'He's not here,' old Mr Runciman shouted from the back of the shop. 'Maybe fishing with that no-good Pa of his. Amos Philander owes me money. I'll dock it from his boy's pay next time.'

I turned and began to push against the mass.

People called out – perhaps friends of Ma's thinking I was in trouble – you could never be too careful with daughters – but I ignored them and kept going. I should have worn shoes, the pavement was scalding my bare soles. As the crowd thinned, I began to leap from shade patch to shade patch, my hair working loose from its school ponytail and flying behind me. My side began to hurt. I could have stopped and rested, but then the magic might dissolve, slip out of my grasp before I had the chance to share it . . .

I panted towards the hill above Seaforth. Out in the bay, two minesweepers steamed in line abreast towards the white pillar of Roman Rock Lighthouse.

At last! The jumble of cottages with their lopsided roofs, the barking of yellow-eyed dogs, the chorused shouts of fishermen heaving their net ashore, but no sign of Piet. I bent over and gasped for breath on the grass where he liked to sleep in summer. Amos's boat was pulled above the high-water mark amid strands of seaweed abandoned by the retreating tide.

I ran along the track to their cottage.

'Piet!' I rapped on the door and pushed it open. 'Piet!'

'Louise!' Uncle Den roused himself from a chair by the stove. The interior was dark after the bright sunshine outside. 'Come in, child, Piet's not back from school yet.'

I stood in the doorway, chest heaving. Piet hadn't been at school all day.

'Have a cup of tea,' Uncle Den reached for a battered kettle. 'Amos isn't here. There was a good catch this morning. He said he had business in town.' Den raised a resigned eyebrow.

'I'm too hot for tea, Uncle Den. I'll see Piet tomorrow.'

'Sure,' the old man grinned, and subsided into his chair. 'Give my respects to your ma and pa. Fine folk, your parents.'

I trailed back to the beach where a crowd was milling around the recently landed net. The familiar, pungent whiff of fish, sweat and wet rope drifted off the sand. Children splashed in the shallows, picking up fronds of seaweed and throwing them at one another like Piet and I used to do.

I sat down on the grass.

From the bush on the far side of the beach, in the patch of willow where I usually changed into my swimsuit, two figures emerged. One was a man. The other was Piet. I recognised his faded check shirt, one of his father's, with its sleeves rolled up and its front hanging down over his shorts.

The day brightened. I took a breath to shout out a joyful greeting but—

What were they doing?

Why were they hiding in the bush?

The man was handing something to Piet. Piet was rolling it up and stuffing it into his shirt pocket. The man gave him a slap on the shoulder and disappeared back into the undergrowth.

I waited with a kind of dread.

Piet stood for a moment, staring out to sea. A vee of cormorants skimmed the silver water beyond the breakers, rising and falling in response to the swells. Then he ran down onto the sand, stripped off his shirt – how thin he was – weighted it pocket-side-down under a stone, sprinted into the surf and began swimming out through the incoming waves, his dark head pushing through the creamy foam. Soon he was past the egg rocks and into deeper water, his arms looping over his head in a powerful freestyle as if he was never going to stop until he reached the undulating cormorants, the lighthouse, the racing minesweepers, the far side of the bay.

I stared at the small bundle on the beach: Piet's shirt.

And, in its pocket, whatever the man had given him.

He was so far out he wouldn't be able to see if I ran down onto the beach, and shook out his shirt. And felt in his pocket.

Chapter Six

But I never did.

After several minutes of breathless uncertainty, I scrambled to my feet and sprinted home, my heart pounding harder than the distance and the heat merited. I told myself that doing the opposite would have been worse: if I'd run down and searched his shirt, it would have meant I no longer trusted him. That was an admission far worse than any brief dimming of our friendship.

Or was I simply a coward?

Calculating that what I didn't know, couldn't harm me. Couldn't harm him?

'What's with you and Piet?' Vera raised her eyebrows as I walked home alone from school. 'Had a fight?'

'He has to help his pa,' I hedged.

'So? Go to Seaforth,' she retorted. 'When you land a boy you've still got to work to keep him.'

The heat of summer wilted, the black southeasters blew themselves out.

I didn't follow Vera's advice and haunt the beach. I didn't face up to Piet. Instead, I let a deep unease lurk in my heart for a time, then fade. I told myself there was time for things to get better on their own. The inviting months that stretched ahead would surely take care of what needed to happen. Forcing a confrontation might drive Piet away from me for good.

At least that's what I told myself.

Into this lonely vacuum swept autumn's sea fogs, creeping over the bay, inundating the town and swirling about me. A different pressure began to build. I avoided Vera and Lola by taking a different route home from school, rushing through the opaque air along minor lanes, scrabbling my key at the front door and rifling through the letters pushed underneath for one addressed to me. I didn't want to set my sights lower. I wanted to shake the pyramid. If necessary I'd try another hospital, and then another, until someone said yes. When there was no immediate reply from the Victoria, I began to compose fresh letters of application while Ma and Pa were at work. I hid them face down in my bookcase, neatly addressed to other matrons at random Cape hospitals I'd found in the telephone directory at the post office.

Then a letter arrived forty-one days later, on an afternoon when the fog draped like thickened cream over the dockyard and the foghorn bayed into the menacing gloom.

I stood holding it with stiff fingers, then ripped it open.

Dear Miss Ahrendts,

Thank you for your letter.

Applicants to the Victoria Hospital are assessed on examination results and on the outcome of a face-to-face interview. The more A grades a candidate achieves, the better her prospects will be. We also look for a positive demeanour, good health and deportment, a respect for discipline and a commitment to moral rectitude.

For successful applicants, the hospital funds the cost of training other than for incidental expenses. There is a small monthly salary, which ought to cover these if your needs are modest. Lodging in the nurses' home is also provided if required.

We believe the Victoria Hospital is the premier training institution in the Union.

Miss Ahrendts, while I commend your enthusiasm I must caution you that no coloured applicant from a Simon's Town school has ever been accepted, so you would be well advised to have alternative employment plans in place.

Yours faithfully,

A. S. Winthrow (Matron)

Matron's signature blurred under my hot tears.

I rushed into my bedroom, slammed the door and buried my head in my pillow. I shouldn't bother to apply. I wasn't rich enough or white enough. And perhaps they doubted my moral rectitude, whatever that was—

'Louise?' Ma burst through the door, 'has someone hurt you? Where's Piet – he's supposed to walk you back!'

'Why aren't you at work, Ma?' I choked.

'Mrs H saw you running back from school. She thought something was wrong!' Ma shook me vigorously. 'I shouldn't have trusted that Piet!'

I fished out the letter and gave it to her.

Ma's reading is not as good as mine and it took her a while to get through it, especially some of the longer words like demeanour and incidental. Then she sighed and pulled out a handkerchief to dry my tears.

'Why didn't you tell us about this, child?'

'I thought you wouldn't understand,' I sobbed. 'You want me to be a maid or a nanny. And get married straightaway.'

Ma wrapped me in her arms and rocked me gently.

'You're a good girl, Lou, but why do you always want to swim before you can walk?'

'I'll work hard,' I cried. 'I can be as smart as any of the girls that apply!'

'*Ja*,' Ma kissed me on the top of my head, 'that may be so. But they probably want only white girls at that hospital and not brown ones. This isn't your pa's British Navy, you know, where they treat everyone the same.'

'Then why don't they say so?' I pulled out of her embrace. 'Why hide the real reason?'

Ma smiled grimly and reached for the brush and began to sweep it through my tangled hair. Ma often saved her most important words for when she was brushing my hair.

'Because, my Lou, no one ever says so. Not outright.' She wrestled with a knot. 'Whites are always chosen first, coloureds second and blacks last. You should know that by now. You can't push too far from where you're supposed to be.'

'That's not fair!'

Progress, Ma was saying, had nothing to do with brains. It was only about the rules of colour.

'Now be sensible, Louise,' Ma frowned. 'You'd have to

pay for extra books to study, and for the train journey to the interview. Is it worth it if they've already decided you don't fit?'

'I want to apply,' I said stubbornly. 'They can't stop me applying.'

'No, they can't. But you should take that fancy matron's advice and have another job waiting. Your pa and I can help you.' She stopped and considered me. I don't think Ma could ever fathom where I got my ideas from. I didn't know, either. They seemed to rise up inside me, sparked by the tumbling of seawater or the healing of ships . . .

'There's a place for all of us in this world, child. If you step outside of it, you get hurt. Like today.'

I bit my lip. I'd never gone against Ma or Pa before. And I shouldn't be worrying them, especially when the news on the radio talked of people losing their jobs, of Simon's Town dockyard cutting back, and of the threat that cutback posed to our choppy sea route and the foreign powers who coveted it.

'I want to try, Ma.'

'Then you'd better keep quiet about it,' she said shortly, getting off the bed and smoothing the cover. 'Terrace girls with big ideas make others jealous. Don't lose friends over something that may never happen.'

I nodded.

Ma stopped at the door and looked back at me.

Mr Venter had looked at me with pity. Ma's eyes showed the same – but laced with a disappointment she couldn't quite mask. I was letting Ma down by daring to be different.

Chapter Seven

It took a year, but Piet finally said yes to the flashy man who haunted the boats at Seaforth beach. A year while Piet grew taller and – the man indicated with a knowing slide of his eyes over Piet's frame – less useful for the job; a year in which Amos's drinking worsened, the cottage sprang new leaks during the winter rains, and Piet increasingly missed school to take odd jobs.

'It will give you a regular income,' the flash man said, shrugging. 'But don't do it if you've got something else . . .'

But Piet had nothing else. His father's boat – promised to Piet one day – might not last much longer. He could have spoken to his teachers, but they were always angry at him and probably wouldn't listen. Amos Philander had never bothered with religion of any sort so there was no Imam or minister that Piet could ask about the difference between right and wrong in an unjust world. And he was too ashamed to speak to Solly Ahrendts. As for Louise, he could still see the hurt on her face when he told her she could go and swim on her own if she liked.

Luckily Mrs Ahrendts still occasionally invited him to eat with them – succulent *bobotie*, sometimes an apple pie – but those were his only proper meals and for the rest of the time he starved. The hunger made him edgy, made him lash out or be rude. If he could just eat more, Piet reckoned, his life would get back on track. And then he'd make up with Lou and they wouldn't need to avoid each other's eyes any longer.

The flash man gave him a little cash up front, and promised one night job per week at an agreed rate. Piet told himself that this new job would only be for a while. Lots of people did this kind of thing when they were down on their luck.

There was no moon that night, and the overhanging Simonsberg helped by blocking out the stars in half of the sky, including the Southern Cross and its watchful pointers. Piet and the flash man crept along a paved road in a smarter part of town than the crowded shanties of Seaforth. The flash man halted, looked about and then pressed down the sagging fence around a small, dark house. They stepped over. Piet examined the darting shadows for animals, then forced his eyes to pick a route through the garden even as his ears strained for the murmur of human talk.

The flash man motioned him forward.

An object, about a foot in height, erupted from a bush, its arched back bristling with black-and-white quills. Piet gasped and choked back a scream.

The porcupine blundered away.

He bent over, chest heaving. Was there a mate? Did they gather in groups? Would his first job be sunk by a troop of wild porcupines?

The flash man shrugged and tapped his wrist to indicate he should get moving.

Piet's narrow body – one advantage of being hungry, he grimaced – twisted its way through the open fanlight with no difficulty. He landed lightly on carpet, stifling a gasp, and stared about him.

A bed, empty.

He sniffed for the possibility of cigarettes, or the gamey breath of a dog leaping from its basket, teeth bared . . .

Nothing, just the pounding of his heart, loud enough to wake the neighbourhood.

He tiptoed into the passageway.

Wall-mounted pictures leant off their hooks towards him.

He edged forward, off the carpet now, his bare feet feeling ahead for squeaks in the wooden floorboards that would give him away. Sweat was gathering in the crease of his neck and on his palms. He'd often smelt cloying fear on the bodies of his fellow fishermen when the waves were so huge they blotted out the sky. He wiped his hands on his shorts.

Here, on his right, was a door. Ajar.

He listened for breathing, but all that emerged was his own fevered panting. He put his head around the door, ready to flee, but the bed, like the first one, was empty.

Across the passage was a bathroom.

He leapt back as a mirror reflected a pinched, wide-eyed face back at him.

But he was getting used to the darkness now. He stole through the well-furnished lounge with growing confidence, then through the kitchen with its gleaming fridge and an oven far smarter than the Ahrendts's, checked the back door was locked, then bumped against a wicker washing basket and almost toppled it. He froze, bent over, hands squeezing the basket hard enough to crush it.

No one shouted. No light was switched on.

No footsteps ran to investigate.

The place was empty.

He breathed out, padded to the front door, ran his hands over it to check for chains or bolts, then unlatched it slowly. The garden leapt dark and forbidding towards him, the only light coming from the glow of a street lamp as it fell onto a stretch of pavement beyond the fence. In the distance, the sea he knew so well was a vast, mute pool of black punctured only by the sweeping beam from the lighthouse.

A shape detached itself from the shrubbery. The flash man slipped inside.

Between them, they emptied the place of jewellery found in the bedroom, a wad of banknotes left in a drawer, and several bottles of liquor from a kitchen cupboard – all of which was swiftly tucked away by the flash man into a sack.

Then they left, closing the front door quietly behind them.

The heavy cough of a baboon sounded from the mountaintop. Then several more coughs. Alarm calls – Piet forced himself to be calm – but not for him. There must be leopard about. He wrestled the sack across the fence, careful not to allow the bottles inside to chink against one another. A car drove along a nearby road, the engine fading into the night. Once they were concealed within the swaying tree shadows, the flash man counted out some notes to pay him.

'Like taking sweets from a baby, hey?' the man whispered, and slapped Piet on the back. 'Wear gloves next time. Sleep tight.'

He was back in bed in his tiny room well before sunrise, before the first raucous chants of the guinea fowl that might rouse a neighbour, who might spot Piet returning, who might tell his father . . .

He stroked the notes under his blanket with trembling fingers. This was riches! But he mustn't arouse suspicion by appearing flush. He would spend part of it on food, and the rest would be saved for a shirt or shoes from the second-hand store, bought gradually so as not to attract attention.

Snores rose from his father and Uncle Den in the two front rooms.

He held up his hands in front of his face, willing his guilty fingers to relax.

He realised he was waiting for something: for the sound of a whistle, for pounding footsteps, for barking police dogs. For discovery.

But none came, only the regular thunder of the sea.

Tomorrow – today – he was going back to school.

Chapter Eight

'Louise?' Piet appeared at my side in the corridor, after class was dismissed. 'Walk you home?'

His black eyes held mine and didn't slide away. I felt my heart lift. It must be part of growing up, this pulling away and coming together again. I'd been right to let him find his own way back, in his own time.

But what of the unknown man on the beach?

And the furtive exchange between them?

Piet stood tall and keen in front of me, his narrow face alert. Here was the Piet I'd grown up with, the boy I'd shared my secret with, the boy who perhaps had the right to keep a secret from me.

'I've missed you,' I said, on an impulse, linking my arm through his.

He grinned, and reached down to hug me.

His arms felt warm, true.

'Me, too. I'm sorry for the way I've been. Let's go for a swim?'

Seaforth Beach was deserted when we arrived, the sand bare of any footprints apart from the delicate pockmarks of seagulls. A meandering line of shell fragments – periwinkles, purple turbans, ridged limpets – studded the high-water mark where Piet laid down our towels. The Simonsberg flew a ribbon of cloud. We swam out past the egg rocks, the swells lifting us up and bearing us along with the outgoing tide. The sun was lowering and amber shafts of light probed all the way to the seabed. Piet dived into the sun-dappled depths to bring up a pair of *perlemoen* shells, each hollowed lobe glistening with mother-of-pearl.

'You can be a better fisherman than your father, Piet Philander!' I called as he surfaced, churning through the water in front of me.

'Race you back,' he shouted, kicking for the shore. I plunged after him. Silver-and-yellow *strepies* flickered past my legs in darting, oval shoals and disappeared among the kelp.

We flung ourselves onto the sand, panting from the struggle against the outgoing tide. Beyond the breakers, the resident flock of streamlined terns took off from their rock, circled, and landed once more.

'Or,' I levered myself up on my elbows, 'you could try for an apprenticeship in the dockyard like my pa.' I reached over and grabbed his arm. 'You've got to stay at school, Piet, you can't give up!'

'Yes,' he replied quickly, grabbing one of the mother-of-pearl shells and running to where the sand was harder, its glistening crystals packed smooth by the retreating tide. He bent down. I shaded my eyes to make out what he was doing. Two jet-black, red-beaked oystercatchers piped and strutted at the water's edge.

'Come and look,' he called.

I ran to his side.

He had used the shell to draw an outsize heart in the wet sand.

'I love you, Lou. I'm sorry I've been so bad. But everything's better now.'

I took his hand and rubbed the place where the skin had broken and then healed. I was wrong to doubt him. And maybe magic disappears for a while, and then returns when you least expect it.

'I love you, too, Piet. Don't leave me alone again.'

He reached for me, his hands warm on my skin, his lips finding mine for the first time.

Chapter Nine

I turned fifteen towards the end of 1933. There was no birthday treat and no money in the tin box for Cape Town excursions. A foreign Depression, first broadcast on the radio in 1929, had flung its cold shadow across the sea, and thrown people into fear of losing their jobs. Terrace men who were less qualified than Pa found themselves out of work. Nobody wanted to buy Mr Phillips' pipes or order new frocks from Mrs Hewson. More people responded to the muezzin's call, or flocked to St Francis Church to hear the dockyard chaplain and pray to be spared the shame of being let go.

'It's a disgrace,' Pa declared as we walked back from church one Sunday. 'A disgrace! All that swindling far away – nothing whatsoever to do with us! But now the patrols are being cut back, there's no money for new tools or even enough paint to touch up the crests on the dry dock wall. Why, do you know, HMS *Acorn*'s almost invisible?'

'Pipe down, Solly,' said Ma crisply. 'Your daughter's

almost fifteen and top of her class. You and I still have jobs. Remember the sermon. Be grateful.'

Pa sighed and gave Ma a fat kiss. His dismay, of course, was about more than tools and paint and out-of-work neighbours. He'd read the letter from Matron. Unlike Ma, he was proud of me for my brave application. But he suspected that the Depression would make it even less likely the Victoria Hospital would find me worthy. Pa knew how hard I wanted it. Pa knew, because he'd once wanted to get ahead as much as I did. And I think he felt guilty for having encouraged me too far; for having stoked too bold a dream for a brown girl.

Surprisingly, Piet and his family hadn't been as hard hit by the Depression. Perhaps, when you had very little to start with, there was less to lose. And fish, it seemed, were always in demand whatever happened on the other side of the ocean. Amos still drank away his profits, but somehow the boat stayed afloat and the cottage held together. He and Piet had declared a truce, Piet told me with a grimace, and fixed the leaks in both.

'Piet,' I hissed from my desk in the row behind his, for my birthday fell on a school day, 'I've got something to tell you!'

'Oh yes?' Piet inclined his head but didn't turn round.

'Ma says we can go on our own to the bioscope on Friday nights!'

My friends were already walking out alone with boys, but up to now Ma had chaperoned me, and frowned at Vera and her latest flame who sat upstairs at the Criterion and – between clinches – passed cheeky comments about the smart white folk in the reserved seats below. There'll be trouble, Ma would mutter with a knowing glance at their entwined limbs, you mark my words. Pa was just as protective. He insisted I was home by sunset, even on summer evenings when Piet and I liked to swim under fresh stars, and hold hands in the lengthening shadows where no one could spot us. We were officially boyfriend and girlfriend, and Piet was eager for more. I could feel it in the tingle of his skin against mine, the way his eyes lingered on my body and the flush that rose in my face when he looked at me like that. Ma watched and privately warned about the perils of looseness before marriage.

'He won't respect you,' she insisted. 'Make him wait.'

Piet turned and shot me a quick grin.

Heavy boots stamped along the corridor. The steps slowed and a white policeman in a dark-blue uniform halted in the doorway, hands on hips. He began to scan the rows of desks.

Mr Venter hurried over, muttered something and then very deliberately closed the door.

'Quiet,' he ordered, as excited talk broke out. 'Return to your exercise.'

The class subsided. Piet settled lower into his seat, burying his head in his book.

The bell rang.

'Finish this for homework,' Mr Venter raised his voice over the growing hubbub, 'and I will test you tomorrow. No shirking! Good afternoon, class.'

'Good afternoon, Mr Venter,' we chorused.

Piet leapt up, rammed his belongings into his rucksack and joined the rush to leave the classroom.

'Wait!' I called, loading up my books, for the demands of being top of the class meant weekends-worth of studying, especially now that I had a job most afternoons. 'Wait for me!'

But he was already pushing through the crush at the door.

The policeman stood across the passageway, his head turning left and right. I craned above the crowd as I reached the door. A boy with Piet's black hair was bobbing down the stairs, a boy far shorter than Piet, a boy perhaps crouching down to escape notice.

There was still no sign of him as I hurried home past Runciman's, and then past Sartorial House where I worked for a small wage, dusting the shelves, measuring lengths of cloth to save old Mr Bennett's eyes, and sweeping out the leaves that blew in on the southeaster. I saved every penny I earned . . .

'The police were here,' Mrs Hewson shouted from her front step, 'wanting Piet!'

I stopped.

'What do you mean? At our house?'

Mrs Hewson shrugged and went back to her sewing. 'I knew he was no good. I warned your pa!'

I scooped my key from under the rock by the front door.

A pair of red-winged starlings rooting in the dirt took off with a startled squeal.

Even though it was my birthday, there was laundry soaking in the sink, expecting to be rinsed. A pile of shirts sat on the kitchen table, ready to be ironed. I flung off my clothes, raced into shorts and a blouse, didn't bother with shoes and was off again, past Mrs Hewson's shouted warnings, down Alfred Lane and along Grandpa Ahrendts's wall, with the memory of another day hammering in my head: the letter sent in hope, the sprint to Seaforth to share it – then the sight of Piet taking something from a man in the bushes and thrashing out to sea.

I hadn't checked his shirt. I still didn't know what he'd done. Even now. Even though he said he loved me, and I loved him back and we were set to be married one day.

Near Tredree Steps I almost collided with a sailor walking towards me.

'Careful, miss!' he cried.

'Sorry!'

Piet didn't want to be a fisherman, he wanted to work onshore, in the dockyard, or go to sea like that sailor. Anything but fishing, he'd finally confessed, his black eyes holding mine, his hands twisting together. Anything. I love the sea, but I don't want to fish it.

I stopped for a second to catch my breath, to steady my heart.

Seagulls hovered above the anchored ships, holding their positions against the wind with uncanny skill. It's their air perch, Pa once said. See? They work out how strong the wind is, and then they flap just enough to keep themselves in one place instead of being blown away.

Had Piet lost his balance and been blown away while I chose not to look?

Was he lying to me when he said that everything was better . . . ?

I ran on.

A yacht knifed across the bay, its sail swollen with the freshening breeze.

The noise reached my ears before I reached the Philander cottage.

'Piet!' I shouted, pushing my way through a heaving mass of fishermen, neighbours, dogs and chickens crowding the front door. A large policeman barred the way, legs astride, beefy arms pressed against the door frame. I darted under his arm. 'Piet?'

'Hey,' the policeman cried, grabbing after me, 'you can't go in there!'

I strained to adjust to the gloom, but I didn't need eyes to sense the gathering storm. Amos and Piet were squaring up in the corner. A chair had been overturned. Dishcloths lay strewn on the floor. Uncle Den peered around the door of his room, his gaze flicking nervously between the men and a pot bubbling on the stove, the lid popping up and down for the steam to escape. In front of me, a second policeman, this time with a notebook and a pair of handcuffs dangling from his pocket, watched with hands on hips as Amos shook Piet and yelled, 'You *bliksem*! That's what you've been doing!'

And then Amos took a swing and hit Piet square across the face.

The crowd shrieked and heaved towards the door. Dogs set up a volley of barking.

'No,' I screamed, flinging myself between them, 'leave him alone!'

The policeman leapt forward to strong-arm Amos aside and pull me away.

'Young lady – this is no place for you!'

'Stay out of this, Lou!' Piet bent over and clutched his inflamed face.

Amos, chest heaving, stumbled backwards. I could smell drink on his breath. One flailing arm caught me on the ear. Pain lanced up my temple, down my neck. I fought to keep my balance.

'I won't go,' I gritted, 'till you tell me what he's done.'

'Tell us what he's done, tell us!' Scuffles broke out amongst the onlookers as they jostled for a view. 'Off!' The inside officer lost his composure and turned to yell out the door. 'All of you! Otherwise we'll bring the dogs!'

There was a scrambling. The crowd dispersed.

Den crept to the stove and hauled the exhaling pot from the hotplate.

I grabbed hold of Piet's rough hand. He was panting in and out, noisily.

I love you, Lou, he'd said, after drawing a heart in the sand. Everything's better.

'Now,' the policeman turned back, 'we'll take this nice and slow.'

Amos righted the overturned chair and sat down heavily.

A chicken wandered past the feet of the policeman at the door and he kicked it away.

'I can make some tea,' Den said in a small voice, from the kitchen.

'No thank you, sir. You are Amos Philander,' he pointed at Amos, 'and this is your son, Piet Philander?'

Amos mumbled a yes.

'It's my duty to tell you that your son's fingerprints have been found at several addresses where there have been break-ins—'

'How do you know they're Piet's?' I interrupted. His hand, clasped with mine, briefly twitched.

'Miss, we've had our suspicions for some time.' The policeman shifted his glance to take in Den as well. 'We've seen this boy returning home very late at night. On the same night as these places were burgled.'

Amos made to get up again, but saw the policeman's frown, and shouted at Piet instead. 'We thought you were in bed but you're running around, thieving! If your mother knew this—' he broke off.

'But the fingerprints?' I forced the words out past my aching temple.

The policeman consulted his notes.

'On Tuesday of last week, I was authorised to gather fingerprints from these premises.'

A roaring filled my ears, like when a wave knocks you off your feet and pitches you into its depths.

'You've been in my house?' Amos yelled, this time lumbering to his feet. Uncle Den flapped a calming hand at him.

I turned to Piet. He raised his eyes from the floor to meet mine. Guilt etched his face, carving it along strangely adult lines. My hand shook inside his.

The policeman swatted Amos back into his seat.

I pulled my hand away. Piet flinched as if my fingers were wet rope slipping out of his grasp, flaying the skin left behind.

'We found prints that matched the burglar's in your son's room. Now,' he looked at each of us in turn, his glance lingering on Piet the longest, 'we can do this the easy way. Or we can do this the hard way.'

Amos hunched into his chair. 'I did my best,' he whined. 'I did all I could to bring the boy up right – you saw that, Den, you saw that?'

'*Ja*, Amos. Let's hear what the officer says.'

The policeman nodded in Den's direction.

'Your son is sixteen. If,' he leant forward and tapped Amos's knee to make sure he was paying attention, 'if he admits to all this thieving, then there's a way I can keep him out of prison.'

'How?' Amos growled.

Uncle Den shuffled across in front of his nephew. 'Did you do this, Pietie?' his voice was gentle.

'Yes,' Piet mumbled, 'I wanted to make money for food, and to buy clothes for school so I could stay and pass my exams.'

Den rested a hand on the boy's bowed head.

'Oh, Piet,' I cried out, 'why didn't you say?' I rounded on Amos. 'You drank all your money away! Piet was forced to do this, you never gave him enough—'

Amos opened his mouth.

'Now you keep quiet, brother!' Den cut in with surprising force. 'The girl's right and you know it. Officer,' he turned to the policeman, 'tell us what you can do for our Piet.'

The policeman steered Piet towards a chair at the ancient kitchen table. 'Juvenile delinquents like this boy can be helped if they go somewhere with strict discipline,' he stated, as if Piet was simply a blunt tool needing to be sent to the workshop for sharpening. 'When they come out, they can rebuild their lives.'

'What is this place?' I asked, with growing unease. The

pain in my ear was lessening, but my heart felt swollen, as if it was trying to hold onto something that was too huge, too overwhelming to be contained.

'A reformatory.'

'A borstal?' Amos shouted. 'My boy in a borstal?'

The policeman shrugged. 'It's more like a school. Where boys learn the error of their ways—'

'How long?' put in Piet, crushed. 'When will I get out?'

'Depends how you do,' the policeman pulled out a pencil and began to write. 'Two years at least.'

'Will he have a criminal record?' asked Den.

'Not if he admits everything now and helps us with our investigations.'

Amos moaned, his head in his hands.

'But if he comes out and reoffends,' the policeman wagged a warning finger, 'then he'll go to prison.' He stowed his notebook and opened the handcuffs.

'He won't do that,' I spoke up. 'He's going to come out and get a proper job. There won't be any more thieving.'

Piet lifted his head and stared at me.

'I know why he did this,' I cast a scornful glance at the moping Amos, 'and it won't happen again.'

But could I be sure?

I gave my heart to Piet, I thought I knew him . . .

The policeman shrugged and motioned to Piet. Piet hung his head and held out his hands, damaged palms touching, as if he was about to pray. The handcuffs went round his thin wrists and engaged with a metallic click.

'We'll wait outside while you help him pack a case and say goodbye.'

The policemen stepped through the front door. Waves crashed in the background. One of the policemen stretched. The other lit a cigarette. The *kek-kek-kek* of an approaching flock of guinea fowl sounded from further up the lane.

Den moved across to Amos. 'Louise will help Piet. We'll stay here.'

Piet's room was at the back of the cottage. There was only space for a single bed and a stack of old wooden apple boxes piled one on top of one another as makeshift drawers. I had never been there. Ma always said that unmarried girls who visited boys' rooms were for ever tarnished.

'I could run away,' Piet jerked at his tethered wrists. 'Climb out of the kitchen window and swim across the bay—' He turned desperate eyes on me. The sea was his friend, he could cut through the water, fast as any fish, probably even with his hands cuffed. 'Why not? If you distract the cops—'

'You'll drown!' It was several miles to Fish Hoek beach and over twenty miles to the far side of False Bay. 'Or they'd find you and put you in jail.'

He subsided onto the bed.

I sat down beside him, and took his hands, easing the cold metal where it bit into his wrists. Piet's hands held the story of his life. Fishing. Robbery.

'Will you wait for me, Lou?'

I stared at him. I wanted to say yes. I wanted to tell him that I loved him despite everything, that I understood why he'd become a criminal.

Because I did.

But I couldn't understand what came after. What he'd

encouraged me to believe. He took a precious mother-of-pearl shell and drew a heart in the sand and told me everything was better . . . while living the secret life of a thief.

It was a monstrous betrayal.

Far worse than my early neglect in favour of my dream; far worse than my cowardice in not confronting him over his accomplice in the bushes, for that is who it must have been.

'Say you'll wait,' he implored. 'I want to marry you, Lou!'

He didn't wait for my reaction but leant forward and kissed me greedily, as if to hoard the taste of my lips, the feel of my skin, the slip of my hair against his inflamed cheek.

'I'll go straight. This won't happen again—'

I drew back and touched a finger to my lips.

I don't know why I did that. Was it to remember the imprint of where his mouth crushed mine? Or was it to stop him saying anything more, making promises I couldn't trust.

I got up and opened his brown school suitcase and began to pack a few clothes into it.

'Wait for me!' he pleaded, wringing his confined hands. 'Wait for me!'

Chapter Ten

Winter arrived soon after Piet's departure for the reformatory. The southeasters that had whipped the sea into the kind of waves he loved to surf disappeared, replaced by north winds that deadened the bay and drove sharp squalls across its moody surface.

In town, another kind of squall caused mothers with young children to hurry away from me in the street. On the Terrace, our neighbours avoided my eye.

Piet's disgrace settled on me.

'I've done nothing wrong!' I cried to Ma.

'It's the way it is,' she shrugged. 'With Piet gone, you're the closest target.'

I hadn't known this about the world: that crime is catching, even if you're innocent.

'Louise!' Mr Bennett shouted out of the doorway of Sartorial House one soggy afternoon as I headed home from school. He wasn't in his usual apron, and the shop was dark behind him.

'I won't be late, sir, I'm going home to change,' I called, hurrying towards him. My shift was due to start shortly. 'I'll be back soon.'

He shook his head and gestured up to the Simonsberg with a resigned flap of his hand.

'No, you better stay at home—'

He went back inside, shut the door, and hung up the 'Closed' sign. I stared at him, then out past the dockyard. The beam of Roman Rock Lighthouse rotated palely through the rain and fell on a warship slicing towards the harbour, its outline barely visible against the flecked pewter of the sea.

I began to run. Maybe he didn't want me any more. Maybe he thought I was a thief, too.

An angry torrent was racing down the side of Alfred Lane. I took the steps two at a time, my school shoes skidding on the wet stone, bitter tears choking my throat. The mountainside had slipped in several places the day before, heaping wet soil and rock against the back of the Terrace, and causing an extra call to prayers from the mosque. Mr Phillips' cottage, missing foundations, was pushed forward until it stuck out like a ship's prow over the slope. Perhaps – I swiped my face to get rid of the rain, the tears – our Terrace guardians Jesus and Allah were too busy elsewhere, the mountain had slipped again, swept into our sitting room, found Ma at her sewing machine—

Mr Bennett knew.

This wasn't about Piet or thieving.

It was God's punishment for my reckless ambition: to

take Ma, to destroy our home, the one place in the world where we truly belonged.

Brown water eddied around the Hewsons' front door, eating away at the soil beneath the steps and carrying it off to darken the torrent pouring down Alfred Lane. I leapt across. My feet slipped and I put out a hand to stop myself falling. Wet stone sliced my skin.

'Ma?' I screamed, scrabbling away from the rushing water.

I should have listened to her, recognised my place in the world, been grateful . . .

Mrs Hewson poked her head out of the doorway. The hem of her dress dragged wetly.

'Go home!' She swept a broom across her flooded floor. 'I heard your pa just now—'

I recovered my balance and slithered the final yards to our front door. The water was exposing the roots of the palm trees where Piet and his friends had played hide-and-seek on my seventh birthday, and where Ma used to lay me down to sleep when I was a baby.

Ma—

'Thank God!' Pa reached down to scoop me out of the wet and tried to make a joke. 'I thought I'd have to go back out with a search party and a fishing rod!'

'Where's Ma?' I clung to him. 'Has there been a landslide through the back?'

'One of these days the whole Terrace will go down the mountain and into the sea!' Pa set me down and stamped his wet shoes on the mat.

'Ma?' I cried.

'Don't frighten her, Solly! We're fine,' Ma bustled in, reaching for my raincoat. 'Hewsons' is flooded, but nothing that can't be dried out. Now get out of those muddy shoes. I'm making strong tea.'

My legs buckled and I sank onto the floor, pressing my hand where the blood welled.

'If we think we've had it bad,' Pa shouted over the drumming rain, and pointed out of the doorway, 'there's a ship just arrived that's been in the thick of it for days! Gale-force winds, huge seas!'

Ma was safe. Our home was upright. If the mountain fell, at least it would fall on us together. And maybe I was not bad or ungrateful.

'HMS *Durban*,' Pa leant across to kiss Ma and squeezed her shoulder. 'One of our regulars. Tea *asseblief*, Sheila. Then I'll check on the Phillipses, and see what I can do for Mrs H.'

I stared out at the rain and the hungry sea that I loved and feared.

'Come, Louise,' Ma laid a gentle hand on my shoulder, 'let's dry your hair. And put a plaster on that nasty cut. Why do you run when there's no need?'

'HMS *Durban*,' my voice shook, 'I saw its crest on the dry dock wall when I was seven.'

I keep seeing signs. But I must be brave. Not all of them are warnings.

Chapter Eleven

The thing that haunted Piet most in the early days at the reformatory was that the flash man had warned him to use gloves.

Mostly he had, but not always. He'd got careless.

And now he risked losing Lou, his magnificent almond-eyed Lou, who'd stood up and defended him despite his guilt.

He gripped the bars on the window. The tiny view it allowed of the Hottentots Holland Mountains was a mean substitute for the sea. Piet had never been away from the sea for more than a day in his life. Not seeing it, not being able to swim through it, felt like losing an arm or a leg.

He stared out. It had been raining all day. There was nothing to be seen.

And soon they'd yell at him for being late.

Or for not being more grateful for what they were doing for him.

He wondered where she was, what she was doing.

He'd make it up to her, whatever it took.

She was his. He'd kill anybody that took her away from him.

Liewe Lou,

I hate this place. The cops said it would make me better but all they do is treat me like a prisoner. They call me by a number. Sometimes I want to hit them or run away but I know I can't because then I'll be in bigger trouble than I am already. Please don't give up on me. When they let me out I'll go back to school and then get a proper job like you said. The only thing that keeps me going here is you. I love you, Lou, and I want to marry you and look after you all our lives and make a family with you. Nothing will change that. Tell your parents I'm sorry.

All my love,

Piet

Chapter Twelve

Our cottage survived the landslide like it survived the black southeasters: only just.

Pa and the other Terrace men spent several arduous weekends shovelling soil, stabilising the slope, trying to push the Phillipses place back into the mountainside.

'Until next time,' Pa leant down to nuzzle Ma as he scrubbed his hands in the sink. 'Then it'll be kaput.'

While they laboured, I studied indoors at the kitchen table. There could be no slacking, especially as my formal letter of application to the Victoria had been acknowledged. I was now, officially, a candidate. But there was no softening in Matron's reply. She repeated her warning almost word for word from her previous letter: no coloured Simon's Town girl had ever been accepted, I would be well advised to have other work waiting. If she'd wanted to toy with me, there was no crueller way than this: to give me hope but then prepare to dash it. Ma and Pa shook their heads at the wickedness of it.

Beyond our cottage, the gossip converged into its own landslide.

'She must have known!'

'Maybe she took money from Piet? For this nursing idea? Solly and Sheila never knew—'

'Have the police searched the cottage?'

'Too fancy to apply to a coloured hospital?'

'But Piet deceived me,' I protested, forcing back the tears that threatened to spill over. 'I'm innocent! And why shouldn't I train at the Victoria?'

But people – even those who've known me since childhood – prefer conspiracy. It's more interesting than honesty. Why should we believe you? they said with a shrug. After all, you didn't tell your parents what you were up to.

Vera was clear on what had to be done to restore my reputation.

'You should find someone else,' she ordered. 'People will feel better about you with a new boy.'

'Otherwise they'll know I'm still keen on a thief?'

The sea languished.

I watched it from the living room between study sessions.

Grey, choppy, flecked with white horses from an erratic wind.

The reformatory allowed one visit per month.

Amos was still too angry to waste money on the train ticket, and Den's bad back didn't allow him to sit on the train for several hours, so Ma, Pa and I were Piet's only visitors. None of our school friends went, or the adults who knew Amos and should have felt some responsibility to the errant boy. It wasn't the cost of the fare that kept them away. It was what I'd discovered: the risk of guilt by association. Better to stay away. Avoid giving the rampant police any fresh meat.

'I hope Piet appreciates us visiting,' sniffed Ma on one of our trips.

'Come on, everyone deserves a second chance,' Pa protested, 'he's not a bad boy—'

But I knew Pa was equally upset. He'd encouraged Piet, hoping he'd break free of the Philander dependence on leaky boats and drink. When we sat in the plain visitors' lounge and Pa saw how Piet's eyes followed me, I could tell he was torn between what he'd said out loud and the private fear of me promising myself to a damaged boy.

'I fed him,' Ma retorted when she thought I wasn't listening. 'And we trusted him. How could he lie to Lou? She must end this . . .'

I was frightened, too. So far in my life, I'd mostly been scared of outside things like mist sneaking over the Simonsberg, or wily butcher birds, or landslides that might snatch Ma from me before I could rescue her. But this was different. I was afraid because there was no forgiveness in my heart.

Only coldness.

To cover it up, I forced myself to smile and say I still loved Piet – how could I abandon him like the others? – and that he could make a fresh start once he came out.

Was it right to lie? Yet it wasn't lying in the way he'd lied to me.

I lied out of kindness.

And guilt for not confronting him, for not saving him when I had the chance.

The reformatory lay across False Bay, and required two trains and several hours to reach. First, a trundle around the bay and across the Constantia Valley to vibrant Cape Town; then a trek across the Cape Flats towards Somerset West. I secretly loved the journey, especially when I turned eighteen and Ma and Pa reluctantly allowed me to go on my own in order to save money. Free from supervision, I could lean out of the window and feel the sea spray on my face, and laugh at the seagulls screaming narrowly over the carriage roof. On the inland leg, I stared at emerald vines wandering across the Constantia hills, and arum lilies lifting cream trumpets to the sun, and imagined – with a hunger that seemed to rise up in my throat of its own accord – another journey that might take me much further.

There'd been a letter.

Out of the blue, and not in response to one of mine.

It said, once again, that I was unlikely to win a place. But it also said I was being offered an interview.

To assess your fitness, Miss Ahrendts, for nursing training.
I must remind you that attendance at an interview is not a guarantee of success.

'Now don't go getting your hopes up,' warned Ma, touching my carefully plaited hair and fussing over my blazer as she saw me onto the train. White-tipped waves thrashed the shore below the railway line. None of the fishing boats were out. 'It's probably just for show.'

'For show?'

'*Ja*. To pretend they're open to all, even though they aren't.' Ma shrugged and slipped a hard-earned shilling into my pocket for emergencies. 'It makes them feel better.'

'Or maybe they really want me, Ma!'

She tried to smile. I hugged her. Poor Ma hated when I was out of her protective range. Mr Venter, on the other hand, was cautiously optimistic. He told me to sit straight in my chair, meet the interviewer's eyes and speak clearly.

'They want to be sure you'll complete your training,' he said. 'They don't want to waste time and money on girls who give up halfway.' It was a reference to Lola and Susan, both of whom had left school to have unexpected but, I suspect, secretly contrived babies.

'I won't get caught so easily,' Vera scoffed, pouting into the mirror in her mother's tiny bathroom. 'I want to try out lots of boyfriends first, and so should you. My ma says there's ways to avoid a baby until you want one.'

The interview was frightening at first – the cold windowless room, the sceptical eyes of Matron – but I remembered Mr Venter's advice and gave my answers clearly and respectfully, and perhaps surprised her with my Simon's Town brand of moral rectitude. Luckily Matron couldn't divine the lustiness of Vera and wonder if I was the same, nor could she see the disgrace that Piet's crime had pinned on me.

'We will await your results, Miss Ahrendts,' she

announced after it was done, looking me over from my well-polished shoes to my least-darned school uniform and my bolt-upright posture. 'But I must warn you that there is no guarantee that you will win a place.'

'Thank you, Matron,' I replied, holding her gaze. Her iron-grey hair glinted beneath the overhead light. 'If I'm beaten to a place, then I know the other girls are more deserving than me.'

Her eyes flickered away from mine.

The conductor came through the carriage and shouted out the reformatory station. I got up, ignoring the suspicious glances of the other passengers – more guilt by association – and stepped off the train. It was a half-mile walk to the entrance along a dirt road flanked by peeling gums. Despite Piet's loathing, it wasn't a bad place. There was plenty of food. The teachers were strict, so Piet was learning something in class. And his bed was near a window in the dormitory so he could look out. But even when he tried to be positive, there was no spark. Piet was a boy made for the outdoors, for the tumbling sea, for the howling gale. Caging him in took away the part that made him who he was.

'Louise Ahrendts,' I said for the guard at the entrance. 'Coming to see Piet Philander.'

The gate clanged open.

'Lou!' Piet grasped my hands, and looked past me for Pa and Ma. 'On your own?'

'Yes,' I reached up and kissed him on the cheek.

He was wearing the standard uniform, even though it was a Saturday: a grey shirt and striped tie, and grey shorts.

His wild black hair was closely cropped. His hands, once noticeable for their scarred palms, were now rough all over from the manual labour that was part of the curriculum: gardening, digging, chopping wood, bricklaying.

'Was it high tide when you left?' His restless eyes swept away from me.

'Almost. Breaking well up the sand,' I said, pretending I'd run down to Seaforth in advance of catching the train. I'd hardly swum since Piet left. It seemed selfish to enjoy the sea while he was locked up; to float on my back and feel the swells lift me while he yearned for even a glimpse of it. I now went to the beach early in the morning when no one else was about, to comb for fragments of the shells he used to collect for me, or sit on the grass and stare out at the breakers we used to surf.

'Was the lighthouse flashing when you woke up this morning?'

'Yes.'

'I think I see the light coming through my window. I count the seconds until it should flash again—'

I reached into my bag. 'I brought you some books.'

He fingered them, then laid them aside.

'Do you still love me?'

The lines on his face were permanent, now, branded into his forehead and cheeks like the scars that criss-crossed his palms. I felt my throat contract. All that was left – all he clung to from one visit to the next – was not his own self-worth, but the thin veneer of whether I said I loved him or not.

'Yes, I love you, Piet.'

He leant forward, urgently, and grabbed my arms. 'Then

let's get engaged! They'll let us see each other privately! We can start making a baby, Lou!'

I stared at him, aghast.

'Please, Lou, it would give me something to fight for. And we'd be a family when I come out . . .' He kept hold of my arms and motioned with his head around the room where other boys were huddled with their visitors.

'But I'm going to be a nurse,' I broke free. 'I've worked so hard, I've been interviewed!'

If the Victoria didn't want me, somewhere else would. I was on my way, how could I let up now?

He jumped up, retaking my hands, crushing them in his grip. 'You can start a year later.'

'No!'

How could he expect me to give up before I'd even started? And what of forgiveness?

A bell rang. It was the signal that there was fifteen minutes of visiting time left.

'Please, Lou! If you love me, you'll do this for me.'

The heat rushed into my cheeks.

How dare he imply that if I refused it meant I didn't love him! How dare he set a test?

His eyes, more alive than they'd been for months, roamed over my inflamed face. He put his hand at the back of my neck, leant forward and kissed me like on the day of his arrest. Deliberately, with an undercurrent of anger. And more hungrily than when Pa and Ma were present.

'I must go,' I wrenched myself away, my mouth bruised. There was a splatter of rain on the windows. The wind was gaining strength, moaning around the side of the building and bending the few scrappy trees on the perimeter.

'If you love me, you'll do this! I know you will.'

'That's not fair!' I leapt up, desperate for my own escape. Seaforth. The unblemished sand. The forgiving sea.

Disbelief followed by despair spread across his face.

My outrage throbbed and then faded into pity.

'I won't have a baby yet, Piet. I'm going to be a nurse.'

He looked down at his hands, then up at me defiantly.

'And when you leave here,' I pointed at the spartan setting, 'you're going to finish school and get a proper job.'

The downpour that pelted me on the long dash back to the reformatory station soon swept across False Bay and enveloped Simon's Town. Ma tutted and made tea while I tore off my wet clothes as if they were somehow contaminated.

'How's Piet?' she asked casually over supper. Rain hammered on the roof.

Pa flicked her a glance.

I straightened my back. Ma wasn't concerned with Piet's state of mind. She was worried about exactly the situation that had come about. On past visits, the procession of young, pregnant visitors to the reformatory had not escaped her notice.

'He's fine, Ma,' I replied evenly. 'But he still hates the place.'

'Of course he does! He's there to learn a lesson.' She spooned mashed potato decisively onto my plate. 'I was talking to Den the other day. He says Amos needs Piet back even though he's still angry with him. Amos's legs are playing up,' she directed a cynical look at Pa.

'Piet must finish school first,' I put in. 'Then he can decide what to do. Maybe not fishing.'

'Quite right,' Pa nodded at me as he forked up his carrots. 'Give the boy a chance to make good on his own.'

'He's got a lot of making good to do before I'll have him back at this table,' Ma snorted and drew herself up, 'or near my daughter!'

'Sheila!'

Ma smacked her serviette down on the table and faced up to Pa. 'I want the best for Lou. She doesn't have to settle for Piet!'

'Ma, please!' I leant over and grabbed her arm. 'I'll wait for Piet to get out. But I haven't promised anything more.'

'Just as well!' Ma picked up the discarded napkin and thrust it back on her lap. 'Your pa knows some respectable men—'

'I'm going to be a nurse,' I shouted, jumping up from the table. 'Why won't anyone listen? Not a wife! Not yet!' I ran to my room and slammed the door.

Chapter Thirteen

The season turned.

Summer's southeasters began to build behind the Simonsberg and the sun danced across a newly enlivened bay. I thrust Piet aside and took to watching for the post as I'd done four years earlier. In the newspapers, there were stories about a German leader called Hitler who wanted to conquer land beyond his country's border. Pa shook his head and wondered about the sea route.

Ma said nothing more about Piet or respectable men, or my chances at the Victoria.

'Leave it,' she whispered to Pa. 'She'll learn the hard way.'

Others were less discreet.

My future was public property.

'The Victoria will never take you!' laughed Vera, as we fought along St George's Street against a spring gale. 'Don't waste your time! And if you won't give up Piet, tell him to stay out of trouble so you can start making babies when he gets out. That's what he wants, doesn't he?'

Were the walls at the reformatory some sort of loudspeaker? But then Vera often surprised me with her careless insights.

'I want to make more of myself—'

'Why?' she teased, hands on hips, hair flying about her face. 'Are you better than the rest of us?'

'Of course not!'

That's what they all thought: that I believed I was too good for them. Too good for Ricketts Terrace. Too good for Simon's Town.

'Don't leave here!' Mrs Hewson shouted from her step. 'What's wrong with working in town, among people you know?'

'She wants to get ahead,' Lola muttered to Susan, as the new baby tugged at her breast, 'but these places only take whites. Lou's clever, but she's too pushy.'

'You can go full time with me,' offered Mr Bennett, from among the bolts of cloth at Sartorial House. 'You're a good worker despite that boyfriend. Five days a week, eight until six, and Saturdays till one. Better than nannying or cooking.'

'I can't decide yet, Mr Bennett. I've been interviewed for nurses' training at the Victoria.'

'The Victoria?' The corners of his mouth curled. 'You're bright enough. But too brown, if you ask me.'

I bit down a retort. Was no one in our world prepared to challenge the colour bar? Surely it wasn't my place to fight such injustice on my own. Older, experienced people should be resisting, they should show the way. But they never came forward.

Even so – my heart quickened – if the government of our Great War hero, General Smuts, suddenly changed its mind and swept away the bias that kept whites at the top, coloureds in the middle and blacks at the bottom, I'd have a chance!

The Victoria would have to choose on merit. I wondered about writing a letter.

Dear Prime Minster . . . why must I always be second?

Why should you be first?

This time, it took only twenty-eight days from the submission of my exam results to the letter arriving. I found it under the door after school and sat at the kitchen table with it in front of me, unopened, all afternoon until Ma and Pa returned home.

Waiting kept the dream alive for a few more hours.

'Be prepared,' warned Ma, as I took up the crested envelope. 'You tried your best.'

'We're proud of you, Lou,' added Pa heartily, flinging an arm around my shoulders. 'You've done better at school than your ma or me by far.'

Dear Miss Ahrendts,
We have pleasure in offering you a place to train at the Victoria Hospital, subject to a successful probation period of three months.

'They want me,' I threw the single sheet of paper in the air and burst into tears, 'they want me!' I'd been steeling myself so hard against rejection – and the need to hold up my head despite it – that when acceptance came there was nothing to do but cry. At last, through the tears, I could claim slippery revenge for every slur I'd shouldered or pretended not to hear, every year I'd waited to be judged good enough.

'That's my girl!' Pa swept me up in his arms and whirled me around. 'Of course they want you!'

Ma grabbed the letter. Her lips made out the words in astonishment.

> *Miss Ahrendts, you will be our first coloured student nurse, and we must stress the need for focus and dedication. Failure to achieve the required standards at any time during your training will result in dismissal from the programme.*

'Get out the Old Brown!' Pa bellowed. 'Invite the Terrace!'

He put me down and bustled into the kitchen for the sherry and glasses.

Ma knelt down in front of me, drew my hands to her and kissed them.

'Well done,' she choked, 'brave, foolish child!'

I dashed a hand across my face and gathered her to me, stroking her wiry hair. Comforting her. In one fleeting moment, via the words on a single page, Ma and I had changed places . . .

'What's this noise, Solly Ahrendts?' Mrs Hewson poked her head around the front door. 'Even I can hear you with my bad ears.'

'It's Louise!' Ma wiped her eyes and scrambled up. 'She's been accepted for nurse's training!'

Mrs Hewson limped inside and wagged a finger at Pa, who was pouring generous tots. 'Look what you've raised, Solly. She might even outdo you.'

She turned to me and patted my head.

'Beware, young miss,' she declared, 'the outside world is full of sin.'

I began to laugh through my tears.

'But an exciting place, they say.' She accepted a glass from Pa and raised it to me. 'Bigger fish. You won't need to run after that good-for-nothing Piet any more.'

Chapter Fourteen

'Nurse Ahrendts!'

'Yes, Sister?'

'Matron wishes to see you. Immediately.'

I froze.

'Nurse?'

I'd served my probation and passed my exams with distinction, I'd proved myself in every way to be as good, or better, than the nurses who were paler than me, and yet . . . Ma's words rang in my ears. *You should have learnt that by now*.

'Nurse? Are you unwell?'

'No, Sister. I'm on my way.'

I breathed out, straightened my apron and walked smartly out of the ward. The polished floor clicked under my heels. Never run, Sister Tutor had drummed into us. Nurses walk – swiftly in an emergency – but they never run.

And certainly not in bare feet!

Never in my life had my feet been confined for such long periods.

It was two years since I'd first paced carefully along the corridors as a nervous eighteen-year-old, my brown skin gleaming – or so it seemed to me – far more conspicuously than it ever did in Simon's Town. Just as skipping stones across the sea is an art more than a science, so it was with nursing. You can learn the mechanics to mend broken bones, but true healing turns out to be something altogether different. In those two years I learnt the practical skills but also, thrillingly, found an instinct that went beyond the book learning Sister Tutor hammered into us. My fellow nurses wondered why my patients' wounds mended better than theirs, or how I used my training to such effect in an emergency. Sister Tutor knew, but she didn't say. Perhaps, like the stones, it's something from God. And perhaps He decided I deserved a break.

But my art wasn't enough for those around me.

'Why's she here? Aren't there coloured hospitals?'

'It's shocking! Taking a white place!' Nurse Phipps tossed her blonde hair and brushed past.

Barely muffled rebuke followed me like the mist after a southeaster, especially when it became clear I didn't have the good sense to fail and slink back, tail between my legs, to the poor community from where I'd sprung. There were times when I imagined I was closing in on acceptance – the nod of recognition, the word of praise – only to have it snatched away from me.

'Good work, Nurse. But Nurse Mullins has been selected for advanced training. Dismissed.'

I was caught between success and ostracism. It became necessary to construct a pretence for those in Simon's Town who saw only the success.

'I've found my place,' I cried cheerfully on my home leaves, as Ma sat on the end of my bed and listened to my contrived tales with astonishment. 'They want me there! They know I'm good enough!'

'Well then, don't let up,' she exclaimed. For all her earlier misgivings, Ma had developed a powerful determination on my behalf. 'Don't give them a chance to change their minds!'

Piet, back from the reformatory and struggling to get ahead, didn't ask about my career other than to envy the money it brought in. I told him very little about my work, it was easier that way. Not because I'd have to lie as with Ma, but because my prospects, even with the opposition I faced, were so much better than his. I told myself to give him time, not to be disappointed at his lack of progress. He, meanwhile, pressed for marriage and a firm commitment. 'How much longer must I wait, Lou?'

Strangely, the harder it was for me to fit in, the more respect I had for Matron. She'd been brave enough to offer me a place. I wondered if she was still taking criticism. Perhaps this summons was to say I was no longer worth the trouble.

I put up a hand up to check that my cap was secure, and knocked.

I must be grateful. Not bitter.

'Come in.'

Matron was the same iron-grey-haired lady who'd

interviewed me for moral rectitude and a positive demeanour. She opened a Manila folder on her desk and looked up. Her gaze swept over me, from my carefully whitened shoes, past my uniform bib, and up to my cap. She nodded. In Matron's view, a tidy uniform begat a tidy mind, and a tidy mind made for an efficient nurse.

'You come from Simon's Town, Nurse?'

'Yes, Matron,' I replied.

If it wasn't about work, had they found out about Piet? Was he to be the excuse? The lack of moral rectitude of my young man. I'd never breathed a word about him, even to those few who liked me well enough to see I was no different from them.

Matron took off her glasses and laid them down on the desk.

'False Bay Hospital in Simon's Town is short-staffed, Nurse. Would you be willing to transfer there for the completion of your training?'

My heart leapt. Seaforth! The cool water, the sand between my toes . . .

'I'd be delighted, Matron.' From my small room at the back of the nurses' home in Wynberg it wasn't possible to see the ebb and flow of the tide, or watch the first tingling brush of the southeaster on the water.

Matron put her glasses back on, and looked at me over the top of them. 'You will sit the same tests as your fellow nurses here, and complete the same training.' Her voice strengthened. 'We will expect the same level of commitment from you, Nurse, as you have shown at the Victoria.'

'Yes, Matron. I will continue to work hard.'

Was she, in effect, rescuing me from her own, unbending, staff?

'Very well.' She closed the folder. 'You will complete your duties at the end of the week, then transfer. The nurses' home at False Bay can accommodate you if you have no lodgings.'

'Thank you, Matron, but I'll be able to stay at home. My parents live near the hospital, and I can walk to work every day.'

'Then this arrangement should suit you very well.' She gave a thin smile. 'Good luck, Nurse.'

She rose from her chair.

I waited for her to dismiss me, but she seemed to be weighing up something more.

'You will be the first local nurse to serve at False Bay.' She looked me over again. 'Be careful to maintain appropriate behaviour with your patients. Familiarity should not compromise conduct. Under the right circumstances, you have the makings of a promising career. You may return to your ward.'

I struggled to keep my face neutral.

Was she implying that, provided I behaved, I'd be treated more kindly closer to home – and progress further as a result? Find true acceptance?

Or was it simply the fact that the other hospital was so desperate for staff they'd take any nurse, even a non-white, and that my transfer would also save Matron the aggravation of having to constantly defend her decision to accept me in the first place.

I'm adept, you see, at winkling out the reasons for my alienation.

Yet for the thrill of seeing the sea each day, I could live with whichever it turned out to be.

'Good afternoon, Matron.'

I closed the door and struggled not to skip down the corridor, much less run.

Chapter Fifteen

Piet and his friend Abie pulled the fishing boat up the sand at Seaforth. It was nearly spring tide, and many a boat, carelessly parked, had been swept away in the past. Abie grabbed his set-aside share of the catch and trudged up the grass slope.

Piet looked up.

The north wind was still in charge. Already a squall was blurring the horizon over Fish Hoek and Elsie's Peak, smudging brown earth, green mountain and blue sky into a single shade of grey. The Simonsberg remained clear of cloud, its slopes thick with pincushions, their tightly folded buds holding out for warmer weather.

'How much fish, Piet?' Amos Philander lumbered down the slope from the cottage. Amos no longer went out in the boat. It was his legs, he said. They couldn't handle the hauling in of the nets, or the bracing required to keep your balance on a heaving deck. All the fishing was now done by Piet.

It wasn't always going to be so.

When Piet returned from the reformatory, he went back to school to try and get his matric. But he was older than his classmates, and it soon became clear that even if he passed the exam, it would never be enough to persuade an employer to overlook his history as a thief. Solly Ahrendts put in a word for him but Piet was not invited to apply for an apprenticeship. So he left school and queued for manual labour at the Queen Vic gate in the dockyard – and was rejected.

All the while, his father complained that Piet was only good for fishing and should be grateful to have the chance even to scrub the boat let alone take it over. Uncle Den tried to keep the peace. And Louise continued to tell him that she loved him but wouldn't get married or have a baby until she was a proper nurse with all the badges she needed to say so.

'Enough,' Piet grunted at his father, and felt in his pocket for the money he'd received. 'Enough to buy food.'

So there it was.

Back to the dreary days of making only enough to buy food, or the medicine Uncle Den needed for his weak heart, or some second-hand shoes when his only pair rotted from the salt water. Certainly nothing for booze. And that was part of the problem: Amos, retired and forced to be sober, was miserable all day, full and free with his complaints about his disappointing son. It was truc that the cottage above Seaforth no longer sounded to the drunken breakages of Piet's youth, but the replacement was a sullen silence that wrapped itself around the three men and drove Piet to spend more time on the beach. Mending nets, caulking leaks on the boat . . .

When he tried to persuade Louise to change her mind, promising that they would take precautions to avoid a baby until she finished her training, the first thing she asked was where they would live.

'In my room, Lou, at the back of the house. Pa and Uncle Den won't mind.'

'But we can't see the sea from there!' The Philander place was blind, hidden behind a series of dwellings that led down to the shore in jumbled disarray.

'What difference does a view make when we're together?' Piet had countered, desperate for her, desperate for her body.

But it seemed it did. And when Louise tried to explain that their lives would be confined to the cramped back room, while in her parents' home the whole household had the run of the sitting room from where the door and the windows gave onto the shining bay below – Piet had been mystified.

And angry.

Maybe it wasn't about the view, or the reality of sharing with Amos and Uncle Den, or the risk of a baby interrupting her training. Maybe it was because she didn't want to be his wife, full stop, and didn't know how to say so without upsetting him.

But he wouldn't let her go without a fight.

She was his.

Chapter Sixteen

I pulled my nurse's cloak tightly about me. The town had been covered in a chilly sea fog all morning, deepened by the sound of the foghorn wailing across the bay and echoing off the hidden Simonsberg like a dirge.

Fittingly so, given the news.

False Bay Matron swiftly called us together to say that regulations would be put in place declaring Simon's Town a closed port; staff would have to show identity papers and a valid permit before being allowed onto the train at Fish Hoek. There would be no exceptions. Already, blackout shutters were being hammered into place at Admiralty House.

I stopped on my way to the nurses' home and peered through the murk. The tumbled shacks of Seaforth were hidden but Ricketts Terrace hovered between ribbons of mist, like a ghostly frieze propped against the mountain, waiting for its first blacked-out night. The mosque was extra crowded as I set off for work this morning, and Ma spoke of a well-attended prayer vigil at St Francis Church last evening where the minister prayed for a short war. Pa had been saying for weeks that the word in the dockyard was it was only a matter of time. He also said that confidence was strangely muted.

'Why? They're the greatest navy in the world – they should strike first. Imagine that! HMS *Hood* could *donner* Hitler's fleet before he gets the covers off his guns!'

Yet no impending war – or the spider-like tendrils of fog – could dampen my mood.

The change happened slowly at first, then gathered pace. A word here, a glance there.

'We're very pleased you've joined us, Nurse,' Senior Sister pulled me aside a few weeks after I arrived. 'I hope you're being made to feel welcome.'

'Yes, thank you, Sister.' I hesitated. 'More than I expected.'

She raised an eyebrow, but smiled. 'Excellent.'

'Lou!' Vera shouted from behind me. 'Are you going to listen?' Her normally teased hair trailed against her neck from the damp.

'Yes. Why don't you come with me?'

'Maybe it's only for nurses, not for cleaners –' she sniffed, fiddling with her skirt. Vera had forgiven me my ambition when she saw where it led and the rewards it delivered. A smart uniform. Far more money than a cleaner's wage. Respect, even.

'It's war, Vee. They'll never ask you to leave.'

'Will our boys have to fight?' Vera asked, trying to fluff up her hair. 'How will we go out at night if there's a blackout?'

'I think we'll all be fighting, in our own way.'

I pushed open the door to the nurses' home. She adjusted

her apron and strutted in behind me. The common room was packed. Nurses sat two to a chair, aproned cleaners like Vera hovered on the margins, cooks in their white overalls perched on the window sills. Black porters leant against the walls or sat, cross-legged, on the floor in front of the radio. War was already shaking the traditional pyramid. A group of off-duty doctors, uncertain in this female bastion, crowded on the sagging sofa.

The radio crackled. From many thousands of miles away came a man's voice, hesitant at first, then growing in conviction.

In this grave hour . . .

Everyone leant forward, as if there might be a last-minute reprieve.

For the second time in the lives of most of us, we are at war . . .

I felt a sharp intake of breath around me, a collective lift of shoulders, as if that previous war was still lurking, still exacting its price. I was born at the end of the Great War. Pa said it should have been the war to end all wars. One of the older nurses stifled a sob. A doctor rested his head in his hands.

Stand calm and firm and united . . .

I put my arm around Vera's shoulders. She leant against me. A pair of red-winged starlings competed noisily for worms on the soaked grass outside the window.

With God's help, we shall prevail . . .

For a moment, no one moved or spoke. The foghorn swelled and faded off the encircling mountains. The starlings continued their private battle, unaware that the world had changed in the time it took them to root out another worm. Then one of the doctors rose, glanced around, nodded as if in thanks, and walked to the door.

'You should marry Piet now,' Vera announced, as we made our way out. 'With more ships calling, they'll need plenty more fish. He'll make stacks of money!' She nudged me. 'Do it quickly before some other girl gets her claws into him!'

I fought down a wild desire to laugh. Vera, for all her flightiness, had a ruthless practicality: if war meant money, then it should be treated as a springboard for marriage. But I didn't need a man to support me. Ma regularly gasped at the novelty of this – and the danger inherent in an independent daughter. Who would take such a girl on? Especially one already approaching her twenty-first birthday.

'Lou?' Vera linked an arm with me and adopted an arch tone. 'You still want him, don't you, Lou?'

And the war would only extend my independence! I pulled myself up short. I was no better than Vera, with her calculations.

'Lou!'

I might even save enough to buy my own cottage . . .

Vera stopped and eyed me irritably, hands on hips.

'He's served his time. You should say if you've gone off him.' She shrugged. 'There are always others in line. I've got my eye on Abie.'

'I want him to do well, to have some success,' I raised my voice over the rushing of Admiral's Waterfall. I'd promised to wait, but surely I'd exhausted that. Yet I couldn't take the decisive step. The guilt lingered. I hadn't saved him back then, so I ought to give him more time to save himself now.

'Don't wait too long! He might decide to throw you

over!' Vera laughed, then wagged a finger above her head and swung off in the direction of the kitchens, hips undulating beneath the shorter-than-regulation skirt.

I watched her go, and turned down the path.

'Nurse Ahrendts?' Sister Roberts beckoned from the side entrance to the lower wards. In the distance a rain shower was advancing along the coast from Fish Hoek, blotting out the boundary between mountain and sky. I picked my way across the grass, my shoes squelching. A pair of rotund guinea fowl scuttled past, red crops quivering, spotted flanks glistening with beads of moisture.

'Yes, Sister?'

'I'm so sorry, Nurse, I know you're going off duty, but I wonder if you can help one of our VADs with a jaw bandage?'

'Of course, Sister.'

I hid a smile. Matron from the Victoria had indeed done me a favour. Slowly, one person at a time, False Bay Hospital was learning to value my ability rather than scorning my background.

'Splendid. Ward Two. Then you may leave, naturally,' Sister Roberts eyes flickered over me, 'I'm sure you wish to get home—'

Her voice struggled with the word *home*, as if the outbreak of war was already threatening its walls, invading its hearth, sharpening its worth. As if home – however humble – would never be quite as safe again.

Chapter Seventeen

Before you knew it, Piet thought exultantly as he loped along St George's Street, the dockyard was a war zone patrolled by military police and crackling with an urgency Piet was eager to share. Scores of ships – too many names for Lou to remember, even if they weren't supposed to be secret – arrived and departed in a rush of refuelling and repair. Solly Ahrendts's machine shop went on extended shifts. And now, in a stroke, Piet himself was going to benefit. Never mind the thieving, the reformatory, the disgrace.

Their Lordships didn't seem to care!

War wiped the slate clean.

'Lou!' he dashed up to the Victoria Gate where Louise was waiting for her father in the waning afternoon sun, and bent down to kiss her. She blushed and edged away. 'I'm in uniform, Piet!'

He looked down at himself. He should have smartened up. He was still in his fishing clothes, a sagging red jersey over baggy trousers. His feet were bare. Like hers used to be, once upon a time.

'I was looking for you – I've got some news, Lou!'

'Oh, yes?'

'I've got a proper job!' He rumpled his fingers excitedly through his hair, then grabbed her shoulders. She shifted under his grasp.

'What sort of job?'

'It's the war!' he shouted. The guards at the gate turned and frowned. 'Our boat's being taken over – requisitioned they call it – I'm going to fish for the navy, they'll help fix the boat and,' he lowered his voice because the deal might be withdrawn if he yelled too loudly about it, 'they're going to pay me even if the fish don't bite!'

'That's wonderful!' Louise reached for his hand and squeezed it. But,' she pulled back and examined him, 'you still hate fishing, don't you?'

'Not as much as I hate being poor!' Piet grinned. If only he could close his arms around her properly, rest his cheek against the cotton material of her nurse's cap, feel her body pulse against his despite the starchy uniform covering it so rigidly from neck to knee. Let's swim, he felt like saying. Let's go swim at Seaforth and I'll dive for sea urchin shells like I haven't done for so long, and your hair will escape from this silly cap and spread out on the water like silk and everything will be like it used to be—

'What's this, now?' Solly bustled through the gate.

'I've got a proper job, Mr Ahrendts,' Piet said triumphantly. 'Supplying fish to the navy.'

'Well,' Solly slapped him on the back. 'That's certainly good news. Just you stick to it!'

He glanced at his daughter, her face flushed beneath her cap. 'You must be proud of Piet!'

'Of course!' she smiled up at him, the triangle of her nurse's cap bobbing against her neck. 'And I've also got some news. I'm being seconded from False Bay Hospital.'

'Where to?' Piet blurted out.

Not somewhere in Cape Town!

Not that!

Lou would meet all sorts of smarter people, he'd never be able to keep her, even with extra money from the war—

'There!' She pointed in the direction of the old aerial ropeway and a cluster of buildings against the mountain. 'The Royal Naval Hospital!'

Piet gaped. British staff served at the RNH. Locals only got to make the deliveries or do the ironing.

'Now, that's my girl!' Solly shouted and opened his arms to envelop Louise with swelling pride.

Piet's mood plunged. Just when he thought he might catch up with her, she leapt forward again. Like a *klipspringer* one bound ahead of him. It wasn't right.

Louise freed herself from her father and turned to him.

Piet forced a smile as she let him hug her. She wore her hair up these days, beneath her cap in a sort of bun that left her neck slender and exposed. Men looked at her with greed, as they'd always done. She didn't know it, but he'd had to reach out and grab one or two of them by the throat when they looked too long and hard. Just as a warning. Even though they were already walking away, still panting for Lou, and didn't see him coming . . .

'It's a day for celebration!' Solly bellowed, ignoring the curious glances levelled at him by sailors coming and going through the Queen Victoria gate. 'Let's go tell your ma, Lou!'

He grabbed his daughter's arm and turned to cross St George's Street.

'Come along, Piet!' he flung over his shoulder.

'Sure?'

Like Amos, Mrs Ahrendts had never forgiven him.

She might still feed him, but it was with *lang tande* – grudgingly.

This job, though, would change everything.

Now he could show he was good enough! He could insist that Louise marry him, because with two salaries they could look for their own place with a view, far away from his father's grumbling. Then, once they were settled, she could give up work and have his babies while the war raged and the fishing money rolled in. They might not manage it straightaway, of course, they'd have to move in with Amos for a while until they found the right cottage—

'Absolutely!' Solly piloted his daughter triumphantly across the road as a convoy of rumbling trucks approached. 'It's not every day life hands out a bonus. For both of you!'

'That's for sure,' Piet laughed.

'Don't waste it!' Solly shot Piet a glance over the top of Louise's head.

Why would he waste it, Piet chuckled to himself as he darted across the road after them.

This was easy money.

When the Royal Navy sought him out, he hadn't hesitated.

Without telling Amos, he signed to say that the boat was his. That he would fish for the navy for the length of the war, and that he, Piet, was the official skipper. The navy promised to fix the leaks and provide fresh ropes. He got to earn regular wages however much fish he chose to catch – Their Lordships seemed uncommonly ignorant about the size of local catches and Piet was in no hurry to enlighten them – and at the end of the war he'd have a boat that was seaworthy and could be sold if he fancied doing something different. Or just having a rest.

Amos and his complaints and his reluctance to transfer ownership had been sidestepped thanks to the war. If there were questions, Piet could say he'd had no choice. The requisitioning had been imposed.

It was the chance – and the recognition – he'd been denied for too long.

Chapter Eighteen

'Nurse! Staff Nurse Ahrendts!'

I put down the sheet I'd been folding and hurried out of the linen room. Sister Graham did not like to be kept waiting. Response time, for Sister, was calibrated in seconds.

'Tidy up number four; Doctor will be here on his round shortly and we can't have an unmade bed. I expect hospital corners on the sheets, Staff Nurse, hospital corners—'

Kek, kek, kek, kek, kaaaa, ka, ka, ka! came the competing squawk of guinea fowl from outside.

Sister halted in mid-flow. I battled to keep a straight face. Most of the British staff had never been to Africa before and, to their horror, our peninsula was rife with alien species. The hairy baboons that traipsed down from the upper slopes of the mountain were the worst offenders. They sometimes chased one another friskily across the ward roofs or tried to bathe in the hospital's water supply. 'Scram!' the orderlies would yell and clap their hands at the beasts while the foreign nurses cowered, 'Scram!'

I glanced around for the VAD whose job it was to deal with the beds, but she was nowhere to be seen. Very well, then. No point in antagonising Sister, especially as she still regarded me as an outsider – not, in this case, for my lack of paleness but because I was not British-trained.

'Surely,' I overheard her hissing at our matron, 'this girl won't be good enough!'

I contrived deafness.

'Yes, Sister.'

Would I ever be in a place where I was completely acceptable?

Don't count on it, I told myself, keeping my gaze respectfully aimed at Sister's collar.

'Number eight needs his dressing changed,' she went on, after the guinea fowl gave up. Patients, for Sister, never achieved human status; they were identified only by bed numbers.

'Yes, Sister,' to her departing, well-starched back.

The severity of Sister's discipline was quickly matched by the grim nature of my work at the Royal Naval Hospital. This was no civilian establishment with a routine quota of tonsils and broken legs. This was nursing on the edge.

'Miss?' Seaman Wills croaked from bed three. His ship had been sunk by a German pocket battleship in the Indian Ocean. Globules of oil continued to leach, pungently, from his skin and hair even though he'd been rescued from the burning sea weeks before.

'Could I have some water, Nurse?'

I leant over and held the cup to his ravaged face. There seemed to be no limit to the way flesh could be cleaved by shell splinters, sometimes jaggedly, but more often as cleanly as a knife through watermelon. This was the side of war not reported in the newspapers, the battles fought out of the light. And there was no time for sympathy: if our patients didn't die, they were expected to cope with their torn flesh and return to duty. Despite the horror on display and Sister's doubts about my training, this was the calling I'd dreamt of as a child, fulfilled and expanded by the tragedy of war – and a shortage of qualified staff. I wasn't naive. The opportunity wouldn't last for ever. I'd be moved out when the war ended.

'Staff Nurse Ahrendts?'

I snapped to attention beside the unmade bed. The surgeon commander strode up, white coat flapping, a stethoscope dangling from his side pocket. 'I'll be operating on Signalman Jamieson shortly. When he comes out of theatre he'll require someone to sit with him until he wakens. I don't want him left on his own.' He leant forward. 'Sister will frighten the poor young man to death, I've suggested you keep an eye on him.'

'Of course, sir.'

'Good.' The doctor gave me a quick, tired smile. 'Carry on.'

'Thank you, sir.'

It wasn't all grim.

My patients, mostly young lads, were unfailingly cheerful. I grew to love their banter, even if I couldn't always make out the words they used – *moother* and *bairns* – when I wrote letters home for them, my hands substituting for their bandaged ones. And the hospital's setting, high above the bay and prey to the antics of baboons, gave us all – patients and staff, although perhaps not Sister – a bracing lift whenever we happened to glance out of the window or cock an ear to the roof.

For a few moments, the war faded, the suffering eased.

'Do many of your patients die?' Ma ventured as we did the dishes one evening in the narrow, candlelit kitchen on Ricketts Terrace.

'Sometimes,' I touched her shoulder. 'But our doctors are clever and we have the very best equipment from England. If anyone's going to save them, we will.'

'I don't think I could do it, Lou,' Ma shuddered. 'See boys die.'

'It's my war, Ma.' I put an arm around her and rested my cheek on her hair. 'Pa fights for every ship, I fight for every sailor. I look past their wounds. I imagine how they'll be when they're healed.'

Ma nodded and blinked away unexpected tears. 'And how do the staff treat you?'

'Mostly fine.' I hesitated. 'Sister isn't sure if I'm good enough but I'll show her!' I laughed, and passed Ma a dirty plate. 'Luckily, the doctors trust me.'

'And so they should,' Ma said severely, bending over the sink. 'War has no time for a colour bar. Just make sure you store up good references, Lou. The old ways will return in peacetime, you mark my words. Leopards don't change their spots.'

'Well, they offer sister training, so if I get in fast I could qualify before the war's over and those spotty leopards come back!' I teased Ma gently.

She pursed her lips and added more hot water.

'And Piet? What does he think of your new job?'

I put away the glasses in the cupboard Pa had mounted above the sink. Piet was proud of me, and greedy for my earning power, but he blamed my work for my reluctance to commit.

'He wants us to get married and move to Seaforth until we get our own place.' I glanced at Ma. 'He says I can keep on nursing.'

Lately, he'd taken to kissing me and whispering in my ear how much he needed me with a violence he'd never shown before.

'Let's do it now, Lou,' he'd mutter, his lips crushing mine, his scarred hands gripping my waist. 'I won't get you pregnant.' He pressed the length of his body against me.

'No!' I fought not to struggle out of his arms and sprint away, 'you're hurting me—'

It was a version of love that was hard to like. And if I agreed to sleep with him and found no tenderness but only the same hot demands, I wouldn't be able to extricate myself as easily as Vera, say, who readily turfed her boyfriends out of her bed. I was respectable. Respectable girls who went into men's rooms were expected to marry – or be for ever second-hand. Ma had taught me well.

'And what do you say?' Ma shot a quick glance at me.

I put a hand up to my flushed face.

'I don't want to move in with Amos and Den. Am I selfish, Ma?'

But it wasn't about selfishness. Or guilt.

I caught my breath.

It was mostly, now, about who we'd become.

'I don't think you want to marry him at all. Wherever you might end up living.'

Ma's words sliced through the close air of the cottage like the hot metal that had cut down Seaman Wills. From the docks came the resonating thud of hammers as Pa's late shift completed repairs on HMS *Dorsetshire*. Boiler, Pa had said.

Ma patted my hand and left the kitchen.

I hung up the tea towels and checked the curtains were tightly drawn. German raiders were hunting in Cape waters, which meant that the Terrace had to be rigorous about blackout, especially when the wind was up. It'll only take one stray light, Pa used to wag his finger at our neighbours, especially old Gamiel who was more devoted to his brandy than to the war, to guide the enemy to the rich pickings below.

Ma's words refused to go away, even as I prepared the ward the next day for the surgeon commander's round. Patients were to be medicated strictly according to their bed letters, able to respond to questions if awake, and freshly pyjama-ed.

I don't think you want to marry him.

How had she known, how had she divined, my very thoughts? The moment when I cut loose from the guilt I felt for neglecting Piet, for not saving him . . .

I focused on changing Able Seaman Hill's – number eight's – dressings.

'It's healing well, Able Seaman.' The ruthless path of shrapnel unfolded like braille beneath my fingers. 'Just be patient and you'll soon be as good as new.'

The young man tried to smile through swollen lips. He'd be scarred for life. I wondered if he was married, if his wife would recoil . . .

'God bless you, Nurse,' he struggled and I leant closer, 'for everything.'

The ward radio crackled with the latest war reports. Our

walking patients clustered around, avid for better news. I listened as I continued around the ward. England remained alone, threatened with invasion. Mr Churchill, his voice rumbling with defiance, confirmed more sinkings in the Atlantic. He gave no figures, but if, like Pa, you worked in the dockyard you soon found out. '*Belfast, Courageous, Rawalpindi . . .*' Pa regularly recited the lost ships' names in disbelief, 'half a million tons in the first three months of the war, Lou, including the *Royal Oak*! Captain sneaked past the anti-submarine nets, picked his target cool as you like, torpedoed the *Oak*, and accepted a medal from Herr Hitler himself!'

Closer to home, on our north-western border, German South West Africa lurked, surely a springboard for further aggression. Every day, after maintenance was completed on our shore batteries, the guns were trained on the approaches. We had no other heavy defences apart from ships in port. Pa's docks would be the first target, the naval buildings, the workshops.

'Nurse?' Signalman Jamieson winced as he shifted his weight. 'Can I get up?'

I closed my mind to the possibility of treating people I loved.

'Tomorrow, Signalman,' I lifted his wrist to check his pulse. 'You can sit on the verandah if the weather's fine.'

'Beautiful out there, I wish I was on the beach,' the signalman said longingly as he subsided onto his pillow.

I glanced out of the ward window. Crystal sky, the southeaster muted behind the Simonsberg, the sea lightly ruffled, limpets and whelks and clam shells stippling the high tide mark. I felt the familiar tug of my first love.

I placed the signalman's wrist back onto the covers. He held on to my hand.

'Nurse? Is it true you can hear the sea if you hold a shell to your ear?'

'Yes, I've heard it myself,' I smiled, gently extricating my hand.

You could even pretend it was the whisper of someone who loved you.

I moved to the last bed. Petty Officer Forbes. Leg in traction. Awake, medicated. I wiped my forehead and straightened my skirt. The ward was ready. Sister might even go so far as to approve. And somehow, amid the dressing of wounds and the talk of worsening conflict and echoing seashells, I'd finally made a decision. I glanced out of the window once more and felt my spirits lift. We were at war, but the sun was climbing towards its zenith and the colour of the water was changing from turquoise to lapis.

There was no time to lose.

I once believed I was being kind by telling Piet I still loved him. But perhaps that sort of lie offers only a drawn-out cruelty. The truth was that the old Piet was gone, and I no longer loved the new, angry one. Gone, too, was the girl he taught to skip stones, the one who ran barefoot over scalding tarmac to meet him. Our Seaforth childhood could never bridge the gap between us. And now that he had a proper job, he no longer needed sparing.

Chapter Nineteen

'Lou!' Pa called, as I came down the driveway of the RNH at the end of my duty. He got up stiffly from the rock he'd been resting on. The rating at the guardhouse poked his head out, raised his hand to Pa and saluted as I went by. 'Goodnight, Ma'am.'

'Goodnight! You don't need to fetch me, Pa!' I reached up and kissed his weather-beaten cheek. 'Not up the mountain after your shift. I can walk back on my own.'

'Ah, but then you don't get to hear the latest news. I can't tell you at home, it'd be around the Terrace in no time. You know how your ma can't keep secrets. Here,' Pa pretended to look around conspiratorially, 'only the baboons are listening!'

'What news?'

Not worse than I'd been hearing, surely?

We turned onto a path that cut diagonally across the mountain towards Ricketts Terrace. Sugarbirds, their long tails waving in the breeze like streamers, perched on the pincushion proteas that dotted the slope.

'It's the German battleship *Graf Spee*,' Pa hissed with satisfaction. 'She's been sunk!'

'What? The same one that attacked our ships in the Indian Ocean?' The one that injured Seaman Wills, I wanted to add. The one that might slip into False Bay at night searching for more prey . . .

'The same. And,' Pa leant closer, '*Exeter*, *Achilles* and *Ajax* did it! At last, some revenge!'

'Were many killed?'

'*Ja*, so they say.' Pa's face sobered. 'Terrible business. *Exeter* badly shelled, direct hits to her forward turrets. *Achilles*, too. They got the gun director tower. They've gone to the Falklands to repair. But don't say anything till it's official. Careless talk, as they say.'

'I remember,' I stared out over the bay. '*Ajax* and *Achilles* have called here before.'

'We've repaired their engines, I've had their oil on my hands. We must paint a special mark on their crests to show they've knocked off a battleship!' Pa chuckled. 'Let's raise a secret glass, Lou. Why don't you invite Piet for supper? He's doing better, now.'

I turned back down the path. Pa stumped after me.

'You must decide soon, Lou-Lou. You can't keep him on a string for ever. Come, sit down.' Pa patted a convenient rock by the path. I lifted my cloak and sat down beside him. The sea's glittering surface was roughening with whitecaps. Above the haze of sea spray, the Hottentots Holland Mountains were black against the clear, purple twilight.

'I can't forgive him, Pa,' I said. 'And I don't love him. Not any more.'

'Lou!' Pa gaped. 'He's a sure thing! There aren't many good boys left, not in Simon's Town—'

'Are you certain Piet's good? How can I trust him?'

Pa passed a hand over his thinning hair. I knew what he was thinking. No local girl in her right mind would turn down a sure match, even one that had been through a rocky period. Perhaps girls from rich, leafy suburbs below Table Mountain, where family money would paper over any disappointment, but not girls from Simon's Town where the wind blew everyone's secrets into the open, and the pool of eligible bachelors was small and ever-shrinking. A whistle sounded and we watched the late afternoon train edge out of the station and crawl around the margin of the bay. Smoke puffed in fat ovals from its locomotive. If I'm honest – and this seems to be my time for honesty – I admit I was keener on the vivid journey to the reformatory than on seeing Piet at the other end.

'You're clever, Lou,' Pa said finally, and rather sadly. 'And beautiful. Clever, beautiful girls can often do what plainer, sillier girls can't. But,' his broad fingers twisted together, 'if you're too choosy, you'll find yourself alone one of these days. Stuck on a narrow shelf, like Mrs Hewson says.'

I reached for his anxious hands and stilled them. Dear Pa! Like Ma, he can't help being afraid of what lies ahead each time I step out of my place.

'They say *Graf Spee* scuttled herself,' Pa said, returning to the war. 'Couldn't break out past the British. Serves that Hitler right for starting the fight in the first place.' He sighed and straightened his back. 'Be careful, Lou. That's all I'm going to say. Be careful you don't throw away something you might regret. Once Piet's gone, he'll be gone for good. Now, we should get home. Your ma'll be cross if we keep supper waiting.'

Around the bay, a swathe of cloud was piping itself above the distant Muizenberg Mountain like one of Ma's crisp dessert meringues.

'Wait!' I reached out and stopped him. 'There's something else – I don't need to get married, Pa. I can earn enough on my own. And when the war's over, the world will be different. I'm sure of it! It's happening already.' I flung my arms wide, embracing the town at our feet and the country to the north as if I was the equal of anyone in it. If I worked hard, why shouldn't I be?

Pa stared at me in dismay. I jumped up and hugged him close, feeling the bulky chest and the arms that had held me so lovingly all my life. Pa's view was confined to Simon's Town. I'd begun to see a wider, more generous world.

'So I won't marry anyone unless we can be partners, and love each other equally.'

Pa was silent.

I watched the train disappear around the lower flank of Elsie's Peak. Its trailing smoke drifted and dissolved against the mountainside. I kept my arm linked with Pa's, and nudged him down the path.

'Please don't worry about me, Pa. And don't say anything yet to Ma.'

'As you wish. What about Piet?'

'He'll have to find someone new.' I glanced towards Seaforth. 'Someone who will love him for who he is now.'

Chapter Twenty

For as long as he could remember, Piet and his fellow fishermen had always put to sea at Seaforth, but nowadays there was a navy inspection point close to his favourite fishing spot where all vessels approaching the harbour had to be checked because, with cheeky Germans off the Cape coast, Their Lordships were taking no chances. Even the massive *Queen Mary*, still unmistakeable despite her battleship grey and crammed with troops, had to stop. So Piet and his fellow fishermen moved around the bay and launched from Long Beach on the sea side of the railway station, beneath the severe, white-pillared gaze of Admiralty House.

It was the combination of the railway and a nearby admiral that got Piet thinking.

What if he could profit from his fish twice over?

Right under the admiral's nose?

The navy was paying him to go out every day to where the sea floor shelved and the upwelling water drove not just ordinary stockfish and *snoek* into his nets, but the sweetest *kabeljou* and Cape salmon as well. Their Lordships in London did not seem to mind which fish Piet provided to the sailors in town or to the hungry troops that called in to Cape Town on their way to North Africa, or from Australia. And he was paid the same whatever the size or the content of his catch – Their Lordships clearly appreciated that fish did not always leap into your nets when you expected them to.

It turned out that the restaurants at the far end of the railway line in Cape Town were pickier than the navy. They only wanted top fish like Cape salmon or kingklip. The fishing boats going out from Cape Town harbour were heavily checked when they returned and so the eateries had to stand in line behind the navy and the army and any other military that got first choice.

A fair proportion of Simon's Town fish travelled to Cape Town by train. Packed in ice, ready for the troopships. The admiral – and the admiral's staff – would never dream that anyone could be so stupid as to try and divert some of the priciest *vis* from under their noses. But there had to be a plan, Piet warned himself, a means of escape if something went wrong. Like the pair of gloves he should have worn first time around.

The key would be to start with the quartermaster, slip him the odd fish, and then, if questions were asked, lay the blame elsewhere – like on Abie Meintjies, or Trev Olifant, both fellow fishermen with supply contracts, even though Vera was now Abie's girl and Lou would be cross on

Vera's behalf if Abie got the blame. Piet and Abie and Trev worked side by side, helped row the boats out, helped to pull the nets back in. It was easy to get fish mixed up. They were slippery, after all. They could fall into the wrong crate by themselves. Or out of it. And fingerprints would never be an issue.

Piet stowed his net inside the boat and stared up at the low buildings of the Royal Naval Hospital, where he was due to meet Louise when she came off duty, stepping down the stone path from the upper wards. She said she wanted to talk about something so maybe they could do that at Seaforth, before they swam. It was mid-tide, not too rough, Lou an eyeful in her bathing costume . . .

This time she must not find out, even if it went wrong.

He was being careful to play her game. She wanted freedom? He was giving her freedom. She didn't want to get engaged or start a baby? He was keeping his trousers buttoned up. Just.

She said it was because of the war, and that she must play her part, especially now she was at the naval hospital. So he waited. But it couldn't go on like this for ever. Not even Their Lordships would expect him to set aside marriage and a family for their sakes. Lou's Matron would just have to find someone else. Lou would miss her salary when she gave up, but they'd have her savings, which, by now, must be a pretty pile.

He took a last look over the boat, then waded across the soft sand to the quartermaster's store and stood in line with the other fisherman and labourers. On Friday nights they were always prompt.

'Abie,' he muttered to the man in front of him. 'Good night for stockfish supper?'

Abie glanced around, gave Piet a wink, and casually patted his pocket. They all smelt of fish anyway, who was to know?

The queue moved closer to the quartermaster's desk.

'Piet Philander. Weekly fish, sir.'

He presented his chits and the quartermaster checked his records and counted out Piet's wages and marked them in a book. 'Don't spend it all at once!'

'Not me, sir. Saving for a rainy day.'

He gave the man a loose salute.

Next time, he'd set aside a small fish, wrap it in newspaper and take it across on Wednesday, say, when the man wasn't busy with weekly wages. Tell him he couldn't promise it every week, but that he'd try.

He hung back from the crowds heading home and leant against the fence by the railway station. A train was working up steam. The guard was inspecting travel papers at the entrance to the platform before allowing passengers on board. At the back of the train, a second guard was checking crates and baskets against a list in his hand and then heaving them aboard the goods carriage. Doors slammed and the whistle blew. The engine gave a wheeze. A last sailor dashed on board. The train began to pull out.

Piet turned away and headed along St George's Street, past the gleaming walls of Admiralty House. The biggest challenge was the two railway stations: how to smuggle a private crate past the guards here, and then past the checkpoint at Cape Town station. It wouldn't be possible for Piet to accompany his fish each time because you needed a permit to get back into Simon's Town and someone would get suspicious: why was this fisherman going all the way into Cape Town when his fish were quite happy in their ice and would be picked up at the other end and find their way into the stomachs of the troops without his help? It made no sense.

Maybe, Piet grinned to himself, he was being greedy.

Maybe he needed to scale back.

If he only went into Cape Town every two weeks or so, when there was a particularly rich catch, it would work. He could say he was being diligent, keeping an eye from time to time so that there was no funny business, no black market stuff going on. The navy would be pleased, they would say it showed 'dedication to the war effort'.

Piet began to trot past his old school, where Sheila Ahrendts used to panic about bad men eyeing her daughter in the lane nearby. A group of sailors crowded into the noisy Ratings' Club, accompanied by a huge dog they called Just Nuisance. He, Piet, would never be welcome in such places, but then he, Piet, didn't have to go out in ships and get shot at.

He bounded up Quarry Road.

He must start straightaway, travelling once every two weeks with the fish into Cape Town. Make friends with the guards, with the military police, with the permit inspectors. Be patient, do it enough times so it seemed a regular thing, so even Abie and Trev got used to it – even were grateful to him for taking the trouble? And then, only then, do it for real. After all his groundwork, it wouldn't be too hard to confuse the guards about the number of crates, or that he or they had made a mistake.

Why, if he got to know the guards well enough, there could be a fish in it for them, too.

And if he got caught, he could claim innocence, or a lack of arithmetic in the adding up.

The admiral would forgive him because the navy needed his fish, in fact they needed more fish than he or Abie or Trev could ever pull out of the water. And the sea didn't care where its fish were going. This was not robbery, it was redistribution.

Piet stroked his weekly pay, the coins satisfyingly solid beneath his rough palm.

Everybody kept saying how the war was the making of Louise.

Why couldn't it be the making of him?

And if he didn't get caught, it could be the making of them both, together.

Chapter Twenty-One

Number three, as Sister Graham referred to him, was Lieutenant David Horrocks DSO, gunnery officer. Emergency appendectomy transferred from HMS *Dorsetshire*, Sister announced. Reached us just in time.

I scanned the bed letter and glanced at the patient.

Handsome, thirty-one years old, scar on the temple, wary blue eyes, fair hair tinged with grey. In this war, you didn't need to be old to be grey. I readied the dressing tray. Antiseptic, cotton swabs, dressings, tweezers. I'd have to be quick. It was already eleven o'clock and the ward floor still had to be scrubbed, but the sick berth ratings were down at Medical Stores' tallying stock. I'd need to get on with it alongside the VAD, if she could be pried away from sorting Christmas decorations. Sister would be generous with her criticism if it wasn't done by noon.

'Good morning, Lieutenant. Are you feeling better today?'

'Yes. No more nausea, thank goodness.'

He wore a carved gold ring on his left hand, and spoke

quietly. A quietly spoken gunnery officer. I nodded and set down the tray on his bedside table. The poor man had been intermittently sick for two days after his operation. I'd been finishing my night duty roster on his first post-operative night when he woke the ward with his screaming. I grabbed my torch and a bowl and raced down the row of beds.

'Ssh,' I held him gently and wiped his sweating face and unravelled the twisted sheets. 'Do you want to be sick?'

'What?' he muttered, wincing at the pain of his wound. 'Nott? Tompkins?'

'You've had an operation, sir. You're going to be fine.'

He fell back on the pillows. The distant boom of waves rolled through the open window on the back of an onshore wind, layering a briny sharpness over the usual smell of disinfectant. I held his hand while his breathing returned to normal. The other patients turned over and went back to sleep.

'Do you live here, in Simon's Town?' he asked two days later as I lifted his wrist to check his pulse before changing the dressing. I don't think he recognised me from the night.

'Yes.' I laid his hand back on the covers. Pulse normal. Skin cool. At least he was easy to understand, and didn't mangle his vowels as some of the other sailors did from the northern parts of their island. 'I was born nearby, just along the mountain.'

A gust of wind rattled the windows. I bent over his wound. His torso tensed.

'Hold still, please, Lieutenant.'

I began to ease the old dressing off. He flinched as it tugged on the stitches.

'Did you live by the sea, sir? Is that why you joined the navy?' This to be polite, but also to distract him from the painful business at hand.

'No . . .' his hands were gripping the bed covers.

The corners of the dressing came away and I concentrated on removing the whole of it without opening the wound. It peeled off, revealing a livid, weeping scar. I reached for the antiseptic and dripped it onto a cotton square. He must have much to think about besides getting well again. His next ship, for instance. *Dorsetshire* had already departed without him. No officer felt comfortable being unassigned. Pa kept me privately up to date on my patients' ships. So did Vera, who was always on the lookout for a new admirer apart from Abie, who smelt too much of fish, she said.

'I joined the navy to escape.'

I looked up, startled. Officers were not inclined to confide, even when ill; unlike the ordinary seamen who wanted to hold my hand or spin me a story whenever Sister's back was turned. 'Never should 'ave done it, Nurse. But just for the sight of your pretty face . . .'

I glanced down the ward. I wasn't supposed to engage in personal conversation with patients. Sister had ears in the back of her head.

'What were you escaping from?'

He gave a rueful smile, but didn't reply.

I focused on the puckered flesh, and reapplied a fresh square. The skin was healing, but rather slowly. It hadn't been helped by the retching. Or the disturbed sleep.

He averted his eyes from what I was doing and gazed out of the window to where the navy flag snapped above

Admiralty House and the waves rode towards Long Beach in glistening ranks. When the wind was blowing from the east, the muezzin's call often drifted faintly into the ward.

'If I lived somewhere like this, I'd never want to leave,' he murmured.

I felt a curious spark of indignation. Surely it ought to take a while for a place to get under your skin? He hadn't fallen in love with this particular sea as a child like I had, or the *fynbos*-cloaked mountains, or the seagulls that cruised the southeaster searching for their air perch.

'All done,' I said. 'It's getting better, the skin is starting to knit.'

'Thank you, Nurse. You're very kind.'

He took a week to reply to my impulsive question. By that time, I assumed he'd chosen to ignore it. The night staff continued to report his nightmares, but he was an easy patient by day. Quiet, undemanding, and grateful even though the regular changing of his dressing continued to be painful, as the skin tightened and wept and tightened further.

It was during that week that I realised I'd heard of him.

Some of my former patients, transferred to the RNH from the Falklands, had served on *Achilles* when he won his medal. 'No panic, miss, just got on with it. Saved Nott's leg. If it wasn't for the lieutenant, we'd all have been cooked.'

Pa confirmed it was the Battle of the River Plate, when *Graf Spee* was sunk. The gun director tower had been hit, but he kept on firing – *alle wêreld*, what bravery, Pa marvelled – despite being wounded by an incoming shell.

'Good morning, Lieutenant. How are you today?'

'Less sore, thank you, Nurse. I can sit up and look out more easily.'

I smiled. He liked our sea. Intermittent whitecaps were freckling the bay beyond the ward windows. Down on Long Beach, Piet and his fellow fishermen would be dragging their boats across the sand, sniffing the breeze and squinting at the sky, and arguing about the particular spot of ocean where the *snoek* and the stockfish might best be lured into the navy's nets. Piet was increasingly transformed by his navy contract. Money seemed to breed confidence and was even tempering his demands. But it didn't change the decision I'd made, though I was struggling to tell him. The last time I tried, at the beach with the water lapping coolly about our feet, he interrupted me and said I didn't need to explain it again, and that I'd be ready soon enough. The war, he shrugged. It makes you rich, but it upsets your plans.

'You asked why I joined the navy.'

I nodded and reached for the tweezers. Piet often brought fish for Ma and Pa. He was trying . . .

'I love the sea and I wanted to serve. But it was also to escape from my future.'

I stopped, my hands in mid-air, struck by the seeming lightness of Lieutenant Horrocks's voice and simultaneously aware of a line being tested. A line that not even the lower-ranked patients, for all their familiarity, were willing to cross.

Sister Tutor's stern warning from training echoed in my ears.

'No fraternisation, nurses! Hard work and compassion – nothing more.'

In the bed on the right, Lieutenant Roche was asleep. Across the way, Petty Officer Talbot was in the bathroom. I stared at my fingers as they went about their task of removing the old dressing, checking for infection, cleaning the wound. It would be better to say nothing, better to avoid those wary blue eyes and give him no encouragement.

But, my hands slowed once more, imagine if I was to cross that line?

And tell him the secret I'd told no one yet?

It was often easier confiding in a stranger.

It began a week before the lieutenant arrived, on a day when the air hung hot and breathless over the docks and the regular theatre sister was suddenly taken ill. A day, initially, like any other: admissions at 08.30, rounds soon after, linen changing, cleaning and stacking of porringers while the hammering of steel-on-steel in the dockyard floated up the mountainside . . . interrupted by a request, delivered urgently, after an ambulance screeched to a halt outside.

'But I have no theatre experience, sir!'

And, I wanted to add, you know I was only assigned here to cover for the shortage of British nurses. When they found I was useful, they decided to keep me on quietly when the new ward opened. So, although I'm valued for my nursing skill, I'm not *officially* here, Doctor.

'No matter, we'll manage,' the surgeon commander flung over his shoulder as he supervised the unloading of the patient from the ambulance. 'Seaman Lincoln may die unless we operate now. Get scrubbed up. Now, steady with that stretcher—'

I hurried to the theatre, my mind racing to identify the lancet, clamps, suture needles.

'Good work, Staff Nurse,' he said afterwards with an approving nod, stripping off his bloody gloves as I gathered the instruments for sterilisation and hoped my hands had been steady. 'You did well.'

'Thank you, sir.'

It was a sign. Surely? Like in the dockyard?

Or, at the very least, an opportunity.

And if Matron agreed, it could cement my place at the RNH, while lifting me beyond the petty tyranny of Sister and onto a fresh path.

Later that night, I drafted the second secret application of my life.

Dear Matron, it began, each line carefully blotted before proceeding.

I was asked by the surgeon commander to assist in an operation today when Sister Hargreaves was ill. It was a perforated ulcer and the patient was in a critical condition when admitted.

I was not nervous, and I found that I was able to fulfil the surgeon's commands accurately and quickly. While I have not had theatre experience apart from a period during my initial training, it is a specialisation that has always interested me, and where I believe I could make a contribution.

Since my secondment last year, I have been honoured to serve at the Royal Naval Hospital. While I continue to enjoy my work on the ward, I am keen to learn a new skill. If it would be possible, I would like to train to be a theatre nurse and then a theatre sister. I am prepared to work extra hours to do so.

I have no family commitments at this time, or in the future.

Yours faithfully

Louise Ahrendts (Miss) Staff Nurse

I have no family commitments at this time, or in the future. There it was, in black and white, the decision I'd taken in my heart but failed, yet, to say out loud. Piet would be livid. He'd see it as a treachery far worse than his own, earlier, deceit. Ma and Pa, for their part, would be horrified at my spurning of family. Only Vera might approve. 'Poor Piet! But more money as a sister!'

I darted a keen glance at the lieutenant but he was preoccupied with the view outside the sash window, entranced by the play of sunlight on choppy water. He seemed forever captivated by the outdoors, by the clouds, or the wind that rattled the shutters and defied the draught excluders knitted by our occupational therapy patients. He never spoke of home, despite the gold ring.

If I shared my secret with him, I'd be guilty of the fraternisation Sister Tutor had banned.

I glanced at him again, more clinically, noting the jagged scar near his hairline that marked the DSO wound, surely the spur for his nightmares.

'It does bad things to them, Lou,' Pa said of gunners in

general. 'Not just because they sit in a closed turret waiting to be hit. They fire on other young men just like themselves. Now that,' Pa wagged a finger, 'is what bothers you later. It never goes away.'

Perhaps the chaplain could visit him, especially with Christmas coming.

Up on the mountain the guinea fowl started their regular chant, *kek, kek, kek* . . .

'Would you like to go for a walk one day, when you're better?'

Oh God, why speak out? Why take such a risk in my position? And he'd probably think I was being forward, like Vera with her red lips and her turned-out foot . . .

'I only meant, if you have nothing else to do—'

I brushed my apron, glanced round, but Sister was otherwise occupied.

The lieutenant was smiling at me, his eyes no longer guarded. He had regained colour in the last week, although his face was still too thin.

'I'd like that very much.'

I seized the dressing tray, and hurried away.

Chapter Twenty-Two

There was an open-air verandah in front of the ward and, once he was mobile, David Horrocks liked to sit there in the mornings while the ward cleaning was going on. A tiny jewelled sunbird would bury its beak in a flowering shrub nearby – although shrub was far too pedestrian a word to describe the plants that rampaged through the hospital grounds. Even the local word, *fynbos*, struggled to describe a vegetation topped with flowers more feathered than petalled, in which squadrons of long-tailed birds fought one another over the nectar. Between the boisterous foraging, it was just possible to monitor the movement of ships to and from the naval dockyard below. Certainly he could never have recovered in time to rejoin *Dorsetshire*, but now he found himself watching the warships from the verandah with something approaching greed. He hated being out of it.

Actually, if he was honest, his decamp was due to Sister's officious attitude towards her nurses and orderlies:

he preferred not to have to watch Louise Ahrendts on her knees scrubbing the floor round his bed—

'Attention!'

David turned. A braided uniform was marching through the ward. A moment later Matron and the senior naval officer in Simon's Town, closely followed by Sister and more languidly by a man in a dark suit, stepped onto the verandah. David made to get up but Commodore Budgen waved him back.

'At ease, Lieutenant! Thank you Matron, Sister. Well now, Lieutenant, on the road to recovery?'

'Yes thank you, sir.' David held himself upright. 'The surgeon commander says I'll be discharged in a few days.'

'Excellent.'

David waited. In the naval scheme of things, SNOs did not go around visiting obscure Lieutenants, even obscure lieutenants with DSOs.

'Now,' the SNO spotted two chairs and drew them up, 'a word, if I may.'

This appeared to be the signal for the man in the suit. He shook David's hand but did not introduce himself, then reached out and closed the verandah door behind him with an apologetic smile at Sister, who was hovering on the threshold.

'Shortly,' Commodore Budgen glanced at the stranger, who nodded, 'a ship is going to dock here to embark a special cargo to be transported to the United States. You will report for duty on this vessel as liaison officer.'

'I will not be serving as gunnery officer?'

'No,' the stranger spoke for the first time, revealing a

strong American accent. 'We have our own, sir. You will be a guest of the US Navy.'

'You will represent His Majesty's Government,' Budgen continued, 'and ensure this cargo reaches its destination in good order.'

'See,' the stranger leant forward and favoured David with a gentle smile, 'we could also use some of your combat experience on the way. Just in case. This is one cargo we don't want to lose.'

'I understand, sir. May I know the nature of the cargo?'

'Only once on board, sir,' the man said, with an air of regret, 'if you don't mind.'

Budgen cleared his throat. 'I have also been instructed by the Admiralty to inform you that you are being promoted to lieutenant commander with immediate effect. Congratulations.'

David fought to keep his expression neutral. 'Thank you, sir.'

A promotion while sidelined from active duty? His friend Bob would have a spicy comment to make about that.

Budgen and the American stood up. David managed to get to his feet in time.

'You will be informed when to report for duty, Lieutenant Commander. And congratulations, belatedly, for your action at the River Plate.'

'Thank you, sir. And sir,' he nodded to the American who inclined his head, opened the door to the ward, and slipped through.

'Good luck,' Commodore Budgen adjusted his gold-encrusted headgear. 'My compliments to your uncle at the Admiralty when you see him.'

David watched them make their way through the ward, herded by Sister.

He turned to stare over the bay. A flock of seagulls was circling above a fishing boat off Long Beach. Their raucous cries echoed up the mountainside.

The first time he wore the DSO on his uniform, Elizabeth ran her fingers over it and then hovered the same fingers over the scar that snaked across his temple.

'Does it still hurt?'

'No, not any more.'

The pain was deeper inside now, and more complicated; partly assuaged by the kindness of Sub Lieutenant Owen's parents when he met them, but revived every time Tompkins's shattered torso rose before him, or when he recalled the courage of the now deaf Nott – his hearing destroyed in the blast – as he learnt to walk again with a cane.

'Have to learn to dance,' Nott whispered, when David visited him in hospital, 'seeing as I can't hold a tune any more . . .'

In newspapers, the battle was trumpeted as a resounding and long-awaited Allied success. The private tragedies that lay behind it were known only to those directly involved and they, like David, mostly kept quiet.

'Lieutenant?'

Staff Nurse Ahrendts was standing by his chair.

'I go off duty at four-thirty tomorrow,' she glanced back at the ward. 'Would you like to take a walk? To help you get fitter,' she added, a faint blush staining her cheeks.

'Thank you,' he said. 'That's very generous.'

She glanced around again, clearly worried about being overheard.

'I'll be on the path by the old aerial ropeway,' she said, then stepped back through the door.

Chapter Twenty-Three

Cloud was heaping itself in stratified layers on top of the mountain as I climbed towards the ropeway at the appointed time. Lieutenant Horrocks was waiting for me. Wind tossed the pines behind him. I glanced around swiftly. No one else about. And no sign of marauding baboons. A walk would be fine but he was in no shape for evasive action.

'Good afternoon, Lieutenant,' I lofted my voice above the wind.

'Hello,' he said, then gestured to the *fynbos*-clad slopes, the limpid bay. 'I imagine you must be used to all this splendour?'

'Oh no, it's always special to me. And the sea is never the same.'

I stopped at his side, but a little further away from him than would be customary for two people about to take a walk. He was wearing a pair of light trousers and an open-necked shirt. It hadn't occurred to me that he might be in civilian clothes rather than the anonymity of hospital pyjamas or his regular uniform. He looked at me directly, his eyes free of the wariness of the ward.

'Is this difficult for you, being here with me? Would you rather I went on alone?'

'You can't walk alone,' I said, glancing at the way he was standing, favouring his right side where the wound was.

'I'm fine, really. But I could use a guide,' he smiled, trying to set me at my ease.

I began to walk slowly along a gravel track that rose at a gentle incline above the hospital. Serrated-leaf proteas rose on either side of us, screening the row of wards below and the rocky heights of the Simonsberg above. The crisp, resin scent of the pines floated down. I took care to place my feet deliberately between the stones on the path, and hoped that he would follow my route. It wouldn't do for him to fall, or sprain an ankle.

'I see you're working more in theatre these days. Do you like it?'

'Oh, yes! It's wonderful.' I stopped and turned back to him. 'They're training me. The surgeon commander says I have an instinct—' I broke off. 'I like being on the ward, too.'

'It gets you away from Sister Graham,' he observed, amusement flickering in his eyes.

'Sister is very efficient.'

He raised his eyebrows. 'Well, she may be efficient, but she treats her staff poorly. I know nothing about hospitals, but if they're anything like ships, a dictatorship doesn't work.'

I stared at him. He plucked a leaf from a nearby protea and rolled it between his fingers and sniffed. I wasn't used to patients expressing opinions. Or speaking to me as if I was an equal.

'It's an honour for me to be at the hospital.'

He examined me. I became aware that the breeze had teased part of my hair from beneath my cap. This man had no physical secrets from me, and yet here I was, embarrassed that he should see my hair unpinned.

'You're very loyal, Nurse Ahrendts.'

'Grateful, actually,' I looked away from his appraisal. 'The war's given me an opportunity I wouldn't have had in peacetime. A little . . . difficulty . . . isn't going to put me off.'

The wind gusted. I reached behind to unfasten my cloak. He made to help but then withdrew his hand. I looped the cloak over my arm. A pair of sugarbirds swooped down to perch on top of a nearby protea, their ribbon tails flying up in the wind.

'Cape sugarbirds,' I said, following his gaze. 'Do you miss your home? Or is that what you're escaping from?'

'How do you know that?' He gave me a wry glance.

'Look,' I said, pointing to a flat rock further along the path, 'we can stop there for a moment. You don't want to do too much on your first outing.'

I folded my cloak inside out and sat on it. He levered himself carefully down at my side, but not too close. The setting sun began to strike the bay horizontally, deepening the troughs between the turquoise swells and turning them a rich indigo.

'I've been escaping since I was eighteen,' he remarked. 'I presume your life wasn't mapped out for you from birth?'

'Oh yes, it was!' I laughed. 'You were expected to know your place. Women like me have only ever been destined for domestic service.'

'So you've broken the mould?'

'I have! I had a dream, and I managed to follow it. My family and friends were upset, of course – you can't break away without causing some resentment – but now I'm independent. Well,' I tilted my head and flashed him a glance, 'almost.'

David Horrocks grinned. It made him look younger, the scar no longer dominating.

'And if you married? What then?'

I gasped.

'I'm sorry,' he put in quickly. 'I don't mean to be impolite. But I've seen how good you are, and I think you could reach the top of your profession. Be a matron one day.'

I clapped a hand across my mouth.

'Why not?' he smiled. 'You have all the qualities.'

But the wrong colour, I wanted to shout, whatever my qualities! Sister, yes. But matron?

'Whereas I,' he went on lightly, as if he sensed he'd touched a nerve, 'have no choice. I have to leave the sea when the war's over.' He got stiffly to his feet. 'Shall we go a little further? It's wonderful to be outside.'

'Of course.' I scrambled to my feet and followed him. He walked steadily, but with a slight limp. St George's Street unwound like a ribbon below us, crowded with workers heading from the dockyard towards the station. A pair of minesweepers bustled out of the harbour entrance. Just up from St George's, our row of whitewashed cottages perched against the lower slope. I recognised our washing flapping on the line.

Lieutenant Horrocks sat down gingerly on a convenient rock. The sun glanced off a window.

He flinched and touched his scar.

'Lieutenant?'

He bent his head and pressed his fists against his eyes. His hair, longer than it would normally be because of the stay in hospital, fell forward, curtaining the side of his face.

'Lieutenant?' I laid my hand on his shoulder.

He didn't react.

I rubbed gently. 'You're safe here.'

'Sorry.' He straightened up, unclenching his hands. 'For a moment there, the reflection—'

'Tell me.' I crouched down at his side.

His eyes – so pale you could almost see through them – met mine. He looked away, towards the docks and the cluster of warships, as if searching for something. His voice, when it came, was steady.

'I was back on *Achilles*. My sub lieutenant was killed, Nott was wounded and Tompkins was screaming for his mother. I couldn't see through the blood in my eyes,' he lifted his hand to tap the scar. 'I'm sorry to be so graphic.'

'Don't apologise,' I said, and paused before going on. 'I know about your battle. The seamen from your ship said you saved their lives.'

'What?'

'I nursed them,' I replied gently. 'They arrived from the

Falklands. They talked of their lieutenant who kept firing, who won the DSO.'

He stared at me. The sun slipped away from the reflecting window that had so bothered him, and hovered above Red Hill in preparation for its evening plunge towards the Atlantic.

'You are my patient,' I murmured, 'please don't be embarrassed.'

David Horrocks' breathing returned to normal. His shoulders relaxed. I knew we should return, it was getting late and the wind was rising. Soon it would be dangerous to be on the mountain if you were uncertain on your feet. But, at this moment, he shouldn't be alone. I remained on my haunches by his side, but no longer touching him.

'That's where I live,' I said, pointing out Ricketts Terrace. 'I was born there. I see the sea every morning from our doorstep.'

A wisp of smoke curled from a lopsided chimney. The younger Gamiels were playing hide-and-seek beneath the palm trees, their shouts drifting up the mountain. I wondered what he saw, or what any stranger would see. Only the poverty? Or would he sense beneath it the warmth – and occasional friction – of close neighbours who looked out for one another? I felt a strange wash of emotion, a longing for something that was slipping away even as I sat looking at it. I reached down to rub the familiar, gritty soil of the path between my fingers but I knew that wouldn't bring it back. I'd outstripped Ricketts Terrace. I still loved it, it was my home, but it couldn't hold me any longer, or dictate what I'd do. Like Piet could no longer hold me. It was exhilarating – frightening—

'Shall we go back?' he asked, getting to his feet and holding out a hand to help me up. If he sensed the turmoil beneath my silence, he gave no sign.

I swung my cloak back about me and led the way. From further along the mountain came the steady hoot of guinea fowl heading to their roosts. As we approached the spot from where we'd set off, he spoke from behind me.

'Thank you,' he said. 'Thank you for bringing me here.'

I turned to face him. He was calm, back in control. 'Not at all. You can make your own way back to the ward?'

'Yes.' He hesitated, searching my face. 'You shouldn't give up on your dream. We only get one chance to make something of ourselves.'

My eyes fell on the ring on his finger.

'You, too. Good evening, Lieutenant.'

We shook hands formally, his skin cool against my palm.

Chapter Twenty-Four

I have never intentionally breached nursing etiquette. My blurted invitation to David Horrocks was as much of a shock to me as it was to him. I told myself it came from sympathy, a desire to be kind. Not Piet-kindness – pretending to love him until he got back on his feet – but genuine kindness. David Horrocks needed taking out of himself. And so it proved. The flashback to his battle may have been distressing, but perhaps it served a purpose in coming by day instead of by night. Perhaps he'd sleep easier.

I don't regret doing what I did.

'Thank you, Staff Nurse,' the surgeon commander dropped his gloves into the kidney bowl, 'excellent anticipation. Stay with Seaman Dawson until he recovers consciousness and then wheel him back. No solids.'

'Yes, Doctor.'

The surgeon commander stopped at the door. 'I never wanted to send you back to False Bay Hospital.' He pushed through the door against a gusting wind.

'Thank you, sir.'

I watched the steady rise and fall of Dawson's chest, savouring the lull after the urgency of surgery. Even without the order, I always stayed with my patient so he saw a familiar face when he came round. That hadn't been the case with David Horrocks. I first caught sight of him, barely conscious, as he was wheeled by an orderly into the ward following his emergency operation. The theatre nurse was already scrubbing up for another procedure. As I moved towards him, Sister Graham ordered me to help one of the juniors fix a cast and so the lieutenant had woken up, disoriented, before I could get to him. That night, his screams for his injured crew woke the ward. I'm not saying his nightmares could have been prevented, or the damaging flashbacks reversed, but healing often hangs by an elusive thread.

The seaman's eyes flickered.

'Seaman Dawson?' I took his hand.

The young man opened his eyes, stared about wildly, then registered me at his side.

'You've had your operation. You're going to be fine.' I squeezed his hand gently. 'I'm going to wheel you back to the ward now.'

I propped open the door and manoeuvred the trolley through. Post-operatives were usually put close to the nurses' station. I'd settle Dawson, then return to sterilise the instruments and scrub the theatre. As I straightened the trolley, I noticed the empty bed at the far end of the ward.

'Nurse?' I said to the VAD emerging from the sluice, 'where is Lieutenant Horrocks?'

'Discharged,' VAD Wilson said, over her shoulder.

'This morning. Promoted, too. Didn't you hear?'

'Staff Nurse Ahrendts!' Sister Graham came up at a clip. 'I trust you will be with us for the afternoon round?'

'I have to sterilise the instruments first, Sister, and then clean the theatre—'

'Well, look smart, Nurse. We can't have the ward round delayed.'

'Seaman Dawson is just conscious, Sister. I'll check him and then finish in theatre.'

'As quickly as possible.' Sister swept off with a rustle of starched skirt.

In the quiet of the operating theatre, I boiled the surgical instruments for the specified time, lifted them out with tongs and laid them carefully side by side in the correct order on metal trays. There was no reason why Lieutenant Horrocks should have waited to speak to me before being discharged. In fact, it would have been unprofessional of him to do so. I boiled more water, collected a brush and began to scrub the floor in sweeping arcs, reversing on my knees from the far end of the theatre. A fine layer of dust had blown in under the door. My collar dampened with perspiration.

He was refreshing. On our walk, he hadn't behaved like a patient at all, in fact more like someone walking out with me for pleasure. His blue eyes met mine directly, he even felt comfortable enough to criticise – actually, to neatly skewer – Sister. I smiled as I scrubbed. Sister as dictator! How apt! I plunged the brush into the soapy water for one final pass, then washed the bucket and cloths and returned them to their cupboard.

The wind raised its voice to a new pitch.

I think he enjoyed talking to me. And I—

But perhaps he'd had second thoughts, and felt it wiser to impose some distance. He was an officer, after all. I was only a respite, a temporary bandage against the war and the future that held him captive. The afternoon ward round proceeded on schedule. While grouped around the final patient's bed, Matron's discerning eye picked up a ball of fluff on the floor, and, to Sister's mortification, lectured the company on the importance of twice-daily sweeping during windy periods. Worse was to follow because Seaman Dawson, after being moved from the trolley to a bed, suffered an attack of nausea and vomited before I could get a bowl to him. It took close on an hour to change his sheets and pyjamas, clean the trolley and bed, dispose of the soiled linen, mop the floor, and settle the poor young man down. And all this had to be accomplished under the irate eye of Sister, still smarting from the incident with the fluff ball.

An hour later I spotted Pa waiting for me halfway up Rectory Steps. He shaded his eyes against the late-afternoon glare and the rising southeaster, and waved. Whenever our shifts coincided, he always climbed up to meet me even though his knees ached from crouching over hot machines and all he longed to do was rest and let Ma fuss around him.

'Pa,' I hugged him, 'will it be a black wind?'

'Probably,' Pa squinted up at the cloudy Simonsberg. 'Now sit down with me for a moment – here, on my jacket, don't mess your uniform. Can you see what's tied up?'

I examined the array of warships. One stood out. Plain, not

camouflaged, and with a Stars-and-Stripes streaming at its mast.

'American? We're offloading American goods?'

'Now that would be good,' Pa chuckled. 'They make the best ice cream in the world! But no, they're not unloading anything. That's all I'm going to say. Come . . .' he got up and tucked his arm through mine as we went down the last set of steps.

'By the way,' he said, 'I met one of your patients today. The DSO man, handsome fellow with a scar. He remembered me from before the war. I'd fixed the machine gun mounts on his ship, HMS *Durban*, when it was damaged in a storm. Remember the time of the landslide behind the Terrace? Anyhow, he was officer-in-charge when I did the repairs.'

'What did he want, Pa?'

'He said he didn't get the chance to say thank you before being discharged. Nice manners, eh? He asked me to give you this,' Pa fished into his pocket and handed over a letter inscribed with my name and title. 'I wished him safe passage, told him to take care. Now let's hurry. Piet's waiting,' Pa shot me a questioning glance. 'He's staying for supper.'

I once blamed myself for being a coward, for not being brave enough to speak up. But bravery, I've discovered, is a quality that's learnt, not something that's inherited from your parents or conferred by God as He passes by. It takes time to build, especially when it means hurting someone.

'I love you, Lou,' Piet said, his voice defiant rather than tender.

We'd had supper and Ma and Pa had left for choir practice at St Francis Church. Piet was sitting on the edge of Pa's armchair opposite me in the sitting room. He'd taken some trouble with his clothes, and wore a pair of ironed trousers. His black hair was brushed flat against his head. Piet had never been handsome, but there was a tall, raw energy to him that drew you in, and made you ignore his tattered appearance. Lately, the navy's steady pay was even filling out the lines on his face. Along with this new prosperity, maybe he'd found – I felt an unexpected stab – someone else. Maybe he was working up to tell me that, despite his love for me, he'd found a woman who would marry him without delay and be grateful to take over the Philander household. Or maybe he'd been stung to see me walking on the mountain with an officer of the Royal Navy, an officer whose letter I hadn't had the chance to read because of the lively demands of a family supper, Pa and Ma's departure, and this moment.

'But do you really love me?' His eyes flashed in the candlelight. 'That's what I don't know. You say you do, but—'

The wind thrashed in the palms, ceased, thrashed again. The front door banged against its hinges. Piet didn't know about the letter I'd written to Matron. *I have no family commitments at this time, or in the future* . . . I must tell him now. Not let him interrupt me this time, or manoeuvre me into silence. I must end it now.

'I care for you,' I reached a hand towards him, 'but the war's changed things—'

'It hasn't changed what matters to me,' he broke in, his dark eyes boring into me. A sheen of sweat beaded his forehead. 'I waited for you to get your training, but Lou-*tjie*,' his voice cracked over his private nickname for me, 'I can't wait for ever.'

He knelt in front of me, took my hands, then drew me to my feet and wrapped me in his arms. 'You're so beautiful, I see how they look at you.' His hands roamed down my back, over my hips.

I felt his breath quicken against my face.

'Piet, no—'

'Your pa and ma will be gone for ages,' he breathed into my ear, 'we've waited so long.' He kissed me and I felt his hand hard against my waist and then he undid the top button of my blouse and pushed his hand inside, kneading my breast. I stifled a cry. He'd never been this bold, never taken hold of me so demandingly, never with such a sense of ownership.

Maybe that was what did it. The entitlement in his hands, his body, his lips.

'No!' I gasped, twisting my head away, but it had no effect. His lips were now devouring my neck, my throat, he pushed my bodice aside and I felt the wet flicker of his tongue against my nipple. A seductive heat began to rise through my body. It was going to happen, and I was going to let it happen unless I stopped him now.

I pressed both hands and forearms on his chest and pushed. 'No! Not like this!'

He staggered backwards. Nurses aren't without a wiry strength.

I stared at him, shocked at myself, shocked at him, for we'd never been so rough with one another before. I'm not sure he saw me, though, because his eyes were unfocused, cloudy, like a patient emerging from a coma. We stood, facing each other, panting.

'Why not?' he shouted, breaking the trance. 'I've waited long enough!'

'I don't want to get pregnant, Piet. And we must talk.'

The pulsing flame of the candle on the kitchen table – or maybe it was my words – split his face into ugly planes.

'I'd be careful – you wouldn't get pregnant first time,' he retorted, waving his arm like Amos had done when he hit me by accident on the day Piet was arrested.

I rebuttoned my blouse with shaky fingers.

'Don't you want me?'

Rain began to splatter against the windows like it had that day at the reformatory.

I swallowed. 'I can't marry you, Piet.'

His eyes focused and met mine in disbelief, as if I'd struck him rather than just pushed him away.

A sharp banging sounded at the front door.

'What's going on in there, Solly Ahrendts?'

Piet threw himself down on the sofa.

I rushed over and opened the door a crack. Mrs Hewson, her hair in curlers beneath a rain-flecked scarf, stood outside, a walking stick gripped in her right hand like a weapon.

'I was passing by, I heard shouting—'

'It's alright, it's just Piet. He's upset,' I cast a glance over my shoulder. Piet remained hunched on the sofa, turned away from the door. The wind whistled through the sitting room and plucked at the curtains drawn tight for the blackout.

'Where's your father?' She poked her head inside. 'He shouldn't leave you alone.'

'Choir practice. He'll be back soon. Please, Mrs H, go home, now. We'll be fine.'

She shook her head, sniffed, and hobbled back through the darkness.

I closed the door and turned to face Piet. His hands were balled into fists, the knuckles showing white. I walked slowly across the room, telling myself that he'd never hurt me, never hit me the way his father had once hit him. But we were alone. I'd just sent Mrs Hewson away, and the wind was howling at a pitch that would mask any upheaval. I sat down on the edge of the chair opposite him. Usually I could read Piet's moods like I could gauge the regular ebb and surge of the tide; sometimes choppy, but always to a pattern. This was a different Piet. Churning, unpredictable as a freak wave, the sort of Piet that Ma feared might emerge from the reformatory and never be tamed.

'I've changed, Piet. So have you. We're different from who we were. But I hope we'll always be friends.'

Outrage flared in his eyes.

'Friends?'

'Yes. I still care about you.'

How could I say I didn't even trust him any more? Nothing would be gained by that kind of cruelty.

He stared at me with a hostility I'd never seen before, then looked down at his clenched fists.

I felt my legs tense. I gripped the arms of the chair.

'I don't want to be friends with you, Lou. I want a wife.'

He got up, brushed past me, yanked the door open and strode out into the night.

The door swung on the gusting wind and slammed shut. The candle flared and blew out.

* * *

Dear Miss Ahrendts,

Please forgive me for leaving the RNH without saying goodbye. I needed to report for duty sooner than expected and will be departing Simon's Town shortly. I can't say when I will pass through again.

So please accept these hasty words as my heartfelt thanks for your dedicated care, and your understanding over my shell shock. I'd hoped that the memories of last year's battle were fading, but my illness seemed to bring them back. Once I'm on active duty they will disappear, I'm sure, but for the moment the flashbacks are all too real, as you noticed.

I've been blessed to be treated here in the beautiful Cape, and I shan't forget your kindness in getting me out of the hospital for a breath of fresh air. On a professional note, I've no doubt that your skills will indeed take you far. In time you will surely be promoted to the highest levels of nursing. And I wish you fulfilment in other ways as well, in the future.

I trust you won't think it a breach of hospital rules if I say that I hope we meet again one day. I would very much like to take another walk on the mountain with you.

Yours sincerely,

David Horrocks

Chapter Twenty-Five

I was coming out of Sartorial House when I saw him. I'd dropped in to chat to Mr Bennett as I did whenever I was off duty, and there he was, wearing the insignia of his new rank, and walking slowly along the pavement amid the lunchtime crowd. A tall, formal figure with a slight limp. He didn't see me at first, and I nearly turned and went back inside. Perhaps it was because I was in my own clothes, a sleeveless blue dress that Mrs Hewson had sewed for me, with a border of white at the neck. Without a uniform, I ought to have no right to speak to him.

But then he saw me, and he smiled. 'Good afternoon, Nurse Ahrendts.'

'Lieutenant Commander? You haven't sailed yet?'

'No,' he replied, stepping out of the noisy foot traffic and into the mouth of a lane alongside Sartorial House. 'Not yet.'

I scanned the crowds and then followed him. Curtains billowed from an upstairs window. He noticed my dress and my bare arms, usually hidden beneath starched cotton.

'Congratulations on your promotion,' I said hurriedly, wanting to get away but not be impolite, 'and thank you for your letter. It was very kind—'

'I meant it,' he interrupted.

'I know. It's nice to be thanked.' I smiled, nurse to patient, and held out my hand. 'Good luck, sir.'

'No,' he shook his head, then glanced around, distracted by the sound of an approaching convoy of trucks. 'I meant I'd like to see you again, I'd like to walk with you.'

I stepped away from him, poised to run like I used to towards Piet and Seaforth, or whenever I needed to feel the breeze in my face rather than the heat of those who said I was pushing too far.

A line of covered trucks laboured to a halt outside the Queen Victoria gate, their engines idling roughly. The wind tore at a line of washing strung between the buildings up the lane.

'I've no right to ask you,' he murmured, 'but I've seen enough death to value moments when life counts for something.'

I stared at him, at the scar.

He glanced at the convoy of trucks at the gate.

'My cargo,' he said wryly, pointing. 'My war.'

'But I think you have a wife,' I gestured to the ring on his finger. 'I don't want to deceive anyone.'

'Neither do I. But I'd like to talk to you again. Could we be friends? Is that wrong?'

The wind eddied dead leaves around our feet. He

didn't shift, or look away from my eyes or my colour.

'If you pass through Simon's Town, come and see me. Maybe we'll walk again.'

'That American ship,' I said to Pa the next morning as we ate breakfast at the kitchen table, 'I looked, but it's gone.'

Ma smiled as she served the scrambled eggs. She knew I liked to check on the ships every morning, as if they were patients.

'*Ja*,' sniffed Pa. 'Wouldn't let us near it. Must have been loading a secret cargo, or a new weapon.' He tucked his napkin into his collar and attacked his eggs.

'I never saw any of the crew downtown.'

'Restricted,' mumbled Pa, crunching his toast. 'Hush-hush, that's what they call it. Are you going to Vera's tonight for supper?'

'No other ships have moved,' I went on. 'HMS *Dragon* is still there—'

Pa laid down his fork. 'Now why are you so curious?'

'Lou's right to be curious,' Ma put in. 'Mrs Hewson said old man Phillips' daughter Milly told her there were armed soldiers guarding each of those trucks. She thought they must be carrying gold, the cranes struggled so much!'

Pa choked on his toast.

Ma shrugged. 'If you want to know what's happening in the docks, just ask a woman. Milly was delivering eggs for the American ship.' She winked at me and began to gather the dirty dishes. 'They love their eggs.'

An hour later I stopped by the aerial ropeway before going on duty. The southeaster had abated to leave clear skies and only a light breeze. A change in the wind . . .

The rupture of a lifelong friendship.

The unexpected hint of another.

I found myself veering between a spark kindled on the mountainside, the tense break with Piet, a risky exchange in an alley while crowds thronged nearby . . . But I'm not fickle, tossing out one man to cast my eyes at another. Perhaps the incidents were simply unrelated. Perhaps I was reading too much into their concurrence. Even so, local brown girls did not take walks with British officers – even innocently, even as friends. Not if they wanted to keep their jobs, and the respect of their families.

I smoothed my uniform bib, conscious of being deeply tired.

'You can't stay up all hours and then do a full day's work,' Ma had scolded over the breakfast washing up, noting my hollow eyes and imagining that I'd been reading too late.

'Don't fuss, Ma.'

The split would come out soon enough. I had enough to think about without Ma's reaction.

A gust tugged at my skirt.

Down on Long Beach, the distant figures of Piet and his fellow fishermen were dragging their boats across the sand. Piet would be tilting his head back to examine the Simonsberg for a hint of the day's weather, and probably complaining to his mates about the treachery of girls no matter how long you'd known them. Or maybe he was too hurt to say anything at all. But that way lay guilt, and I was done with guilt.

Chapter Twenty-Six

Piet's fury took some time to subside. He tried to distract himself by thinking about the other available girls he knew – that tarty Vera, for one, but she was fixed on Abie. None of them really compared with Louise, but what was he to do? He'd hung on for Lou while the other good ones got taken, and now here he was, left high and dry like a boat that had missed the tide. And just because he wanted his reward for waiting all these years. He deserved her! She was his, she always had been.

Instead, all he got for his patience was rejection.

He forced himself to unclench his jaw.

Of course, if he was desperate, he could go visit the girls on Paradise Road. They would be only too pleased to see him. But that wasn't a long-term solution. He needed a wife. Someone to take over the Philander household. And someone to make the next generation of Philanders.

'Return to Cape Town,' he said morosely, pushing

his money across the wooden counter at Simon's Town station. 'Third class.'

At least there was his business to keep him occupied. Pocketing his change and the ticket, he strode onto the platform. The afternoon train wasn't due to leave for another twenty minutes but he'd followed exactly the same process two weeks before – and two weeks before that – and was determined to do nothing different. He might be making a good living, keeping Den in heart pills and himself in decent clothes and Amos in the odd beer but there was always room for a little extra egg on the *bobotie*, especially seeing he'd need to provide for a wife one day, whoever that turned out to be.

He made his way to the end of the platform where goods were piled for loading into the guard's van. People remembered surprises, changes to a routine, but they didn't notice when you did the same thing every time. Like fish, he chuckled to himself, cheering up. Hang around them long enough and they get used to you. Dive among them unexpectedly and they *skrik*. Fish, people, they were all the same.

'Hey,' he called out to a sweating guard who was heaving boxes aboard. It was a man he recognised. Piet knew them all, now.

'You can't come aboard, this is private,' the guard puffed. 'Oh, it's you, Piet. Come to check on your fish?'

'*Ja*,' said Piet. 'In the meantime, why don't I help you with these?'

He picked up a box clanking with metal and swung it into the carriage with ease. Then a second. And a third. Then a set marked keep upright.

The guard leant against the door and lit a cigarette.

Piet looked about. 'My four crates. 'Specially for the navy in Cape Town. And also crates for Meintjies and Olifant?'

'Over there,' the guard pointed his smoke at the last pile, under a tarpaulin.

Piet strode over, lifted the cover. 'Always want to make sure they have enough ice. Can't have the fish fried before they arrive – ha ha!'

The guard smirked and ground out his cigarette. 'Pass them up, then, we'll get them out of the sun.'

'Thanks, I can manage,' Piet said.

He lifted the crates up one by one as the guard watched.

'Good to know you look out for the fresh stuff. There, all aboard.' Piet stretched his arms above his head and cracked his knuckles. 'Good day for the fish, we couldn't keep them out of our nets. Can I travel in here, like before? Then I can help you unload at thc other end.'

'Have you got a ticket?'

Piet showed him.

The guard shrugged and picked up a clipboard with a list attached. He glanced vaguely over the packed carriage, then pulled a pencil from behind his ear and ticked off the list. 'All the same to me. I can always use some help.'

'My pleasure,' grinned Piet. 'Don't worry, now. If you've got other stuff to do, I'll look after the goods.' He clapped the fellow on the back and settled himself on the floor alongside the fish as if it was as comfortable as a seat in first class.

The guard nodded, and jumped down onto the platform.

Fifteen minutes later, the train jerked out of the station. Piet leant out of the window, sniffing the briny air. An hour or so of boredom and then the meeting with the Cape Town guards and the play-acting over the fish and how cold were they and making sure they were going to the right place and why do you need to bother counting the crates? Where would they be if they weren't here? And the joking that next time he would quietly slip them all a fish – why, he actually had one to spare, look . . .

And then the trip back.

Again in the guard's van but with a different guard that he'd help to load the crates going back to Simon's Town because of course he would help even if he had no need to check on the empties or get a numb backside on the hard floor. They were all in this together, weren't they?

Like taking sweets from a baby, the flash man had once said to Piet.

Not quite.

This time he was being much more careful. And he wouldn't take the rap alone. He would bring them all down with him, even the admiral who regularly enjoyed a special gift of fish from Piet, delivered in person, and lovingly prepared by his navy chef.

Chapter Twenty-Seven

'Where are the Yanks?' groused Pa, as we listened to Churchill on the radio talking about fighting in the fields and never giving up, 'Don't they care? Or are they just after our gold?'

With the war going so badly, gossip was a bracing diversion. Luckily, the whispers centred on the cargo loaded onto the American ship – and not the deployment to that same ship of a British officer who'd been foolish enough to talk to a local nurse in the centre of town. Gold, they speculated, or maybe diamonds from the mines at Kimberley, although you wouldn't need trucks to deliver a load of tiny stones, would you?

I was lucky.

No one saw me in the lane downtown.

I prepared an answer just in case. He was my patient, he wanted to thank me – though anyone seeing us together would be suspicious. After all, I had form in this kind of rebellion: I applied to be a nurse without telling my parents, and it was now common knowledge that I'd rejected a man who'd come good despite a difficult patch. Folk were proud of me but it wouldn't take much to reignite gossip.

Too *slim*, too crafty, again.

Meanwhile, our enemy came closer, fighting our troops in the deserts around Tobruk, and threatening Egypt. Wounded men from hotter battles began to populate my ward.

'Nurse?' Petty Officer Talbot, wounded off East Africa, stood in front of the ward table in his naval rig and turned his cap in his hand.

'Yes, Petty Officer Talbot? Are you all set?'

'Oh, yes, Nurse, can't wait to go . . . begging your pardon, Ma'am. But I wanted to say thank you before I left.' He blushed all the way up to his ear tips.

'Good luck, Petty Officer,' I offered my hand. 'Take care of yourself and come and see us when you pass through again.'

'Certainly will, Ma'am.'

'Staff Nurse Ahrendts!' Sister Graham's voice rang down the passage. 'Petty Officer Talbot will be late if you continue to detain him.'

Talbot, his back to Sister, winked at me before executing a sharp about turn.

'I would have thought, Staff Nurse,' remarked Sister, bearing down as Talbot disappeared, 'that you had sufficient duties to keep you busy without gossiping with discharged patients.'

'I was wishing Petty Officer Talbot good luck, Sister.'

Sister Graham regarded Louise coldly. 'Too much

empathising with patients is unprofessional, Nurse.' The girl's beauty was a distraction, making patients more likely to linger. 'Discharge should be treated in the same way as admission: efficiently and, most importantly, swiftly.'

'Yes, Sister.'

'Do not turn patients into pets, Staff Nurse.'

I gritted my teeth. Sister Graham would have been better suited to theatre work where patients were usually comatose.

'And this came for you.' She slapped an envelope addressed to me on the ward table. 'Kindly don't use this hospital as a post office.'

Dear Nurse Ahrendts, I read by candlelight later. *Forgive me for writing to you via the hospital, but I have no other address for you.*

I realised, after we met on St George's Street, that you may have found my behaviour improper. That was not my intention. I would not wish to repay your kindness by embarrassing you in any way. Please accept my apologies.

I cannot tell you where we are, other than to say that we are steaming off the coast of Africa. There is a strange mist clinging to the coastal hills. It reminds me of the cloud that used to pour over your mountains whenever the wind was in the right direction and cold sea air rose up over the land. Less about science, I always felt, and more about an extraordinary, riotous beauty.

I expect to rejoin my ship at some stage. Thank you, again, for everything you've done for me. I send you my very best wishes.

Yours sincerely,

David Horrocks

I was walking on the mountain when I saw him.

It was six months since he'd left, and four months since the letter which seemed to say he wouldn't seek me out for another walk. And here he was, alone, sitting on the ledge by the aerial ropeway, staring at the thicket of warships clustered within the dockyard. Although his back was to me, I recognised the angle of his head, the fair hair. I was about a hundred feet above him, on a path I often followed below Grandpa Ahrendts's quarry. If he didn't turn, he wouldn't see me. If I turned and went back the way I'd come, he wouldn't see me either.

I waited, one moment willing him to turn, the next willing myself to be sensible and go back . . .

'Lieutenant Commander?'

He swung round, breaking into a smile, and climbed quickly up to me with no sign of the limp.

'Nurse Ahrendts! How good to see you!' We shook hands. He was in uniform, and his face had lost the pinched look from the hospital. I became aware that the tail of my white shirt had pulled out of the waistband of my shorts and that my hair had partly fallen out of its ponytail. The last time, it was his casual clothes that had unnerved me. If he noticed my untidiness, or felt disconcerted by it, he gave no sign.

'When did you arrive?'

'Last night. We hit a storm off Madagascar and were diverted here for repairs.'

A baboon barked further up the mountain.

'Aren't you worried,' he said, gesturing upwards, 'walking on your own?'

'No, they don't bother you if you leave them alone. Are you well?' I glanced down at his waist.

'Yes, thank you, fully healed. And sleeping better,' he shot me a quick grin, 'when the war allows.'

'Did you deliver your gold safely?'

His eyes sparked but he didn't reply. I laughed.

'It's hard to keep a secret when we see everything that goes on from our front door!'

'You do have a ringside seat,' he acknowledged, glancing down at the Terrace row.

I sat on the ledge and lifted my face to the sun. He remained standing, staring out to sea. He was silent, and I wondered if I'd somehow disappointed him, perhaps he was comparing me to a more sophisticated companion, a wife he'd seen in the interim . . .

'Thank you for your letter,' I said. 'It wasn't necessary, but it was good to hear that you were alive and well.'

'I've been very lucky. Some of my friends less so.'

'Enough of the war!' I said lightly, not wanting to stir his memories. 'Will you tell me about your home, Lieutenant Commander?'

He turned to me with a smile and sat down by my side.

'Corbey has been in my family for almost two hundred years,' he began. 'It's beautiful but in a smaller, gentler way than this,' he swept an arm to encompass the bay and the mountains.

I glanced at him, the uniform, the ribbon of his medal.

'And one day it will be yours?'

'Yes,' he said. 'If I survive the war I will become the earl, as my father is now.'

Earl of Corbey. A titled gentleman. If he survived the war? I shivered, wondering if his healing was, in fact, complete. The losses on *Achilles*, the losses still to come . . . And if it ever could be complete, for any of my patients.

'But you don't want to?'

'You must think me very odd,' he said quietly. 'I don't mean to be ungrateful. But I love the navy. And I've found life at sea much more rewarding. I suspect,' he gave me a sideways glance, 'you feel the same way about nursing.'

A jackal buzzard glided by, its charcoal wingtips splayed to catch the updraft. I watched its graceful upwards spiral until it disappeared over the ridge of the mountain.

'What would you do about Corbey, if you stayed at sea?'

He turned to me eagerly. 'I'd consolidate it with the neighbouring farm, bring in a manager with modern ideas to run it. If the Hall itself became too expensive to restore, I'd let it become a ruined monument. We could preserve the lawns, the oaks. It would be striking,' he paused, 'but in a different way. And then I'd build a small farmhouse further off.'

A silence built between us. But not an awkward one, nor one I felt the need to break.

'What does the land look like, over there?' I asked after a while, glancing around at the lively proteas, the green limbs of the Simonsberg running down to the sea.

'Ah,' he touched my arm, 'it's lovely. Rolling hills, a stream in a small wood where I used to fish as a boy, oak trees that are lime green in the spring. My mother used to show me the bare branches swelling at the nodes, how the buds would wait until a warm moment and then burst open, and we could declare spring.'

'But I thought you hated it! When you were on the ward, you always talked of escaping!' I covered my mouth. 'I'm so sorry, I've no right—'

'Please don't apologise,' he broke in. His eyes met mine. 'I love the land, it's the commitment I've tried to escape.' He looked away, then added lightly, 'You must have found me a confusing patient. I don't know how you managed.'

I giggled. He grinned. A striped lizard darted onto a rock near our feet, basked for a moment, then scuttled away. One of the warships in the bay hauled up its anchor and began to manoeuvre to enter the docks.

'I know some of the ships that've been sunk,' I murmured, 'I've seen their crests on the dry dock wall. It's like losing a friend.'

He touched his hand briefly on mine, then withdrew it.

The warship glided through the dockyard entrance and nudged into its mooring. Faint shouts from the docking party floated up the mountain.

'I feel a little ashamed,' I admitted, 'this war has ruined so many lives but it's helped me.'

'You've more than repaid your promotion,' he said warmly.

I felt myself blushing. I straightened my shoulders and stood up.

'I must say goodbye, Lieutenant Commander. And good luck wherever you're going.'

'Thank you,' he said. 'And please call me David.'

I hesitated, then put out my hand. 'David.'

We shook, and I began to head down the uneven path, aware of him watching me from behind. How long would I remember his face? That quiet, measured voice? Already he was being replaced by other patients, other young men needing to be healed. But David Horrocks was different. There was something special about him, and about the ease I felt with him. Yet this was surely the end. We'd had our second walk on the mountain, as he'd hoped. Using his name for the first time was a poignant kind of farewell.

'When can we meet again?'

I turned around. His white uniform was stark against the *fynbos*, his eyes challenged mine across the few yards that separated us. Didn't he understand? Friendship between a brown girl and an earl's son was madness! It could destroy our careers, risk the marriage he'd yet to acknowledge.

'If there's one thing this war has taught me,' he came a few steps closer, 'it's that our lives are shockingly temporary. What we are, what we've built, can be easily swept away.'

He glanced at the far mountains, then gave me a surprisingly tender smile.

'Only the natural elements – sea, land, the human spirit – will survive.'

And love, I told myself. Don't forget love.

The pines rustled behind us.

'If you're still here,' I said as I turned down the path, 'I walk at Seaforth on Thursday mornings.'

I felt his gaze on me as I descended. The ground blurred in front of my feet and I found that I was crying. Was it about him, or was it a delayed reaction to the break-up with Piet? Or the cheerfulness required to buoy up my patients, the resilience required to withstand Sister Graham, the grim roll of war dead . . .

I fought not to lift my hand and wipe away the tears.

Perhaps it was simply the sun in my eyes.

Chapter Twenty-Eight

Piet crouched in the undergrowth beside a eucalyptus tree, his heart thudding with a savagery that was making him feel sicker than the first time he'd burgled a house. He strained through the leaves, up the hill, to see the man she'd been talking to. An officer, judging by the uniform. They sat side by side as if they knew each other, as if they were friends.

What the hell was she playing at?

He, Piet, had just come off a hard morning's fishing when he spotted her coming down the path below the quarry. But then she stopped for several minutes. Why was she waiting? Admiring the view? Views were always big for Lou.

He was just about to turn away – but then she called out to someone he hadn't noticed, an officer sitting on the ledge by the ropeway. The man jumped up, and took her hand. Then they sat down on the ledge and talked for far longer than if he was just an old patient and she was just being polite.

He touched her arm. She didn't stop him. They laughed together.

The train with Piet's fish left the station in a squeal of metal.

He watched through the leaves as Louise stood up, stepped down the track, then onto the road and headed towards the Terrace. The officer got up, watched her disappear, then walked briskly down the path past the hospital, turned in the opposite direction, and made for St George's Street. He was tall and looked more than thirty, with light hair and the badges and braid of a lieutenant commander. He had a scar on the side of his face but even so he carried himself with the confidence that rich folk seemed to drink with their mother's milk. He passed quite close by. Piet parted the branches and watched him walk away.

It must have been planned.

Maybe this was what her rejection had been about. Not him, but some white bastard!

God help her if she fancied him. And God help the officer. The Royal Navy didn't like its heroes messing with the local talent. He realised that he was clenching his fists. He'd clenched his fists a lot lately.

Amos had hit him once, with an open palm across the face. In front of Louise.

Piet had learnt to use his fists very effectively in the reformatory but so far, apart from some near misses when he saw people leering at Lou, and the odd time when he'd needed to defend his catch, he'd held back.

He climbed out of his hiding place and turned to look down at the dockyard.

It wouldn't be difficult to find out what ship he was on.

Chapter Twenty-Nine

The good weather continued for the rest of the week – no mist and a molten-sapphire bay – making the erratic movements of *Dorsetshire* all the more obvious as I watched her on my way to and from the hospital.

'Trials,' Pa explained. 'They've had an engine problem. They fix it in port and then they go out to test it, then they come back and tighten it up some more. Fiddly stuff.'

'You know that one?' Ma came up behind me on Wednesday morning and stroked my hair. Any relief she felt over my split with Piet had been quickly overwhelmed by the question of what to do about a defiant, newly single daughter. I overheard her badgering Pa. 'We need to find someone soon!' she urged. 'Lou's almost twenty-three!' Poor Pa found himself caught between her insistence and my resolve to make my own choice.

Why must marriage be such a relentless business for girls?

'Yes, *Dorsetshire*. One of my old patients is on her.'

'He even wrote her a letter,' Pa called from the table. 'To

say thank you. Now that's good manners, don't you think?'

Ma arched an eyebrow at him and patted my shoulder.

I fought to keep my expression neutral as I took my place at the table.

'Is the *Dorsetshire* fixed, now, Pa?'

'Maybe.' Pa shrugged. 'They were in a hurry to get it done. The captain was standing over us in the engine room. She's needed for convoy duty.'

An hour later I stopped on the path to the hospital.

The cruiser sketched a tiny outline on the horizon.

For the last few nights, I'd lain awake and imagined the worst outcome of my latest invitation to David Horrocks. He'd probably get away with a rebuke and a discreet reassignment, but my punishment would be far harsher. I'd abused my unofficial acceptance by the hospital and compounded the sin by making friends with a patient from a higher tier of the pyramid. I'd be swiftly removed from the RNH and sent in disgrace to somewhere obscure where I'd never come into contact with a decorated, white officer again. 'Totally unacceptable!' I could hear Sister Graham snap. 'A mistake to bring her here. She's better off amongst her own.'

On the streets of Simon's Town, where the wind blows everyone's secrets into the open, I'd be attacked once more for my unruliness. We always knew it, they'd say. Got her comeuppance, now. Ma and Pa would be crushed with shame.

I turned away from the sea.

The best outcome would be for the *Dorsetshire* to leave and never return.

'Sister Graham.' The surgeon commander hurried into the ward late in the day. 'May I borrow Staff Nurse Ahrendts for the theatre?'

Sister looked up at the ward clock.

'I can stay,' I put in and the surgeon nodded, 'if Sister will release me?'

'Very well,' Sister pursed her lips. 'You will report for duty tomorrow afternoon as usual.'

'Yes, Sister.'

'It's an emergency,' the surgeon commander muttered as he strode out with me. 'I wouldn't impose on you otherwise, Nurse. Not after a long day. Could you scrub up, please?'

The emergency operation stretched into the early evening and by the time I'd waited for Able Seaman Lane to regain consciousness and then settled him in the ward, it was dusk. I stepped wearily down the path, stumbling a little in the gloom, even though my feet knew the route well. Ma and Pa would be wondering where I was. I sat down to rest my legs and stared over the purple bay. One vessel, with the outline of a frigate, was just visible at anchor, its hull darker than the surrounding sea. Closer in, the ships in the dockyard had already fused into an indistinct tangle of funnels and masts.

He was surely gone.

The next day being Thursday, I was able to sleep through the dawn call to prayers and Ma and Pa's departure for work. By the time I woke, sunshine was already bathing the dockyard, and *Dorsetshire* was at her usual mooring. I wolfed down a piece of toast, threw on a wide skirt and a shirt and ran – like in the old barefoot days – past the mosque, down Alfred Lane and along St George's Street. Seagulls swooped above my head, searching but not finding their air perch in a breeze that was too light to hold them steady. The familiar grain of tar bit into my feet as I diverted off the pavement to go past a man wheeling a bicycle. Reality travelled from my bare soles to my brain. Turn around! Don't risk everything!

I stopped, glanced back.

The hospital glimmered against the slope. The Simonsberg brooded in its grey fastness.

I ran on.

Seaforth loomed, with its tumble of cottages. I avoided the Philander place and headed straight for the hidden vantage of the grass verge from where I'd seen Piet and his accomplice in the bushes. The beach below was deserted, the tide low to middling, the sand pristine. Morning sun tinted the rocks in creeping stripes of gold and rose-pink. I've always felt closer to God at Seaforth than in the confines of St Francis Church or under the watchful gaze of the mosque. If David Horrocks didn't come, this place was enough. I'd find comfort here, like I always had.

I walked towards the water, my footsteps sinking into the crystal sand, the first prints to touch the beach since the last high tide. I reached down to splash my face and the water hit my skin with an astringent shock. If I'd brought my swimsuit, I could have taken a quick, restoring plunge before work. A shell was protruding from the sand near my feet and I knelt down and dug it out. These days I was responsible for my own shell gathering. It was a Pink Lady, an elongated, jagged teardrop of a shell. I rinsed it off and held its cavern to my ear. A shadow fell across the sand.

'Hello,' David Horrocks smiled and squatted beside me. He was wearing white tropical rig and he'd taken off his shoes. The sight of his feet was somehow disconcerting, even though I'd seen them bare so often. I felt myself blushing.

'What do you have there?'

'It's called a Pink Lady. Normally you don't find them, they get broken up before they reach shore.'

I handed it to him and he ran a finger along its sharp ridges. 'Beautiful. Fierce, but beautiful.'

'I didn't think you'd be here,' I looked down, conscious of a stealing shyness, feeling the surface of the sand for more hidden shells. 'I saw your ship go out yesterday—'

'Yes. We did a full day at sea and got back rather late.'

He stood and walked closer to the water's edge, and let the wavelets wash over his feet. I followed him. It was a strangely intimate act to stand fully clothed yet barefoot alongside a man whose body I knew almost as well as my own.

'Can I ask you something,' I paused, 'David?'

'Of course.'

When he smiled at my use of his name, his face changed utterly. I could see what he must have looked like as a young man, when there was no scar.

'What is it like, to wage war at sea?'

He looked at me in surprise, then stared out towards the rim of mountains on the far side of the bay.

'There's no set battlefield. You have to be on constant alert. I think of it as a blind chess match, where you can't see the other man's pieces. You try to stay out of his sights, *here*' – he gestured left – 'but within your own range to knock him out of the water, *there*,' he pointed right.

A blind chess match, I shivered, with death the price of miscalculation.

'And in the case of submarines, the horizontal becomes the vertical.'

Layers of water, like those through which Piet used to dive for shells, but multiplied a hundred times in depth, and made for an ambush.

'I hate to think of the sea being used like that.' I reached down and ran my hands through the familiar, lapping tide. Fragments of brown kelp and green sea lettuce, churned up by the recent spring tides, were beginning to deposit a frilly line at the dying edge of the wavelets.

'I know what you mean,' he glanced at me. 'When the water closes over a sinking ship, it feels like an outrage. And all that remains is a streak of oil, a few spars of wood. And memories.'

I closed my eyes for a moment, recalling the ships' crests on the dry dock wall, the pride of the sailors in keeping them touched up, Pa's dismay when a lack of paint prevented them doing so.

'And then it becomes my war,' I said. 'Nursing the survivors.'

He nodded, bent and gathered a handful of wet sand and let it dribble through his fingers.

I wondered how much he told his wife. And if she understood the visceral connection he felt to water, to the elements, to his men.

The incoming tide began to lick higher up the egg rocks. A feather of cloud briefly covered the sun. Where we were standing, we'd be clearly visible to anyone looking down from the cottages. But it could still be classed as a chance encounter . . .

'When it's over, how will you look at the oceans? Won't they be too damaged for you?'

'Oh no,' his blue eyes sparked. 'Thank God I don't look at it like that! The sea recovers despite how we use it.'

'I like that,' I smiled. 'I like the thought of water being forgiving.'

His eyes rested on me warmly. I fought the urge to slip my arm through his.

'What is it?' he asked. 'What are you thinking?'

I inhaled the crisp, salty air and felt its freshness lift me.

'I'm starting to feel that I know you. And yet that can't be right. We only ever meet here.' I pointed at the green slopes, the dancing sea, the hospital.

'It's strange for me, too, Louise.'

'In what way?'

He sighed, gave a wry smile and touched my hand.

'I should go,' I began to edge away. I shouldn't have pressed. And it was long past the moment to reinstate the distance Sister Tutor had drummed into me, and Matron had warned me to observe. I'd crossed every boundary, Vera would call me a fool—

'No, don't,' he ran a hand through his fair hair, exposing the pale terminus of his scar, 'not yet.'

His eyes roamed over my face.

I wavered, poised to run, my toes digging into the sand.

'I didn't plan on falling in love with my nurse, beautiful and accomplished though she is.'

The rosy morning exploded, peppering me with a brief, gasping brilliance. I wanted to leap and catch its shards, as if they held the magic I'd called up as a child. Bright. Promising. Reckless . . .

'You can't!' I stumbled backwards. The sand became heavy, clinging. 'You're married, I'm coloured, we mustn't meet like this again—'

'Please,' he caught my arm urgently. 'Don't go till I tell you why.'

I pulled away, pressure building in my chest. Pa would soon find out, so would Ma, Matron and Sister Graham at the hospital, Piet on Long Beach, Vera, the rest of the Terrace.

'Forgive me,' he lowered his voice. 'Shall we go and sit down?'

I followed him up the beach and squatted on my haunches, a little away from him, still ready to run. But it might be too late for escape.

He stared into the blue distance.

I closed my eyes briefly and listened for the healing rush and retreat of the waves.

'My wife,' he touched the gold ring on his finger, 'is the daughter of our neighbour. My father encouraged the match because it would benefit both properties, but Elizabeth has always been more of a younger sister to me. We married at the time of Dunkirk.'

He hesitated.

'I think we both hoped my affection for her would

turn into love, but it's never reached more than fondness.'

I sank down. He watched as I spread my skirt over my legs, then reached across the distance I'd imposed and touched his fingers on the side of my cheek.

'It must sound silly from someone over thirty – but I've never been in love before.'

I felt my skin respond.

Perhaps he felt it, too, for he began to speak more intently.

'The war has made me realise how precious love is when you happen to find it. The men who died on *Achilles* will never know it again.'

I touched the sand, let it slide through my fingers. 'You told me, on the mountain, that all that will remain are the elements. Land, sea, and now love?'

'Yes,' he rubbed a hand across his scar. 'I couldn't say so at the time, it was too soon. I'd have shocked you.'

'But I thought it.'

'You did?' His voice leapt.

The waves began to push further up the beach. A cormorant landed on one of the egg rocks and extended its wings to dry them in the passing breeze. I wanted him to keep talking, I wanted to hear more of that quiet, fervent voice.

'You said you only wanted to be friends.'

'Yes,' he admitted, 'maybe that's all I can hope for. Even so, you deserve to know the truth.'

I realised I was still clutching the Pink Lady in my left hand. I opened my palm. The shell's ridges had driven red indentations into my flesh. He leant closer and rubbed them with his thumb.

'Louise,' his voice lingered over my name, 'I know you can't feel the same way about me. I saw you, once, with a young man. He seemed very keen.'

He looked away from me like he used to on the ward, searching the cloud-topped mountains, the ships that came and went. I sensed he was releasing me back to Piet, like a bird tossed into the sky to rejoin its mate; offering me the chance to leave without embarrassment – after all, I'd said that I wanted to go, that we shouldn't meet again . . .

'Piet and I aren't together any more.'

He turned to me in surprise.

The heaviness ebbed out of my body and an altogether new emotion took hold. I fingered the shell and held it out to him. 'If you hold it to your ear, you can hear the sea. Perfect. Unspoilt. Wherever you are in the world.'

Or the whisper of someone who loves you.

He searched my face as he slipped the shell into his pocket. 'I'll treasure it.'

He lifted one hand to stroke my hair.

Then he reached across and kissed me on the lips. His mouth was tender.

I pulled away, scrambled to my feet.

'We can't meet again like this, not in the open—'

I left him on the sand and raced up the grass verge, up the lane past the Philander cottage and along St George's Street, wondering who had seen me, who would be the first to tell.

Who might guess just by looking at me . . .

A gum tree was shedding feathery red blossoms onto the pavement, making it slippery. I stopped to brush the underside of my feet. A black motor car with a pennant flying on its hood, drove by. I caught a glimpse of gold braid. Vera, loitering by Sartorial House, watched it pass with her hands on her hips, then spotted me and beckoned. I waved back but continued on my way, ignoring her shouted invitations for a gossip. I turned up Alfred Lane, hurried past the mosque and into Ricketts Terrace beneath the quiet fronds of our palm and surely beneath the sceptical gaze of Jesus and Allah, feeling all the while a deep, wondrous, dangerous, elation.

Chapter Thirty

Dear Louise,

It is night here, and while the Southern Cross has dipped below the horizon, you have not left my thoughts since we parted on Seaforth Beach. It's not just the feel of you, the brief kiss we exchanged, it's a deeper current.

I realise this is a breach of my vows to my wife. Even so, I can't shake off the feeling that when one finds love – however unexpectedly – one should cherish it. I've no sense, though, how to take it further without hurting you or Elizabeth. I know we run the risk of severe reprimand if we're discovered together, and that the cost for you will be greater than for me. War may have shaken much of the old world and its ways, but I would never want to endanger your career, not after you've broken down so many barriers to achieve so much.

What should we do?

I nearly died on Achilles. *At the moment, the only anchors I have are the sea, my ship and the pull towards you. So, although I've no clear answer, I must see you and hold you again.*

Shall we wait to see how the wind blows?

There may be possibilities for us that we cannot yet imagine.

Thank you for the time we spent together.

Whatever happens, it will remain the most precious of my life.

My love,

David

I sat on my bed, holding the letter.

Why? What possibilities could there be? He was married, his family was titled, many hundreds of acres waited for him after the war.

In the sitting room, Ma's sewing machine competed with the rumble of Pa talking with Mr Phillips about foundations and plaster and how to stabilise the Terrace against the mountain. There'd been more slippages.

'Louise?' Ma called. 'Old man Phillips has gone. Can you help lay the table?'

'Have you heard?' Pa muttered to me as he clattered knives and forks. 'There's a huge flap on. The battleship *Bismarck*'s got out. They think she's making a run for the Atlantic through the Iceland gap.'

'So what'll you do?' asked Vera as we sat on the sea wall below Jubilee Square a week later. Gulls bobbed on the swells. A crane manoeuvred above a moored warship with a squeal of metal.

'About what?'

'Well,' Vera considered, as she pointed her bare feet, 'you've thrown over Piet, you won't go out with anyone else, you're making a good living. What'll you do now?'

I looked across the bay towards Muizenberg, nestling below its ridge of mountain, and laughed.

'I'll buy my own cottage, and then I'll marry someone I haven't met yet!'

'What about someone at work?'

I darted her a glance.

'I knew it!' Vera squirmed around to face me. 'You're blushing!'

'I'm not!' But Vera has known me all my life.

'Why should it always be a secret with you, Lou? Is he a porter? One of the storemen?'

'Nothing will come of it,' I said, swinging my feet back over the wall and gathering up my bag.

Vera scrambled after me and grabbed my hand. 'He's married?'

'I don't want to talk about it, Vee.'

'Why not? Why should it be a secret?'

'I'll see you tomorrow.' I leant down and kissed her on the cheek.

Vera ran in front of me.

'I know why,' she breathed triumphantly. 'It's because he's white!'

War log

North Atlantic, 48 degrees north, 16 degrees west

Fog. A freezing wind out of the north.

Bismarck *has sunk HMS* Hood, *with 1400 men lost. I pray my old Dartmouth friend, Bob, was spared. We're racing at full speed to join the attack.* Bismarck*'s shells have a range of thirty miles. We must close inside that to fire on her. There will be more losses.*

Does unfaithfulness to my wife require an act of betrayal, or merely the thought of it?

Elizabeth haunts me in the cold daylight.

Louise fills my dreams.

It was the not knowing that was the worst.

'Lou?'

Pa stumbled through the darkness to where I was sitting on a ledge above the Terrace. I'd taken to going there after supper, wrapped in an old blanket against the winter cold. The blackout meant that the stars glittered with a stark brilliance I'd never seen in peacetime.

'This is not good, my Lou, you out here moping every night.' He settled down beside me. 'Your ma and I are worried. Is it because of Piet? Are you sorry you gave him up?'

'No, Pa. It's just the war. It seems never-ending.'

'I know,' Pa put an arm around me. 'And HMS *Hood*. I can't believe she's gone.'

'She was my seven-years-and-one-day birthday treat.'

'*Ja*,' he considered, 'so she was. But here's some interesting news on that front. When *Bismarck* was finally sunk, remember that lieutenant commander you nursed, the one with the DSO? His cruiser fired the final torpedoes. Fancy that!'

I fell against Pa, turned my head into his shoulder.

'Lou?' Pa rocked me gently. 'What's the matter? It'll be over one day. Then you'll meet another young man, better than Piet. I'm sure of it.'

Chapter Thirty-One

I didn't reply to David's letter immediately. I hid it inside a book beneath my shell collection and left it to brew. I wanted some time to go by. I wanted to be sure I wasn't simply succumbing to the elation without an appreciation of the danger it carried, not to mention the practical barriers. I looked for distraction. I began to go out more. I swam every day at Seaforth, even though it was strange to be on my own in the water. In the evening, sitting alongside Vera at the Criterion bioscope, I watched Judy Garland fall in love and Hedy Lamarr smoulder, but I knew there was no connection between the silver screen and real life.

'You're mad!' Vera declared during the interval. 'You'll lose everything if they find out.'

I said nothing.

She unwrapped a toffee and sucked it noisily and leant closer to me. 'Listen, Lou, we all thought you were too cocky wanting to get ahead but it turns out you were right. You're a nurse and we're cleaners or nothing at all. But this is different.' She glanced around at the upper floor with its single-colour audience. 'This is dangerous.'

'I know,' I whispered. 'Now hush.'

'I won't hush,' Vera's voice rose and several people looked around, 'because now it's about more than you. Don't you see?'

'What do you mean?'

Vera rolled her eyes. 'People look up to you. Kids want to be like you, with a career and all. If you're disgraced, you set them back. You set us all back because the whites think there's a girl we gave a chance to, and look how she repays us?' Vera jiggled her feet. 'Dipping her toes in places where she shouldn't be!'

'Ssh!' I glanced around.

'Don't do it, Lou! Don't touch him and,' she pinched my arm, 'don't let him touch you.'

'Even if I love him?' the words slipped out.

'Oh dear Lord, especially if you love him,' Vera spluttered under her breath as the lights dimmed. 'For a clever girl you're not showing much brain any more.'

Later in the week, I asked for an interview with Matron at the RNH. She received me in her office overlooking a tranquil slice of the bay.

'I'm grateful, Matron, for my theatre training.'

Matron inclined her head. She was younger than my Victoria matron, and spoke with a strong Scottish accent like some of my patients. My file lay open on the desk in front of her.

'You'll be fully qualified by the end of the year, Staff

Nurse Ahrendts. We're very pleased with your progress. Now, is there anything else?'

I glanced over her shoulder and out of the window. A light rain began to fall, smudging the horizon.

'With your permission, Matron, may I speak candidly?'

'Certainly.'

'Can you advise me what my prospects might be after the war? As a local nurse, will I be able to stay at the RNH or will I have to leave?'

She smiled, revealing neat teeth. Matrons don't often smile, so you rarely get to see their teeth.

'I think that you have an excellent chance of staying. Your background is of no consequence in that decision. Given that most of our staff will return home, we'll need experience to cover the transition and you've proved yourself to be outstanding. By that time, Nurse, you'll be well on your way to Sister registration. Any hospital would be keen to recruit you.'

'Thank you, Matron.'

She put on her glasses and looked down at my file. 'I see the surgeon commander has recommended you for two days of advanced theatre training at the Victoria. We will try to accommodate that in the next few weeks.'

'Thank you, Matron.' I rose to my feet, trying to suppress a smile.

'Just one thing, Staff Nurse,' she looked at me carefully. 'Sister Graham believes you allow too much familiarity with your patients. I don't happen to agree, having observed you on the ward. But it's worth being on your guard.'

'Yes, Matron. I understand.'

But what about outside the ward, I wanted to ask.

Have I built up sufficient credit to be kept on if you find out I've crossed that particular line?

Later that night, after Ma and Pa had gone to bed, I took the letter out of its hiding place and read it through once more, tracing the angular strokes with my finger, imagining him sitting in his cabin, deciding which words to use, or even whether to write at all.

When one finds love – however unexpectedly – one should cherish it.

What should we do?

I picked up my hand mirror and looked at my face.

I'd taken risks to break free, to claw my way up the pyramid.

But there was still something missing.

It demanded the biggest risk of all.

I put down the mirror and took a piece of paper and a pen.

When you come back, I wrote,

We should be together.

But not in Simon's Town.

Chapter Thirty-Two

Even in wartime, there are days in early spring when the Cape shrugs off the raw north wind and reaches for quiet, limpid sunshine and peace seems close enough to touch. The mountains abandon their clouds and scratch sharp outlines against the sky, and the guinea fowl start to *kek* hopefully for a mate. In St Francis Church in the spring of 1941, the pews were glowing yellow beneath the stained glass windows. I glanced about while the minister exhorted us to pray for the triumph of Allied good over Axis fascism, and wondered how God managed to support the devout on both sides of a war. Today there were fewer worshippers. Perhaps it was war-weariness or perhaps folk preferred to petition their God outdoors when the weather was fine. For me, that was true all year round.

'Louise?' Ma linked her arm through mine as we left the service. Pa was working an emergency shift. 'Let's take a walk. It's such a lovely morning.'

She patted Mrs Hewson, who was shouting with one of

the Phillips daughters, pointed up the mountain and cupped her hand to Mrs H's ear. 'We're going the long way!'

We climbed up Victoria Lane and onto one of the elevated paths towards the Terrace.

'There's no getting away from it, Lou,' Ma picked her way between the rocks, trying not to scuff her shoes, 'you're working too hard. You need to get out and about more.'

I smiled, perhaps the sermon had failed to hold her attention as well. There was no doubt where this conversation was heading. Also, in the months since the sinking of *Bismarck*, David had written me several letters, addressed to Ricketts Terrace. Ma noticed one, and gave it to me with a questioning look; the rest I managed to pick up before she got home from work.

There will be no memorials for Bismarck, *or for HMS* Hood, *he wrote.*

Just the longitude and latitude of where they went down. We picked up as many German survivors as we could, but there was a U-boat alert and we had to leave some behind. It's not a sight I'll forget, men tossed off the scrambling nets and left to die. Will we find humanity again at the end of this?

On a more cheerful note, I have a confession. I saw you once before on a previous visit by Dorsetshire, *just after Dunkirk. You were in uniform, with your young man downtown. You didn't see me but I couldn't help noticing you. Your extraordinary eyes. Your graceful beauty. There's a strange postscript to this. When I was ill with appendicitis before we put in to Simon's Town, I imagined you again in my feverish moments. And when I woke up in hospital after the operation, you were there.*

I wonder if you received my letter after Seaforth? The post takes months, I know. Perhaps I've been getting ahead of myself with the recollection above, please forgive me if I have.

I told myself I owed Ma no explanation.

I was doing nothing wrong, correspondence was not a sin. But I'm not a natural dissembler like Piet. Or Vera, who can lie without a qualm if it suits her, or choose to tell the truth in the most unvarnished way. Vera, though, was being kind and discreet, inviting me out to the cinema or to tea in the cafe near Sartorial House, as if keeping me close by her side would reduce the opportunity for me to stray in the direction of my white admirer. She hated the colour bar as much as I did, but whereas I'd discovered it was bendable to an extent, she saw it as implacable at best, destructive at worst. Vera worried I'd be broken and never recover.

'Will you please slow down, Louise?'

'Sorry, Ma!' I waited for her to catch up. 'The only new men I meet are my patients.'

'Exactly! And they're no good for anything,' Ma snorted, 'except writing nice thank you notes! It's a shame you don't have any of our Cape Corps servicemen at the RNH.'

A pair of sugarbirds alighted on a protea. I pointed them out to David the first time we walked here.

'Nothing will happen till after the war, Ma.'

'That's what everyone says, especially your pa.' She

mimicked his gravelly voice. 'Wait for the war to be over, Sheila, then this will happen, or that might happen.' A strand of wiry hair escaped from beneath her battered straw hat.

'He's right,' I said gently, putting my arm around her and trying to lighten the moment. 'And I'm too tired for a romance right now.'

'Nonsense,' Ma retorted, giving me a brisk nudge. 'It's only marriage that needs stamina.'

I laughed and looked about for a level rock and the distraction of a view. 'Let's stop here for a bit.'

Ma gathered her skirt and sat down gingerly. I perched beside her.

'I'm serious, Louise. You must get out more. You won't meet anyone new until you go out and try.' A tugboat curved out of the harbour and slowed in the approaches, pitching in its creamy wash. 'Is there something bothering you, child? Something you want to talk about?'

As I said, I'm not a good liar. Like Vera, Ma knew me too well not to suspect something was amiss. But the questions I'd like to have asked were too revealing.

Had Ma ever done anything she knew was wrong?

Does God reserve a special punishment for those who contemplate their sin with the kind of longing that gripped me every time I reread David's letters?

'Ma, when you fell in love, did you know it straightaway?'

'Of course!' She chuckled. 'I took one look at your pa and knew he was the one. And so will you, when the time comes.' She paused and shot me a quick glance. 'Or perhaps it has and you're not telling.'

My heart lurched. I stared at the sea.

'I'm heart sore about Piet, though,' Ma went on, motioning vaguely toward the Philander place, 'all the times we fed him and trusted him, when he was just a common thief.'

Ma, I reflected, would be horrified to know that Piet and I were not all that different.

Stealing is stealing, whether it's property or a husband.

'You mustn't worry about me,' I said with a show of firmness. 'I'm doing fine.'

Away to the east, where Cape Hangklip marked the far entrance to the bay, a vessel poked above the sea horizon. With a puff of smoke, the tug got underway again. We watched it sweep past the lighthouse towards the distant ship.

'You're twenty-three,' Ma said crisply, swatting away a persistent bee. 'Make an effort! The war can't stop you going to Cape Town. Or visit Lola and her husband in Grassy Park. Mrs Phillips says there are heaps of decent young men in Grassy Park. We'd have to find out about their families, of course—'

'Maybe I will. Shall we carry on, Ma? Pa will be home soon.'

I helped her to her feet.

She held on to my hand.

'I couldn't be more proud of you, Lou. I've said it before but I'll say it again. You're making a mistake if you think you can manage on your own for ever.' She gripped my hand more tightly. 'This is a hard place to be brown and female and alone, even if you're the prettiest and cleverest in the room.'

* * *

4th December, 1941

Dear Louise,

I'm writing this hurriedly in the hope of catching the last collection.

We docked in Cape Town this morning, and there's a week's leave for all but a skeleton crew. Thanks to your wonderful South African hospitality, some of my shipmates are going upcountry to stay with farming families and I've received the offer of a garden cottage in Oranjezicht, below Table Mountain. It's fully equipped and the owners will be away.

I know this is sudden, but can you spend a few hours, a day – or more – with me? I long to see you.

From tomorrow, I will wait every day at noon in the Dutch East India Company Gardens, next to St George's Cathedral. Please come.

In haste, with love,

David

I've lied in the past to bolster Piet's self-esteem, and to convince Ma I was acceptable to my white peers. And I've concealed dreams, letters of application, David . . .

But I've never lied outright for my own benefit. My own pleasure.

'This is most inconvenient, Staff Nurse,' Sister Graham frowned. The VAD clattered pans in the sluice. 'Could you not have given more warning?'

'I'm sorry, Sister. It's a friend who's taken ill.'

'Do you have sufficient leave?'

'Yes, Sister,' I replied, making respectful eye contact. 'I've taken no leave since I was assigned to the RNH.'

She gave me a sharp look. She herself was not averse to the odd day off.

'Can't you fit this – extracurricular – nursing around your existing shifts?'

'My friend lives in Cape Town, Sister. I will need to go by train.'

My dual role as both ward and theatre nurse gave me useful leverage over Sister. I'd taken care to get the approval of the surgeon commander in advance, an approval that I could cite if she chose to refuse.

Sister pursed her lips. 'Very well. Two days, taken from tomorrow. And in future, kindly avoid commitments that will interfere with the smooth running of this ward.'

'Yes, Sister.'

I turned around smartly and walked back to my post, astonished at how easy it was. Maybe this was why lying could become addictive: if the first time is simple, you want to test your ability again, even increase the stakes.

And so I did.

'I've planned a little trip,' I said later that day, darting a glance at Ma, who beamed. 'I'm going to see Lola and then I'll spend the night at the nurses' home at the Victoria. I've got theatre training the next day. Like last time.'

'Well that's kind, Lou,' Pa said heartily. 'Lola must be miserable, stuck so far from her friends.'

'She should have been more careful who she ran about with,' Ma observed tartly, 'but it'll be a good break for Lou. Won't it be lovely if the weather holds?'

And that was the end of it, although Ma popped her head into my bedroom while I was gathering myself and said she was pleased I'd taken her advice to heart, and reminded me to include a long-sleeved jersey in case the December heat were suddenly to vanish.

What do you pack when you're going to meet a man who may – will? – become your lover? I had no smart clothing, in fact my nurse's uniform was probably the smartest outfit I possessed. And there was no time to buy anything new. But I had a sleeveless blue dress, made by Mrs Hewson, the one I was wearing when we met on the street. I saw how he noticed it, how his eyes approved. That could be my day dress. There was also a deception to maintain, so I packed a uniform for the mythical day's work at the Victoria, praying that no twist of fate intervened to reveal the lie.

Then a nightgown, a brush, the best of my simple underwear . . .

In fact, the preparations stopped me from dwelling on what might actually happen. The touch of skin on skin, the thrill I could hardly bear to imagine.

I've never lied like this before. And I've never done anything so shameless.

But, if I look into my heart, I was committed from the moment I gave him the seashell.

Beautiful, he said, as he ran his finger over its sharp ridges. Fierce, but beautiful.

Chapter Thirty-Three

I examined each one of my fellow passengers on the train to Cape Town. An elderly couple, a labourer, a mother with a child in school uniform, and a pair of teenage girls who got off at Fish Hoek. No one recognised me. I hardly recognised myself, caught up in such deliberate deceit. And yet, as we passed each station, my heart raced with the possibility of a successful escape – and the simple thrill of a journey beyond Simon's Town. The summit of Devil's Peak posed above wispy cloud just for me, the massive rampart of Table Mountain leant protectively over the train as we drew into the city.

When does a lie become the right thing to do?

December heat shimmered. I hurried up Adderley Street, longing to peer about at the lively crowds, but keeping my head down. I was wearing a scarf that matched my blue dress and covered my forehead. Hopefully just another nondescript coloured woman heading to work.

He was waiting for me on a bench beneath the line of

trees that flanked the main walk through the Gardens. I glanced around. It was midday but the office crowds had yet to arrive. There was no one about. I'd stayed close to the shrubbery, so he didn't spot me at first. He was gazing up at the Cathedral.

He turned.

'Louise!' he leapt up and hurried over. He put his hands on my shoulders but we didn't embrace. We could never embrace in public. He glanced down at my suitcase. I felt myself flush.

'Thank you,' he said. 'Thank you.'

He picked up my case.

'Shall we go?'

The cottage David had been lent lay off a side road in a garden thick with proteas, and shadowed by the face of the mountain. It took us about twenty minutes to get there, but we didn't hurry. He talked quietly, about rejoining his ship in Scotland, about being presented to the King while His Majesty was inspecting the fleet, about the purple heather that coloured the mountains like our ericas did here . . . gentle conversation, designed to set me at ease, and requiring no particular response. He was in uniform – if anything more elegantly handsome than I remembered – and he was careful not to walk too close to me. To an outsider, we could have been simply friends or perhaps, if I'd been white and less scarved, a brother and sister meeting after a long absence.

He put my suitcase in a small bedroom that led off the sitting room. I don't know if it was where he was sleeping and I didn't ask, just nodded when he offered to make tea and wandered out into the secluded garden.

He brought a tray with tea and buttered bread, and set it down on a table.

'It's a year since we first met,' he said, raising his cup to me. 'You came to me when I had a nightmare after the operation.'

'But I thought you didn't know me!'

He smiled. 'Ah, but I did, even though I was hallucinating. And the next day, when you changed my dressing, I closed my eyes and recognised your voice.'

I looked at the lush garden and the pretty cottage with its shuttered windows. A white-browed robin hopped amongst the foliage, piping a call more delicate than the birds I was used to in Simon's Town.

'I wasn't expecting it to lead here.'

'Neither was I,' he leant forward and touched my arm. He hadn't touched me on the way here and our fingers only briefly brushed as he gave me my tea. 'So let's live for this moment, for however long we have together, however long you'd like to stay.' His eyes never left mine and I saw his need, but also a readiness for me to set the limits of our togetherness. As he had on the beach, he was giving me the chance to leave whenever I chose.

'I have two days!' I felt the unexpected prick of tears. 'We have two days!'

He reached forward and took my hands in his.

We didn't kiss at first. He untied my scarf at the nape of my neck and let it fall onto the chair. My hair tumbled forward and he ran his fingers through it and lifted it away and behind my ears, and cupped my face between his palms.

'We have now,' he murmured.

I have mostly been kissed by Piet. And those kisses tended to be quick, pressured, greedy.

David kissed me slowly, lips meeting and parting, our breath mingling, his skin cool and sharp against my cheek. I felt the tears again and let them flow, and I laughed and he laughed and we kissed through their saltiness.

We didn't make love straightaway. The sun sank behind the mountain and a violet shade invaded the garden. The robin fell silent. Below us, the city receded into the pitch-darkness of the blackout. A fragrance of lilies from a nearby garden drifted on the cooling air.

He sat me down, went inside and brought out a blanket to tuck round me.

'I'm going to make us some supper. You stay here. Watch for the stars to come out.'

We ate scrambled eggs – he said he'd learnt to make it as a child with his mother – and drank a tart white wine. We finished the buttered bread from teatime, and then he brought out grapes and peaches he'd bought from the Parade downtown.

And we talked.

As if – now the decision had been made and we knew we would soon be lovers – we were free to discover one another afresh in words, gestures, and laughter.

The sky became sequinned velvet. Table Mountain hovered, palely lit by a half-moon. He brought out another blanket and we sat side by side, wrapped up. After a time he reached under the blanket, drew out my hand, kissed it.

'I'm going to clear up. Would you like to take a bath?'

I nodded and we bundled up the blankets and went inside. He showed me the bathroom, gave me a candle, and disappeared into the kitchen to wash up.

After bathing, I stepped out onto the terrace in my white dressing gown. The paving stones still held the day's heat and were warm beneath my bare feet. The Southern Cross had already sunk behind the mountain but Sirius was up, directly overhead. Towards the eastern horizon shone the hard, unwavering disc of a planet, probably Mars. Soon, before the stars turned much further—

I felt David's arms go around me from behind. I leant back against him.

'Are you worried about a baby?' he asked quietly.

'No, it's not the right time.'

He turned me around and held me at arm's length. He touched my hair, its ends damp from the bath. 'And if it had been?'

'I wouldn't have stayed,' I said simply. 'We would have had to wait.'

He hugged me close. 'You go in. I'll lock up, then have a quick shower.'

I was waiting by the open window when he came into the bedroom in his pyjama trousers. The candle flickered on the bedside table. He lifted the curtain of my hair and kissed my neck. I touched the livid scar on his hip, then turned away from him and undid my dressing gown and stepped out of it. He rested his hands on my shoulders, not rushing me. After a moment, I lifted my sleeveless nightdress and pulled it over my head and turned around to face him. My hair fell forward across one breast.

He gathered me carefully into his arms. I was trembling, and he whispered to me until I relaxed against his bare chest. Presently I held myself away from him and said, with a glint, 'You're a little overdressed.'

He smiled, led me over to the bed, and took off his pyjama trousers. I stretched out, and he ran a finger from my throat, around my breasts, to my waist and flanks. Then traced the same path with his lips.

I began to tremble again.

'Shall I stop?'

'No,' I breathed, 'please don't stop—'

But he waited, kissed my lips, then the swell of my breasts, the contraction of my stomach.

I felt the urgency begin to build within us both.

'Don't let me hurt you.'

'You won't hurt me.'

A faint breeze rustled the garden beyond the window. The candlelight danced across our moulded bodies, played on my legs, brightened the contrast between my skin and his as we moved, catching us in a transience of light and shade, heat and chill, advance and retreat.

He stopped for a moment, searching my eyes, wanting to see deeper than he had before, but I didn't want him to stop and I grasped his shoulders and together we moved again.

When it was over, it wasn't just I who wept but David as well.

I folded him in my arms. The candle, burnt down to

a stump, gave a final flare and died. The night expanded about us. A dog barked in the distance.

David's pounding heart began to ease.

After a while he moved, lay on his side and pulled me close.

'I didn't know I'd cry,' I whispered. Or that tears could be like this. Warm. Unbidden.

He kissed me on the forehead. 'The best tears, my darling.'

I closed my eyes. He stroked my hair, rested a hand on my waist.

'I love you, Louise.'

We slept.

The first streaks of dawn were just probing the darkness when I woke.

For a moment, I was disorientated. A soft, broad bed. No clatter of Pa and Ma. Beside me, and around me, warmth. I turned carefully. David lay on his side, the lower half of his body swathed in a sheet, the upper half naked and pressed against me. He'd slung one arm across my waist. He was breathing deeply and evenly. I lay and watched the rise and fall of his chest. After a while, his breathing changed and I lifted the sheet to cover him against the morning chill. From the garden came the first notes of a different dawn chorus from Simon's Town.

He stirred, opened his eyes, registered me with an intimacy I'd never seen before.

'Good morning, my love.'

'And to you.' I leant over him, traced the scar on his temple with my fingers, then touched my lips along its length. 'You slept well.'

'Yes, I think I'm over my wounds.' He touched a hand to the scar. 'And I was tired,' he grinned.

I lay back beside him. 'Can I close my eyes, just for a little longer?'

'Of course.' He lifted his arm and drew me close. I rested my hand on his chest.

'Tell me about a different ocean from mine.'

And so he described the calm shallows of the Adriatic; the mean waves of the South China Sea; the ice-swollen swells of the Arctic . . .

And presently, my body began to spark against his and he stopped talking and we made love in the fragile clasp of a new day.

I borrowed a shirt of his and tucked it into the shorts I'd packed along with my walking shoes, and we headed up the mountain on a deserted path. He walked ahead, striding out, turning every so often to catch me in his arms and kiss me. Above us, the sun struck Table Mountain squarely, picking out the rocky ledges and pinnacles jutting from its face. Different pincushion proteas from our yellow ones clung to the slopes. They'd mostly finished flowering but here and there a conical bloom opened stiff petals to the light.

It was a golden morning.

We reached the gravel road that traversed the mountain and sat down in the shade of a pine tree. The city glittered below, diffusing a muted clamour of car horns, clanking machinery and sirens. But we were elevated, adrift in our own precious space, not of the city and not of the mountain.

'I can't say when I'll be back,' he said, taking my hand.

Across Table Bay, Robben Island floated like a rough-cut jewel.

'I know,' I replied. 'We'll have to wait for a favourable wind.'

He smiled. I leant against him.

'Shall we head down?'

We retraced our steps, stopping for him to point out the familiar grey lines of the *Dorsetshire* tied up among a huddle of warships.

'I love you, David.'

And, once back in the cottage, he undressed me and led me back to bed while the butterflies flickered outside our window in the tawny sunshine.

We walked slowly through the Gardens, David carrying my suitcase. I was wearing the same blue dress I'd arrived in, and I'd tied my hair into the scarf.

I sensed he was struggling not to touch my hand, take my arm, kiss me.

'The first time I saw you,' he said as we walked through the dappled shade, 'I thought of it as a once-in-a-lifetime enchantment. A fleeting glimpse that would never be repeated.'

I darted a glance at him and smiled.

'You look so beautiful, your parents will guess something has happened.'

The solitude of the Gardens gave way to the bustle of Adderley Street, then the station, the press of crowds, the shunting of trains beneath balloons of steam. And the newspaper boys, yelling 'Read all about it! Pearl Harbour bombed! America in the War!'

He dropped my suitcase, abandoned caution, seized me.

'This is it, my darling! We can't lose! Not now!'

He rifled in his pocket for change and bought us papers. My train was already working up steam as we rushed to the platform. He went on board, lifted my suitcase into the rack despite the stares of other passengers.

'I could come with you as far as Fish Hoek,' he'd offered earlier, but we both knew that would be crazy. Our luck couldn't last. Someone would see us, recognise me.

I went with him to the carriage door.

The whistle blew.

'I love you,' he whispered against my cheek. 'I'll find a way. Please wait for me.'

He jumped down, slammed the door closed. The train began to move.

I lifted my hand, kissed the tips of my fingers.

Chapter Thirty-Four

My darling,
It's hard to know where to start, in writing to you!

Thank you, first of all, for coming to me, for giving yourself in the way you did. I know that the fact of my marriage means we have to conduct our love in the shadows, but the war will end eventually and I'll find a way to obtain my freedom while protecting the interests of Elizabeth. I know this period of limbo is difficult for you but please believe me when I say I'll return. The miracle of war and illness that brought us together is far from fulfilled.

I can't say where we are, except that it's hot and humid.

I love you,
David

His touch, his voice, stayed with me.

No one discovered my lie – or, rather, no one expressed

any suspicions. With Ma and Pa, I pretended my visit to Lola had been brief but happy, and my training at the Victoria had gone well. To Sister Graham, I said that my friend was doing better since my visit. I avoided Vera, who would have guessed straightaway. But Ma suspected something, as David thought she might. When I stared into the mirror as I brushed my hair, I could see why. I tried to damp it down, but my eyes glistened with a restless joy that was plain to see.

Less obvious was the guilt.

If you loved a man and he happened to be married, was that a sin?

And if David hadn't been honest with me about being married, was I less of a sinner?

In the weeks that followed, I often went to Seaforth to swim and to run my fingers through the sand and listen for His verdict – damnation, forgiveness – but I heard only the rush of the tide.

Wait, he said. *I will find a way*.

And so I waited.

Piet once asked me to wait . . . I pushed the memory aside.

1941 became 1942.

I threw myself into work and completed my training as a theatre nurse.

'Well done,' said Matron with a brisk handshake and a formal smile. 'But your duties will continue to be divided between the ward and the theatre, Staff Nurse.'

Sister looked on with barely hidden irritation.

In the dockyard, the unsettling buzz grew that although the Americans were building ships faster than they could train sailors to crew them, their efforts might not come in time.

'It's bad,' Pa said darkly. 'Those Japs will take as much beating as Hitler. Remember how they sank *Prince of Wales* and *Repulse* – great big ships – with aeroplanes only?'

They're on the march, David wrote.

You'll have read of our losses. I'm devastated about the fall of Singapore, I went there before the war. No one expected the Japanese to come down through the jungle. It was brilliant tactics and it's no secret we were caught napping.

It's very hot where I am. Flat, greasy, unappetising sea. Sharks.

I long for the fresh waves of the Cape.

As I long for you, my darling.

'Lou?' Pa waved to me from the path as I came off duty. Pa still liked to meet me on the mountain when our shifts coincided, especially if it was calm and he could point out the vessels in dock and tell me their wounds. Today was just such a day, and the seagulls cawed in disappointment at the lack of a breeze.

'Let's sit down for a bit.'

'You should get your knee looked at, Pa.'

He flapped a hand impatiently.

'My knee isn't the bother. It's this war.'

'What now?'

Pa shouldn't have been telling me, of course, but I know it helped him to talk, so I listened and never passed on anything he said, especially to Ma.

'There's been another disaster. Japs caught some of our ships off Ceylon. At least two bombed.'

'What ships?' I grabbed his arm.

He sighed. 'I probably shouldn't say. It's not official.'

'What ships, Pa?'

He glanced at me, patted my leg. 'One of ours. That gunnery officer you nursed was on her. The *Dorsetshire*.'

I fell against him.

'Lou?' he struggled to hold me up. 'What's this now?'

The mountain bore down on me, the sea that I loved began to rise up towards me.

'It's sad, child, but lots of your patients have got hit. Come now . . .'

The seagulls were crying. I covered my ears to block out their hard, sharp wails.

Pa hugged me to him.

'Let's get you home, it's been a long day.'

I stared at his kind, worried face and then down at the tiny ants scurrying along the dirt track. A grasshopper whirred past.

He pulled me to my feet.

'Come. Not far to go.'

We stumbled down the mountain.

I could see the path clearly, and which rocks to avoid, but my feet didn't want to obey my brain. Pa began to breathe heavily as he battled to keep me upright. It wasn't fair on Pa, the strain on him and his knee. The Phillips' grandchildren were playing behind the Terrace as we went by. The oldest called out to me, offered to help but Pa waved him away.

Mrs Hewson spotted us from her step.

'What's wrong?' she shouted. 'Have you turned your ankle?'

'*Ja*,' Pa gasped. 'Sheila can look at it.'

'They're working you too hard,' Mrs H snorted. 'Nothing good's come of this war.'

'What in heaven's name?' Ma ran to help me inside. Pa wiped his forehead and fell into a chair. Ma led me into my bedroom, sat me on the bed, drew off my shoes, unpinned my cap, eased me lengthways. She felt my ankle, stroked the hair away from my face.

'I'll make tea. Then you can tell me what's the matter.'

Ma tapped on my door a little later and came in with cups for us both. I'd taken off my uniform, hung it up and changed into a skirt and shirt. I was sitting on the bed. Ma handed me a cup and sat down beside me.

'There's nothing wrong with your ankle, Louise. Are you going to tell me what's really going on?'

There was no point in lying. Dry, hacking sobs broke inside me. Not tears, just recurring, lung-deep shudders. Ma stroked my arm and sipped her tea and waited.

'I've fallen in love with a British naval officer. His ship's been sunk.'

Shock leapt in her eyes, followed by a dawning recognition. She drew me to her, rocked me gently but I knew I'd gone too far this time. Reaching for a career had been narrowly possible, but loving someone foreign, way above my station, someone white to my coloured, was out of the question. And inexcusable. *You should know that by now.*

'I'm guessing this is the man who wrote to you?'

I struggled to banish the image of David wounded, his blue eyes losing focus, the sea closing over him until all that was left was the memory.

'It wasn't planned, Ma. And I'm not ashamed. He loves me, too.'

'Ah, child, they all do.' She gave a weary smile. 'You're beautiful. Of course they love you! But it's only while they're sick.'

I looked down at my hands. David and I were long past patient–nurse gratitude. And, if Ma was looking for reasons why it wouldn't work, the differences of colour and background were less important. It was the fact of his marriage that would keep us apart.

Ma waited for me to respond.

She sighed.

'I'm so sorry, Lou,' she kissed the top of my head. 'I'm sure he's a good man. But it would never have gone anywhere. Not with a white officer. Try to get some rest. I'll bring you supper a little later.'

She gathered the cups, then stopped at the door.

'When the war's over, you're sure to find someone who'll make a fine husband.'

I sat in the gathering darkness.

The last time I was at Seaforth beach, I'd found another Pink Lady, a twin of the one I'd given him. I reached over to my shell collection and picked it up, fingered its spine, held it to my ear.

It wouldn't help to let my distress show. Pa said the news wasn't official.

I must hold on until the formal announcement.

And even then, I mustn't give way. There was still too much to lose.

For three days, there was no word. Then it came. The Admiralty announced with regret . . . HMS *Dorsetshire* and HMS *Cornwall* sunk by enemy action in the Indian Ocean . . . no information yet on survivors.

Ma came into my bedroom that evening and wordlessly brushed my hair.

I didn't tell her that David and I were lovers. There was no point. If he was gone, there was no need for anyone but myself to know. The candlelit bedroom of a cottage beneath Table Mountain would be mine alone, to cherish for ever.

Pa asked no questions, but he walked me to hospital each morning, and walked me home at the end of my shift. I don't know how he rearranged his work to do so, but whenever I came off duty, he was there, sitting on a rock below the entrance.

'Thank you, Pa.'

I sat down beside him and leant my head on his shoulder.

He patted me and hauled himself up.

'Let's get back. Your ma's making apple pie.'

Pa eventually found out that there were survivors but the navy hadn't released names.

'HMS *Enterprise* and her destroyers picked them up.'

'Where are they, Pa?'

He wrinkled his forehead. 'Addu Atoll in the Maldives,

probably. The wounded will go to Ceylon or India. I'm sorry, Lou, that's all I could find out.'

I looked out of our front door. The season was on the turn. Soon the mists would roll in from the sea and blanket the docks, and the foghorn would sound during the day.

'When will I know?'

He put his arm around my shoulders, shook his head.

'*Dorsetshire* was being refitted in Colombo,' he murmured. 'Better radar, more anti-aircraft guns. But then the Jap fleet came through the Malacca Straits, heading for Ceylon. She had to leave before the work was done. I'm sorry, Lou. He was a good man.'

Chapter Thirty-Five

When there was no word from David, I told myself that he might be injured and unable to write. Perhaps there weren't enough nurses where he was, to allow one of them to write on his behalf. Or maybe his letters were lost in transit, sunk by enemy shipping.

But as the weeks went by it became harder to convince myself he was alive.

I went to Seaforth. I stared at the sea I loved and tried not to hold it responsible.

Against her natural instincts, Ma kept my secret liaison strictly to herself and Pa. None of us needed a scandal. And if she and Pa wondered about the extent of my friendship with David, they never asked.

Vera visited. She was the only outsider I told. But, as with Ma, only part of the truth.

'He's dead, V.' I picked up the Pink Lady and smoothed it. 'His ship was sunk off Ceylon.'

She sat down beside me on the bed and leant her shoulder

against mine. 'I'm so sorry, Lou.' She waited a while, then nudged me. 'Maybe it's for the best? You could never have married him.'

'No, I could never have married him.'

Two months of silence passed. I performed my duties in theatre, I nursed my patients on the ward and I smiled at their jokes. I swept floors, gave medicines, helped VADs change dressings, even shooed the baboons from the slopes behind the ward. 'Dreadful beasts!' shuddered Sister.

I became a good actor – no one noticed my lack of delight in my work.

It was a form of lying, I suppose. But lying, in this case, to myself.

Winter blew in and our convalescing patients were forced to retreat from the verandah. The flags on the ships streamed permanently from the north. I began to notice that I was thinking of David in the past tense.

In the dockyard, Pa cocked an ear to every passing officer's conversation and it turned out that the surviving *Dorsetshire* and *Cornwall* crews had indeed been split up between the Maldives and India or were already returning to the UK. But unless you knew someone who knew someone, there was no way to find out whether David was alive.

'It's tricky to get names, Lou,' Pa said quietly. 'That's only for next of kin.'

'Don't do anything to get in trouble, Pa.'

By contrast, Ma believed that even if David had survived against the odds, the romance was surely doomed. There could be no future for a brown girl and a white officer. It was now a matter of kindly distraction and diversion.

She took me to Bible study classes in order to rekindle my sense of right and wrong. She made comforting soups. She invited friends to the cottage for tea. She treated me as if I was a child who'd strayed, and needed fattening.

'Your ma's right,' said Vera, munching one of Ma's scones. 'You need building up.'

In my life, I've only allowed myself to cry with joy – or the anticipation of it. Except for when the mountain slipped and I thought Ma was dead and I couldn't stop weeping as the rain poured down and the stream at the Hewsons' tried to wash me away.

But now I cried at night over anticipated loss.

Ma looked at my face in the morning and wondered why it was taking me so long to get over a man I knew only superficially and who was never destined to be with me anyway.

Chapter Thirty-Six

My darling Louise,

I hope this letter finds you soon, I know the post out of India is unreliable so I've been writing every week. I hate to imagine what you've been going through, knowing that my ship had gone down. I hope, somehow, you may have got word through your father that I was lucky enough to survive. I've written to Elizabeth, of course, and I'm sure my uncle at the Admiralty will have told her.

Two hundred of our crew died in the attack, and many were injured. I am beyond sadness for them and their families. I don't know why I was spared while so many were not. Our rescue, after a day and a half, came just in time. Our water was almost out and we had to take turns in the sea because only two whalers survived.

One of the outcomes is that our close-knit group is now being broken up and sent to other ships. I will miss them. It looks like I'll be reassigned shortly, too. War allows for no respite.

But you were with me, my beloved L, through all those hours in the water. I saw you walking towards me in your blue dress, carrying your suitcase. I felt your touch, I relived our time together. How we talked, how we loved!

What I said at the station in Cape Town holds true now more than ever.

Please wait for me. I will come back.

All my love,

David

Chapter Thirty-Seven

Piet leant back against the empty crates and began to laugh.

The conductor was down the train, probably having a smoke with the engine driver, or laughing with the passengers about the travelling Great Dane called Just Nuisance, with his navy pass and his doting audience of able seamen.

Once again, it had gone perfectly.

The Simon's Town guard, growing fat on a weekly gift of fish, hadn't even bothered to check the number of crates. At the Cape Town end, the paperwork was quickly signed by a second guard who also regularly benefitted from Piet's generosity.

Piet spotted his contact on the station concourse. In the confusion of trolleys and scurrying passengers, and while wheeling his particular trolley towards the navy's truck, it was child's play to lift the tarpaulin, hand one crate over and trouser the payment.

He felt into his pocket for the reassuring crinkle of a note.

A week's wages for one day's work. And then, on Friday, his regular navy pay.

If the war went on long enough, he'd be a wealthy man.

And then – who's to say Louise wouldn't come running back?

He didn't intend to save himself for that – there were several girls already pleasuring him for the chance to become Mrs Philander – but it was worth bearing in mind.

The train shunted and then began to gather itself for the final run from Fish Hoek into Simon's Town.

He didn't want to think of Lou, but he couldn't help casting his mind back.

It had been an accidental sighting. And for months Piet said nothing even while he once again harboured thoughts of following the man when his ship next visited Simon's Town, contriving an accidental stumble-and-punch in a dark alley by the Officers' Club.

It came about because the *Dorsetshire* chose, for once, to moor in Cape Town.

He'd been taking a short cut through the Company Gardens after visiting the restaurant that was keen on his fish.

They were walking side by side, the man was the same one she'd met in Simon's Town on the mountain. The same one she'd laughed with. He was carrying a suitcase.

Piet hid behind a bush as they passed, then followed them to a fancy cottage up the mountain. He watched them go through the gate. This was no casual visit, he could tell. That was Louise's case the man was carrying. She was staying with him.

He turned away and went to spend the night with a girl he knew in District Six.

And now the man was probably dead, if the rumours about the losses on *Dorsetshire* were true. So there was nothing to be done, no anonymous revenge to be taken. He felt sorry for Lou, but she'd taken a step too far. She probably got what she deserved.

Even so, for the moment, he'd keep quiet.

Knowledge was different from fish, it wasn't perishable.

The longer you held onto it, the more valuable it became.

Chapter Thirty-Eight

'Staff Nurse Ahrendts?' Sister called from her table one midday. 'We have an urgent admission from the *Duchess of York*, just docked. A captain with sepsis of the leg and damaged lungs. A hero, VC in the Great War. We'll put him in number eight.'

'Yes, Sister. I'll make sure everything is ready.'

Sister nodded and bent to her ward notes.

When he arrived, Sister, mindful of the VC, went to meet the ambulance personally. The other patients craned as the stretcher was brought in. The captain was coughing heavily. I waited by the empty bed with a dressing tray nearby. And, following the stretcher, came a tall, fair-haired man in uniform with the rank of a lieutenant commander.

I clutched the railing of the bed.

Sister bustled alongside. The orderlies lifted the injured man from the stretcher onto the bed.

'Staff Nurse! What are you waiting for? Draw the curtains!'

He had stopped halfway down the ward. And – I caught my breath – he showed no sign of injury.

I felt his eyes rest on me like a caress.

'Nurse!'

I drew the curtains.

Sister glared at me, then addressed the ill man. 'The surgeon commander will be here soon, Captain. In the meantime, Staff Nurse will attend to your wound.'

She swept aside the curtain and marched off. I heard her steps slow.

'Why, Lieutenant Commander Horrocks. I trust you don't need our attention at this time?'

'No thank you, Sister. I've been accompanying Captain Agar.'

'I can assure you that the captain is now in safe hands. You must have other duties, I'm sure. Good afternoon.'

I placed the dressing tray on the side table with a shaky clatter.

Captain Agar cleared his throat.

'Do you know, Nurse, my lieutenant commander out there was once a patient here?'

I flashed him a quick glance. 'Yes, he was. How did you get this wound, sir?'

'I was hit by a bomb fragment,' he grimaced. 'Then my leg got infected in India. Not surprising, in that heat.'

'I'm so sorry, sir. Please hold still.'

I don't remember how I got through the rest of my duty. The air in the ward shimmered with a radiance that's only blessed me a few times in my life. Luckily, Sister appeared not to notice and made no reference to my tardiness with the bed curtains other than to give me a questioning look after I finished with the captain.

A drizzle began to shroud the bay and obscure the mountain path where David and I had walked. Where else would we be able to meet within the goldfish bowl that was Simon's Town? And why was I contemplating such a dangerous possibility . . .

At the end of my shift I fastened my cloak and left by the lower entrance. I would go down to St George's Street and walk along the tarmac road rather than risk the slippery mountain path, and pray that he would be discreet enough not to meet me in town, because I wouldn't be able to hold back from running to him.

'Lou?' Pa stepped out of the guardhouse where he'd been sheltering.

'Pa!' I gasped. 'He's alive, Pa!' I flung myself in his arms.

'Come, child,' he muttered, disengaging himself and giving an embarrassed grin to the guard who was watching us. 'Let's get home. Lord knows what we're going to do, but standing here and getting wet isn't going to help.'

It was only when we got home that I realised what Pa meant.

For, sitting on a chair in the lounge was David, his beribboned uniform resplendent against our shabby upholstery. Ma perched nervously nearby. I stopped in the doorway, my cloak dripping, my white shoes rimed with mud from the leap across the stream at the Hewsons'.

Ma pursed her lips and looked at me with a tension that I recognised from my teenage years: pride, in this case that I could have attracted such a fine man, but fear, as ever, of where my ambition might lead.

No one spoke. Pa shook out his raincoat.

David leapt up and gathered me gently, wet cloak and all, into his arms.

There was no time to protest or wonder at his recklessness, because I heard the front door close and a key turn in the lock and then we were alone and he was kissing me with passion.

'Wait!' I pulled away. 'You're not wounded? I've been desperate—' I ran my hands over his arms and chest, down his back. He was thin but reassuringly whole, and his face bore the remains of severe sunburn. His eyes were clear, thank God, undamaged by splinters or fire. Whatever retribution was due to come my way, it hadn't chosen David as its victim.

'I'm well!' He chuckled at my impromptu check-up. 'I wrote every week while we were in India.'

'I never received a word!'

He drew me down beside him on the sofa.

'Listen, my darling. We haven't much time. It took a while but I've persuaded your mother,' he grinned, 'to give us two hours together.'

It wasn't long enough.

He carried me through to my bedroom and we made love on the narrow bed, alongside the bookshelf with my seashells and his hidden letters. And afterwards he told me about the *Dorsetshire*, his stark words piercing the bray of the foghorn and the patter of rain and the tender aftermath of love.

The thirst, the deaths, the brutal silence of water and sky.

'But the sea didn't take you,' I touched his scar, 'it kept you alive.'

'And so did you,' he said. 'Without you, I would've died.'

Then we dressed, and remade the bed.

There wasn't much time left.

He stood behind me as I brushed my hair. I looked at him in the mirror.

'What are we going to do? How are we going to get you out of here?'

He rested a calming hand on the top of my head. 'No one saw me arrive, darling – they were all indoors because of the rain. And I'll leave under the blackout.'

But he didn't know how close the Terrace was, how the curtains at every front window twitched whatever the weather and blackout. Especially over me. I'd have to contrive a story, tell a lie . . .

We went back to the sitting room. I lit candles, made tea, and wondered why being with him like this in my own home, in my own bed, felt proper rather than forbidden; meant-to-be rather than outrageous.

The rain stopped, but the wind began to pick up. He turned his head to listen to the flailing palms.

'We have oaks around Corbey,' he mused. 'The wind is different, less energetic. I want to take you there.'

I poured him more tea. There was so much – and yet so little – that needed to be said.

'When must you leave?'

He put a finger to my lips. 'Soon, I'm afraid.'

My cup shook slightly in my hands. He took it from me and placed it back on the tray.

'A love like ours must be fought for, my darling.' His hands, hard from the business of guns and survival, gentled mine. 'I will be asking Elizabeth for a divorce at the end of the war.'

I stared at him, the hair noticeably more silver than when we last met.

'Will you take a risk?' His eyes searched mine. 'Will you marry me once I'm free?'

'But I'm mixed-race, and from a poor background, no one will want me there—'

And his family will think that people like me have no shame in seducing a husband away from his wife. They will treat me like the sinner that I am.

'I love you for everything that you are,' he said firmly. 'And we'll decide together about Corbey, and the navy. And where you can work. We'll be a team, my darling.'

I won't marry anyone unless we can be partners, and love each other equally, I'd declared to Pa.

I felt my heart race with the now-familiar elation.

We'd face the world together. Any joy or punishment would be shared.

'Yes,' I breathed. And if our secret escaped before the end of the war, I'd defend it with every truth or lie I could muster. There was no going back.

'It will be our journey,' he cupped my face, 'side by side.'

I heard footsteps outside, then Pa's key in the lock.

'Yes,' I repeated, clasping my hands around his, 'I'll marry you, David.'

In that moment, we both believed that anything was possible.

Chapter Thirty-Nine

But possibilities had to wait.

The war ground on. Two years passed. Two years from the rainy night in Simon's Town when we last saw each other, last lay together, last made love. I've waited a lot in my life: to be a nurse, to find true love. And very often, when I'm on the edge of it, there's a lull, a postponement. Or a barrier. Sometimes it's because I've pushed too far, other times it's because the world has other matters to resolve before my turn can come around again.

It was hard.

I never believed love could hurt so much, that the pain of separation could be such a constant companion. David wrote often, and his letters were a partial salve, a slice of London and a war that now seemed a long way from Simon's Town. I worried he might have second thoughts, especially if he was able to spend more time at home. I knew his guilt about Elizabeth. And I would always be coloured, an outsider in his world.

My darling Louise,
How are you, my love? I think of you constantly. I imagine you at Seaforth looking for shells, watching the waves and wondering, as I do, when we'll see each other again.

I'm desperate to get to South Africa but I find myself chained to a desk job for the foreseeable future. You'll have heard about our successes in France. It's a start, but there's still a long way to go. I am hopeful of a return to sea if the focus shifts towards the Far East. You'll know what I mean. In the interim, our lives are spooling out and there is little we can do but keep faith.

My father has passed away. He'd been poorly for some time, as you know, and he died in his sleep last week. I've just returned from the funeral. Father and I had an up-and-down relationship – we never shared the kind of warmth you have with your parents – but lately we'd found a tentative understanding. I suspect he knew I had ideas for Corbey of which he wouldn't approve, but we tacitly avoided the subject. I was loath to initiate anything while he was still alive but now is the time to plan for their implementation once the war ends. I'd like Corbey to be self-managing as far as possible, to free me up either for the navy or for a position where we can best be together. I will also be seeing my solicitor shortly to discuss a divorce, and how to protect Elizabeth and ensure her financial future. Only once I have this clear in my mind, will I speak. It will be a hard blow for her.

But I can no more imagine life after the war with

her than I could ever imagine giving you up. Or forgetting the souls of Tompkins, Owen, the men on Hood, Dorsetshire—

When one finds love – however unexpectedly – one should cherish it . . .

Please keep writing to me, my darling, this is a difficult time. I hate continuing to deceive Elizabeth but there seems no alternative. She's running Corbey on my behalf, and I cannot pull it from under her feet while this war is raging and I'm posted in London or elsewhere.

Thank you for your patience and your courage

All my love,

David

I folded the letter and put it into my pocket. It was dangerous to bring it to work, but I felt stronger when his words were nearby, tight against my skin. And he was right about Seaforth. I went there often. Not necessarily to swim or discern some kind of divine direction – I fear God and Allah have probably given up on me – but to feel David's presence. The sea was the element that connected us. Even though he was in a shore job, he liked to walk down to the Thames to trace the ebb of water into an ocean that I imagined circling the globe and eventually finding its way to False Bay.

'Sister!'

'Sister Ahrendts!'

It had taken the same two years of separation from David to complete my qualification. I looked about. I wasn't used to my new title.

Matron bustled up. 'Sister, would you kindly join the ward round this morning? There are no operations planned, and Sister Graham is not well.'

Matron kept me involved in ward nursing when my theatre duties allowed. I think she knew I enjoyed being with my patients when they were awake.

'Of course, Matron.'

While my role expanded at the RNH, two years saw the war diminish Simon's Town. Pa and his fellow workers were permanently hollow-eyed from the long hours, and his ships suffered the demands of a conflict that gave no respite. Rust spread, and hurried repairs were unavoidable. Those of us on land noticed, too. Our formerly smooth tarmac roads had to bear their cracks for 'the duration'. The flags at Admiralty House, once regularly replaced, flew until they disintegrated in the southeaster. And despite Pa's entreaties, there were no plans or resources to stabilise the mountain behind the Terrace. Each winter, more soil compacted behind our row of cottages.

'We mustn't complain, we're winning the war,' Pa said with guarded satisfaction at the kitchen table. 'Hitler's on his way out, it's just the Japs now.'

'The Americans are winning, aren't they?' asked Ma.

Pa sniffed. 'Not quickly enough.'

We never talked about David Horrocks. But he was there, a silent presence at our table.

'I hope you know what you're doing, Lou,' was all Ma said as the door closed behind David that night. 'This won't end well.'

Dearest Ma has never understood why I do what I do. To her credit, she's warned me of the dangers – and been proved right, sometimes – but she's never forbidden me from following my own course. Or threatened to cast me out when I didn't take her advice. Even over David.

'We must wait until the war's over,' I replied. It's what I said to Vera, too, when she asked what I was going to do about the married white man who still wrote to me.

I fingered his letter in my pocket.

The silence between Ma, Pa and myself served another purpose.

There was still a secret to keep.

I'd entertained a white man in our family cottage and although the law did not explicitly ban sex between whites and coloureds at the time, the price was high. Morals were defined by colour. If my secret got out, Matron would have no choice but to dismiss me for improper conduct. The disgrace would reach further. Just as I'd suffered by my association with Piet, so Ma and Pa would be condemned because of me. Pa might be hurried into retirement, Ma would be quietly let go. We could lose our cottage. We'd almost certainly lose our position in the community and Pa would shrivel without the standing he'd worked so hard to achieve. If I was to ride this out, we three were bound together by the necessity to keep my recklessness quiet.

Chapter Forty

Piet was hauled before the lieutenant who was the quartermaster's boss, a young squirt with a smooth chin and a chest full of ribbons. He looked at Piet across his desk with distaste.

'We know what you've been up to, Mr Philander.'

'I don't know what you're talking about, sir,' Piet said heartily, folding his arms and stretching out his legs beneath the officer's table. 'I fish for you like I always have, and I deliver my crates to Cape Town like you want.'

'You've been selling fish on the side.'

Piet grinned. 'I've been giving a few fish away. That's a different thing.'

The officer pursed his lips. 'Giving away the odd fish and selling entire crates on the black market are two separate matters.'

'Crates?' Piet frowned. 'How could I sell crates? Your guards, sir, they count the crates in and out. Maybe they made a mistake. I'm an honest man, sir. I fish for the war effort.'

'You've been seen handing over a crate.'

'Ah,' said Piet, 'now it's only one crate, sir?'

The lieutenant gave him a sharp look and shuffled paper on his desk. Piet strained to read upside down but he was pretty sure that the train manifests had long been filed somewhere obscure or discarded completely once the transaction was complete.

Piet adopted a wheedling tone. He had this fellow's number.

'Sir, once a week I give my best fish to the admiral. No charge. I go up to Admiralty House,' Piet waved a hand at the window, 'and I go round to the kitchen and I talk to the chef and he cooks it for the admiral. The admiral,' Piet leant forward, 'knows me. He likes my fish. No one takes the trouble to bring him top fish. Free and gratis.'

The lieutenant shifted in his seat.

'We'll be watching you, Philander. Any more trouble, and we'll tear up your contract.' He stood, indicating the meeting was over. Piet slowly got to his feet.

'I'll be extra careful, sir. I'll make sure the guards write down the correct number of crates. You can depend on me, sir.'

The lieutenant sat down and turned back to his papers.

Piet walked out, closing the door carefully when he really would have liked to slam it shut.

But he must be careful. His defence had worked – this time.

He must tell the restaurant that there'd be a break in deliveries. Just until things settled down.

He strolled across the warehouse, chock-a-block with goods the like of which most folk hadn't seen for years.

Paint, rubber, wire— 'Philander?' the quartermaster beckoned to him. Piet hurried over. The man pulled him out of sight behind a stack of boxes.

'I know what you've been up to,' he hissed, thrusting his face into Piet's. 'I didn't give the lieutenant all the papers, I've got them safe. But I want a cut. Otherwise I hand them over and you're out.'

Piet looked into the man's greedy face and felt something snap.

'Sure,' he said loudly. 'And when I go and give the admiral his fish I'll be sure to tell him he only gets second-best fish – his quartermaster gets the best. And then I'll also tell him that one of his officers has been sleeping with a coloured nurse at the RNH!'

The quartermaster's eyes bulged.

Piet stormed off, pushing past a group of ratings who stopped unpacking metal pipes to stare at him.

The sky above the Simonsberg was grey, and a thin drizzle sifted down.

He shouldn't have, he told himself as the wind cooled his face, he really shouldn't have.

Chapter Forty-One

War log
No particular date
Private hostilities

On my last leave, I asked Elizabeth to give me my freedom. I stressed it wasn't her fault, that I'd been wrong to marry her without loving her as a husband should, and I promised her a generous settlement. She was rigid with anger and accused me of using her, while feathering a love nest at the Admiralty. I can't blame her. She has only ever wanted Corbey and a life as my wife.

But someone else has my heart. Must I give Louise up for the sake of convention? Duty? Must I pay for my mistake with the rest of my life?

I'm being reassigned, thank God. Back to sea.

I was sitting with a patient while he regained consciousness when Sister Graham marched down the ward towards me.

'Sister Ahrendts,' she addressed my rank with sarcastic emphasis, 'Matron would like to see you. I'm sure the able seaman can wake up without your help.'

'Yes, Sister.'

I was still careful to defer to her, although these days there was no reason to do so other than courtesy. I walked out of the ward, conscious of her eyes on my back.

Every encounter with authority carried the risk of unmasking. Even when Matron congratulated me on making Sister, I searched her face for some hint of knowing, some edge of the castigation to come. In our letters, neither David nor I referred to our secret assignation. The chance of a censor reading and passing it along was too great a risk.

I straightened my cap and knocked on Matron's door.

'Come in. Please sit down, Sister.'

Matron folded her hands beneath her chin and looked at me over the top of them for several moments. My file was open in front of her.

'I have cautioned you before, Sister, that your relationship with your patients should remain above board in every way, have I not?'

Here it was.

'Yes, Matron.'

She glanced out of her window. A fat wedge of cloud hung above the bay, painting the water beneath it in tones of steel blue and grey.

'It has come to my knowledge that you may have formed an attachment with a patient.'

I breathed deeply. To lie, or tell the truth? But perhaps there was a middle way—

'Sister? What do you say to that?'

I have found, thanks to the advice of my old schoolteacher and from a lifetime of not being pale enough, that unwavering eye contact is the best weapon when under attack.

'I have only ever been professional in my work, Matron. I have not encouraged familiar behaviour while I've been on duty.'

'And off duty?' She regarded me keenly.

I lifted my chin. 'I have no attachment with any patient, Matron, or any local young man. I am single, and I live with my parents.'

She put on her glasses and picked up her pen and wrote a few sentences in my file.

Then she took off her glasses, stood up and went to the window and looked out over the sweep of the bay. She addressed me with her back turned.

'You know, of course, that if found guilty of this sort of behaviour, you would be dismissed.'

'Yes, Matron.'

She continued to speak while facing away from me.

'We would be very sorry to lose you, because you're an outstanding nurse.'

I kept quiet.

She turned back to me, her eyes puzzled, her voice softer. 'Surely you must know, Sister, that any understanding between yourself and a white man, while not strictly against the law, is certainly . . .' she searched for a word, 'frowned upon?'

Again I made no reply.

She sat down. I continued to meet her eyes without looking away.

'You know better than me the ways of this country.' She shook her head. 'I make no bones about the fact that I find exclusion on the basis of colour or any other trait to be abhorrent. It offends my Scottishness.' She tapped her fingers on her desk. 'But you are playing with fire in several directions if this report is true.'

She looked down at the desk, then appeared to make a decision.

'I don't listen to gossip about my staff.' She closed my file with a snap. 'Unless I'm offered proof, I regard it as hearsay. But,' she fixed me with a severe look, 'I warn you this has been noted on your record. If proof is subsequently provided to me, I will have no choice but to dismiss you. You must now regard yourself as on probation.'

I struggled to keep my expression neutral.

'I understand, Matron.'

'That is all.'

'Thank you, Matron.'

I stood up. The sea folded into languid swells beyond the window.

'It would be an immense waste to throw away everything you've achieved, Sister.'

I turned and left her office, closing the door quietly behind me.

Our secret has been discovered, I wrote.

I don't know how, David, it certainly wasn't anything my parents or I revealed.

I was warned by Matron that if she receives further proof, I'll be dismissed. I'm therefore on probation until the end of the war. While I know my training will allow me to get another post, a dismissal from the RNH will be a stigma. I may have to leave the peninsula, and work at a lesser salary in a remoter area.

But, dearest, the bigger issue is you and me.

We can't be together if you happen to visit Simon's Town.

And perhaps, given the situation with your wife, that may be sensible anyway.

But how will I stay away from you?

Chapter Forty-Two

I stood in the doorway of our cottage and looked down on the docks with that lurch of the heart that came whenever a new ship arrived. Maybe him, maybe not. This time, it was a three-funnelled heavy cruiser that was nosing to her mooring. Pa came to stand alongside me, chewing a piece of toast. He lifted his spare hand to shade his eyes and squinted. '*Cumberland*,' he announced. 'Eastern Fleet.'

'It's David,' I gasped and clutched him.

Pa stiffened.

I stared at him.

'It's been two years, Lou – I thought you'd given him up?'

I shook my head. Pa sighed explosively.

'Someone will find out,' he grimaced. 'You were lucky last time.'

'They already have,' I replied crisply. 'Matron received information. I've been warned.'

Pa looked bleakly at the toast cooling in his hand. 'It's my fault, I told you if you worked hard you'd go far. I put ideas into your head when you were little – and now look where it's led?'

Cumberland's gangway swivelled down onto the wharf.

'Don't be silly, Pa,' I gave him a pat that was more reassuring than I felt inside. 'It's nothing to do with you. Or what you said. And I know I can't meet him here. In fact, we may not be able to meet at all.'

'*Agh*, my Lou . . .'

But we did see each other, later that same day.

A cool breeze was whipping the sea into a light chop as I finished my duty and walked along St George's Street towards Alfred Lane. Streamers of cloud flew from the top of the Simonsberg like ships' pennants advertising his return. A group of seamen were standing outside the Officers' Club. I recognised his silvered hair before I saw his face, the scar, the blue eyes. I stopped.

He spotted me.

The group jostled about him. Pints of beer were passed from hand to hand.

I crossed over the road and stood by the harbour wall, as if I was waiting for someone.

We were about fifteen yards apart.

Sailors brushed past me. Someone called my name from the direction of Runciman's General Dealers but I pretended not to hear. Every so often David would be obscured by his lively companions and he'd move slightly so that we could see each other again.

His eyes have this tremendous ability to caress from a distance.

Mine began to blur with tears. Someone would notice. I began to edge away.

He lifted a hand and touched his lips.

I walked away.

The next day I received a note, saying that if I was able to come to Cape Town at the weekend, he'd wait for me in the Gardens like before. We can talk, he wrote, and I can tell you that I love you, my darling, even if we can't touch.

'I'm going into Cape Town for the day,' I announced at our family supper the next night.

'You're going to see him?' Ma frowned and exchanged a glance with Pa. 'Is that wise?'

'Leave her, Sheila,' Pa warned. 'This is Lou's life. She must decide for herself.'

The Gardens looked different from when we last met there. In December of 1941 they'd been lush with the bounty of summer. Now they looked tired, as did the slopes of Table Mountain, baked brown from the heat and the relentless wind. I felt weary, too. Weary of waiting; of being unable to run across the road into his arms. Even meeting here – at arm's-length if we could manage – was a strain, not to mention risky. But there was no alternative. *Cumberland* was due to sail within the next few days. The war was about to enter its final, grisly act. If David survived, he would return to Corbey to his own confrontation that would seal the divorce. Then, only then, would he be able to come back to Simon's Town as a free man and make me his own.

But where would we live, I wondered as I hurried to

meet him, where would we work, how would I manage as the coloured wife of a white man in places that were foreign, privileged . . . ?

'Louise!' he called.

I'd approached from the upper end of the Gardens, like I'd once surprised him from higher on the Simonsberg, but this time he was expecting it. He jumped up. I was wearing my blue dress again, but with a different scarf.

'Lieutenant Commander!'

'My darling!' he breathed, his eyes alight.

I extended my hand formally and he shook it. I sat down at the opposite end of the bench.

'You look stunning!'

I darted a quick glance at him. 'You're a little older than before.'

'Can you face marrying a man with grey hair?'

'I think so!'

He grinned ruefully, and ran a hand through his hair. There were two years for us to cover but the memories would have to wait until we were together, and intimate. It was enough just to be beside him. And, as to the future . . .

'I can't give you a timetable,' he said regretfully. 'Although Europe will soon be liberated, the war in the Far East must take its course. Only then can I get extended leave to settle matters at Corbey, and with Elizabeth.'

'You don't need to explain,' I said, moving my hand along the bench towards him. 'I'll stay at the RNH for as long as they'll have me.'

'You've had no further warnings?'

'No. I'll be fine,' I said. 'Please don't worry about me.'

He reached out and touched my hand, curling his fingers over mine.

'But I do,' he said softly, leaning towards me. 'I've made you wait long enough.' A squirrel darted across the grass in front of us. He smiled, then glanced at the blue-grey mountain with its layer of whipped cloud, the wild profusion of Cape honeysuckle surrounding our bench. 'Can you bear to leave this, my darling?'

I looked down at my lap.

'My dearest girl,' he murmured, 'I'll do all I can. Bring you back often, once we're married. But please don't try to cover up how you feel. I'd rather know you're homesick than have you suffer by keeping it hidden. I want no secrets between us.'

I turned to him, my eyes blurring with unshed tears.

He reached across the space between us and touched my cheek.

Cumberland was delayed in Simon's Town a little longer than expected. Pa said there was a problem with the propeller shaft. I watched the docks and wondered about seeing him again.

David's note reached me a day later.

Can you join me in Cape Town if you're free over the weekend? That cottage is available again. My darling, I know it's a risk, but this will surely be the last one you'll have to take. But we must travel from Simon's Town separately. I'll be waiting for you.

I walked to the cottage on my own, again dressed to avoid detection: a scarf tied low over my forehead, my head bent. One day I'd be able to stand tall beside David, and walk with him wherever we chose. Ma and Pa said nothing as I left, but I saw the fear in Ma's eyes, and the confusion in Pa's.

I bumped into Vera at the station.

'Lou!'

We kissed. Vera examined my smart dress and conservative scarf.

'Where are you going dressed like that?'

'To Cape Town for the weekend.'

'To Lola?'

'No,' I lied. 'A nursing friend. Someone from the hospital.'

'Ah!' she laughed. 'Well, it's about time you had some fun!'

He was waiting for me in the doorway. He'd changed out of his uniform and was wearing the kind of clothes that I imagined he'd wear in England in the summer. A shirt with the sleeves rolled up. Light trousers. The scar gleamed palely against his tan. He opened his arms.

I dropped my case and ran to him.

As before, we sat outside in the fragrant garden, waiting for the stars to appear.

And we loved each other, and fell asleep in each other's arms.

It was a day and night that made me giddy with the possibility that marriage to him might fulfil, every day, the promise of these snatched meetings.

And then we left separately.

This was the time to be most on guard. To make a mistake now, so close . . .

David didn't come to the station with me or wave to me from the cottage door. He planned to wait an hour before leaving, so that there was no chance we'd be on the same train. I latched the garden gate behind me without looking back, took up my case and walked away.

Wild pink belladonna lilies nodded from the dry verges of the railway line as I travelled home. There would be lilies wherever I went. Perhaps not as beautiful as these, but I could learn to love the substitutes like I loved all the ones I'd grown up with – regal Cape arums in winter, burnt orange clivias in spring.

David held the letter in his hand. The Sumatran heat, so unpleasant after the freshness of the Cape, pressed down like a blanket.

Dear David,

We parted on such bad terms when you left in January but I hope you will understand it was caused by the shock of what you told me.

I haven't written since then because I've been so hurt and so angry that you don't want to be married to me any more, despite seeming to care for me. But I'd like to ask you to reconsider. Circumstances have changed. I am expecting our baby before the end of the year. He will be the heir to Corbey, and will carry on the traditions that your family have laid down over the generations. I am thrilled and honoured to have this child. I want us to give him a healthy upbringing and prepare him for his role one day as earl.

And I do mean us. This is your child, David. He belongs here at Corbey with his parents, you and me. I believe we can still make a good life together as a family. I promise never to speak of your affair, or hold it against you. Please don't throw away the chance to build on what your father worked so hard to preserve.

Always yours,
Elizabeth

Chapter Forty-Three

I stood on the front of the Terrace, and watched victory in Europe erupt in Simon's Town. One by one, streetlights that had been dark for more than five years flickered into life. Hoarded firecrackers exploded. On cue, the ships in the harbour began to sound their horns and send up flares that hung in the sky like slowly revolving stars. Up on the mountain, the RNH's wards glowed with electric light.

'What a show!' shouted Pa exultantly. 'Can you see, Sheila? Mrs H – come and have a toast!' He flourished the sherry bottle at Mrs Hewson who was watching from her front step.

Not to be outdone, our tugs turned on their hoses and sprayed great arches of water within the illuminated harbour basin. Ma wiped away a tear and clung to my arm. Dogs barked at the frenzy. 'Happy peace, Mr Ahrendts, Mrs Ahrendts!' The Phillips' grandchildren linked arms and dashed along the path.

'Lou!' yelled Vera from a group gathering near the mosque.

I dropped a kiss on Ma's cheek, and ran to join her. She grabbed my hand and we hurried down Alfred Lane and onto St George's Street. Revellers packed the street, occasionally rocking a slow procession of tooting motor cars. A choir of ratings began to sing 'Rule Britannia' at the tops of their voices, in between frequent swigs of beer.

'Listen, Vera!'

A ship's band was marching out of the Queen Victoria gate playing Vera's famous namesake's hits. 'The White Cliffs of Dover', 'A Nightingale Sang in Berkeley Square', 'Lili Marlene' . . .

'Let's dance!' shouted Vera, gyrating to the music. 'There's Abie! I'm going to marry him before he spends all his fishing money!'

Mr Bennett from Sartorial House was climbing up a rickety ladder to drape a huge Union Jack across the front of his store. In the distance I spotted Piet and a girl that I recognised from the laundry. He lifted a hand to me, but was swallowed up in the crowd before I could wave back. Vera wiggled to the music and rubbed her body against the eager Abie.

'Hello, Sister!' a group of VADs from the hospital giggled past, waving flags.

The band exhausted their supply of Blitz tunes and swung into Great War favourites.

I stared up.

Sirius blazed amid the glittering Milky Way. Even though the war with Japan ground on, were David and his crew pausing to celebrate? He must surely feel the approach of victory, the exhilarating sense of a fresh start.

It was a sign. I was sure of it.

Like the signs that had lit my path since childhood.

We danced and sang on the heaving streets for hours. Firecrackers popped, sirens blared, the whiff of gunpowder drifted, star shells continued to burst against an infinite sky. No one bothered with partners. No one worried about work the next day. Men, women, children, sailors, officers – from every level of society – abandoned their reserve and came together in raw, joyous celebration.

War log
July 1945
Off Burma

Escort for our aircraft carriers striking enemy shipping near Diamond Point.

Victory in Europe, but not for us. They'll fight to the last man, the last bowl of rice.

I've replied to Elizabeth and assured her of my affection and care for her and our child now and into the future. I also said I couldn't let go of the love I've found and still wish to obtain my freedom.

Surely, on reflection, Elizabeth will see that our happiness, and the happiness of the child, will be better served by us being apart and content rather than together and forever at war?

Chapter Forty-Four

When is a sign not a sign at all – but a tipping point?

Victory ushered in the first spring of peacetime, rich with shower flurries and a pod of dolphins leaping across the bay in graceful arcs. Seagulls swooped, alert for scraps stirred up in their wake. I sat on the mountain path above the aerial ropeway and watched them, with David's letter in my hand. It was loving, it was devoted, and it chilled my heart.

My darling Louise,

It's over at last, you'll have the read the news. Two new American bombs did the job, and the destruction has been massive. Please God this will turn mankind against war for ever. There's no need for secrecy any more so I can tell you we're in Singapore, handling the Jap surrender and handover of Java. We're then scheduled to return to Britain.

I have other news, which has shocked me deeply. I received a letter from Elizabeth to say that she is expecting our child before the end of the year. The arrival of new life can only ever be greeted with joy, especially at this time, but I'm also torn with regret.

My darling, please be in no doubt as to my love for you. You are the delight of my life, and I haven't altered my determination for us to marry once I've gained my freedom. But I can't pretend that Elizabeth's pregnancy hasn't changed the situation. You will have to be patient for a little while longer, I'm afraid. I must go back to Corbey, welcome my child, and come to a resolution with Elizabeth.

Wait for me, please. I will return.

My love,

David

I folded up the sheets and put them in my pocket, willing my hands to stay as steady as they'd been in the operating theatre earlier. There was no need to panic, David would do what had to be done and our future was still bright; as bright as the promise of that spring – pincushions in bloom, southeasters girding themselves behind the mountain. But, on the streets of Simon's Town, the promise quickly dissolved into an end-of-war malaise. As swiftly as it had filled in 1939, the dockyard emptied. Ships called, but left swiftly for their home ports. The cheerful legions of off-duty ratings disappeared from St George's Street and our British staff began to be repatriated. Sister Graham departed in the first group.

I held out my hand. 'Goodbye, Sister. I hope you find your home and family well.'

She looked at me with suspicion, and favoured me with an icy smile.

'Thank you, Sister.'

The opposite of malaise, however, gripped me.

Elizabeth Horrocks' pregnancy changed everything.

I'd already prayed to any God who was willing to listen to forgive me for my part in breaking up David's marriage, but now there was a child to consider. While I was ready to be a step-parent, every child needs his own mother, not a substitute. David's child deserved to have his parents on hand, together, to bring him up. Like my parents had done with me, like David's had done with him.

I couldn't share these thoughts with anyone. When you deliberately step out of your place, there are no friends or family who've travelled with you or who understand your new destination. Ma would be upset by the tangle of allegiances, Vera would throw up her hands and say that if I was still set on this man then I should wave goodbye to my old life and get out of the country and arrive on his doorstep before he changed his mind.

The more I thought about it, as I stood barefoot in the shallows at Seaforth and watched the terns circle and land on the egg rocks, the more I began to realise that my role was not simply to wait, as David asked of me. I didn't have to be a bystander. I had a choice, too. Especially as I was now guarding my own secret.

The easier option – the one my heart most desired – was to do as he suggested, and hold on. Hope that he negotiated his freedom, and marry him at the first opportunity.

The harder one was to do what I knew to be honourable:

release David from his commitment to me. Give him my blessing to remain with his wife for the sake of their unborn child.

But I didn't do it. I didn't choose the honourable course. I left it up to him.

And, unlike me, he didn't have the option to wait.

He was forced to choose.

Chapter Forty-Five

I waited and hoped through September and into October. The sun glared down from an unseasonally cloudless sky and the sea was lulled into glass. Then the few spring showers dried up and summer burst on us as if it couldn't wait any longer. We left the ward doors open at night to steal whatever cool air might waft up from the bay. The temperature hit the high eighties and refused to abate.

'Water jugs for each patient,' Matron ordered. 'And get them onto the verandah where possible.'

I swam at Seaforth every evening after work, lying on my back and letting the water cool my skin and ease my anxiety. Gentle waves broke and carried me to shore amid a welter of bubbles to where Pa waited on the sand for me.

'Do you know, Pa,' I asked as I towelled my hair, 'if *Cumberland* has returned home?'

'Yes, so they say. But you must get over this, Lou,' he caught my arm, his face furrowed, 'it's not sensible, this longing for someone you can't have. What good will it do?

Your ma and I are worried. Why don't you make a fresh start? Somewhere in Cape Town?'

I stared over the bay. No ships in the approaches, just an endless stretch of brilliant, empty water. 'Maybe.' I squeezed his hand.

Perhaps it was the sun glancing off a piece of glass on the mountain that caused the spark.

Without wind, of course, it could be stamped out quickly. Add a raging southeaster and it would leap from a spark to an inferno in minutes. We thought we were safe that October, because there was so little breeze and the damp of winter would still be in the soil.

'Fire!' shouted the rating from the guardhouse below the hospital.

I dashed to the rear door of the ward. Above the aerial ropeway, beyond the path where David and I had walked, a wisp of smoke was spiralling above a clump of trees. No flames yet, just an ominous, drifting streak. Then, as I watched, there was an explosion. Flames burst through the leafy canopy like myriad orange umbrellas unfurling against the white-hot sky.

'Call the fire brigade!' yelled a porter, abandoning his trolley and running to alert the office. 'Fire!'

There were buckets with sand along the back wall, but they were for small-scale accidents. I licked my finger and held it up. Not much, but definitely downhill. Forgetting my training that nurses never ran, I raced back inside and almost collided with Matron.

'It'll head this way, Matron,' I said urgently, 'the wind's in this direction.'

She looked at me, and I realised she probably didn't know about African fire. Its speed. Its hunger. The way it ran before the wind.

'The walking patients, Matron?'

'Good thinking, Sister. The brigade are on their way but we shouldn't wait. Assemble everyone out front. As a precaution.'

I moved from bed to bed. Thank God for peace. If this had happened during the war we'd have had a full ward, mostly too injured to walk.

'Able Seaman, can you get up and move onto the verandah? Petty Officer, let me help you. We need to get you all outside.'

The approaching bell of a fire engine cut through the heavy air. But there was another sound, too, not the hum of Christmas beetles or the moan of the southeaster, but a slowly building crackle. I began to smell smoke.

'Nurse?' I caught up with one of our juniors. 'Get the medicine trolley. Roll it outside. Then check the other wards and take theirs out as well. Quickly, but don't run.'

'Yes, Sister.' Her eyes were round with fright.

More fire engines clanged. Shouts came from outside. As I helped patients onto the verandah, I saw firemen racing up the path with coiled hoses to plunge into our reservoir where the baboons liked to splash. Sirens sounded from the dockyard. The navy were mobilising.

'Sister?' Seaman Irvin croaked. He was immobile after an operation the day before. 'Don't leave me.'

'Of course not!' I laughed. 'I'm going to give you a ride outside.' I began to wheel his bed gently towards the door.

Sweat trickled down my neck. The smoke was making me feel ill. 'There'll be a little bump as we go over the step.'

The sick-berth attendants were already shepherding patients down towards Cornwall Road. One of them took over Seaman Irvin. 'Find a shady spot,' I muttered. 'Make sure someone is with him.'

The sky took on a sludgy shade of brown. Our aromatic *fynbos* fizzed and popped like firecrackers celebrating the end of the war. The back of my uniform clung to me.

The operating theatre—

I rushed inside. Smoke was seeping beneath the door that faced the mountain. The surgeon commander was already there, piling instruments into boxes.

'Take some dressings, swabs,' he tossed a canvas bag at me. 'Then get out, Sister.'

'Don't stay too long, sir!' I heaved the bag over my shoulder.

'Sister!' Matron called. Her hair had escaped from its starched cap. 'After you're done, inspect the upper wards. Make sure everyone is out. Check the linen rooms, the sluices. Sister Chisholm will do the lower wards.'

'Yes, Matron.'

Above the *fynbos*, clumps of pines succumbed quickly, their branches tumbling into the scrub. Lone gum trees tried to resist, standing tall and proud until their sap ignited, sending flames racing up their trunks, showering the undergrowth with glowing ash – and spreading the fire further.

I dumped my surgical bag with an orderly and ran back inside. Skewed beds were cluttering the aisles, their bedclothes thrust aside or onto the floor in the haste to evacuate. The flammable linen would need only a single spark to ignite the entire place. Smoke eddied and attacked my throat and I began to cough. I raced through the first ward – empty – then the next, and the next, stopping out of habit to turn off a sluice tap that had been left dripping. All clear. The hiss of the burning *fynbos* was close, now. Thank God, the last linen room! My eyes were streaming and I was heaving for breath. White towels sat on their designated shelves in neatly stacked piles. I grabbed some, and several rolls of dressings, and dashed outside.

'All clear, Matron!' I rasped, finding her supervising the last of the ambulant patients.

'Good work, Sister. Now get into clearer air,' she looked at me with concern. I bent over and tried to steady my breathing. More sirens. Frenzied shouting from the firefighters.

The dressings.

I pulled open a pack, tore off strips and began to distribute them.

'Tie around your mouth and nose! Breathe normally!'

An explosion ripped through a tree close to the upper wards I'd just checked. A nurse screamed. 'Steady,' came Matron's voice as she herded patients downhill. 'No need to rush.'

'God Almighty,' breathed the surgeon commander, seeking me out amongst the crowd shuffling past the guardhouse. 'We've had it.'

Chapter Forty-Six

Piet was out in the boat with Abie. The navy contract was still in force – all those troops returning from the Far East fancied fish on their way home – but rumour had it the powers-that-be would cancel at the end of the year. Not surprising. The number of troopships was reducing every month. Piet and Abie had, of course, already deliberately reduced their catches to give the impression of a shortage. After all, they were paid the same however much or little they caught, so there was no sense in flooding a smaller market and then being laid off because the navy was awash with too much fish and too few soldiers and sailors to eat it.

He could always steer the excess towards his private clients, but Piet had the feeling he should be cautious. With the war winding down, people had time on their hands. The new quartermaster who'd arrived recently might get a little bored and start to examine his paperwork more carefully. Maybe even take a trip to the station to watch the goods being put on the train.

Pity, thought Piet. He'd bagged a tidy packet while keeping one step ahead of the snotty lieutenant who'd accused him of robbery. Piet was all in favour of a chase, just as long as he ended up the victor.

He and Abie were just about to lay their nets when the first orange glimmer appeared on the Simonsberg above Louise's hospital. He still felt bad, but at least she hadn't lost her job so no damage done other than to Lou's heart. He'd heard that the *Dorsetshire* officer survived, but there'd been no sign of him around Simon's Town so he must have scuttled off home. It really didn't matter any more. Lou must make her own bed. She'd pushed Piet out, and now she was left high and dry while he, Piet, had other irons in the fire. The laundress from the hospital was coming along nicely, she wasn't Louise but she'd be good enough. He wasn't in the mood to be fussy at this stage.

The glimmer grew, and burst into life.

'Let's go!' shouted Piet. 'To hell with the fish. Row, Abie, row!'

They leant on their oars. A threat to one part of the mountain threatened the whole of it, especially where the houses were cramped like at Seaforth. Or Ricketts Terrace. He hoped to God his father or Den had spotted the smoke and were collecting buckets of water to throw on the roof. If you didn't damp the roof, the place could go up before you'd even got out of your chair.

By the time they beached the boat, stowed the nets and ran up Cable Hill, three fire engines and scores of firemen and volunteer beaters were already fighting the flames. A navy commander was in charge, directing operations, supervising the newly arrived volunteers, keeping away onlookers.

'Cover your mouths and noses! Keep to your line! Look out for your neighbour!'

Piet stared up at the peak as he joined the latest beating party.

Abie tossed him a rough-cut branch of green foliage.

Crucially, no streamers of cloud to show a rising wind.

Chapter Forty-Seven

We had no time to watch the progress of the fire because the nurses' home on Cornwall Road had to be turned into an emergency hospital. We put serious cases in the common room, while the shady garden became a refuge for those less injured who coughed through their makeshift face masks and asked for water as they peered up at the flames.

'There's no need for alarm, Seaman Irvin. The firefighters will bring it under control.'

'But the buildings, ma'am? What if they burn down? Where will we go?'

'We'll worry about that later,' I said briskly. 'Now, let's look at that dressing.'

We imposed a routine. Medicines were dispensed via an informal ward round. The surgeon commander monitored those patients most affected by the choking smoke and moved them to naval houses further down the mountain. Matron organised soup from the dockyard canteen for those on liquid diets, and sandwiches from the Officers' Club for the rest.

It wasn't just our patients who needed help.

Firefighters began to stumble down the mountain, dizzy from smoke inhalation, cut and burnt by the smouldering *fynbos*. There was no time for sympathy. We patched them up and sent them back out.

The night nurses arrived early and were put to work.

Ash drifted on the air and settled in my hair, on my uniform.

Sunset painted the sky with an ugly patina of ochre.

'Sister Ahrendts!' Matron waved me over. Her eyes were bloodshot. I suppose mine were, too. Unusually, she caught my arm. 'Sister, go and check on your family. I know you live along the mountain. Please go,' she nodded and gave me a little push, 'that's an order. You've been here long enough.'

I nodded and rushed out of the garden and wondered whether to risk the lower path across the mountain. It would be faster than going down to St George's Street and then up Alfred Lane. As I strode, the heat and crackle of the fire faded behind me. The path was clear, although lone rabbits and whole families of field mice were using it with me to flee the flames, scuttling past me with no fear. The baboons had presumably headed over the peak. Apart from the receding fire, there was no sound. No sugarbirds on the proteas, no seagulls soaring on the wind.

I looked back. The brown smoke was spreading into a mantle over the surrounding mountains. A wavering line of flame edged closer to the upper wards. A quarter-moon loomed opaquely.

* * *

'Ma! Pa!' I shouted as I came round the corner of the Terrace. Mr Phillips and Mr Gamiel and the older children were filling buckets of water and sloshing them onto the roofs.

'Your ma and pa have gone to help at the church, making sandwiches for the firemen!' Mrs Hewson bellowed from her front step. 'You're filthy, child, what have you been doing?'

I looked down at my uniform in surprise. My skirt was stained, my shoes crusted in dirt. I wiped my face, and my hand came away black with grime and sweat. I'd quickly wash and change into a fresh uniform, run down to check on Ma and Pa, and then back to the hospital.

A letter was waiting on my pillow.

It would only take a moment to read, but I forced myself to wash my face and change my clothes first. I could hear his voice in my ear, soon I'd touch the words he'd written and imagine, for a brief moment, his lips on mine. Then I could go back to my patients.

I sat on the bed and reached out a hand to touch the spiral curves of the Pink Lady seashell. Soon . . .

I ripped open his letter.

Beloved Louise,

This is a letter that I never wanted to write, and never wanted you to read. But I have to write it, and you, my darling, must read it.

I have now been at home for three weeks. My daughter, Ella, is a healthy and beautiful baby. Elizabeth and I have spoken at length about the way forward. She has laid down a condition for our divorce. She will agree only if I give up my right to see Ella or play any part in her upbringing. She insists I surrender Ella to her entirely. This means, my darling, that I have to choose between my daughter and you.

At first, I thought I'd be able to agree to her demand – marrying you is the deepest desire of my heart. I've also been given the chance of a position at the Admiralty, which would allow us to be together and build a life in London. Ella could have joined us there from time to time.

I've asked Elizabeth to reconsider but she is adamant. I've offered her a generous settlement and the right to remain at Corbey with Ella for as long as she wishes and with no responsibility for the estate unless she chooses it. She has refused. My solicitor says I have no legal recourse, given the circumstances.

Elizabeth is exerting a cruel revenge.

I love Ella, who's an innocent victim of this terrible bargaining. I hold her in my arms and she already knows who I am, and falls asleep on my shoulder. I realise I have a responsibility to her to be an active father, not a ghost. I also realise that no child should be left solely in the care of someone who can impose such a brutal ultimatum.

This means that we can never marry – I am weeping as I write these words, as you can probably see.

Please don't wait for me any longer, my beautiful, glorious Louise. I cannot come back for you. Forgive me for allowing us to believe that I could, and that we could be together. Forgive me for betraying our love.

I will leave the navy and return to Corbey for good. Elizabeth and I will live under the same roof but apart. There will be no more children.

Forgive me, my darling. I will love you for ever.

David

I crushed the single sheet of paper with its smudged words and thrust it into my pocket.

I don't remember leaving the cottage.

I only remember the steepness of the slope behind the Terrace and my feet slipping on the dry earth, and the smoke irritating my nose – and the need to climb upwards, ever upwards. After a while, I came to a flat plateau of grass, and lay on my back in my nurse's uniform and looked up. To my left, in the direction of the hospital, the stars were obscured. But directly above, they blazed down on me with such intensity that I thought I'd be able to reach up my hand and brush them one way and then the other. Like jewelled curtains.

Or the tears that David and I would shed for each other.

Perhaps, finally, this was God's punishment. Perhaps my failure to release David to his daughter had been the last straw, the tipping point of lies, concealment and illicit love. But why did He wait until I got so close to my future that I could almost smell the foreign grass, see the ripples on the Thames, feel David's hair beneath my fingers . . . and then wrench it away? Punishment should be immediate, not deferred.

If I wanted to, I could impose the punishment on myself. I could keep climbing until there was no more mountain above me and I could slip off the edge into the sea and let myself sink down, find the etched seabed beneath my fingers, and drift on the tide until I fell asleep.

There was a shudder.

The ground shifted beneath me. Stones rattled past.

Yet above, the Southern Cross hung steady, like an anchor on its side. Orion's belt curved among the sea of stars, an infant wave breaking at Seaforth beach. David would see the same stars, but arranged upside down. He might show his daughter—

I hauled my gaze down to earth and saw flickering tongues of orange, and heard distant shouts. Maybe I wouldn't need to go further up the mountain, or find a cliff with the sea lapping at its foot and the rocks rising like eggs out of the water. Maybe if I lay here and held on to the stars until they disappeared—

'Louise!'

It was my mind playing tricks. Nobody knew I was here. Ma and Pa thought I was at work. Mrs Hewson thought I'd gone to see Ma and Pa. It was the slippery earth teasing me.

'Lou!'

A familiar face loomed over me.

'What are you doing up here?'

I stared at him, the wild hair, the familiar black eyes. 'I'm waiting to die,' I said to Piet.

'Why?' he demanded, gathering me in his arms. 'Why do you want to die?'

'He's gone, I've lost him.'

Piet said nothing. But his arms were comforting. I used to love David's arms around me, the way he was gentle but also strong, the way his fingers could convey so much with just a touch of skin on skin. The way his lips curved, even the line of his scar.

'The fire's under control,' he pointed up to where the orange flickers were subsiding. 'But there's been a landslide. Come, Lou, we must go back. Check on your folks.'

'I don't want to go back.'

He stared at me, his eyes running over my face, my body. He looked different. Older. There came a rumbling from higher up the mountain. Piet leapt to his feet and dragged me up with him.

'Hold on to me!'

It was harder heading downhill because the gravel kept slipping beneath my feet. Piet clamped me to his side and we edged down. I could hear shouts on the left but my eyes were too blurred from the smoke and tears to make out the cause.

'When the trees burn, the soil slips,' Piet muttered, 'nothing to hold it back.'

The face of the moon was brightening.

'Wait!' I stared at the dockyard, trying to make out the ships. *Durban*, *Achilles*, *Dorsetshire*, *Cumberland*.

'We can't stop,' Piet urged, pulling me forward.

A crowd was gathering around the Gamiel place at the end of the Terrace.

'I must help!' I cried, pulling away from Piet.

'No, Lou! Come inside. Trust me.'

Trust Piet?

I let him lead me inside. He took me to the kitchen sink where he rinsed out a cloth and began to wipe my face and my hands and arms. Then he took me to my bedroom and sat me on the bed.

'You need to take off your dirty clothes,' he said, squatting down in front of me. 'People will wonder. And then you must rest for a bit.'

'I don't want to be alone,' I said.

David didn't want his daughter to be alone, either. It was her or me.

'I'll stay with you.' Piet handed me my dressing gown from a hook on the back of the door.

I took off my uniform in front of him, wrapped the gown around me and lay down on the bed. He bent over and stroked my hair like Ma often did. Then he lay down beside me. I was grateful for his kindness, his warmth.

I closed my eyes and thought of David with his daughter. He might describe Simon's Town to her, conjuring up yellow proteas, turquoise water, red-beaked oystercatchers strutting across the sand.

'Don't cry for some foreigner,' Piet said, burying his face in my hair.

Would David tell her, one day, about me?

I turned my head and let Piet kiss my lips. It didn't matter any more who kissed me.

I felt his breathing quicken.

'Lou?' he said thickly, 'do you want this?'

I kept my eyes closed. I could imagine it was David, tender David, who'd come back for me after all.

I felt Piet's hand on my thigh.

I let him kiss my lips more feverishly.

Perhaps this was my punishment.

He got up and closed my bedroom door. Fumbled with his clothes.

I didn't stop him.

I let him have me.

It was the only option I had.

I have always kept secret what I most want – until I could savour its arrival. Now I must conceal how close I came, and how much I've lost.

Ma never asked me about the contents of David's letter. But when Piet described how he'd found me, dishevelled and incoherent, close to the fire line, I'm sure she knew. Perhaps Ma knew everything – even what happened afterwards.

Neither Piet nor I ever spoke of it.

When viewed against the demands of cleaning the hospital, which narrowly escaped destruction, and digging out Mr Gamiel and his cottage from the landslide that buried them both, my stumble on the mountainside was insignificant. I'd been overcome by smoke. I'd taken a wrong turning. I was spotted by Piet who brought me home.

And there was a happy ending – especially after the sad end to one of our neighbours.

Piet and I were married quietly at St Francis Church.

My parents, Amos and Den Philander and our closest friends attended. Pa gave me away in his pre-war suit. Ma wept the whole way through. With joy, she told anyone who tried to comfort her.

'God, Lou!' giggled Vera, now engaged to Abie. 'You're a dark horse!'

Mrs Hewson made my wedding dress of white cotton

with an empire line that concealed my four months' pregnancy. I'd love this child, it was all I had left.

I kept my view of the sea, because I got Piet to agree that we'd live with my parents at Ricketts Terrace. After all, it made sense with Ma looking after the baby once I returned to work.

'We don't keep posts open as a rule,' Matron frowned, 'but perhaps in this case we can make an exception.'

'I'm grateful, Matron. I will be the breadwinner in my family.'

Piet, these days, seemed more keen on drinking with his friends than fishing.

I didn't expect any more letters from David, and none arrived.

Chapter Forty-Eight

Republic of South Africa, 1967

'Sam! Sam!'

Sam Philander poked his head out of the front of the cottage. Solly, his grandfather, lurched across the stream from next door.

'I heard from the church! They want you to carve the new lectern!'

Sam grinned and clapped the old man on his shoulder. Not too hard, for Grandpa was getting on, even though his enthusiasm for life was as keen as ever. He spent most of his waking moments as Sam's promoter-in-chief.

'Thanks, Grandpa. How did you persuade the minister?'

'I told him it was his responsibility.' Solly drew himself up. 'Your grandma and I were married there, we've sung in the St Francis choir for forty years, so the least he can do is give my grandson work.'

'And Ma and Pa were married there,' reminded Sam. Grandpa threw up his hands and shot Sam an apologetic look. That marriage, Sam reflected, was never celebrated.

'What work?' Sam's mother stepped through the doorway in her uniform.

Even though she was almost fifty, Ma's beauty still caused the chattering crowds on St George's Street stop in their tracks and stare. His pa was a fool. And the government was an even bigger fool to overlook her for Matron at the False Bay. However bright you were, Sam gritted his teeth beneath his welcoming grin, they made you sweat in the shadows when you deserved the chance to be recognised for what you did and be properly paid for it. Like Grandpa used to be, when the Royal Navy was in charge of the dockyard before it was handed over to South Africa in the fifties.

The only answer was to work for yourself.

Sam knew, without being boastful, that he could restore an antique wardrobe better than anyone else, or work a fresh block of timber into curves and angles that regular workmen never tried. He'd taught himself from books out of the library, with pictures of British church carvings and Polynesian canoes. If you were good enough, customers ran after you and the government left you alone, especially in a small place like Simon's Town.

His friend Benji Olifant, son of Pa's old fishing friend from the war, said Communism was the only solution, and he dragged Sam along to well-funded, secret meetings where people waved their fists for equality and sang 'The Internationale'.

Sam didn't want to be equal, he didn't want to be like everyone else.

He wanted the chance to stand out.

'Sam's going to carve the new lectern at the church. Fancy that!'

Ma's weary eyes sparkled and she came over to hug him.

'I'll get on, now,' Solly said. 'We'll see you later for supper.'

'Thanks, Grandpa. You're the best.' The old man winked and stumped off.

Sam turned to his mother.

'Ma? Is everything alright?'

She put down the bag of vegetables she'd picked up from Runciman's on the way home. Her hair, pulled back under her cap, had traces of grey over the ears. She sat down at the table and rested her chin in her hands.

'Ma?' Sam put an arm across her shoulders.

She looked up at him. Her eyes were that amazing shade of almond that he loved when he found it in wood. Not as bright as *podocarpus* – yellow-wood – but not as deep as mahogany. And with flecks, like the grain that ran through oak.

'I've received a letter,' Ma said.

She shifted her gaze from his and looked out of the door towards the sea, roughened with white horses from the north wind. Sam knew that meant rain tomorrow, sweeping from the Muizenberg Mountain. Up there, in the ravines, were extraordinary patches of forest, packed with indigenous beauties whose trunks he loved to stroke, imagining the glow of the wood within . . .

'We're being evicted.'

'What?'

'Simon's Town is to be declared a white area.'

Chapter Forty-Nine

I've never been afraid of going against the tide. After all, I challenged – and bent – unwritten laws of gender and colour and pyramids.

I won those battles, didn't I?

Of course I was younger, then, and this was something different; something that couldn't be fought, or moulded to my will. This was an attack on colour by means of geography.

The letter was perfectly clear.

And its power lay in the fact that it was also perfectly, brazenly, legal.

Under the terms of the Group Areas Act, passed by the white parliament of South Africa in 1950 and now being enforced some fifteen years later, all coloureds living south of the line between Chapman's Peak and Kalk Bay were to be expelled to a new place called Ocean View. If you didn't want to go to Ocean View, you must leave the area entirely and fend for yourself in a coloured township further away. They even specified the contour line below which you would be forcibly removed.

Presumably, if you were brave enough to live on the mountain summits amongst the baboons and the odd elusive leopard, you could stay put until you were thinned out by natural selection.

The process was given a fresh name. It wasn't called eviction, it was called resettlement – supposedly a kinder form of expulsion.

It was the law.

I touched my brown skin, then took out the letter and read it again, between the lines.

Simon's Town, named by the Dutch, built up by the British, and defended by a rich palette of black, white, Hottentot, Malay, Indian and every shade in between, was no longer to be shared. It was to be the sole preserve of white people.

The blacks must leave their mountain shacks and go to Nyanga, miles away on the Cape Flats, the coloureds to Ocean View and the Indians to a suburb that hadn't yet been specified. Sam and I in the late Mrs Hewson's cottage, Ma and Pa in our original family home, the Phillipses down the way, old Gamiel's grandchildren in the rebuilt cottage – we'd all have to leave. Even Piet, living a shrunken life in the Philander cottage, would be scooped up and deposited far from the sea he loved and which I hoped might yet save him.

Piet . . .

I suppose I could have tried harder and for longer, but there was Sam to consider. When unfair laws can trap you in their web, you need a steady family if you want to teach your child the difference between right and wrong.

I touched the ring that still encircled my finger.

Vera says that I've grown more impatient as I've grown older. It's true: I've no time for silly rules and lost causes. To me they're beached seaweed, the flotsam of others trying to tell me what I must or mustn't do, or who I should or shouldn't save. I've learnt to skip over their strands, or toss them aside more quickly than I did as a young woman. I'm not proud of what happened with Piet, and I take most of the blame, but there's no point in indulging a mistake once it's been made.

'But I rescued you!' Piet shouted more than once, coming closer, the brandy sloshing in his glass. 'If it wasn't for me you'd still be disgraced and weeping for that Pommy!'

Piet realised my secret, of course, soon after we married and my pregnancy began to show too quickly for him to have been the father.

'The fancy British officer,' he said bitterly, 'you slept with him in secret. I saw you, once,' he leapt to his feet and began to pace around the kitchen, 'on the mountain. So where is he now you need him? Why did he leave you high and dry?'

'I'm grateful to you, Piet,' I said, meeting his eyes. 'I'll be a good wife if you take the child as your own. Say that we anticipated our wedding by a few months.'

He stared at me, his hands flexing. I remembered Amos slapping Piet across the face, and Piet's coiled fists when I refused to marry him. I waited. This time, I was too heavy with child to sprint away. But he didn't hit me. And in a month or so, he started to enjoy the back slaps and the winks of his mates as they noticed my growing belly. Even Ma and Pa and Vera accepted the lie that, in a moment of weakness, I'd allowed Piet too much freedom with my body. 'I warned you,' said Ma, taking refuge in bent morals and avoiding the trickier question of who the father was, 'you should have known better, being a Sister and all.'

'Why didn't you say you and Piet were back together?' Vera giggled, 'Sneaking around, too!'

To my work colleagues and our Terrace neighbours, my indiscretion was, briefly, a scandal. Matron frowned when I updated her on my due date, and certain folk took it as another example of my talent for stepping out of line. But there seemed to be no dispute that marriage and a family was the sensible outcome for two people who'd known each other all their lives and turned to one another as the war faded. The usual order of events had simply been reversed.

'That Piet's a lucky *skelm*!' Mrs Hewson shook her head. 'And a child's a blessing, even if you weren't wearing a ring.'

But I know it's more complicated. I have the broken heart and the later wounds to show for it. David shouldn't have married Elizabeth without loving her completely, and I shouldn't have married Piet when I was carrying David's child. Both of us have had to make hard choices as a result.

David stayed with Elizabeth to raise Ella.

I cast out Piet so Sam might become a better man than his stepfather.

And now the life I'd reforged was about to splinter in a way that none of us had ever imagined. With the arrival of the eviction notices, our tight Terrace watched over so democratically by Jesus and Allah was to be scattered like the stones that slid down the Simonsberg on the night Piet found me. Once we were gone – discarded – the cottages we'd shored up against the slippery mountain for so long would be demolished.

I felt a chill on the back of my neck that wasn't the wind.

But I try not to take heed of signs any more, or potential

tipping points. They're too fickle to be trusted. Like the worst – and best – of lovers? I'm grateful for what I have, I hold Ma and Pa and Sam close and only let my mind drift with the tide at Seaforth.

And yet this removal . . .

I reached across to the bookcase and fingered my shells. The apple-green urchins. The toothed cowries. The Pink Lady. In the future, where would we go to swim if the beach was closed to coloureds?

The shell's ridges pressed into my hand.

Sometimes David surprises me . . . in the passing slide of blue eyes, the timbre of a man's voice, the line of a warship slicing across the bay.

Or the expression on the face of his son.

I can almost believe he is here.

Should I contact him? A secret letter, via the Admiralty, so there was no chance of it falling into the wrong hands?

Not for myself – there would be no point – but for Sam.

Thirty years ago, Matron at the Victoria took a risk and gave me a chance. I was lucky. These days, youngsters like Sam were actively barred from decent work, discouraged from shining in even the smallest way. And soon we were to be removed to a place far from potential employment. There was no future, there, for a young man with talent.

But what would I say?

Dear David,

You can't have me, but here is our son . . .

Chapter Fifty

My darling,

I have written so many letters to you . . .

They sit locked away in my desk, a diary of my life since the end of the war and a reflection on the loss we've shared for over twenty years. I realise it's selfish of me to use you as my longed-for correspondent like this, without your knowing, but it's the only way I can keep you alive. I don't expect you to have forgiven me – I've never forgiven myself. And so I've never posted the letters.

However, this is one that I shall send.

I can't sit by any longer, watching images of apartheid brutality on television, and not worry about you. The papers are full of the deliberate ill-treatment of anyone who isn't white. The Cape landmarks, the beaches – even Seaforth with its lively waves that I remember so well – may now be out of bounds to you. How is it possible that the country I grew to love can have descended into such madness?

My beloved L, please let me help.

If you want to get out of South Africa and start afresh, I'll pay for you to leave. If you have children, I'll help them find their feet somewhere new.

This is about more than you and me. It's about human decency, and the irrelevance of colour.

I hope I'm not too late. I hope you're still on Ricketts Terrace.

Write to me. Please.

My love,

David

Chapter Fifty-One

The eviction notices were served at Seaforth too. Piet didn't get much post so he was surprised to see the letter pushed under his door.

And it occurred to him that he'd be able to concentrate on an official piece of paper far better if he had a full stomach. But he hadn't been out in the boat for a while so there was no fresh fish or the money to buy anything as a substitute.

He could go up to Lou's and beg some grub. See the boy – handsome fellow, looked more like Piet with his black hair than the foreigner – but then he'd have to clean himself up. Lou wouldn't allow him in if he hadn't bathed recently. Piet couldn't remember when he last took a bath, actually. Or when he last shaved.

It was her fault, of course.

She'd driven him to it. Actually, she'd calculated every move.

Letting him have his way with her, asking him to marry her and take over the child, but then telling him to leave a few years later when he had some temporary problems. Told him he was a bad example for the child. Told him if he cleaned himself up and worked proper hours and contributed instead of leaving it all to her, then he could come back and they could be a family again.

But, Piet scratched himself and yawned, he couldn't be bothered.

It was all too much trouble, especially for a boy who wasn't his and a wife who didn't love him. After all, there were no more children. No Philander to call his own. It wasn't for want of trying, at least Lou had lived up to that side of the bargain, allowing him access to her body whenever he chose. But her heart wasn't in it, and maybe the flesh knows and won't play along.

He once said he wouldn't let her go without a fight, that she was his, but having her second-hand turned out to be not worth fighting for. She still carried a candle for the British officer. Much good that had done her. Or him, for that matter. If she'd stuck with her own and not had fancy ideas, they'd both have been better off. Why, just look at Abie and Vera! She'd opened a beauty parlour and was rubbing cream into the faces of women searching for eternal youth, while Abie sat on his backside and counted the money!

Once upon a time, he and Lou had been the golden couple.

He dragged himself up and went over to the stove.

He'd make some tea. Black, because there was no milk. But somewhere – he rummaged through a cupboard filled with empty brandy bottles and brown packets saved for

God-knows-what – there was some sugar. He lit a match. His hands shook a lot these days. Maybe it was his eyes that were the problem, not his hands.

Bloody stove didn't light.

He struck another match.

It wasn't right. This was woman's work. He shouldn't be forced to make his own tea, cook his own food. If the navy had kept buying his fish, he'd be a wealthy man and other people could make his tea for him.

He struck another match, and then another.

He threw the matches down, some went out on the floor, others flickered.

And then he fell over. Like when Amos hit him the day he was arrested.

But somehow he'd managed to light the stove. Or had he? If he could find a kettle he'd fill it with water and then make tea and use the spare hot water to shave. But he was feeling sleepy. He'd just curl up here, on the floor.

The kettle would whistle when the water was boiling.

Chapter Fifty-Two

After the eviction notices, Simon's Town went about its business like the sea recovering from a storm: the surface smooth but the water beneath churning with the remnants of the recent blow. Surely, we told ourselves as we tried to suppress the panic, the whole business would be declared a mistake, surely life would resume as normal?

There were indeed days when I felt hopeful.

But as time went by with no reprieve, they were soon outnumbered by the days when I despaired. Streets I'd run along all my life began to feel alien beneath my feet. Our palms caught the mood and hung dank and lifeless above the cottage. Whites who'd nodded to me and acknowledged my uniform and my service for years, blushed and looked away.

The Post Office stopped making deliveries, as if we'd already left.

We were still part of Simon's Town yet utterly cut off.

Pa said there was a rumour that the Terrace removals

were because our vantage point above the dockyard gave us a view of navy secrets that we could pass on to the Communists.

'Madness!' he cried. 'We're being moved away to protect the dockyard that my pa – all of our pas' – he waved his hand heavenwards – 'actually built?'

The government's fear of Communism knew no bounds. Russia and its proxies were intent upon invading South Africa, they claimed. Simon's Town was to be attacked while the world looked on and did nothing. Yet if they were right, surely everyone – including blacks and coloureds – should be mobilised in the fight, not evicted from the battlefield?

'They won't go ahead,' Vera tried to convince herself. 'Some of the whites have raised petitions. They say the town can't afford to lose us. It'll go bankrupt!'

But petitions, while worthy, don't stir leaders who are certain that they're right. And we coloureds couldn't even speak for ourselves. We'd already been removed from the voters roll some years before, so there was no one to represent us officially or exert pressure. At the time of that particular discardment, a government minister said it was to avoid the collapse of white civilisation across Africa.

'It's worse than we thought it would ever get,' Ma wept as she sorted through a lifetime's clutter in the cottage.

'We must be brave,' said Pa quietly and gave her his best kiss. 'Brave for Lou and for Sam.'

The blows kept coming.

Perhaps that was the intention: to hit us while we were down.

'What's this?' Vera picked up the newspaper from our

kitchen table with long fingers, as if it carried a bad smell.

'It's racial classification,' I said as I brought tea over. 'We have to declare which group we belong to. There are seven to choose from.'

'You can't be serious!' Vera squawked. 'Tell me!'

'Cape Coloured, Malay, Griqua, Indian, Chinese, Other Asian and Other Coloured,' I recited.

'And what if we fit none of those?' Sam threw up his hands. 'What'll they do then?'

'You'll have to be Other Coloured,' piped up Vera's daughter Sandra, who'd inherited her mother's frizzy hair and provocative poses. 'Anyone who doesn't know where they came from can be Other Coloured.'

'Don't talk like that, Sandra,' bristled her mother. 'I know exactly where you came from.'

'Even whites can be Other Coloured,' Sandra pouted, ignoring the interruption, 'if the police decide you're too dark. Serves them right for trying to get away with it.'

Our eviction played on the mind of my matron at the False Bay Hospital.

'Louise,' she chose her words carefully at one of our weekly meetings, 'I've put you forward for advancement many times. This one, for example,' she picked up a letter from a pile at the side of the desk, 'to be part of Professor Barnard's heart transplant team at Groote Schuur. I thought – if you were being forced to move anyway – then why not? But I'm afraid that others, often less outstanding, are chosen ahead of you.'

I clasped my hands in my lap. 'I'm used to it, Sylvia. But thank you for trying.'

Shades of Ma. *You should know that by now.*

Matron was, of course, officially senior to me, but we divided her duties equally between us. I ran the hospital's theatre and intensive care nursing, she ran ward and outpatient nursing. It was a formula that worked, but not one we publicised.

'I've had one small success,' Matron leant forward and her voice took on a conspiratorial note. 'I've finally succeeded in getting your position re-evaluated. Your title will not change,' she raised her eyebrows in rueful exasperation, 'but from now on you'll be earning more.'

'Thank you, Matron. I'm very grateful.'

'No,' she stood up and held out her hand. 'I'm the one who's grateful. You've remained loyal while the politicians have pushed you away. I'm ashamed of what's happening.'

I left the office and stopped in the corridor. Cape Hangklip's peak jutted into the sky on the far side of the bay. Roman Rock Lighthouse gleamed white against the steel-blue water.

I'm ashamed of my country, too.

Vera has a radical solution.

'Cross over! Try for white! Especially you and Sam' – she tossed her head with its beehive hairdo – 'you're gold, not brown. All that Malay blood from your ma.'

We were sitting in Jubilee Square. So far, the benches were still unsegregated.

'You'd have to leave, of course, go somewhere else, up the coast.'

'No!' I cried, grabbing Vera's arm. Passers-by stared.

I lowered my voice. 'I'd never do that. I won't betray my own.'

And leaving the peninsula would mean I could never be found.

'Don't be a fool, Lou! Out of all of us,' she thrust an angry arm at the diverse crowd on the square, 'you'd have the best chance. You're a nurse, there'd be less questions. You'd be free! And with a white salary. Your parents would understand.'

I shot her a glance and then stared out across the bay. A tug was steaming towards a grey warship, its bow wave creaming through the flat sea. Amazingly, no one had guessed about Sam's father. Perhaps it was because he appeared to have inherited Piet's dark hair, although I knew his hair was more like mine, more brown than black. And his blue eyes, initially far lighter than Piet's, had luckily darkened as he got older. For me, the likeness was as clear as the memory of Oranjezicht. I saw David in the line of Sam's nose, the way he held his head, the quiet fervency, at times, in his voice. Ma might have guessed, but she never spoke. The secret remained intact. But it lived in my heart like a knife.

'Millie Phillips' daughter is going to do it.'

'But—'

The Phillips family were darker than Vera and darker than me. Even if she got away with it, the price would be devastating. She'd have to shun every friend she knew, ignore her parents and her brothers and sisters if they happened to walk by on the street. No eye contact. No recognition. They'd be dead to her, as she would be to them.

'Think about it,' Vera repeated intently. 'If I looked like you, I would. True as God is rainbow-coloured. I'd forget Abie, set up on my own somewhere, find myself a rich white man. I can still show some leg . . .' She brandished a mottled ankle. 'Think, Lou! There's not much time left.'

Create a new identity and live brazenly as a white person at the top of the pyramid, ignoring the coloureds and blacks who toiled in its shadow?

'I can't.' I stood up. 'And I won't leave Ma and Pa.'

Vera shrugged and put an arm through mine.

Instead, I began to plan in secret for a different kind of crossing over. Sam was losing heart, I could tell. The first signs were already there. The lectern, while a welcome piece of work, was draining him in a way his other commissions hadn't. He was worried about what he'd do once the project was finished and we were stuck in Ocean View. Who'd employ him there? And I was afraid that a part of Piet that had so far lurked silently about him, could erupt any day. I had to do something before that happened.

I once held on to David and forced him to make a terrible choice. I can't do that with Sam.

However much I love him, however much he evokes David, I must let him go.

Chapter Fifty-Three

My darling, he began, his hand shaking so much that he had to start again on a fresh sheet.

I have written to you so often – indeed, hundreds of letters – but never sent them apart from one, some months ago, when my concern about your situation became acute. I offered financial help to you and your family to leave the country. That offer still stands. The letter was returned to me, saying address unknown. I hope – profoundly – that you are safe.

Many years ago, my lawyer asked me if I had any doubts about my wife's ability to raise our daughter on her own. No, I said out loud. But yes, I said in my heart. I went back to Corbey, desperate for you, and watched Ella asleep in her cot and I realised I could never leave her under Elizabeth's sole influence. My daughter has now grown up into a fine young woman—

He looked up. The rolling fields of Corbey stretched out beyond the study window, ordered, immaculate. How much should he say? How much should he describe Ella, the delight of his life, but the reason he left Louise?

I am soon to be divorced. Elizabeth agreed because, it turns out, she has a new companion. She will remarry once the divorce is final. I'm past feeling bitter, there is only a lasting regret for the wasted years.

If you're free and still love me as I love you, I will come to Simon's Town.

But if you're married, I will leave you be and send you my best love and wishes . . . and thank you, again, for the most precious moments of my life.

I hope you will receive this letter. I realise you may have moved, but perhaps it will be forwarded as your family is well known.

Please reply, even if it is to say no.

It wasn't right. Too stilted. He'd have to start the letter again.

Chapter Fifty-Four

Sam stood back from the new lectern. He'd gone for clean lines, the better to show off the yellow-wood's seductive sheen. A little baroque moulding at the base, then the stem soaring upwards in a simple pillar, discreetly bevelled to reflect the light, and culminating in the angled reading shelf from which a velvet cloth could be draped – although Sam thought, privately, that the piece needed no further embellishment. The gleaming wood was its own adornment.

'Beautiful, Sam. Wonderful work.' The minister walked around, eyeing it from every angle. He stroked a thin hand across the shelf. 'You're an artist, young man.'

'Thank you, sir.'

'I want to consecrate it the first Sunday of next month.'

Sam nodded.

'It will be announced in the parish newsletter.' The minister drew himself up to his full, gaunt, height. 'I intend to dedicate it to the coloured community, staunch members of this congregation. If you don't mind?'

'I'd like that, sir.'

The minister sighed and put a hand on Sam's shoulder to usher him down the aisle. 'I'm so sorry,' he consoled, 'this wrenching of people from their homes. Appalling. We've fought it at the highest level, but there's no swaying the authorities.' He lifted his hands in despair.

Sam felt a flicker of rage. Sympathy and hand-wringing wouldn't stop the bulldozers. Neither would the petitions presented by Simon's Town's whites, lamenting the heart being torn out of their town. It needed more forceful action. Why hadn't the archbishop led a march on parliament? Why hadn't white congregations risen up and said they wouldn't stop until there was fairness for all?

There were only a few weeks left.

'The Nationalists say they're doing God's work,' he said, trying to keep his tone respectful. 'They quote Genesis. They say God directed them to rule over the birds and the animals – and lesser people like us.'

'No! A travesty of the scriptures,' the minister interjected, shaking his head, 'they're perverting the Word of the Lord.'

Sam stopped and looked around the church. He'd come to Sunday school here. His parents and grandparents had been married here. It was his church. But it would be too far to come every week from Ocean View. And as far as he knew, there was no church where they were going.

'So who is right, sir?' he found himself rasping. 'The Church or the government?'

There was a beat of silence. They'd reached the vestibule. The minister's hand trembled as he passed it over his sparse hair. Sam instantly felt ashamed. The minister was a good man. He truly felt the pain of others. It wasn't his fault that he couldn't relieve it. Through the open door came the thunder of waves on Long Beach below the station. After all, the lectern was just another job. He'd been paid, he should leave, not yell at his customer about why he'd failed to halt the eviction of half his congregation.

'I'm sorry, Reverend.'

'The Church is right, Sam,' the minister declared. 'The government will face its sins on Judgement Day.'

Sam looked out of the door towards the restless sea.

'That will be too late for us, sir.'

He stepped outside and began to run.

He sprinted past the side entrance to Admiralty House where his father liked to boast he had special access, and onto the main road. Up the slope, and not far from where the Admiral's Waterfall spewed in winter, lay the low outline of the False Bay Hospital, where Ma worked. Beyond the old Officers' Club, pylons for the aerial ropeway marched up the mountain, passing the former wards of the Royal Naval Hospital, where she served during the war. His old school brooded across the road. He ran on, sweat breaking out on his forehead, the pavement hard beneath his shoes.

This road, this tarmac, was real. It couldn't be taken away from him.

This was his place.

Great Grandpa Ahrendts built the wall around the dockyard, Grandpa fixed the ships inside it, Grandma swept and fed and cleaned its people, Ma healed whoever was sick.

His place.

His mountain.

His world.

How dare anyone say he was no longer welcome?

Maybe Benji's Communists weren't crazy. Maybe they were on the right track.

Chapter Fifty-Five

It's nearly time.

Now, white people don't just blush and avert their eyes, they come up to me on St George's Street and say how shocking it is that we coloureds are being forced to move; that it's a scandal, a blind cruelty imposed by a government that doesn't understand the kinship we've nurtured between the sea, the ships and those who serve them. People usually go on to say that the town will die without us. And they may be right.

We may not have had much money, but through our numbers we swelled the coffers of Sartorial House, Runciman's and the post office, and filled St George's Street for victory celebrations and sang in the church choir and shored up the mountain behind us.

'It will empty the town, sir!' Ma declared, cornering the admiral at the pensioners' annual tea.

'I hope not, ma'am. We must try to be positive.'

'But after all we've been through,' Ma persisted,

clutching her elderly straw hat in the breeze, 'you'd think they'd show some respect.'

'I'm so sorry, Mrs Ahrendts. I'm afraid it's out of my hands. Government policy.'

'Come, Sheila,' Pa put an arm around her ample waist and steered her away. He waved his free hand northwards. 'They don't care.'

For Pa, the eviction was about more than Ricketts Terrace. It was about personal rejection.

His years of service. His pride.

The day dawned bright and clear. I hadn't slept much so I got up early, put a pair of old trousers and a knitted jersey over my swimsuit, grabbed a towel, crept out without waking Sam and headed for Seaforth.

I don't sprint any more but I still love to run.

The odd car passed, the odd person walking a dog nodded to me. The tide was low, licking at the base of the egg rocks, the water tinged with the pink of sunrise. More and more beaches were being closed to non-whites, but it was too early for the enforcers to be out. I'd be safe. I flung off my sweaty clothes as if I was a child again, and dived in and swam out past the forests of kelp. A vee of cormorants hugged the swells as they beat towards the lighthouse. Spirals of smoke and the shouts of parents hustling their children rose from the straggle of cottages above the beach. I rolled onto my back and looked up at the Simonsberg etched sharp against the pale sky, and drifted, letting my hair spread out about my head, relishing the tug of the current and the brisk chill of water not yet warmed by the sun. The young Piet came back, roused from the Philander cottage, diving for shells amid the flickering anemones. David came back, touching my cheek and telling me he loved me as we sat on the polished sand.

I swam to shore and dried myself. Then took a last look at the curling surf . . .

And hurried back to the Terrace which, come sunset, would no longer be home.

Eviction is a humiliating business.

A date is provided.

Trucks will come by on that date.

Anything more than a truckload per household can't be taken.

Perhaps it would have been more fitting if bad weather had shrouded the entire event in mist or deluge, but Jesus and Allah took it upon themselves to bless us by keeping the southeaster at bay, and the dust down, so that it was a perfect day for moving. The sea sparkled, the ships in the dockyard gleamed, and the butcher birds perched and swooped through the palms searching for the fattest of prey.

Fine weather, of course, also allows everyone to see – and linger over – your life; your furniture, your private possessions and the bits and pieces that have little value but are, somehow, essential to every home. The chair with a crooked leg that you can't bear to get rid of, a carpet that usually hides its stain beneath a conveniently placed armchair, the cloudy glasses not shown to visitors.

'Watch yourself,' says Pa to Sam – although Sam is by far

the stronger – as they lift our faded sofa out of the door and lower it onto the earth. David once sat on it, his uniform splendid by contrast.

I follow with the cushions, wrapped in newspaper to try and keep them clean.

Then the linen from both cottages, crammed into lumpen bags.

'Here,' Ma hands me a rattling box of plates. 'Keep it upright.' She is close to tears.

'I'll take it,' Sam lifts it out of my arms and stacks it beside a crate of cutlery.

'*Hou die blink kant bo* – keep smiling!' Pa cries hoarsely to us, and to our neighbours who are also dragging their goods outside.

'I'll miss the sea,' moans old man Phillips, carting his pipe collection. 'And all of you.' His family are going to Grassy Park, a coloured suburb on the Cape Flats beyond Muizenberg. It's closer to one of the younger children's work, but he and his wife have no friends there.

'*Blerrie* fools!' The Gamiels yell at each other as a case bursts open and spills its contents onto the earth; a set of fraying cloth nappies, a purple hat, a tarnished sugar bowl wrapped in a towel. 'Pick everything up before it gets dirty! Why'd you pack it so full?'

Pa shakes his head and stumps back inside to wrap the mirror from our tiny bathroom.

Millie Phillips' daughter – the one Vera says wants to try for white – is standing apart, not helping, dressed in a pale-pink dress.

Her brothers and sisters ignore her.

Maybe she has chosen this day to cross over.

I wipe my forehead and catch her eye. She looks away. It would be the right time. She could leave the Terrace, but never arrive in Grassy Park . . .

'Sure you can manage, Ma?' Sam stands at the end of the table he made for me when he was still a schoolboy. 'Keep looking up when you lift.' He worries the weight is too heavy for me. Piet should be here, helping. But he hardly ever comes to see us, he lives like a hermit in the old Philander place, also scheduled for eviction.

Once our cottage is empty, I rest on the wall in the sunshine.

The sea winks with a brilliance I must try to remember. Ma comes to sit by my side. We take each other's hands. Hammering drifts up from the dockyard.

Sam helps wherever he's needed. I overhear him reassuring Mrs Gamiel. 'It'll be a fresh start, Mrs G. I'll put up your cupboards, just the way you like them.' But the oldies don't want a fresh start. The Terrace, its windblown cottages, its sublime view of False Bay, is all they've ever wanted.

By eleven o' clock, our lives sit pitiful and smouldering in the heat.

An hour passes.

We wait.

I massage my aching hands. Pa finds a plaster for young Phillips who's cut his leg. Ma shares out the sandwiches she made before the last of the kitchen was packed.

'What if they don't come?' someone shouts. 'What if they've changed their minds?'

Ma looks hopefully at Pa. He shakes his head.

The sun passes its zenith.

Millie's daughter sidles away, past the mosque, down Alfred Lane.

Then the trucks labour up the hill, along with a police van to make sure there is no trouble.

'*Maak gou!* We haven't got all day,' a huge sergeant yells as his men stand by and watch.

But no one has the heart or the energy for violence. We are cowed by the weight of leaving.

'Heavy stuff at the bottom!' shouts the foreman in charge of the loaders, but his warning is ignored. All our goods are thrown on the vehicles in a mighty confusion and in the rush some things fall off or are never loaded and disappear for good.

Haste seems to be essential for our evictors. They want us out of here fast.

'The photographs, Lou!' cries Ma, newly distressed.

'In my bag,' I hold her close against me. The sepia pictures of Ma and Pa on their wedding day, a toothy Sam as a baby, David's letters, my most precious shells. . .

'It's not fair,' she weeps, now that there is no going back. I stay close, to shield her from the rough handling and the shouts of the loaders. 'Mrs Hewson would've dug in her heels. Made them carry her out!'

'It'll be over soon,' I murmur, watching our cracked suitcases being tossed aboard along with the furniture, followed by Pa's bundle of overalls tied up with string, Sam's beautifully carved case of woodworking tools. This is what it must have been like for the Jews in Germany. Dear Jesus, I find myself praying to our Terrace guardian for the last time, please let this be as far as it will go. Only banishment . . .

Pa takes a final look inside.

He comes out and stands in the doorway, his rough hands twitching.

I grit my teeth. I refuse to cry.

Chapter Fifty-Six

My darling,

I have written to you twice but, sadly, both of my letters have been returned address unknown. I sent a telegram when I read of the evictions, but I fear I was too late. Apparently the removals in Simon's Town have been going on for some time.

I'm writing again, in the hope that this letter might find you.

My daughter, Ella, and I are coming to South Africa to look for you. This may be foolish, because perhaps the success I predicted for you has indeed materialised and you don't need my help – and would not welcome my unexpected arrival! Forgive me if that turns out to be the case, I'll be overjoyed for you if it is. But I can't escape the feeling that you and your family are in danger. The terrible headlines continue here, I scan the pictures, praying that I won't see you amongst the images of people dragged from their homes.

Ella knows about my love for you, but she doesn't know about the cruel terms imposed by Elizabeth. I would never want to burden her with that. I've encouraged her to believe that I gave you up voluntarily.

And in the matter of giving, you offered me so much that I've never been able to repay or reciprocate. I could never forgive myself if you were in trouble and I didn't come to your help. I can't sleep at night thinking about you. There is a tightness in my heart that's been there since the last letter was returned, as if my body is bracing itself for irrevocable loss. Please God it is not so.

All my love,

David

Chapter Fifty-Seven

We rode on the back of the lorry, wedged between our furniture and suitcases, and clinging on to the less secure packages to stop them from sliding off.

The vehicle lurched down from Ricketts Terrace.

I craned over my shoulder. Palm trees. Gimlet-eyed butcher birds. Simon's Bay.

Our cottage, its door left open.

The jolting lessened when we reached the flat but the pace remained slow as the heavily laden trucks laboured along. White people on St George's Street stopped to watch. Some held their hands over their mouths, others attempted a feeble wave. Apart from the revving of the engines, there was no noise. Even the seagulls were hushed. Mr Bennett's son leant in the doorway of Sartorial House as we went by. Like other shopkeepers, he could stay by special exemption but only for a limited period. Outside the station, a crowd of coloured and black workers stood in silence as we drove past. The blacks had already been removed from their shacks across the mountain to Nyanga Township, more than an hour away by train. The Indians were going to Wynberg. The fabric of Simon's Town was ripping apart before my eyes.

No sooner had we left the surroundings of the bay than the sun found a bank of clouds.

It began to rain.

A sign . . .

I know Ma thought so, huddled beneath a towel hastily pulled from one of our bundles and crying into Pa's shoulder as the downpour worsened. Sam sheltered me with his jacket. I tried not to worry about the state of my carefully packed uniforms. How would I manage to get one dry and ironed in time for work the next day? We were short-staffed in theatre, I hadn't been able to take extra time off. We passed Glencairn, Sunny Cove, and then turned into Fish Hoek. Again, white folk stopped and stared at the line of trucks and leant into one another to speculate on the rough convoy. After a while the neat houses, the crescent beach and the gleam of False Bay disappeared behind us. On our left, scrubby hills poked through the murk. To the right, the outline of Chapman's Peak cleared and blurred behind shifting cloud. The Atlantic was a distant line on the horizon. We skirted Noordhoek and then jolted into the bush down a dirt road lined with gum trees like those that had marked the track to Piet's reformatory. We came to a halt in a clearing.

Up ahead rose two low apartment blocks, surrounded by an expanse of bare ground.

Ocean View.

'Everyone out!' yelled the driver. 'This is the end, no further!'

The loaders became, if anything, more frenzied in their unpacking than in the packing. The police had already abandoned our miserable procession at the limits of Simon's Town, so there was no one to watch or possibly temper the loaders' attitude if they'd been open to persuasion. But it was already late afternoon, and clocking off was uppermost in their minds. Our possessions were hurled off the vehicles with no care at all. Furniture splintered, bags split, suitcases burst open. The Gamiels, in the truck alongside, had used up all their anger at the start of the day and worked silently, gathering up their disarrayed possessions as best they could.

'Come, Sheila,' Pa led Ma away from the mayhem and laid down a cloth for her to sit on beneath one of the straggly gums.

'Mind my plates, Solly,' she cried, 'tell them to mind my plates!'

Sam fished a raincoat out of his case and I wrapped it around me. The rain was still falling steadily. I looked around for the Phillipses, but of course they weren't there. They'd gone to Grassy Park, like Vera and Abie and their children. It would be less lively without Vera nearby.

'Get everything out of the wet into the nearest block!' I shouted to our milling neighbours. 'Then we'll work out what belongs where.'

I picked up two cases and began to trudge towards the closest building.

The trucks roared off, their wheels spinning, their job done. We'd been successfully evicted.

* * *

Ocean View turned out to be little more than a collection of ugly apartment blocks set in a barren valley with few facilities apart from a bus stop. The flats were barely finished, their walls half-painted. Naked light sockets dangled from the ceilings.

'A disgrace!' Pa growled, after we found our allocated place in a dark building. He flicked a disdainful hand at the blistered surfaces. 'I wouldn't leave a ship's badge in this state.'

'Then get on with it, Solly,' ordered Ma, revived by the discovery that we actually had a roof over our heads. Terrace rumours had said we'd be left on the open ground where we'd been dumped, surrounded by our boxes, with no water and furnished only with a long-drop toilet. Site and service, it was called, the bare minimum. This was what most blacks got, and they had to build their own shacks with whatever materials they could scrounge. By comparison, we were fortunate.

'You and Sam better fix everything double quick.'

'Of course we will,' said Pa, bending stiffly to give her a kiss. 'It'll be like a new pin. Better than what we had before.'

But I knew it wouldn't. It could never hope to offer what we'd left behind, even though our cottage used to bend in the southeaster or lurch whenever the mountainside slipped. Ocean View might be steady in the earth but it was sightless. There was no sea view, even from the upper-storey windows. In order to get a decent glimpse of water, you had to trek a good half-hour or more over sand dunes, coastal bush and tangled carpets of sour figs that dragged at your feet. There was no Simonsberg to lift you as you trudged, or shade you in its purple shadow, or funnel the wind over its shoulder to cool you down. We'd been moved to a wasteland.

Would Jesus or Allah be bothered to guard us in such a place?

'We'll manage, Grandma,' Sam said, heaving our linen up the stairs. 'Don't you worry!'

Thank God for Sam. Thank God for strong muscles and the optimism of youth.

'Let's get the beds made up, Ma, then you can rest,' I said. 'Look, I saved some sandwiches for us for supper. And here are your pictures!' I set them on the floor next to where she was sitting with her back against one of the poorly painted walls.

Her wedding photo. One of Sam and myself.

Ma picked them up and clutched them against her breast.

Even though Pa still drew his pension, so far honoured by the South African Navy via the Simon's Town Agreement, the financial burden for the family now swung heavily onto my shoulders, especially as Sam soon lost his customer base. We were too far away for folk to run up Alfred Lane and offer him work. If he took the bus to Simon's Town and walked to some of his old customers, many of them worried about employing a coloured because you never knew what restrictive new law might have been passed while you weren't paying attention. And his woodworking tools were too heavy to take by bus – on the off-chance of finding work.

If you work hard, you can go far . . .

Pa's words rang hollow as I watched my diligent son plod back after each fruitless day.

My route to work began with a ten-minute tramp along the dusty road to the bus stop, then a jerking trip to Simon's Town amid a stream of honking cars. Often, the bus was delayed.

'I'm so sorry, Doctor,' I would gasp, flying into theatre where the team waited. 'The traffic—'

There were days when the late-afternoon bus never arrived and I'd have to walk all the way up Glencairn Valley through thickets of Jackson willow, down into Noordhoek, then a hard mile along the road to Ocean View, my legs aching from a full day's work, my carefully whitened nurse's shoes grimed with brown dust.

Some mornings, for moral support, Pa would travel with me.

After saying goodbye to me at the hospital gates, he'd walk along St George's Street past Grandpa Ahrendts's wall and look out over the sea. It wasn't the same as sitting outside the Terrace and watching the bustle of the dockyard, but it was the next best thing. After his walk he couldn't stop for a cup of tea because all the cafes were whites-only, so Pa would stand in Jubilee Square for a while, and then catch the bus back to Ocean View.

Chapter Fifty-Eight

Sam's father died in a fire at Seaforth before he could be evicted and join the exodus from Simon's Town. The police said they weren't sure of the cause, but that foul play couldn't be ruled out, given Mr Philander's history.

A dispute over a fishing catch, they speculated.

A settling of scores.

Sam hammered the post for the new washing line into the ground. Self-help, Ma called it. No one will fix Ocean View and make it liveable. It's up to us.

He stared up at the sky as a drop of rain fell onto his hand. The only thing he'd truly admired about his father was his unerring ability to read the weather. Ocean View was different, though. Pa's knowledge had been tied up with the Simonsberg and False Bay, and the swings that resulted from their particular interplay. Here, for example, the southeaster didn't obey Pa's rules. It arrived later than it did in Simon's Town, and fully formed – no warning breeze. Sea fogs rolled in from the northwest when you least expected them. Rain fell from clear skies.

He found himself grinning.

At least Pa would have approved of the weather at his funeral.

'What a day, Sam,' Ma said, as unseasonal heat beat down from an autumn sky. She drew his arm through hers as they walked back from the cemetery where they'd laid Pa to rest.

'He always loved my food,' Grandma reminded Grandpa. 'He was a good boy, once.'

Abie Meintjies, looking prosperous in a shiny suit, came over to say Vera was too tied up to come but she sent her love and said Louise was still young enough to find someone new.

Sam led his mother away from the rest of the mourners so they were facing across the bay.

Pink cloud draped the peaks of the Hottentots Holland.

'I love you, Ma,' he said. 'We don't need to worry any more about Pa arriving to ask for money, or to stay.' He took a breath. 'We'll be better off.'

Ma stiffened.

'Don't speak ill of the dead, Sammie,' she murmured, glancing down at the ring on her finger. 'He cared for you, in his own way. And I should have done more when he was a boy. The reformatory broke him,' her voice faltered, 'he was never the same after that.'

'It wasn't your fault.'

'No,' she drew herself up and smiled at Sam shakily and then around at the dispersing mourners, 'but I didn't save him, even when we were a family.'

'And,' Sam pressed on, 'please don't do so much overtime.'

She opened her mouth to protest, then smiled and pointed across the darkening bay towards the north, as if there was a world out there beyond the mountains that she knew about but he didn't. 'There's still a future to save for, Sam.'

Then Grandpa and Grandma bustled over and said there was sherry and *koeksusters* for the funeral guests and that it would soon be dark so they should be getting back.

Perhaps, Sam reflected as he stepped back to check the post was straight, when you were married to someone who was cleverer and more successful than you it was impossible to accept their advice – and especially their criticism – without getting upset. Ma tried to help Pa in the early days. She encouraged him. She bought new nets for the boat. She suggested alternative employment.

'Help me, Piet! Be an example to Sam. If you don't want to fish, grow vegetables! Or fix our roof!'

But in the end it made no difference.

In the noisy days before Pa left the cottage on Ricketts Terrace, he often shouted that Ma was being unfair to expect more from him and that she should be grateful he'd rescued her, which was a cheek considering that Ma had stayed faithful through the reformatory and the war until they could marry. Sometimes, though, he shouted other things that made no sense, about Ma being a cheat, about Ma betraying him and taking advantage. Once he was so enraged that Sam rushed at his father, who – oddly – collapsed on the sofa in laughter. Whenever Piet started shouting, Ma used to send Sam off to Grandma and Grandpa but Sam often waited just outside the front door, listening, in case Pa took a swing at Ma. If Ma hadn't thrown Piet out, there would've been trouble one day between himself and his father. But now, to his great relief and only slight grief, there was no chance of that. No possibility that Pa might hit Ma and then Sam would kill him with his hammer before he could stop himself—

The rain was starting to sift down harder, shrouding the distant Chapman's Peak, their closest approximation to the Simonsberg.

Sam quickly gathered his tools. Where would this self-help effort lead? Installing washing lines was a long way from working with wood to reveal its scars and striations, sanding and polishing until the finished item gleamed with both beauty and usefulness. It would help him to eat but it wouldn't fill a lifetime.

He glanced at the ugly buildings, and down at the barren earth.

The only way to make his mark would be to leave. Abandon Ocean View and his family. Scrape together some money and go to Cape Town. Or further away, like Ma seemed to hint when she pointed north. There he'd find wealthy customers willing to commission bigger lecterns, more elaborate carvings . . .

Ma would encourage him to leave.

But then she'd be alone with old folks. There'd be no one to protect her.

* * *

My campaign among the residents of Ocean View, while raising spirits and improving our spartan surroundings, didn't manage to rouse Ma.

She never saw the sea again, never dipped her toe in the water.

She tried to like the new place, and was grateful for Pa and Sam's fixing, but one day I got home and found she'd taken to her bed. Despite Pa's tender care, and my conviction that she was still healthy, Ma never got up again.

'It's not what I know, child,' she fretted as I brushed her hair and brought her tea and peeled an apple for her. 'I've lost my place in the world.' She pointed at the window that offered no view. 'The palm outside our front door. The sea in the morning.'

We buried Ma on a chilly winter's day, with snow on the distant Hottentots Holland, and a weeping sky over Simon's Town.

She didn't deserve this ending.

She deserved it to come when she was sitting in the shade of the palm trees, shouting with Mrs Hewson and watching the sun set over the sea's cambered swells while a succulent *bobotie* warmed in the oven.

Chapter Fifty-Nine

Ella Horrocks stood at the rail of the Union-Castle liner in the hour before dawn and watched the bow wave carving off the front of the ship. She'd never been on the open ocean before. Strange, that. Dad had been in the navy for almost twenty years and yet she'd never had much to do with the sea other than the odd visit to Dartmouth and a day trip in her great-uncle's yacht. Partly it was because Mum never cared for the sea and preferred to stay at Corbey. Leave your father to it, she'd say to Ella. He needs his annual fix.

But this!

Ella tilted her head back and gazed up at the dramatic red funnels etched against a slowly brightening sky. A stiff breeze lifted her hair. No wonder Dad couldn't get enough of it!

If only he could've been here . . .

But Ella was determined this would not be a wake.

Dad had said so himself.

'You have a job to do for me,' he whispered through the pain. 'Potentially joyful. Potentially life-changing.'

He levered himself up against the pillows. The illness had struck so suddenly, she was often at a loss for words, unable to comprehend her tall, healthy father so quickly diminished. First it was the tiredness, then the pallor to his skin, even though he said he was fine, nothing to worry about. He'd pick up once he was on board ship.

'We could wait until you're better, Dad,' she suggested, as they sat together in the library. His hands, once so strong, now looked skeletal, over-veined.

'No, we must go this year. I should have gone before . . .'

But it was soon clear he'd never make the journey. They both knew it, even as they planned and talked, and read his war logs each afternoon in the creeping autumn light. The doctor said it happened like this, sometimes. Men in their prime cut down for no reason. There was the war, of course. The head wound. The trauma of seeing fellow officers die. Sometimes mental scars take a physical toll many years later. Mum, calling from Scotland, said she was sorry to hear of his illness, and that it was more likely to be bad luck than anything to do with the war. David had put all that behind him years ago. She'd visit the next time she was down south.

'A job? What do you mean, Dad? What do you want me to do?'

He winced, then breathed deeply.

'Go to Simon's Town and find Louise Ahrendts. Give her this letter – the second one that was returned – and,' he pointed to the bedside table where another envelope sat, 'that one as well, which I've just written.'

Ella took his hand and stroked it. 'How will I know her?'

He smiled. His eyes were still a brilliant blue.

'She'll be the loveliest woman you meet.'

Ella lifted his hand and held it against her cheek.

'Can you tell me more? What she was like? I'd love to know, if it's not too painful—'

David stared at Ella. It was time.

'She was a local girl, from a Malay family. What the South Africans call coloured.'

Ella started.

'Did Mummy know that?'

'No,' he said firmly. 'I never told her about Louise's race.'

Ella searched his face. How intense their love must have been to even consider ignoring the conventions! He was married, she was brown. Nowadays, in England at least, mixed-race couples were almost accepted, but back then . . .

'Was her colour going to be an issue? Was that one of the reasons you gave her up?'

'No!' David's eyes flashed. He coughed, put a handkerchief to his mouth. 'I wanted to marry Louise, bring her to England. Her colour was of no consequence. I asked her to wait for me.'

Oh God, Ella thought, getting up and going to the window, I was born in the middle of it.

She stared at the stars pricking between the bare branches of the oaks. Moonlight played on the gravel driveway. Long ago, a young couple hovered, caught in illicit love.

'But then,' she turned, pushing a strand of fair hair behind her ear, 'you did indeed give her up.'

'Yes.' David sank back on his pillows. 'I decided a divorce would be too disruptive. I loved you and Corbey deeply. I couldn't put that at risk. So I asked Louise to forgive me, and to make a life of her own.'

Ella came to sit on the side of the bed.

It wasn't like that.

Dad was bending the truth, to save her from realising he'd given up the woman he loved because his wife refused to set him free. Or – Ella stifled a gasp – because she threatened to take his infant daughter away from him? Surely not even Mum could be so harsh.

'And you gave up the navy, as well?'

'Yes,' he said hoarsely.

She reached for a glass of water and held it to his lips. He swallowed with difficulty. Dad was an admired, decorated officer. She'd heard from Great-Uncle Martin he'd been in line for a top job at the end of the war. Presumably the affair was still secret at the time. Mum probably used the potential for scandal to insist he leave the navy, too.

'Do you know if Louise forgave you, Dad?'

David gave a wry smile, and lifted a hand to touch his daughter's cheek.

'I hope you'll find out.'

Ella nodded. He closed his eyes. A tiny blue vein throbbed at his temple. Never once had she heard him say a mean word to her mother, despite Mum's coldness to him. Never once had she seen him with a woman he truly loved.

'El,' he murmured, opening his eyes. 'Please believe that I wasn't looking to betray your mother. Louise knew I was married. Neither of us planned to fall in love. But what do you do when you find a true partner – a soulmate?'

Separate bedrooms, Ella reflected bleakly. The

formalities observed. A life of civility rather than love. A seashell in the library.

'I'll go to South Africa, Dad. I'll find her.'

David's eyes roamed across her face.

'Tell her the letters are my final gift. She mustn't mourn. And neither,' he felt for her hand, 'must you.'

It ended quickly, far more quickly than Ella was prepared for.

She walked a lot in the days following his death. Into Corbey wood to sit next to the stream; up the ridge through the yellowing trees; along the driveway to catch the splendour of the approach. The emptiness that followed her mother's departure seemed a minor dip compared to the chasm that now yawned. University friends phoned, some visited, but they were tied up in burgeoning careers and the bright lights of London. But at least the responsibility of being owner of Corbey helped. There were decisions to be made with the farm manager about planting cycles, there were tenant farmers to reassure that nothing would change under her ownership. And there was the funeral.

She and the vicar chose rousing sea hymns to send her father on his way. The vicar suggested using the village church to accommodate the expected congregation, but Ella wanted the chapel, and so extra chairs were brought in behind the pews, and some folk stood. Pale sunshine filtered through the stained glass windows and alighted on the crystal vases she'd stuffed with Dad's favourite cow parsley. The vicar, a new man, recited Dad's war record with pride, and framed his life at Corbey thereafter as a longed-for return to his roots. A life, Ella thought with a touch of irreverence as she sat in the front row, free of the controversy that would have infected it if she, Ella, had not been born and David had taken a new wife. If the mourners only knew . . .

Elizabeth Horrocks Parker attended with her husband, kissed Ella on the cheek, congratulated the vicar on his meticulous eulogy, and left straight after the service. Those who stayed included a large contingent of former naval officers whom Ella had never met, including one with a cane, who embraced Ella and told her that her father saved his life.

Don't weep, she told herself fiercely as she saw the last of them off.

Honour his memory.

Find Louise Ahrendts.

Then come home and make Corbey your life's work.

And now here she was, three months later, armed with the war logs for company, sliding down the Skeleton Coast on what Dad called a potentially joyful, potentially life-changing quest.

Life-changing for whom?

She watched the vast dunes of the Namib undulate in ochre waves towards the interior.

He once described this very clash of sea and sand, how the blue and brown faded into pastel and then into hazy monochrome as the day wore on. He'd convoyed down this coast, and chaperoned a shipment of gold in the opposite direction, across the Atlantic to New York, almost drawing neutral America into the war early, he said, when they came across a German oiler and the captain ordered him to lead a drill. They were in my sights, Ella . . .

There was a strange intimacy in following his path across the ocean.

And, she realised with leaping excitement, the journey was swiftly expanding beyond daughterly duty. There was something happening here that was more than a proxy mission. She could feel it in the throb of the engines taking her southwards, and in the plaintive cries of the seagulls that spoke of the approaching Cape. An odd sense that she was searching not only for Louise Ahrendts, but for an essential part of herself, too.

Slowly, the Namib fell away.

A day or so of unremarkable coastline passed, and then Table Mountain loomed on the horizon against a dawn sky streaked with powder blue and apricot. In the east, a fiery semicircle of sun poked above brown hills.

South Africa.

She gripped the railings. Passengers flocked on deck to watch the jagged peninsula reveal itself.

'Why are you coming to Cape Town?' asked one of the young men who'd tried his luck with her earlier in the voyage. He was nice enough, but all this talk of soulmates with Dad had concentrated Ella's mind. Better to wait rather than dally with casual talent.

'It's a research project,' Ella replied, on an impulse. And why not?

'You're a writer?'

'No!' she laughed and tossed her head.

The young man pointed at the purple mountains growing in splendour as the ship approached Table Bay. 'Well, there's everything here. Beauty. Cruelty. Humanity. You won't lack material.'

Chapter Sixty

Sam is all I ever hoped a son to be. Bright. Faithful. Keen. All the more reason not to chain him to me, or to this place. But I won't tell him about his father, not yet.

Perhaps before he leaves? But then he'll know, and David will not, and surely that is too great a burden for any young man to shoulder on his own?

I often look at my son and wonder if there's some part of him that he can't quite identify, some subtle leaning or quality that he hasn't been able to trace to me or Piet or his grandparents, or the Cape he believes is his only home. Without my encouragement, he loves English architecture and carving. I often want to tell him that his attraction is not unexpected.

'Sam,' I said one night when the heat hung over Ocean View like a clammy eiderdown and the beetles screamed in the dry scrub, 'I want to tell you something.'

He came over and sat opposite me at the kitchen table. His dark hair – the only obvious similarity to Piet – flopped over his forehead. He'd just turned twenty-three. I'd already fallen in love by that age, but Sam was a loner. There'd been one or two girls, but they never lasted. Perhaps it was as well, given my hopes for him. He could make a cleaner break if he wasn't looking backwards.

'I've almost saved enough to buy you a ticket overseas. One way.'

For a moment he said nothing, just gasped. But I saw a spark in his eyes. As a child, he brought home library books with pictures of canoes chiselled from the single trunk of a tree, or intricately worked panels from a hall in London. It was the same spark.

'Ma—' he began to protest.

'No! Listen to me.' I leant forward and gripped his hands in mine. 'You must get out. I won't see you ground down, arrested for petty offences. Vera's kids are forever in trouble in Grassy Park, it could happen to you, too.'

'But what about you?'

'I've got a job. I'll manage. You're the future, Sam, and,' I gestured around our gloomy flat, 'the future's not here.'

He stood up and went over to the window, searching for the view.

'I can't leave you.' He turned to look at me, his dark eyes sombre. 'You deserve to get out as well. Think, Ma,' he strode back to the table, 'you're senior enough to find a good job abroad, you could come with me. We'll save a little longer, for two tickets.'

'I can't leave,' I said quietly. 'There's your grandpa.'

And, I wanted to add, the sea. The mountains. Echoes of David. Even though I've been displaced, how can I leave the world that's shaped me?

He bent and put his arms around me. I sensed a wetness against my cheek, a shuddering in his chest.

'My life is here, Sam.' I disentangled myself and smiled at him through my own tears.

He sat down on the chair next to me and wiped his eyes.

I rested my hand on his arm and fought for control. He must not see me cry again.

'You'll need to be careful,' I warned. 'Say nothing to your friends, especially Benji and the Phillipses. Quietly apply for a passport. Tell the authorities you've saved up for a holiday abroad. Then think where you want to go, Sam, find out what country will allow you to work.'

He nodded. I could sense his excitement building.

'Prepare a résumé. Take photographs of your woodwork, write letters. You'll only have one chance.'

There would be enough money for perhaps two weeks' simple accommodation and food.

After that he'd be on his own.

I didn't tell Sam that if he chose England, I'd give him David's address – but only to be used as a last resort. I'll say David is a remote contact from the war. I don't want Sam to be a burden, or a source of renewed tension with Elizabeth Horrocks. I cannot allow that, even after all this time.

David doesn't know he has a son.

Chapter Sixty-One

Ella spent most of the train trip from Cape Town leaping from one side of the empty carriage to the other. On the right was a spine of mountains clothed in green forests, on the left a succession of pretty suburbs, to the right – further on – a valley chock-full of vineyards, to the left the sand-fringed banks of a small stream—

'Excuse me, miss, your ticket?'

'Oh sorry,' Ella rooted in her bag and handed it over.

'First visit, miss?' the conductor asked.

'Yes. It's so beautiful!'

'This is nothing,' he grinned as he headed forward. 'Down south is the best.'

The train came around a bend and there it was, the vast blue horseshoe of False Bay, rimmed by grey-green mountains. Ella remained glued to the sea side as the train chugged past tiny crescents of sand lined with bright beach huts, and negotiated low bridges mere feet above the water. Neat villages clung to the seashore above the railway line.

St James, Kalk Bay, Fish Hoek, Glencairn.

She leant out of the window and closed her eyes, letting the spray speckle her face, imagining Dad's warship sailing through the same waters, battle-scarred, desperate for safety.

Thank God for ST, he wrote in 1941.

Gale-force winds. Massive seas. Constant alerts. Tanker torpedoed, picked up survivors. We need solid earth. An uninterrupted night's sleep.

The port appeared around a headland, tucked into a protective curve of mountains, Simon's Bay at its feet and peacefully dotted with yachts. A cluster of taller naval masts thrust above the harbour wall. Flags flew from poles above a jetty.

'End of the line! All change!'

She stepped off the train with a strange sense of familiarity.

Look up, Dad had said, *always look up!*

The highest peak is the Simonsberg, and if the wind is from the south-east there may be cloud around its peak.

She smiled. A brisk wind was draping a fleecy band at the summit.

She hefted her suitcase and set off along St George's Street. Immaculate, Victorian-era buildings lined the roadway. Whitewashed houses perched on the green slopes of the mountain. A huge flag flew in the grounds of Admiralty House, named on a brass plaque. At ground level, a tide of coloured and black workmen swerved nimbly around her as they headed for the station where, presumably, her train would soon reverse itself for the return journey.

'Ah, Miss Horrocks,' said the receptionist at the Lord Nelson Hotel. 'Welcome to Simon's Town. Did you have a good journey?'

'Yes, it was wonderful.'

'I hope you enjoy your stay.' The receptionist examined Ella's passport and returned it to her. 'And don't hesitate to ask if there's anything you need. The best way to see the town is on foot.'

'Thank you.'

'You'll be quite safe, my dear, walking on your own. We have no vagrants round here any more.'

And very few permanent residents among the workforce either, thought Ella later, as she watched the continuing exodus from a pair of ceremonial gates towards the railway station. This was the daily grind of an evicted community.

She wandered into a well-proportioned, empty square lined with palm trees. A low wall led down to the shallows of the bay, and a scattering of yachts and speedboats moored in the lee of the mountain. Beyond, the superstructures of naval vessels reared between the stone buildings of the dockyard. She sat on the wall and dangled her feet. The afternoon sun glinted off the water. Wind rustled the palms, snapped the flags and delivered a refreshing tang to her nose.

It was exquisite – and yet unsettling at the same time.

Perhaps, she thought, as she hurried back to the hotel along the quiet street, there'd been too much to digest in a single day, from the drama of Table Mountain to the dainty but reduced town at the end of the peninsula where all the tea rooms she passed were resolutely white.

South Africa? Dad had tried to sum it up for her.

Beautiful. Welcoming. He hesitated, then smiled. *Defiant.*

Chapter Sixty-Two

Sam is newly energised by the prospect of leaving. There's a spring in his step. He's applied for a passport without arousing suspicion. Apparently, the authorities have no issue with young people travelling abroad provided they don't cause trouble when they return home. Freedom must not be imported along with souvenirs.

Other young people are off, too.

Vera's daughter, Sandra, has gone to Johannesburg, where she hopes to make it as an actress, and then be plucked by Hollywood, where fame and fortune surely await. Vera shrugs and says drama is in the family. Any path to the outside world is worth a try, even that chosen by the Phillips girl who is still missing. No one talks about her any more.

'I don't want to leave you, Ma,' Sam often murmurs to me as we climb a dusty track to a vantage point above the blocks, where there's a glimpse of the sea.

'Don't be silly. If you find something you love, you should cherish it. And pursue it – even if it means leaving what you know.'

I once imagined leaving.

Home. Family. Country.

The arum lilies that bloom in winter, the orange clivias that light up the spring.

Should I tell Sam?

Do I have the right to keep his father secret from him for the rest of his life? It would mean for ever denying the man who shaped him, a man far finer than poor, broken Piet. There ought to be no debate here. My loss – even if it pierces me when the wind shifts or I catch David in my son's eyes – must have no bearing.

Sam should know the true identity of his father.

David should be told he has a son.

'They offer apprenticeships in England, Ma,' Sam said more cheerily, as he led us back down into Ocean View. 'Would they take foreigners, do you think?'

Any connection abroad, however slim, would be vital for Sam. How their father–son bond developed would be up to them. And to Elizabeth Horrocks. I watched Sam swinging his arms, he was excited but trying not to show it. It'll be a shock, of course, when I first tell him. But perhaps it will confirm a niggling suspicion he might have had for years. I tried to shield him from Piet's accusations, but he must have wondered why his father would call me a cheat.

I paused and took a last look at the silvery line of the Atlantic breaking towards Noordhoek beach. We never hear the sound of the waves, even if the wind is in our direction.

I feel out of place in Ocean View.

Has Sam felt like that all his life?

Chapter Sixty-Three

The breeze eased the following day, allowing the heat to hover, unmoving, over the town. Remnants of cloud dissolved from Simonsberg peak. Ella grabbed her hat and notebook and headed out.

Walk along St George's, beside the high stone wall, and stop beneath one of the pylons of the old aerial ropeway. Look up to follow its route on the mountain.

Ella halted and looked up.

To the left, above the highest of the houses, you'll see the rectangular wards of the Royal Naval Hospital – provided they haven't been swallowed by fynbos.

Ella grinned. There they were. Still visible despite burgeoning vegetation.

She crossed the road, climbed up a set of steps, reached Cornwall Road, and then puffed up a sloping drive past a boarded-up guardhouse. Shrubs bearing stiff, conical blooms grew with abandon between the buildings. Grass erupted from crevices in the tarmac.

'It's been closed for over ten years,' the receptionist said with a curious glance when Ella enquired on her way out. 'There's nothing worth seeing. Rather visit our museum.'

Several of the wards had been converted into accommodation and their verandahs enclosed, with deckchairs angled to enjoy the view. But there were other buildings on the site that were unoccupied and heavily bolted. Peering through a dusty window, Ella spotted an overhead pulley arrangement. The laundry. And poking through the growth were the remains of a trolley system that connected the lower set of wards with the upper, probably for transporting food or stores. She ducked as a pair of chattering birds swooped over her head.

You won't believe the variety, El!

Sugarbirds with tails like streamers. Tiny sunbirds, coloured like jewels.

'Can I help you?' an elderly black man came around the side of the building. 'This is navy land.'

'I'm sorry, am I trespassing?'

The old man grinned. 'A little bit. Are you looking for something, ma'am?'

Ella examined him. Old but clean khaki clothes. Perhaps he was the caretaker.

'I'm looking for someone, actually. A nurse who served here during the war.'

The man shook his head. 'The place closed a long time ago. They all went back to England.'

'There was a nurse from Simon's Town who worked here.'

'Only English nurses here, ma'am.'

'Didn't any . . . local . . . people work here at all?'

'There were cleaners,' he shrugged. 'And kitchen help.'

'I see.'

'You should go back now, ma'am,' the man nodded at her kindly. 'Sometimes the baboons bother folk up here.'

'Thank you,' Ella smiled. 'Goodbye.'

A pattern began to emerge.

The following day, the post office on St George's Street claimed that it had no reliable forwarding addresses for the residents who'd been evicted from Simon's Town. Records were still in the process of being gathered because they could have gone to any one of several areas, the bored clerk behind the counter said – Ocean View, Grassy Park or one of the other townships on the Cape Flats. The young lady should enquire there. Or she could telephone the hundreds of Ahrendtses listed in the telephone directory, bearing in mind that many poorer families could not afford a telephone. The fact that the person in whom she was interested may have married and now be living under another surname was a further obstacle.

A pattern of polite interest, polite dismissal.

The local history group, while charming and eager to help, had no records of staff at the Royal Naval Hospital. They were lodged back in Britain, they said. But in any event, no mixed-race nurse could have served at the hospital. Ella's father must have been mistaken. Perhaps she was a cleaner, they suggested apologetically. Or a washerwoman in the laundry.

Where, Ella changed tack, might a non-British nurse have gone when the hospital closed?

Well, there were any number of hospitals in the Cape

Town area. If she was coloured, then probably to the Cape Flats, the vast plain accommodating the city's non-white population. But certain areas were restricted. And Miss Horrocks would struggle to be allowed access to government employment records for a private enquiry.

Now, would Miss Horrocks like to join the committee for tea? They were keen to hear about her father's naval record. Simon's Town dockyard had repaired over 170 warships during the war. Their crests were painted on the dry dock wall, closed to the public, of course. But they could check on her father's vessel from their list.

Durban
Achilles
Dorsetshire
Cumberland

Ella headed along St George's Street beyond the end of the shops, and up a slight incline. The occasional car passed by. Neat houses, set in well-tended gardens, looked out over the bay.

Keep going, past where the dockyard wall runs out. Look out for the white pillar of the lighthouse. You'll come to a tiny fishing village, above a beach with egg-shaped rocks protruding from the sand.

Get there early, when the sun is less fierce, and the cormorants are skimming the waves.

It's where I told Louise I loved her . . .

Ella turned down a road marked Seaforth.

There might once have been fishermen, but no longer.

Derelict remains were being overtaken by rampant growth or cleared to make way for smart new houses. She crossed a stretch of grass and climbed down to the deserted beach. Low tide. She took off her shoes and wandered towards the water. Shells, fragmented by the surf, etched a necklace on the tideline. The water was cool and startlingly clear. Tiny fish darted past her feet. Next time she'd bring her swimsuit. She could change in one of the bushy copses.

I love you, my darling.

But how can we . . .

'Miss Horrocks?' The head of the history group called back to say that the False Bay Hospital, on the slopes above Admiralty House, might be able to advise about Louise Ahrendts's current employment. It would have been the logical destination for a nurse looking for local work ten years ago, especially if, as Miss Horrocks insisted, she'd served at the prestigious naval hospital.

But before that came the South African Navy, in the person of a suspicious public relations officer who appeared after she enquired at the Queen Victoria gate.

'Why do you want to know about the RNH and its staff?' he demanded in thickly accented Afrikaans. 'The place closed years ago, after the handover of Simon's Town to South Africa.'

'I'm so sorry to bother you,' Ella smiled winningly. 'But I'm trying to trace a nurse who served there before it was closed.'

'Well,' he scratched his head, 'we've got no records of

Royal Navy staff. You should have checked before you left England, ma'am.'

'But when the hospital was closed, the local staff would have been given some sort of compensation, surely?' She hesitated. 'As part of the Handover Agreement?'

'How do you know that?'

'My father was in the Royal Navy,' Ella paused and chose her next words with care. 'He was aware of the terms of the Agreement.'

'Are you looking to make a claim, miss?'

'No,' Ella laughed, with as much humour as she could muster. 'I was simply hoping you might have the contact details of those who were let go. To help me find this particular nurse.'

He rose and went around the desk and opened the door.

'I'm sorry, ma'am. I'm not able to provide that kind of information.'

'I see. Thank you for your time.'

His eye fell upon her camera and he shook his head.

'You mustn't take photos of navy installations, ma'am, even those in view around the coastline.' He went on to say that such photographs would be a breach of security and could result in her being detained under various laws pertaining to the fight against Communism.

'Now, you have a pleasant holiday, Miss Horrocks. Go to Cape Point and see where the Indian and Atlantic oceans meet. Watch for dolphins in the bay. This is the best time to visit.'

Ella told herself it was early days. She ought not to overreact to the polite rebuff as soon as she mentioned she was looking for a non-white; or the sense that she was interfering in matters she couldn't hope to understand and which ought not to concern her. Worse, though, was a realisation that history – the stuff she'd chafed against at university for being too distant and too boring – was being erased here, in plain sight and within living memory. Anything that pre-dated apartheid or clashed with its central goal of separation was being diminished. Whether it was a single evicted woman or an entire community, they were being purged from the public record as if their contribution was as insubstantial as the mist that hovered and then dissolved above the sea every morning.

Have a pleasant holiday, she grumbled to herself as she walked back through the Queen Victoria gate. Stop asking questions.

At least they couldn't dictate what she read.

War log
48 degrees 10 minutes north, 16 degrees 12 minutes west

I don't hate the Bismarck *but I can't deny this is revenge. Bitter, bloody revenge.*

For HMS Hood, *for HMS* Royal Oak. *For Tompkins, Owen and Nott on* Achilles. *And so many more.*

If this is what it takes, we will finish the job.

'Your tea, Miss Horrocks.'

The hotel's coloured waiter set down a tray as she sat on the hotel's verandah with her reading. Freshly baked scones nestled in a small wicker basket. Unlike the officious navy man or the bored postal clerk, he'd been unfailingly concerned, and warned that she shouldn't spend too much time in the sun at midday, or walk around on her own after dark. *Skollies*, he said, with a glance up the mountain. No respect, ma'am.

'Thank you. That looks delicious.'

She watched as he went inside.

How do you deal with a place where prejudice and generosity rub so closely together?

You have a job to do.

The letters were in her bag. Dad was counting on her. If the False Bay hospital proved a dead end, she would move on. The hospitals and clinics in the coloured areas would be next.

But first, Ricketts Terrace.

Chapter Sixty-Four

Sam walked along the road towards town. He'd just finished a job in Murdoch Valley, above the winding route that led to Smitswinkel Bay and Cape Point. Sam loved that part of the coast. It was wilder than the town side, with huge sandy cliffs that sometimes shed great chunks into the sea. He liked watching the penguins that lived in the bush above Boulders Beach and waddled into the sea every morning to hunt for fish far out in the bay. Lumpy seals, basking on the offshore rocks, occasionally lumbered into the water to chase them as they passed.

There might be more work at the same house, a wardrobe that needed repairing, so Sam had promised to go back the next day. It wasn't much, and not very demanding, but any work was better than no work at this stage. He needed to save as much as possible to take with him to England, for that was now his preferred destination. He'd written letters enquiring about apprenticeships, and there'd been a reply telling him that he could present himself and perhaps there would be an opportunity if he was found to be good enough. He'd made sure to say he was coloured. A white South African applying wouldn't have had a chance.

Reverse discrimination! Sam chuckled. He'd be judged for the skills of his hands – but their colour might very well turn out to be an advantage!

His real fear was the prospect of leaving Ma behind. God knows what further restrictions the government had in store for non-whites. But he knew she was right to push him: this might be the only chance he got to make something of himself. If he'd been the parent, and Ma his daughter, he'd have done the same thing.

He squinted up at the Simonsberg. Clear. And no wind at all. If they'd still been at Ricketts Terrace, he'd have persuaded Ma to come with him to Seaforth for an early evening swim. Ma adored the sea, and could surf the waves like a teenager.

He kept up a good pace along St George's Street.

The police were quick to suspect you of loitering if you didn't look sharp.

He reached Alfred Lane and glanced up at the mosque.

Why not?

Ma and his Grandpa never came back, but he liked to see the old place, even if it was in ruins. It reminded him of the happy times when Pa was sober, and Ma used to laugh more, and Grandpa Solly first told him he had a talent for woodworking.

The palms were still there, but their trunks were no longer trimmed and old fronds dragged on the ground like broken bones. A pair of starlings burst from a tangle of undergrowth and shot over his head. The end cottages were in the best shape, but the Phillipses was completely derelict. A clump of prickly pears was gaining a foothold where Ma's washing line used to be. But the view—

Sam stopped.

There was a girl sitting on the wall.

Ella hadn't gone to Ricketts Terrace – or what remained of it – straightaway. She'd wanted to absorb the atmosphere of the town and try to recreate the British naval base in her mind via Dad's words, before turning to more recent events. The abandoned Terrace would be a depressing sight, and one she'd have preferred to deal with only after finding Louise alive and well.

But it was now over a week into her stay and Louise was still elusive.

She couldn't put it off any longer.

The Terrace had to be faced.

Listen for the muezzin's call when the wind blows in your direction.

The mosque will still be there, El.

Places of worship are the only structures exempt from demolition.

On a glorious afternoon – were there ever afternoons in this part of the world that weren't? – she walked along St George's Street past the string of family-run stores – Runciman's, Sartorial House – until she found Alfred Lane. A small, elegant mosque sat at its head. She climbed up the lane and turned right. Unkempt palm trees drooped over a row of broken-down cottages that had once been painted white. She stepped over a small stream and picked her way along a dirt path. Even though it was only a hundred yards or so above the town centre, the place was silent. Eerily so. Weeds sprouted at the base of the tumbledown walls. Several of the roofs had collapsed and were cantilevered at odd angles to the rest. A fallen washing line poked from scrappy vegetation. A pair of greasy-looking black birds squawked in a doorway. The mountain rose steeply behind.

Ricketts Terrace.

The words on her father's returned letter sprang at Ella.

'Gone. Address unknown'.

'Who do you know in South Africa, Dad?' Ella remembered her casual query as she looked over his shoulder.

There was a pole in the ground, but the street name had been removed.

Grief, deep and painful, rose up in Ella's throat.

Would he know, if she failed in her mission?

She sat down on a crumbling wall below the end cottage and gazed at the stupendous view. The stone buildings of the dockyard spread in an orderly pattern. Beyond the harbour wall, the sea laid a satin quilt to distant mountains. As she watched, an eddy of wind flickered across its surface like the casual brush of a hand.

How could anyone survive the loss of this?

He should go.

She was white.

He didn't need some kind of accusation so close to his escape.

'Wait!' the girl called as he was about to turn away. 'Please, wait!'

He turned back. She wasn't South African, her accent was British. She was fair and very pretty under a floppy sunhat. She came towards him. She wore a white dress that showed off her small frame.

'Excuse me, do you know this place? Do you know the people who lived here?'

He hesitated. Some kind of activist? That wouldn't help him either. Any questionable contacts, and they'd refuse his passport. Or serve him with a banning order like what had happened recently to Benji and several of the Communists. Confined to home. No contact with anyone, let alone meeting friends outdoors. That was considered by the law as a 'riotous assembly'.

'Please,' the girl was wringing her hands, now. 'I'm trying to trace a family who lived here. My father knew them in the war. I don't know where they've gone.'

'Why do you want to know?'

She sighed, and looked out over the bay. 'My father loved a woman here. He wanted to come back to find her, but he died before it was possible.' She looked at Sam, and there were tears in her eyes.

He stared at her.

'What was her name?'

'It was Ahrendts. Louise Ahrendts.'

Sam sat down on the wall, thrust his hands through his hair, and tried to order his churning thoughts. His father, in a moment of self-pity, had once shouted that Louise had never stopped loving an officer and how could anyone compete with that? Grandma, hearing the commotion, had quickly hustled Sam out of the room. When he asked Ma, she would say only that she'd met someone briefly in the war but it wasn't meant to be and she'd returned to Piet. It never occurred to Sam that the officer might be white, and British . . .

'Are you alright?' she bent down to him. 'It's very hot—'

He shook his head. 'I'm fine.'

She sat down next to him. A tug released a plume of smoke and began to edge from its mooring, a vee of wake rippling behind it.

'It's more beautiful than I ever imagined,' she breathed.

He looked at her. He didn't often sit next to pretty white girls – or rather, pretty white girls didn't often choose to sit next to him.

'You should see it at night,' he said. 'The mountain and the sea turn different shades of silver. Sometimes you see dolphins jumping along the path of the moon in the water.'

She looked at him with delight, and smiled. She was different, too. More natural than the girls he knew like Sandra Meintjies, with her poses. A small fishing boat was putting out from Long Beach. He watched it pitch through the breakers, waiting for a sense of whether to be honest or not. Pa used to row out from that very same spot, cast his net and then haul in the catch from shore. Pa, who knew about this girl's father.

'Can you help me find Louise Ahrendts? My father wrote to her but his letters were returned.' She gestured about her at the collapsed cottages.

'Why do you want to find her?'

'I'd like to honour his memory,' she swallowed, then lifted her chin, 'and give her the letters. But no one can help. There are no forwarding addresses.'

The boat was stationary, now. Sam could just make out the lattice disturbance on the surface of the water as the net sank into the sea.

'They wanted us to disappear. They wanted to erase every sign of us.'

'Us? You lived here?' Her eyes bored into his.

The boat began to pull back to shore. He remembered the strain of the oars against his palms when his father took him out as a boy.

'Yes. And Louise Ahrendts is my mother.'

The girl put her hands over her mouth and turned away to look over the bay. She said nothing. He sneaked a glance at her. She was crying silently, the tears pouring down her pale cheeks.

'Please,' he touched her tentatively on the arm, 'don't cry—'

She wiped her face and managed a smile.

'I'm sorry.' She dug into a fabric shoulder bag and pulled out a tissue and blew her nose.

'What is your name?'

'Ella. Ella Horrocks.'

'I'm Sam Philander.'

She stared at him, searching his face, then reached into her bag again. 'I also have this. It comes from my father's desk.'

She held out a beautiful, ribbed shell. A Pink Lady.

The same as the one Ma kept on her bedside table.

Chapter Sixty-Five

Ella took her dinner alone at a corner table. She'd asked Sam Philander if he'd like to join her, but he looked at her oddly and said that it was against the law for him to eat with her in the hotel. The place only served whites. She realised, then, that it was just as well they'd met and talked on the deserted Terrace. No one could see them breaking whatever law applied between whites and coloureds outdoors, food or no food.

As the sun sank towards the western flanks, Sam explained that his father was dead, and he and his mother and grandfather lived in adjoining flats in Ocean View, some miles from Simon's Town. Even though they were clearly alone, Sam seemed nervous about addressing her directly, preferring to talk towards the sea or the mountain.

'I'm a carpenter,' he said. 'I restore furniture and do wood carving.'

She glanced at his hands, broad, strong-fingered, golden-skinned.

'I'm sorry about your father, Sam. And about the eviction.'

When he did manage to look at her, she was struck by his eyes. Dad said Louise had almond eyes. Sam Philander's were a deep steel blue. Not unfriendly but cautious. With his dark hair, they gave him a faintly intimidating look. The sort of man you'd want on your side.

'My father died two months ago, of cancer. But somehow,' she paused, 'it was as if the disease liberated him in the final weeks. He never spoke before, but then he began to tell me about the war, the part he played in the *Bismarck* action, the sinking of his ship off Ceylon.'

One sip of water and half a biscuit per man.

Rescue came late on the second day, just as hope – and water – were almost spent.

'I learnt about his early life, too. How he battled my grandfather for the chance to go to sea. How a picture, amazingly' – she laughed shakily and pointed at the dockyard – 'of HMS *Hood* in Simon's Town, spurred him on.'

'A picture?'

'Yes. It was in the *Illustrated London News*. Dad was fifteen at the time. "Flagship to show colours on world tour", the caption said. There were flags and bunting and cheering crowds. And your mountains,' she waved an arm towards them. 'He was so captivated he found himself crushing the magazine in his hands. And so was I, actually, when he showed me the photos. I wanted to come here and see for myself.'

A light breeze stirred in the overgrown palms.

Sam seemed distracted, watching the train edge slowly out of the station.

Perhaps she'd said too much, too soon.

But even so, maybe he would understand?

'Sam,' she risked touching his arm briefly, 'I know it sounds crazy, but I think their romance was somehow ordained.'

'What do you mean?' He shifted around to face her.

'He knew about Simon's Town long before he ever visited, from that photo. He noticed your mother, too, on an early trip, before he'd even met her.'

Slender, with that twist of the exotic so unmistakeable in the local girls.

'And when he got appendicitis,' she rushed on, 'this was where he was brought. She nursed him. After the *Dorsetshire* sank, he came back here with his captain and they met again.'

'But what about her race?'

'It didn't matter. He said . . .' She stopped and recalled her father's actual words. '"Her colour was of no consequence to me." They were the love of each other's lives. Race, background, marital status . . . all faded.'

'But not enough for them to marry,' he said shortly, after a moment.

'No,' Ella murmured.

It was getting dark. A troop of noisy grouse-like birds flapped to their roosts. Streetlights began to wink along the margin of the bay, picking out the towns and leaving the mountains to recede into the night. Sam got up. His face was hard to read in the lowering light but Ella thought she saw anger.

'It's not what you think!' She jumped up and dashed a

hand to her eyes where the pesky tears were beginning to well again. 'I'm to blame, Sam. It's my fault.'

'How is that?' His eyes met hers coolly.

'They couldn't marry because of me.'

Chapter Sixty-Six

Sometimes significant moments announce themselves with a fanfare. Other times they don't announce themselves at all, they just arrive. After supper, say, once the dishes have been done.

'Goodnight all,' Pa hugged me and patted Sam. '*Bobotie* just like your ma's, Lou.' He shuffled off to his one-roomed flat next door.

'Night, Pa. Sleep well.'

'I went to the Terrace today,' Sam said.

I undid my hair. After a whole day of it being pinned beneath my cap, my scalp ached.

'Tell me.'

'It's still the same. Broken down but not demolished yet.'

I sighed. 'The authorities don't know what to do, it's controversial ground. Whites don't want to build there.'

'The starlings are nesting in the sitting room.'

'Don't go back, Sam, it's too upsetting.'

Opportunistic starlings, black-and-white butcher birds, the view from the doorway . . .

'I met someone there.'

'A vagrant? I knew there'd be problems if the cottages were left vacant.'

'No, it was a young woman. She's from England.'

I stiffened, put a hand out for my tea, then withdrew it.

'You need to be brave, Ma,' Sam said gently and shifted his chair closer. 'She gave me this.' He felt in his pocket and pulled out a seashell and placed it on the table between us.

A Pink Lady.

Still lustrous, still fierce, but smoother than when it was newly found.

For a while I just sat and stared at it. Then I reached out to touch it, but my hand was shaking so much he picked up the shell and put it in my palm and closed my fingers gently around it. Ella Horrocks, here in Simon's Town? Sam's sister! And David? I opened my mouth to confess, to ask forgiveness, but most of all to ask where he was – but Sam spoke first.

'She said her father loved Louise Ahrendts during the war and wanted to come back and find her.'

'He's here?' I felt the familiar leap in my heart.

Sam knelt in front of my chair and reached up to embrace me, gently guide my head to his shoulder. 'No, he's not. Only his daughter. I'm afraid he passed away three months ago.'

The shards of magic that once exploded about me at Seaforth and hovered in my wake for so many years, folded their wings for good and slipped away. I became aware of peripheral things, the dripping of water from our leaky tap, the creak of the stairs, the oppressive weight of silence broken only by my erratic breathing.

I can't say when I'll be back, he'd said, taking my hand as we walked on Table Mountain with the bustling city at our feet.

I know, I replied. *We'll have to wait for a favourable wind.*

Ella Horrocks had told Sam that her parents were divorced earlier in the year. David was planning to come to Simon's Town to find me when he fell ill. He confided in Ella about our love affair and asked her to go in his place.

'She's been searching for you, Ma. All over! The RNH, the navy, the post office. She was about to try False Bay Hospital when I met her.'

Sam found her by chance at Ricketts Terrace, sitting on the wall in front of our broken cottage. Ella wept, Sam said, when she discovered that he was Louise's son, and gave him the seashell that had been on her father's desk since the war.

'She wants to meet you, Ma.'

Yes, I thought, and I need to meet her – but not yet. I must first mourn what I've lost. Sam's sister must wait until I've been alone with David.

Sam sat with me for a while, stroking my hand where it held the Pink Lady. I didn't cry, not then. 'We'll talk more tomorrow, Sammie. You go to bed, now.'

'Will you be okay, Ma? Will you think about meeting Ella?'

'Of course,' I smiled at him and touched his cheek. 'Don't say anything to Grandpa yet.'

What will she carry of David? His fair hair? The warmth

beneath the initial reserve? I searched Sam's worried face as he got up. Had he seen anything of himself in her?

He must be told, of course, but only after I've met Ella and taken her measure. I need to be sure she has room in her life and her heart for a brother.

The secret has to remain mine for a little longer.

I'm still a good actress and prepared to lie if necessary, so no one noticed any difference in my work or my mood the following Monday.

'Very well, thank you, Matron. And yourself? The family?'

I assisted in two operations, checked on the patients in intensive care, and then went home on the bus and made a late lunch for Pa.

'I'm going out for a while, Pa. I just need a walk to clear my head. It's been a busy day.'

'You work too hard, Lou,' Pa grumbled as he gathered our plates. 'They take advantage. You get on then, I'll wash up.'

I knew I had to be near the sea to think about David, with the cries of seagulls in my ears.

Seaforth would have been more fitting, but it was too intimate and, these days, off-limits to me as a woman of colour. An impersonal beach would be better. And Noordhoek was vast, miles of hard-packed sand bordering a fierce ocean too dangerous for swimming. No one would spot me amid its sweep and tell me I was trespassing. It took me three quarters of an hour to reach the beach over rough terrain but I found the sea at the end of it. Cross-currents and backwash ripped through the water, turning it into a mess of half-formed breakers and torn foam. I sat down by the high-tide mark. The spoor of seabirds crossed the sand like delicate train tracks. On this side of the peninsula, the sun sets directly into the Atlantic rather than slipping behind Red Hill as it used to from our vantage point in Simon's Town. I watched its fiery descent, the way the sky flared and then faded in its wake. Slowly, and then with increasing speed, the brilliant circle shrank below the horizon. I felt David reaching for me, his strong hands gentle on my skin, his eyes resting on me warmly, the words we both believed filling my heart.

Wait for me. I will return.

He'd sent his daughter in his place. Sam said she was lovely, and she had letters for me from David. Ella was fulfilling his wishes.

Yet how will I manage to face her and not break down?

And how will she take the revelation that her father betrayed her mother with me, and that she has a brother?

My sin is catching up with me once more.

I will return.

My breath faltered from its normal involuntary rhythm.

I closed my eyes to the shadowy beach and lay back on the cool, yielding sand.

Chapter Sixty-Seven

Sam promised to meet Ella Horrocks again at Ricketts Terrace. It was the safest place. No one went there, not even vagrants, so no one would see them.

Ma had already left for work by the time he woke.

'Is she alright?' he asked Grandpa, who always got up in time to see her off.

'Yes, but tired, I think.' Grandpa frowned. 'The early shift is always hard, your ma worries about the bus being late. I've made toast, Sam. Come sit down.'

'Thanks, Grandpa. I'll take it with me.'

'Wait,' Solly lurched over and held his arm, 'have you heard about Benji?'

'Benji?'

'He's run away. Broke his banning order and disappeared. I haven't told your ma.'

Sam picked his way along the track that led towards Glencairn and Simon's Town. Sometimes, when he needed to think, he avoided the crowded bus and took the bush route. It wasn't as beautiful as walking above Simon's Bay, of course, but there was a rockiness to the path that often matched his mood; and somehow the exercise contrived to settle his mind by the time he came down the stretch into Simon's Town. He ought to be thinking about Benji, and whether his disappearance had implications for Sam himself. The police would interview Benji's friends, questions might be asked about Sam's plans, his quiet passport application. He needed to prepare answers, be ready to deny being a Communist.

But instead all he could think of was Ella Horrocks. Was it ordained – her word – that he'd walk past Alfred Lane on a particular afternoon and decide to visit the ruins of Ricketts Terrace? That she would choose the same afternoon to do so?

Ella.

Surprising, captivating Ella.

She was waiting for him when he arrived, sitting on the same length of wall. A rising wind whipped white horses on the sea. He took the extra precaution of approaching from across the mountain, just in case someone spotted her going up Alfred Lane, and noticed him going the same way. It also gave him the chance to look at her, unobserved. She was wearing blue jeans, a loose white blouse and the floppy hat from before. There was something arresting about her. You didn't want to stop looking. Maybe her father had it, too. Blue eyes with a flash of grey, or perhaps it was green.

Maybe Ma hadn't been able to stop looking, either.

He watched as she turned to follow the flight of a gull,

spotted him and waved, then jumped up and climbed towards him. Her eyes were anxious.

'I thought you might not come.'

'Why?'

'Well,' she looked down awkwardly, 'perhaps you were upset. I talked so much, you probably thought this trip was all about me, but it isn't.'

She sat down on the wall. Sam joined her.

'I told Ma I'd met you. I told her your father had died.'

She put a hand up to her forehead.

He felt ashamed, she was still in mourning, he could have spoken more kindly.

'I'm sorry, Ella. If I haven't said so before.'

She nodded.

'How is she? Will she agree to see me?'

Sam looked at the row of broken cottages. Caved-in roofs. Glassless window cavities. Rubble and dead palm fronds choking what were once carefully swept paths.

'I don't know. Ma's strong. She's fought hard for us. She never talked about your father.'

Ella smiled and touched his arm, like she'd touched him yesterday. She seemed to have no fear, no understanding that even the simplest, kindest gestures could be misconstrued and land you in jail.

'Dad said she was brave and ambitious. That she could keep secrets.' Ella stopped for a moment, distracted by a layer of mist that began to swirl over the ridge at Red Hill. 'He asked her to wait for him. Then he asked my mother for a divorce so he could marry Louise and bring her to England.'

'What?' Sam gasped. 'I know nothing of that, Ella. But my pa sometimes shouted at her, talked about rescuing her—' he bit back what he was about to say. Pa had called Ma a cheat.

From the dockyard came the wail of a hooter as two tugs chivvied a warship from its mooring. Tiny figures lined its deck. A band played faintly.

'But then,' Ella squared her shoulders and addressed the bay, 'Mum became pregnant with me. Dad wouldn't admit it was the turning point, but I know it was. It's the only explanation.'

'What do you mean?'

Ella looked down at her hands, then straight up at him.

'Mum made him choose between me – and your mother.'

Sam felt her words like individual blows of his chisel on hardwood.

'So you see, I'm the reason they never got together.' She smiled at Sam through a veil of tears. 'I need to thank her for letting me have my father. I need to apologise that I came between them.'

Sam stood up and held out his hand.

'You won't need to do that. Ma would never ask that of you.'

She let him lead her up the mountain path to a flat rock where they got an even more splendid view of the shining bay. He waited while she caught her breath and wiped her eyes. Beyond the harbour wall, the warship was peeling away from its escorting tugs and steaming towards the Hangklip–Cape Point gap. A pair of sunbirds buried their beaks in the orange tubules of a Cape honeysuckle.

Here, far above town, only nature's laws ruled. He could be honest. He could be himself.

'Your father sounds like a special man. As special as my mother.'

She smiled. 'He was. He is.'

'Imagine,' he ventured, 'if they'd married, where would you and I be today?'

Chapter Sixty-Eight

It was dark by the time I left the beach. The pale face of Venus rode on the western horizon. I walked back to the flat and told Sam he could arrange for Ella Horrocks to visit.

That was the easy part.

The actual meeting turned out to be tricky to organise.

On Ricketts Terrace, a white visitor would've been unusual but not remarkable. Like Sam's customers, for example, or the odd dockyard colleague of Pa's, or a grateful patient with a small gift. Ocean View, however, was coloured only. I wondered whether there might be a ban on white people visiting, and whether I should try to find out. But an enquiry might simply bring down a further raft of restrictions on our heads. I've discovered it's often best to be determinedly ignorant, then you can't be accused of breaking a law you were aware of.

The most practical problem, though, was that of transport: how to get Ella to Ocean View, and return her safely back to Simon's Town. The train stopped at Fish

Hoek, but the station was several miles from us so a further connection was needed. A bus was a possibility and Sam would need to make sure he was there to meet Ella and accompany her because a lone white woman travelling into a coloured area might not be safe. Or she could take a taxi, but then the taxi would drop her at the entrance to Ocean View and she'd need to find her way to our block, running the risk of robbery if she wandered about alone.

I found myself mystified by the logistics of managing travel based on skin colour.

Maybe we should find a venue in Simon's Town. But where?

'We'll come by bus, Ma,' said Sam firmly. 'I'll meet Ella and bring her with me.'

'She might be nervous—'

'But what else can we do? We can't go to a cafe or a public place. They're whites-only. It's got to be here.'

Yes, I thought, it's got to be here. Also because we need privacy when I tell them, if I tell them . . .

'So we'll make it the bus, Ma? After work?'

'Yes. I'll try to get off early,' I hesitated. 'You must warn her, Sam. She mustn't be too friendly. You never know who could be watching. After Benji and all.'

'I know.' He grimaced and patted my shoulder. 'We can't be seen to know each other too well. I'll put her at the front, near the driver, and then I'll take the seat behind her. And keep my distance when we're walking. Don't worry, Ma, it'll be fine.'

I sat on my bed later that night, fingering the Pink Lady.

I'd saved up enough for Sam to go. The money was sitting

in my bank account. As soon as his passport arrived – any day now, he'd been promised – he could book his ticket and leave. Nothing must endanger his departure.

It's a fine balance.

Ella Horrocks' arrival might be the very best thing that could happen to Sam.

Or it could wreck his chances.

As for me, I must find the strength to see it through.

Chapter Sixty-Nine

War log
August, 1945

We thought the Japs would never surrender, it would be island-to-island, house-to-house.

But the Bomb has ended it. Peace at last.

And Elizabeth is expecting. I have no words to express how I'm feeling. Amid the formal surrender, I must write two letters. I must find a way through. But, as with the war, I fear there'll be no winners. Only the elements – sea, land – will survive.

And, if we're lucky, a slice of love.

'What will you do,' Sam asked on their third meeting at Ricketts Terrace, 'when you return to England?'

She gave a pensive smile and leant against his shoulder briefly. She was so relieved, every time they managed to get together. She still worried he'd disappear; that he and his mother, whom she was about to meet, would sink back into a vast brown population that she would never breach.

'I was going to continue teaching. Near home. But now Dad has died.'

They were again sitting on the uneven wall in front of the ruined cottages. Nimble swallows performed loops against the brilliant sky. The sort of day you wanted to bottle, Ella thought. Yet African weather was so mercurial, it changed without warning. There was no gradual ebb, like at home. No time to get used to one spectacle before a different one presented itself.

'You can still do that. Make a career, something for yourself apart from Corbey.'

'That's what Dad always said, the estate doesn't have to take all my time. But I'm not sure.'

She wanted to say that, in a strange way, nothing could be resolved until she met Louise Ahrendts. It was no longer simply a matter of fulfilling Dad's wishes by handing over the letters and then saying goodbye. Louise was the woman her father adored, the potential stepmother she, Ella, never knew. Dad believed that if she was still alive, Louise might inspire Ella in a way that could be pivotal.

Potentially joyful, potentially life-changing.

She turned around to look up the mountain where Dad said they'd walked unseen amongst the sugarbirds and the yellow proteas.

She turned back and smiled at Sam.

In private, there was a breadth and sensitivity to him she hadn't expected. He had opinions about sculpture and Communism and the design of Viking longships, but he was also adept at reading moods and nuances. What about his future? He wanted to break out, make something of himself. But in order to do so, he'd surely have to leave this gorgeous, troubled place.

And the family he loved.

She stared over the pristine bay.

What had that young man said, as they stood at the ship's rail on their approach into Cape Town?

'There's everything here. Beauty. Cruelty. Humanity.'

Chapter Seventy

Luckily the buses were running on time on the appointed day. I rushed home early and dusted the sitting room, and swept the floor and the landing and the stairs down to the entrance of our building. Ella might recoil from our surroundings, but at least they'd be clean. I'd arranged for Pa to take supper with friends in another block. Then I laid a tray for tea with Ma's best cups and saucers that had survived the move, and made triangular cheese sandwiches. The activity helped take my mind off the coming meeting, but I kept reminding myself not to be shocked when she looked like David, spoke like David.

I waited on the sofa until I heard Sam's key in the lock.

He stood aside and ushered a young woman forward.

'Hello,' the girl said, holding out her hand, 'I'm Ella Horrocks.'

I looked at her, at the eyes that were David's, and I took her in my arms. Ella began to weep, surprisingly noisily. Uncontrollably. I fought to stay dry-eyed. Sam put his arm around her shoulder, so that she was embraced by both of us. We held her until I felt the shudders subside.

She drew back and wiped her eyes. She was slender, with fine features and blonde hair, and she was wearing a plain green dress and sandals. David was in her hair, the line of her nose, the smooth temple before the war wound.

'I'm sorry! I thought I'd never find you—'

'Come, Ella,' I managed. 'Do sit down.'

She glanced around her but didn't register the cramped living room, the small windows. I waited while she gathered herself.

'How long have you been in South Africa, Ella?'

I found myself searching for more of David, but I mustn't do that. She's her own person.

'Two weeks. I was worried I wouldn't find you,' she glanced at Sam.

'You went to Ricketts Terrace.'

'Yes. It was very sad to see it like that. Dad said it had the best view in the world.'

I smiled. She stopped and looked down at her hands. I sensed she'd prepared what she wanted to say, and was steadying herself to do so. Perhaps she'd known the moment would be overwhelming. She was very young to be so astute, and so composed after tears.

I waited.

'I know this can't be easy,' she began hesitantly. 'Thank you for agreeing to see me. I have something for you.'

She opened her bag and took out a letter and handed it to me. 'My father wrote this before he became ill, but it was returned to us, as was an earlier letter, marked address unknown.'

'Yes,' I said. 'The Post Office stopped deliveries.'

'Dad wanted to come to South Africa but he died just before we were due to sail.'

She clasped her hands tightly. I wanted to reach across, comfort her, tell her she was doing well.

'He asked me to find you and give you the letter.'

I looked down at the envelope. Just after the evictions! So close . . .

Ella stared at me with a fervent stillness that I remembered. I swallowed and breathed deeply. David settled about me. His fingers were on the envelope. His love was waiting in the words he'd written. I realised my hands were trembling. They never tremble when I'm in theatre. Sam had his palm over his mouth.

'Thank you, Ella.'

I got to my feet, bracing myself against the side of the chair. 'May I read this in private?'

She nodded.

The sides of the room seemed to close about me.

I forced out the courtesies. 'Sam, please make tea for Ella. And do help yourselves to sandwiches.'

My darling,

I have written to you so often – indeed, hundreds of letters – but never sent them apart from one, some months ago, when my concern about your situation became acute. I offered financial help to you and your family to leave the country. That offer still stands. The letter was returned to me, saying address unknown. I hope – profoundly – that you are safe.

Many years ago, my lawyer asked me if I had any

doubts about my wife's ability to raise our daughter on her own. No, I said out loud. But yes, I said in my heart. I went back to Corbey, desperate for you, and watched Ella asleep in her cot, and I realised I could never leave her under Elizabeth's sole influence. And now my daughter has grown up into a fine young woman, lively, impatient with conceit or dishonesty, and warm-hearted. How much of her has been moulded by chance, and how much by my sacrifice of you for her, I will never know and would not be vain enough to imagine. I'm simply grateful for the lovely person she's become. She shows, incidentally, a similar mix of grace and intent to you, and I hope she may yet develop your steeliness . . .

My situation has altered at last, and I must tell you, even though I risk opening up wounds that have been buried for so long. I am soon to be divorced. Elizabeth agreed because, it turns out, she has a new companion. She will remarry once the divorce is final. I'm past feeling bitter, there is only a lasting regret for the wasted years.

And so I'm writing to say that if you're free and still love me as I love you, I will come to Simon's Town. But if you're married and have a family of your own, or don't need my help, then I will leave you be and send you my best love and wishes . . . and thank you, again, for the most precious moments of my life.

I hope you will receive this letter. I realise you may have moved but perhaps it will be forwarded as your family is well known.

Please reply, even if it is to say no.
All my love,
David

I could hear the murmur of conversation from the young people; Sam's local accent, Ella's polished vowels. I sat on my bed for a while and reached for the two seashells and held them. I wept and wept, silently, painfully, as if my heart were being dragged out of my chest and squeezed of its essence.

I wept for the love, and I wept for the waste.

When there was nothing left, I blotted my eyes, brushed my hair, stood in front of the window for a while, and then rejoined Sam and Ella. I'd been gone for at least half an hour.

They were sitting side by side on the couch. He was describing his work to her.

'Ma!' Sam jumped up and led me to the table, supporting me gently. He poured tea for me.

I sat down opposite Ella.

'Thank you,' I said, 'thank you for coming all this way to bring me your father's letter.'

She gave a sad smile. She was indeed lovely, as both Sam and David, in his letter, had said. There was also a watchful quality about her, as if she'd learnt to wait before making a decision, holding back her opinion until she was sure she could trust you. Rather like the way I'd intended to watch and wait until I'd taken her measure.

They were looking at me, wondering about the letter.

'How long do you plan to be here, Ella?'

I can't tell her yet, I can't tell Sam yet! I need to reread the letter and prepare my confession rather than blurt it out and risk overwhelming this first, tentative contact. We need to build on today before I reveal they are brother and sister.

'I'd like to stay another week or two. Dad gave me a second letter for you. He said it was his final gift.' She pointed to another envelope on the table between us that I hadn't noticed.

I picked it up. This envelope had not been posted, and was marked only with my name. He must have written it when he was ill, when he realised he'd never see me again.

I felt my throat contract. What more was there to say?

Ella put down her cup.

'I'm sure you'd like to be on your own, you and Sam. Can we meet again in a day or two? Will you talk to me a little more? There's so much I don't know,' she stopped, and blushed, 'only if it's not an intrusion.'

I smiled at her. There it was, for a moment, a flash of what the young David must have been like, newly in the navy, eager to learn, avid for the sea.

'Of course.' It could be a gentle route towards revealing my secret.

She nodded and gathered her bag.

'I'll go back with you,' Sam said. 'Won't be too long, Ma.'

He squeezed my hand, and opened the door for Ella.

She hesitated, then came back into the room and kissed me on both cheeks.

'I've never seen Daddy as happy as when he spoke about you,' she murmured. 'You were his soulmate, right to the end.'

Chapter Seventy-One

Still shaken by the experience of meeting Louise – elegant, gracious, utterly out of place in the dank apartment – Ella wasn't prepared for the challenge of the return journey. The sun had gone down and Ocean View now presented a sinister aspect. She and Sam were going the whole way by bus and she'd imagined it would be as straightforward as the train journey. She began to feel uneasy from the moment they arrived at the bus stop, despite his substantial presence beside her. As they waited, she realised he was attempting to shield her paleness from the view of youngsters hanging about under the few dim street lights. When the bus came, they closed in and seemed on the point of some kind of confrontation – Ella shrank against Sam – but then backed off.

She sank down into the front row.

Sam was directly behind her, as he'd been before. The remaining coloured and black passengers looked on them with suspicion and sat as far away as possible, meting out to her the kind of exclusion Sam presumably endured from whites every day.

'I won't be here for much longer,' he muttered, leaning towards her.

'What do you mean?' She didn't look round. She couldn't face meeting the wall of accusing eyes. What is this white woman doing here, she could hear them wondering? Does she think she can share our alienation by taking a single bus trip?

'Ma's been saving for years to get me out of South Africa,' he said, under cover of the rumbling engine. 'There's not enough work. And you've seen the way we're treated.'

She turned to meet his eyes.

'I don't blame you. But what about Louise?'

Sam sighed.

The bus jerked to a halt to pick up more passengers. They stared at Ella. She smiled in what she hoped was a polite way, but no one smiled back.

'Ma doesn't want to leave because of my Grandpa,' Sam said as soon as they moved off. 'And she'd have to save more. But even if she did, I'm not sure she'd go, you know. This is her home. This is where her memories are.'

Living history, thought Ella.

'So where will you go?' she asked over her shoulder.

'To England. There are craftsmen doing the kind of work I like. Restoration. Commissions.'

He'd shown her some of his pieces while they waited for his mother to read the letter. She'd been astonished. Beautiful carving, gleaming joinery of a quality that could grace the finest interiors.

The bus stopped. Old black men in frayed jackets got on, tired-looking coloured women bearing bulky parcels swayed down the aisle, sullen youths with averted eyes flung themselves onto the cracked seats. If it wasn't so frightening being the lone white among them, Ella reflected, it would simply have been unbearably sad.

The numbers thinned after they left the environs of Fish Hoek, and most of the passengers had disembarked by the time the bus eventually reached St George's Street.

Ella stumbled off with relief. Sam walked her across the road to the hotel.

She stopped at the steps and looked back at him. They were about the same age but he looked older, and sure of himself. Perhaps being deprived of your national identity made you more determined to nurture your own.

'Thank you for taking me, Sam, and keeping me safe. I'm very grateful. Goodnight.'

He smiled, nodded, and turned away.

He was finally letting down his guard, she realised, allowing his eyes to rest on her when they spoke. She wanted to kiss him, like she'd kissed Louise, to say thank you but also to let him know . . . what, exactly?

Chapter Seventy-Two

My darling Louise,
If you're reading this, I know that you've met my dear Ella. Apart from you, she has been the light of my life. You will also know that I've succumbed to cancer. It came suddenly, and my greatest regret is that it deprived us of the chance to be in touch, perhaps even to meet again.

I was unable to take care of you in my lifetime, my dearest L, but I'd like to make amends now, even if it is only in a material way. I'm leaving you twenty-five thousand pounds in my will, to be used as you see fit. I hope this money will help at home, or give you the chance to travel abroad to places where you'll be treated with respect.

I often think of the walks we took, my darling, and the days you spent with me in Cape Town. I've never known such joy. Your warmth, your beauty, and the spark in your eyes have never left me. I first thought of you as a once-in-a-lifetime enchantment. I was wrong. The enchantment has been eternal.

Be happy. Please don't mourn me. Rather, take a walk on the beautiful Simonsberg in my memory.

My love, always,

David

I went to sit on a bench in the hospital grounds in my lunch break, with the letter in my pocket. I wonder if David suspected that no marriage – other than to him – would satisfy me?

That I'd end up on my own.

The breeze was picking up, stirring the flat surface of the bay. Soon the southeaster would unleash itself over the mountain. Perhaps he'd described our wind to Ella. Its hunger, its ability to drive fires, whip cloud, fill sails . . .

I felt my numb heart stir, then race with a matching eagerness.

Money may not be essential for happiness, but it does provide cushioning. David's legacy would take care of Pa and me even if I lost my job, and help Sam get established overseas. And one day, if our country came to its senses, David might even help me reclaim what I'd lost. Simon's Town. The soaring mountains. The irresistible sea.

A cottage to embrace them!

There's no time to lose. I must meet the young folk soon. I must give Ella the brother she's never known, and I must give Sam his sister. And then, when we're alone, I'll offer her my memories, the part of her father that I knew. That will be my gift to her.

But I'll tell no one about the windfall.

Not Pa, or Sylvia here at the hospital, or nosy Vera in Grassy Park who will surely have heard about our white visitor by now.

Why should I?

I grinned to myself, and got up from the bench.

It will be my last, most unexpected, secret.

Chapter Seventy-Three

Ella waited with some nervousness on the Terrace wall, turning her back against the raging gale, and pondered her next move. She and Dad had planned to go up the Garden Route, see another part of the country. After all, her task was complete, she'd delivered the shell and the letters. She'd fulfilled all of Dad's hopes.

What she hadn't expected – despite Dad's intuition – was the draw she now felt to Louise and Sam. And the tingling sense that she was on the cusp of something more.

Find what you love, El, and go after it.

Soon after her remarriage, Elizabeth Horrocks Parker had invited Ella to meet her stepsiblings in Scotland. Ella went, hoping for a connection, but they were absorbed in their own lives and politely disinterested in a newcomer. At Corbey, Ella had no particular alliance with the estate manager and his family, it was a business relationship. Great Uncle Martin and his wife never had children.

Ella was the sole surviving Horrocks. Unlikely

as it sounded, Louise and Sam were now the closest approximation she had to a family.

A mighty gust almost propelled her from the wall.

She glanced around. It was too dangerous to take shelter in one of the ruins, they might come down about her head at any moment. The docile bay she'd first admired from the train window was now in a ferment, slashed with foam, mantled in spray. But it was the mountains that made her catch her breath. Cloud churned ceaselessly over the peaks, then dissolved into thin air halfway down their sides.

A silent avalanche, El. You won't believe it 'til you see it. Savage, ethereal beauty.

Dad had a way with words.

'Hello,' Sam appeared from above her.

'Does this often happen?' She spread her arms and shouted through the uproar.

'Every summer!' He laughed. 'It's a tourist attraction. We arrange it specially.'

She pulled her hair into a knot and bundled it under her hat.

'Aren't you ever afraid?'

'No, I grew up with the wind. In a way,' he paused, 'it's like an annoying friend. One you'd probably like to see the back of—'

'But you'll miss, when you go.'

'Yes.'

She watched a massive wave pound against the column of Roman Rock Lighthouse.

'A friend of mine has been in trouble.' He grimaced. 'The police believe in guilt by association. I need to leave as soon as my passport arrives.'

She stared out over the frenzied water. They'd met four times like this, each time more revealing than the last. Sometimes it was what he said, or what she said, but often it was about sitting side by side in a silence that was surprisingly easy. The broken palms shaded them, the gleaming bay watched. They didn't judge her presence here, alongside a coloured man. But there was no denying the whiff of danger, the consequences of discovery. In South Africa, this kind of friendship was forbidden.

It had always been.

But it didn't have to be so in the future.

'Why don't you come to Corbey?' she turned to him, impulsively.

He stared at her in disbelief.

'You could help me restore the Hall.'

Chapter Seventy-Four

Sam told me he and Ella continued to meet at the Terrace.

'We can talk without being seen, Ma.'

Or judged. A coloured man and a white woman, alone.

The wind gusted fiercely. I held on to my cloak and climbed up Alfred Lane for the first time since we were evicted. The mosque sat quietly at its head, serving worshippers from the dockyard and the shopkeepers who'd been allowed to stay, but in dwindling numbers.

'Fewer young people,' lamented Mr Bennett's son. 'How can a mosque survive with only old men?'

I turned past the mosque and walked towards the Terrace.

Crumbling walls. Rampant weeds. The cracked step in front of our gaping doorway.

The bereftness of it.

Sam and Ella were sitting side by side on the wall, beneath the shade of the unkempt palms. There was no obvious resemblance – their hair and eyes were too different – but I could see the parallel in the way they held their heads, and in the line of their mouths when they smiled. I'd told Sam not to mention Ella to Pa yet, we'd introduce her in a while. Because Pa would know. Pa would see it.

'Ma!' Sam jumped up and ran down to me. 'You never come this way!'

'Yes, but I knew you'd be here with Ella.'

He led me up to where she was standing.

'Mrs Philander,' she said, reaching out a hand, once more a little shy.

'Louise, please,' I embraced her gently.

I sat down between them on the wall and gazed over the bay, then checked the docks automatically for ships I might recognise.

'Shall we go somewhere else?' Ella said, glancing at Sam. 'If this is distressing?'

'No,' I said. 'Let's sit here for a while. I've something to tell you both.'

I watched the seagulls for a moment. They were swooping against the gale, searching for their air perch, and then hanging in the same spot until a random gust sent them diving away.

'Your father's last visit to Simon's Town, Ella,' I touched her arm, 'was in the final months of the war. Germany was about to surrender, but HMS *Cumberland* was on her way to the Far East where everyone thought the war would go on for far longer. David said the Japanese would fight to the last rice bowl.'

'Yes,' Ella nodded. 'I've been reading his war logs. But then it ended suddenly, with the atomic bombs. He came home soon after that.'

'He did. But what David didn't know, and what you and Sam have never known,' I laid my hand on Sam's arm and turned deliberately away from Ella to face him, 'is that on that last visit we conceived you. Sammie, darling,' my voice broke, 'David is your father, not Piet!'

Shock, bewilderment and a kind of dawning recognition crowded Sam's face. Next to me, I was dimly aware of Ella's gasp, and that she'd leapt to her feet.

'Sam, forgive me,' the tears began to flow now, 'I had to keep it a secret. I would've been disgraced – you would've been disgraced even before you were born – if it had got out.'

'No one else knows,' Sam said in a strangled voice. 'Except Pa – Piet?'

'Yes.'

'Ella,' I turned to where she was standing. 'I know you must be upset. Please let me explain a little more.'

But she didn't appear upset, in fact she was looking at Sam with growing delight.

'We're brother and sister,' she shouted against the buffeting wind. 'Brother and sister!'

'Yes!' I took her hand and his hand and joined them together. I could sense Sam was overwhelmed but he got up, opened his arms and gathered his sister to him and rocked her against his chest. I've always been proud of him but perhaps this will be my proudest moment.

We were all crying now, Ella in gasping, laughing sobs, Sam with silent emotion.

I found a handkerchief in my pocket and wiped my face. There was more to be said, not about our love affair because that will remain mine, but about the accommodation that both David and I had to make.

'There was a fire,' I said, pointing towards the old RNH and forcing myself to choose my words, not to give too much away. 'We had to evacuate the hospital. I came back here to check on my parents but they were at the church making sandwiches for the firefighters. There was a letter on my bed, from David. I was going to go back on duty but I read it before I left. David said he couldn't come back for me,' my voice broke again and Ella clasped my hand in hers, 'and he asked me to forgive him.'

'Did he say why?' she asked in a low voice. Her face was pale, apprehensive.

I can't tell her, I can't damage a child's love for her mother.

'He was needed at home, Ella. He had to put you and your mother first. I understood that.'

Ella stared at me, then glanced at Sam and I knew she'd already guessed the truth: Elizabeth's ultimatum, the pitting of daughter against lover, David's heartbreaking choice.

'Your father didn't know I was expecting Sam. I kept it a secret.' I turned to Sam and leant against him, feeling the steady warmth of his body against mine. I was cold, for some reason.

'I climbed up the mountain towards the quarry, but I got lost.' I stopped for a moment. The glow of the fire was real, the rocks scuttling past my feet as the mountain slipped, the glitter of stars where the sky was clear of smoke, my desire to slip off the cliffs, to sink into the forgiving sea . . . I shook off the flashback.

'Piet found me and brought me home. He promised to care for you as if you were his own son.'

Sam lifted his arm and put it round me and hugged me to him. Ella was still clinging to my hand. I felt their energy about me. Had I said enough? But not too much?

'I wish Dad had known before he died,' Ella flashed Sam a quick smile. 'He would have loved you, Sam. He would've loved getting to know you.'

Sam didn't respond. He was watching the sea, where the waves were being broken up by the gale into foamy disarray as they neared Long Beach.

'Sam? Will you forgive me for deceiving you?'

'Oh Ma,' he turned to me, 'there's nothing to forgive.'

'And keeping quiet about it for so long?'

'You did what you had to do. You could've lost your job, we'd have had to move away.' He paused. 'Pa once said he'd rescued you. I thought he was joking,' Sam managed a grin in the direction of Seaforth, 'but he did, after all.'

I nodded.

'What about Grandpa and Grandma? Did they know?'

'No one knows. And it's worse than you realise. I might have gone to jail – and what would they have done to you? I couldn't risk it. We still can't risk it.'

'You mean it's got to remain a secret?' Ella broke in. 'We can't say we're brother and sister?'

'No,' I said firmly, 'not while you're in South Africa. You'll have to wait till you're outside the country before you can hug in public.'

'Well then,' she directed a merry glance at Sam, breaking the spell of tears, 'we'll have to have our celebration here – quickly and in private!'

They both began to laugh. She seized Sam's hand and

began to twirl around, her yellow dress flying about her legs. I watched them, loving her spirit. Please, Jesus or Allah, if you're still here on the Terrace, please keep them safe, allow them to leave here and never look back.

'Ella?' I asked, when their impromptu dance ended and they sat down on the wall. 'Will you forgive me for springing this on you, too?'

Ella, remarkable Ella, threw back her head and laughed.

'Why wouldn't I?' she cried joyously 'I've found a brother!'

The wind tugged at my cloak and I pulled it more tightly around me. I'd need to leave soon to make the late-afternoon bus. Pa would be waiting for his supper. I might tell him about Ella tonight, and about Sam's father, before Sam himself got home. I knew Sam would be a while. He'd want to walk home the long way, across the mountain, to absorb the fact of his new half-family.

'I'm going to leave you two.' I looked about but we were still alone. 'Be careful, dears.'

I stood up.

'Shall we meet, Ella? You and I? At the hotel tomorrow afternoon?'

'Yes, of course. I'd be delighted.'

We kissed, her fair hair soft against my cheek, and then I embraced Sam.

'I love you, Ma,' he whispered, only for me to hear. 'You're the bravest person I know.'

Chapter Seventy-Five

The wind swung to the opposite direction overnight, whipping the waves into a different pattern and seeding the air with a fine debris of earth, spray, and shredded vegetation. Unable to sleep, Ella took an early morning walk – more of a stagger – to Jubilee Square, then retreated to the hotel lounge to wait impatiently for Louise Philander and read the last of the war logs. Maybe they would settle her, she reflected. She could do with some steadying. There was a nervous anticipation in her that was running riot.

War log
October, 1945
En route to Britain

I have a beautiful baby daughter, called Ella, just born.

So far, there is no softening from Elizabeth.

But I still believe there's a future for L and I.

A horizon that will no longer have to be secret. Or out of reach.

'Ella?'

Louise stood in front of her, immaculate and graceful in her white uniform. Ella had no idea of nursing hierarchy, but Louise's various brooches must signal a position of considerable seniority.

'How good to see you!' Ella jumped up and took her hand, remembering just in time that they probably shouldn't kiss. 'Do sit down. Would you like some tea?'

'Yes, tea would be lovely. If they can manage it.'

Ella hurried over to reception.

'Could we have some tea in the lounge, please? For two.'

It was a risk, of course, and the receptionist appeared on the edge of an objection – serving a non-white woman in a white hotel etc. – so Ella added, severely, 'It's a business meeting.'

The lounge was empty apart from themselves, and the familiar waiter soon appeared with their tea and a plate of biscuits. He nodded at Louise. She smiled back and raised her eyebrows.

Ella waited. She'd learnt enough of Louise's character in their two meetings to know that this get-together was not an idle arrangement, nor was the venue lightly chosen. It might not involve another secret, but Louise clearly had something more she wished to share, and was not afraid to do so in public.

Louise sipped her tea.

'Do you know the substance of the letter your father wrote to me, Ella?'

'I do,' Ella replied. 'Daddy left you an inheritance. He hoped it would be enough to give you independence.'

'It certainly will,' Louise said with feeling. 'I'm very grateful. Perhaps I might find somewhere better to live one day, when the country changes.' She glanced outside, then across at Ella. 'Somewhere closer to the sea.'

She had the most extraordinary eyes, Ella registered, tilted at the edges, and in a shade of golden brown that highlighted her skin.

'I'm glad. That's what Dad would've wanted.'

'You must be wondering why I asked to meet you.'

'Yes,' Ella replied. 'And without Sam.'

Louise smiled.

'Today isn't about your brother, Ella, or how it'll be between you. You have the rest of your lives to build a lasting bond. No,' she paused, 'I came here today to talk about you.'

'Me?'

'Yes. To say that you're a credit to David, and a credit to yourself.' She reached forward and squeezed Ella's hand. 'Your parents were estranged because of me. A lesser daughter would not have been so generous.'

Ella found herself, for a moment, without words. The apology she'd prepared – about coming between her father and Louise, about being the reason they couldn't marry, slipped away, unneeded. Louise had taken on the last potential barrier between them, and erased it in a few graceful sentences.

The wind moaned around the side of the building.

Louise leant back in her chair and glanced once more out of the window. 'My father, Solly, used to carry me on his shoulders to Seaforth beach in a blow like this. You've been there? That's where I learnt to swim, among the egg rocks. And to collect shells. My late husband,' her voice shook, 'used to dive for shells. Cowries, mussels, apple-coloured urchins.'

'That's where you gave Daddy the Pink Lady.'

'Yes. If you hold it to your ear, you can hear the sea. Wherever you are in the world. Or,' her almond eyes rested on Ella, 'the whisper of someone who loves you.'

Ella repeated the phrase to herself. 'The whisper of someone who loves you.'

How beautiful! Remember it. Remember the words . . .

'The sea,' Louise gestured outside, 'was my first love affair. And maybe your father's, too.'

'You're right,' Ella nodded. 'He said everything began with the sea.'

Louise reached over and poured a second cup of tea for both of them.

'Why did you come, Ella? You could have used a lawyer to find us. Handled everything from abroad. It would've been easier, less harrowing.'

Ella stared at her.

'Daddy wanted me to find you. It wasn't just about delivering the letters. He knew I might find what I was searching for.'

'And what were you searching for?'

Ella shifted in her chair. How to explain that somehow,

somewhere, in the words and gestures of this woman was a piece of her own history, a piece she needed in order for her life to become whole, and for her future to be meaningful?

'I think,' Ella began cautiously, 'I've been searching for you all my life.'

'For me?'

'Yes,' Ella smiled. The tears were close, but she could hold on a little longer. There'd been too many tears of late. 'You've been a silent presence since childhood. Dad knew that. He said meeting you would be potentially life-changing.'

Louise got up from her chair and walked to the window.

Ella grabbed a handkerchief out of her bag and blew her nose.

Louise turned. For a moment she was framed against a sky strewn with pale, wind-blown cloud. Slender, golden, out of reach, as Dad put it. Tears shone in her eyes.

Then she walked back and sat down.

For a moment they were both silent.

'The world turns in strange ways, Ella. I'll take you to meet my father. He met David years before I did.' She paused, as if wondering whether to say more.

'Please go on,' Ella encouraged.

'Your father's ship, HMS *Durban*, arrived in a north wind stronger than this one. I saw his ship in the bay, through the rain squalls. Solly fixed *Durban*'s damaged machine gun mounts. Six years later, David would be my patient.'

Ella felt a rising excitement. Louise's words would elevate the war logs, offer the contrast, the emotion, to balance Dad's fine detail. If Ella could gain her trust, bring the fragments together . . .

'Will you tell me about your life?' she blurted. 'You could come and visit us at Corbey!'

And perhaps, in the telling, there'd be healing for both of them.

Louise's eyes widened in astonishment. She glanced back to the window.

The sea frothed beneath the gale.

'Your father said the wind was different at Corbey, less energetic.'

I want to take you there.

Ella waited in a fever of impatience. Maybe she was selfish, thinking only of her own fulfilment.

Louise turned back. Delight flooded across her face.

'Thank you, Ella. One day I will.'

Chapter Seventy-Six

Sam and Ella met for the last time at Ricketts Terrace. Ella had hoped to stay longer – her conversations with Louise were providing extraordinary insights – but the arrival of a telegram at the hotel meant she had to fly back straightaway instead of returning by sea. It was the Hall's roof. A winter storm had done substantial damage and decisions had to be made. It was her first major challenge as owner.

Sam would be accompanying her, at a distance, to Cape Town airport to see her off. But this was the place where they would say their proper farewell until they met again at Corbey.

His ticket was booked for two months hence, by which time his passport would've been issued, according to the office he'd visited the previous week. There were no outstanding issues, he was assured. No questions being asked. No guilt by association with banned or disappeared individuals, or pretty white girls.

The wind had abated and the bay spread languidly before them. The Simonsberg stretched above.

'I didn't expect this to happen,' she said, nudging his arm.

'It's something in the air,' he replied, caution gone, dark-blue eyes dancing with mischief.

You have a job to do for me, Dad had whispered. *Potentially joyful. Potentially life-changing*.

Seagulls circled above a fishing boat battling through choppy swells.

1969

I sat on the ledge by the aerial ropeway and looked down on the buildings of the old Royal Naval Hospital. A child's tricycle lay outside my old ward. Patterned curtains flew from a window. Beyond the roofs, the sea glistened beneath a hazy sun.

I took the letter from my pocket and read it again.

Dearest Ma,

Corbey changes from season to season, and I'm starting to recognise the signs. The way the trees colour and drop their leaves, the way the frost cuts down tender plants. Nature's workshop, I call it!

Ella has arranged for me to be employed on the restoration of the library, and the panelling in the hallway. The banisters need work, too. But we'll go slowly, and I'm taking on other jobs in the area to build up customers. There's a cottage on the estate that I'd like to buy once I've saved up enough. Even though

Ella would give it to me, I want to make my own way.

I'm so lucky to be here, Ma, and to know I'm a small part of it, and can make a contribution. Ella and I are as close as any brother and sister could be. The weather is awful at times, and there's an ache in my heart for you, and the sea, and the mountains that won't ever go away. But no one looks at me as if I'm second-class any more. People like me as I am. They like my work. I don't have to sit in a separate part of the bioscope.

I'm learning more about David through his war logs. He writes about you, Ma. I can feel his love for you. Do you know he left a stack of letters that he wrote after the war and never posted? When you visit us in the summer, Ella will give them to you.
Here's something I found.

Every word, every moment with her, is a gift.
How could I ever have imagined coming back to Simon's Town – and not meeting her?

Please tell Grandpa I miss him.
All my love,
Sam

Acknowledgements

One of the fascinating challenges of writing *The Girl from Simon's Bay* was to step back in time to create an authentic, wartime version of a modern community. Luckily, much of Simon's Town has been carefully preserved – indeed, many of the buildings that appear in the book are still standing today – so my task was made a little easier. But I would never have been able to pull together the story and its setting without considerable help.

My sincere thanks go to Margaret Constant of the Simon's Town Museum who allowed me access to records on the town, the dockyard, and the ships that called during the war. Audrey Read and David Erickson of the Simon's Town Historical Society answered my questions and, in the case of David, guided me around the former Royal Naval Hospital and offered much invaluable advice from his own research work in SA and the UK. For naval matters, I am grateful to Capt. Terry Korsten SAN (Retd) and Capt. Bill Rice SAN (Retd) for their expert opinions. Patty Davidson, of the Simon's Town Heritage Museum, was immensely generous in helping me recreate the pre-eviction Ricketts Terrace community. The Heritage's impressive collection of genealogy data and photographs were essential for the development of the character of Louise. In the UK, the National Archives, The British Library and the Imperial War Museum all gave me access to their records on a variety of topics: the Simon's Town Agreement negotiations, Royal Naval Hospital reports, recordings of the survivors of the sinking of HMS *Dorsetshire*, to name but a few. To hone the life and service record of David, I followed the actual careers of four young naval officers of a similar age. David's action at the Battle of the River Plate was inspired by the real-life heroism of Lt Richard Washbourn, DSO.

I am most grateful to my agent Judith Murdoch and my editors at A&B for their guidance at all times. Finally, my deepest thanks must go to my family for their unfailing patience, love and support.

Barbara Mutch, London

BARBARA MUTCH was born and brought up in South Africa. Before embarking on a writing career, she launched and managed a number of businesses both in South Africa and the UK. For most of the year the family lives in Surrey but spends time whenever possible at their home in Cape Town.

barbaramutch.com